THE SECRET OF JULES AND JOSEPHINE

To D—,

partner in everything.

GALWAY COUNTY LIBRARIES

The Secret
of
Jules and Josephine

An Art Deco Fairy Tale

by
Artemesia D'Ecca

PHÆTON

The Secret of Jules and Josephine

FIRST PUBLISHED IN THE U.K. & IRELAND 2006
Phaeton Publishing Limited, Dublin.

*

Copyright © Artemesia D' Ecca 2006.
Artemesia D' Ecca has asserted her right
to be identified as the author of this work.

Cover drawings and illustrations copyright
© O'Dwyer & Jones Design Partnership 2006.

Printed and bound in the United Kingdom.

*

*British Library Cataloguing In Publication
Data: a catalogue record for this book
is available from the British Library.*

ISBN⁻¹⁰   0-9553756-0-6 (LIMITED EDITION)
ISBN   978-0-9553756-0-6 (from January 2007)

All rights reserved. No part of this publication may be reproduced, stored in or introduced into a retrieval system, or transmitted, in any form or by any means (electronic, mechanical, photocopying, recording or otherwise) without the prior written permission of the publisher.

This book is sold subject to the condition that it shall not, by way of trade or otherwise, be lent, re-sold, hired out or otherwise circulated, without the publisher's prior consent in any form of binding or cover other than that in which it is published, and with a similar condition imposed on all subsequent purchasers.

This book is a work of fiction: names, characters, places, organisations, and incidents are either products of the author's imagination or are used fictitiously. Any resemblance to actual events, organisations, or persons, living or dead, is entirely coincidental.

Illustrations

'…the apache gangs were very dangerous in Paris in the 1920s.'

Contents

The Secret of Jules and Josephine

Prologue

MURDER AT THE PLACE DE L'OPÉRA

PARIS, MAY 22, 1927.— A man was stabbed to death last night at the Place de l'Opéra in full view of the large crowd gathered there to celebrate the safe arrival of Captain Lindbergh.

Members of an apache gang are being sought for the murder.

Investigators at *La Sûreté* are working on the theory that this was a gangland killing and that the four apaches were paid assassins.

The dead man has not yet been identified, but a bottle of chloroform and a

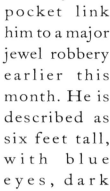
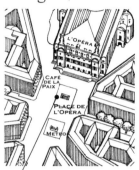
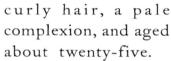

LOCATION OF THE ATTACK

small diamond ring found in his jacket pocket link him to a major jewel robbery earlier this month. He is described as six feet tall, with blue eyes, dark curly hair, a pale complexion, and aged about twenty-five.

Chapter 1

The Plan

DATE: THE PRESENT TIME

'I'M NOT SURE,' May said uneasily, as she looked at the girl with pale skin and dark curly hair sleeping in the crowded bed.

The girl had one arm around a stuffed elephant and an ancient rag doll, and the other resting against a small grey-and-white sheepdog snoring comfortably into her shoulder. A moving bump down near her feet, and a few faint yelps, indicated that a second dog was dreaming vividly under the quilt.

'She's very young, Fuchsia. I'd feel better if we could use an adult human.'

'An adult would never take the risk,' Fuchsia replied. 'Even an older child wouldn't. This one's a perfect age. She's old enough to follow instructions, but too young to be suspicious about what we tell her.'

May and Fuchsia were sitting on the mantelpiece in Cornelia's bedroom, talking about the only subject fairies ever talked about any more—the Great Terror and who would be the next victims. More specifically, they were talking about a complex plan Fuchsia had thought up that might yet save them all.

It involved a big risk for the human in the bed, however, and because of this, he was having a hard time convincing May that they should go ahead with it.

'We have to be ready to act without notice,' he reminded his wife. 'We have to remember we're in danger all the time now, and this mortal and those two flimsy toys are the only things that stand between us and—'

'Oh, don't say it,' May said quickly.

'No, no, I won't,' he agreed. 'But all the same, just look at them,' he added despairingly, pointing both to the sleeping child and to the very odd pair of dolls—an unsmiling man and woman dressed in evening clothes of the 1920s—resting on a pink shelf over her bed. On a piece of folded card standing beside the dolls, the child had written the names '*Jules and Josephine*' with a pink crayon.

'To think that with all our powers and magic, this is what we're depending on now,' he said, shaking his head in disbelief. 'A mortal child and two strange toys that could be gone the next time we put our heads above ground. This human family won't be left here much longer—we know that—and those two dolls will disappear with them. And what happens to us then? I know that what we're planning with her is a big risk, but we have no choice.'

May said nothing for a while. She was as frightened as her husband by what was being done to their world, but if Fuchsia's plan went wrong, they—the fairies—would have caused the death of a human, and who knew what would happen then?

Fairies did not kill. Mortal creatures—humans and animals alike—killed one another all the time, of course, but fairies never interfered with Nature. Even to be thinking about the possibility made her feel strange and shivery, and almost without noticing, she livened up the fire in the grate—a move that brightened and warmed the room, and woke the small sheepdog.

He sat up tiredly, growled as a matter of principle, and if he could have talked, might have said 'here we go again,' as he recognised the same elusive, unidentifiable sense of something in this bedroom that had plagued him for years. He did not bark or try to wake Cornelia, however, because he saw no immediate threat. This annoying presence had been coming and going for most of his life, but had done no harm yet—that he knew of anyway. He would just keep watch for a while.

His growl did, however, wake the other dog, the white terrier that had been asleep under the bedclothes; and wondering what was up, she struggled dozily now to make her way out, pausing only to yawn and scratch her ear as she picked her way with practised delicacy over the stuffed dog held in the girl's right hand as well as the two toys on the pillow.

She found the sheepdog sitting up and on the alert—for the usual reason. The terrier herself never got much sense of this mystery visitor that frustrated her companion, but then she wasn't as smart as the sheepdog, who never missed anything. She settled down beside that venerable animal, prepared to keep watch with him all night if need be; but after a few minutes, the terrier fell back asleep.

'It's a pity those two *old* humans went away,' May said after a time. 'The child's grandparents, I think they were. If we explained the situation to them, they might have done what we wanted, even though they knew what the risks were.'

'Or not,' said Fuchsia sceptically. 'If they knew what we were planning they might have taken the whole family away from here rather than let any one of them get involved with us. No. We'll have no chance if an adult finds out.'

Worried where all this might lead, May swung her feet up on the mantel, and leaned back against her husband's shoulder, feeling an unfamiliar weight of guilt and helplessness.

'I tell you what, May,' Fuchsia said conspiratorially, wanting to cheer his wife up, 'no one needs us back at the fort right now. We could pay a quick visit to the Silver Poodle Club. One fox-trot, and you'd feel like a new fairy.'

May brightened instantly at this suggestion. 'I could wear my gold and black dress,' she said eagerly. 'With the diamond beading.'

'And your diamond earrings, maybe,' Fuchsia suggested, as the two fairies vanished from the mantelpiece.

The sheepdog had allowed his heavy eyelids to drop

shut for a second or two, but now he raised them again quickly as he felt one of those unaccountable breezes over his head that he noticed so often in this room. It was a reason he slept on Cornelia's bed every night, instead of dividing his nights between her bed and her brother's bed as he used to do long ago. There was something in this room that needed watching, he thought, as he rested his chin protectively on Cornelia's shoulder and fell back asleep.

—Chapter 2—

A Time of Crisis

I T WAS THE FIRST DAY of the long Christmas holidays, but it did not feel like it. Indeed, it felt more like the day she got her head caught in the schoolyard railings, the day Oscar the gander landed on her shoulder and pecked at her head all the way up the drive, the day she got lost at the agricultural show, and the day a delivery van ran over their cat, all mixed together into one, Cornelia thought gloomily.

Everybody in the house was unhappy, and her mother was in her room crying. Her father, crosser and more worried than she had ever seen him, had gone outside and was applying his bad temper to a fallen tree he was sawing into logs; and her brother Barry had gone out too, looking red in the face and kicking rugs and slamming doors as he went, and bringing the two dogs, Tickles and Freddy, with him.

It was a pity, she thought unhappily, that Barry had needed to take the dogs. In times of crisis—and there had never been a crisis as bad as this one—the comfort of having a warm, furry dog sitting on one's lap could not be overstated.

Freddy, an all-shades-of-grey sheepdog, was particularly good in such circumstances—licking her face with concentration when she was in a bad way and showing heroic indifference to whistles, his dinner, the arrival of motor-cars, distant sirens, straying geese, visiting humans, wandering dogs, and even trespassing cats until the emergency had passed; and as for Tickles— well, the small white terrier's cheerful self-importance had never yet been touched by outside events, so even at times as dismal as the present, she could be relied on to make Cornelia laugh.

Still, the dogs were not there, so in their place, she gathered up the nearest-to-living creatures in her bedroom—the five eccentric toys that shook and made her feel tingly sometimes when she held them (they really did, and this had nothing to do with '*her imagination*' in spite of what her parents whispered to one another in amused voices when they thought she was not listening)—and told them:

'You know, my mother says it won't be that bad if we have to move to another country. She says it will broaden our minds, and that will be good for us, and eventually we'll live in a place that's just as nice as this, although at first we may be all crowded on top of one another, but that will be an adventure too. Oh yes,' she added, dropping her voice, 'but we're not to talk about any of this to Daddy, because he gets cross if anyone even thinks about leaving here.'

The words were brave enough, but they were delivered without a hint of conviction; and even as Cornelia spoke, she was casting a worried look around her pink bedroom and her important possessions, wondering if she should pack them right now, just to be sure none of them was left behind when she and her parents and Barry and the dogs had to escape the country in a hurry, as most of their friends and relatives had been forced to do already.

Her aunt and uncle had to go last summer. They'd moved to France. Then last month, her grandparents had gone to stay with them when her grandfather got sick, and everyone thought it was too dangerous for him to go to a hospital here in Emeraldia.

Without telling anyone, Cornelia already had made a few discreet preparations for the emergency flight she expected to be making soon. So far, what she had done was to put aside a special knapsack for the unlikely selection of toys she was now holding, and she had secretly practised—like at the fire drills at school—how she would pack it quickly and put it on her shoulders when the moment came that the family had to run for it.

First into the knapsack would be Jules and Josephine from the shelf over her bed; and surrounding and protecting those two elegantly dressed dolls would be the three unprepossessing hand-made toys that shared the bed with her every night—the rag doll, Daisy, made a long time ago by her great-grandmother; the sad-eyed elephant, Zanzibar, made in Africa to raise money for an elephant orphanage there; and Strudel, the tiny cloth dog with crooked legs and one eye higher than the other, which her aunt and uncle had found at a Christmas market in Vienna, and given to her when she was a baby.

These were the five toys that surprised Cornelia

by quivering now and again (and, once again, for the record, it was not '*her imagination*', in spite of what everyone thought); and even if she had to leave behind every other thing she owned in the world, she was never going to leave any one of them.

The bedroom she shared with these toys was at the front of her family's farmhouse, and it was an unusually inviting room, heated still by its old fireplace—a circumstance that entirely suited Cornelia's cosy soul. The O'Hara farm (best known as the producer of Fairy's Leap Organic Free-Range Eggs, Organic Geese and Organic Herbal Tinctures) had its own small woods, and

in the present hard times, their home-grown firewood was the only fuel the family could afford.

Right in front of the fireplace (changed over the two

centuries since the house had been built only by the addition of a sturdy childproof screen) was an ancient wing chair, the seat of which had been covered with a feather cushion to protect against the springs that, several decades earlier, had burst up through its worn-out upholstery. Covering both this cushion and also the chair's wide arms (now so threadbare that interesting strands of horsehair regularly emerged from them) was a folded, homemade patchwork quilt.

In general, Cornelia had this most cosy of chairs positioned so that she could look out the window at the view of the glen if she turned in one direction and look at the fire if she turned in the other, but not today. Today, she knew that if she looked outside, she would see something terrible, so she closed the curtains even tighter and turned the wing chair at such an angle that the tall back of it was solidly between her and what was happening out there, gathered up the quivering toys again, snuggled deep into the chair with them all piled on top of her, and told them:

'If you press your ear hard to the side of the chair, you can't really hear what's happening outside; and if you look straight at the fire and think about nice things, you can see pictures of those things in the fire; and Barry and the dogs will be back before long. That will help too.'

—Chapter 3—

Puffy Pickenose

TWO SCARY THINGS had happened the night before. One of these was serious and the other maybe not so serious, but so weird that no one in the house could stop thinking about it.

The serious scare was that the Ryans, who were both their closest neighbours and their closest friends, and whose land and house chimneys Cornelia (until that morning) could see from her bedroom window, had suddenly fled the country. It was the most surprising and frightening dash yet, the Ryans having slipped from their house in the dark of night, abandoning all their furniture and leaving their farm animals to be taken away in trucks the next morning.

'It's like war has been declared,' her father said. 'I don't see how anyone could be that powerful. Not even the Lawful Guild.'

The Ryans had driven up to the O'Haras' house in the dark and without headlights, unannounced except by the agitated barking of Freddy and Tickles. Their car was overflowing with luggage, and as Mr and Mrs Ryan stepped out of it, they told the frightened-looking six-year-old twins, Mary and Patrick, to stay in the car and to mind the equally worried-looking Labrador and cocker spaniel squeezed in with them. Both of the Ryans looked around them nervously as they approached the O'Haras' kitchen door.

'We can't come in at all,' Mrs Ryan said quickly, 'and we shouldn't even be here, but we couldn't leave the country without seeing you. We're leaving tonight, Kate,' she said, her voice breaking. 'We'll be in France tomorrow, and I don't think we're ever coming back. I'd never feel safe living in Emeraldia again,' she added, miserably. 'Not so long as that Lawful Guild is running it.'

'You're not serious, are you?' asked Cornelia's father, shocked. 'You've left your house?'

Mr Ryan nodded grimly, and looked at his watch. 'We have to catch the late ferry. It's sailing in two hours.'

'We just wanted to give you our address in France,' Mrs Ryan said, 'for when you have to come there yourselves.' She dropped her voice to a whisper. 'I'm afraid your names are on the list, Kate. And Puffy Pickenose herself' (or Pruella Pickenose, as she was more respectfully known within her large and powerful Family) 'has taken charge of the clearances in this area. Listen, do be careful,' she said urgently. 'She—'

But then Mrs Ryan jumped and looked over her shoulder, trying to see out into the darkness. 'What was that?' she asked in a whisper.

Cornelia's mother switched on the outside light, but all she saw was Cornelia and Barry talking to the Ryan children through the car window. 'I didn't hear anything,' she said, dropping her own voice to a whisper as well. 'Do you think there's something there?'

'I don't know. I'm imagining it, I suppose, but that

Pickenose creature has me spooked. She was in our house this morning with a gang of men, and I thought she was even crazier than the last time I saw her. She kept guffawing in that awful way of hers, and told us we'd all be put in jail tomorrow if we were still in the house, and it was obvious she wanted that to happen because she nearly salivated when she said it.

'And just to put the tin hat on everything,' Mrs Ryan finished furiously, 'she *stole* things. She stole a little china figurine from Mary's room, and she even stole our Christmas wreath.'

'Your Christmas wreath,' repeated Cornelia's mother, startled. 'You mean the wreath on your door?'

Mrs Ryan nodded. 'Yanked it right off it when she was leaving.'

Everyone looked at one another.

'They're all three-quarters mad,' said Cornelia's father finally. 'Every one of the Pickenoses. It's like it's their secret weapon. I can't figure any other reason for how they've got so much power.'

'Since this morning, I keep thinking I'm hearing her everywhere,' said Mrs Ryan worriedly. 'Even when we're on the ferry, I think I'll be looking over my shoulder to see if she's there.'

'Couldn't you stay with us tonight?' Cornelia's mother asked. 'We could—'

Mrs Ryan shook her head. 'That's good of you, Kate, but I really won't feel safe until we're all out of the country. The Lawful Guild says our property is theirs now, and they're going to charge us €10,000 a day for every day we stay on it as well as putting us in jail. And you know how powerful they are. They could do it. They say they're sending men with equipment tomorrow morning to knock down our house, just as soon as they've taken everything they want from it.'

'I can't believe any of this is happening,' Cornelia's mother said in a shaky voice. 'It's like a bad dream.'

'This is the address where we'll be staying for a while,' said Mrs Ryan miserably, handing over a piece of paper, 'and we'll—' But then she stopped and turned away, unable to talk any more, and Mr Ryan seemed like he couldn't talk either. The four of them hugged one another silently, except for Cornelia's father and Mr Ryan who shook hands; and then the Ryans left, without anyone saying another word.

After the Ryans had driven off, the dogs stayed outside barking, which made everyone even more uneasy. Cornelia's father went out to look but saw nothing, and came back after a few minutes, calling in the dogs and locking the door behind them. Then he went through the house, locking all the other doors and windows as well, before he joined his shaken family at the kitchen table.

'Mrs Ryan was awfully scared, wasn't she?' Cornelia said in a small voice. 'And Mary and Patrick were so scared they wouldn't even talk to us. They just looked at us like this,' she said, opening her eyes wide, and fixing a frightened stare on her parents to demonstrate.

'I'll bet they close the school,' Barry said, finding a

bright side to the situation. 'With Mary and Patrick gone, there's only five kids left. Everyone used to say that if the number got down to less than ten kids, they'd close the school, and now there's only half that many.'

Their mother hardly heard them. She was wondering what the Ryans would do when they got to France, and how they would be able to support themselves. A law had been passed the year before which stopped people taking money out of the country, and a lot of people who had been forced to leave Emeraldia now were living in great poverty abroad.

She did not like to think what their own position would be if they had to abandon everything and take flight some night. At least here they had a house and, if worst really came to worst, they were just about self-sufficient for food and heating; but it was hard to believe how grim life had become. It was not easy to go through every day worrying and being tired all the time.

The farm was not supporting them any more. Most of the people who used to buy their herbs and their tinctures and their organic eggs and geese already had been forced to leave Emeraldia, and another law had been passed stopping people from exporting anything unless they got a special licence, and nobody could get a licence except members of the Lawful Guild or people who could afford to pay a lot of money to that Guild, or else members of the Pickenose family, who were the most powerful force in the Lawful Guild; and the result of this law was that the O'Haras' out-buildings now were filled to the ceiling with crates and crates of tinctures and dried herbs that they had no hope of selling. They could carry on for about two more months, and then—'

'You look scared, too, Mommy,' Cornelia said worriedly.

'I'm not scared at all,' she said, lying. 'I was just thinking of how much I'm going to miss the Ryans, that's all.'

'I wish Gran and Grandad hadn't gone to France,' Cornelia said wistfully. 'If they were here now—'

'Gran would be baking a cake, like she always does when something bad happens,' Barry interjected quickly.

'Is that a hint?' his mother asked, smiling at him. 'Because if it is—'

But she broke off abruptly then as a startled scream burst from Cornelia, who was staring and pointing at the window. The dogs had been barking angrily at the door since the Ryans left, but now this turned into a frenzy, as both of them threw themselves at it, as if trying to knock it down.

'What is it?' asked her father, as he turned to look at that window, and then, to everyone's astonishment, they all saw something in the lighted yard outside. At first, none of them could believe what they saw, but the fact was, they all saw the same thing. It was Barry who found his voice first.

'That was Puffy Pickenose,' he said. 'Now she's stolen *our* Christmas wreath.'

—*Chapter 4*—

A Reconnoitre

THAT WAS LAST NIGHT. Then this morning, the Ryans' house was knocked down, just as Mrs Ryan was told it would be.

A tall machine with a big metal ball hanging from it had driven noisily onto the property, and the O'Haras had watched from an upstairs window as the heavy ball swung through the air over the roof of their neighbours' house, crashing into one of the two tall chimneys and smashing it to pieces. Hurriedly, Cornelia's mother closed the curtains, and after that, no one even tried to keep a brave face.

Both Barry and her father left the house without saying anything, and her mother went off to her room crying; and that was when Cornelia found herself alone in the fire-lit bedroom.

'I think those Pickenoses are the worst people in the world,' she said heatedly, continuing her conversation with the armful of toys; 'and Puffy Pickenose is crazy and smelly and mean and she picks her nose and she talks like a fat old man and she tells lies and she walks like a big hairy gorilla and I wish she'd never been born and then everything might be all right now.'

She had a lot more to say to say on the subject of

Puffy Pickenose, but she was distracted at that point, and lost her train of thought. What distracted her was that one of the toys—the doll, Josephine—suddenly quivered.

$$= \diamond =$$

'I prefer going into these toys when she's not holding them,' Fuchsia said to May, when he had followed her inside Josephine.

Queen May had gone more or less directly into the doll after coming in Cornelia's window, but King Fuchsia had lingered briefly on the sill, taking a worried look back at his kingdom, which was the prominent grass-covered mound across the glen on the Ryans' land, but which now had almost disappeared under the thick layer of dust that had blown over from the ongoing demolition of the house.

He shook his head as if to clear away an unpleasant sense of foreboding, and then looked around and saw Cornelia holding Josephine up in front of her and studying the doll as if trying to see inside it. Resignedly, he followed May into the toy anyway, although he knew this would cause Josephine to be inspected even more closely.

'She always notices when we go in and out of these dolls. It's fine so long as no one believes her, but if someone ever does, the jig could be up for us. Some meddling human might take them apart to see what's inside them.'

'You worry too much, Fuchsia,' May told him. 'The

adults around here have a lot more to think about now than what a child is saying about some dolls; and if her brother were going to dissect them, he'd have done it by this.'

'I suppose so,' Fuchsia said cautiously. 'But why did you want to come here now, May? I don't feel right about being away from the fort while they're knocking down the humans' house. They're all close to panic back there.'

'Yes, I know. I'm close to panic myself, and that's why we're here. Obviously we have no choice now but to go ahead with your Plan, but I'm very worried about it, Fuchsia. I just want to make sure that we haven't overlooked anything, and that when Tansy takes away the small human, she has the best chance possible of bringing her back in a condition that will allow her to go on living.'

'But what more can we do?' Fuchsia asked, puzzled.

'Probably nothing,' May said resignedly. 'But we've always just accepted that we haven't our full powers when we're inside these dolls and we've never worked at trying to do anything about it. Just bear with me a minute, Fuchsia, while I concentrate hard, and I want you to keep an eye on me in case I do something that I don't notice I'm doing, and it gets a result.'

Fuchsia watched closely. May made no movement, but concentrated so hard and for so long that he thought he saw a tiny wrinkle appear in her forehead, and then he called out to her quickly. 'May, stop immediately,' he said. 'Your forehead's wrinkling.'

GALWAY COUNTY LIBRARIES

S461194

'It's not really, is it?' she asked horrified.

'Well, it's gone now, but I definitely saw a wrinkle appear. My dear, you mustn't hurt yourself. We just have to resign ourselves that, inside here, we have limited powers, but I'm sure they'll be enough for Tansy to get the job done.'

'And you really saw a wrinkle?' she asked.

'Yes I did,' he confirmed. 'My poor May. You must have been concentrating very, very hard.'

'Well, I am feeling a bit beside myself,' she admitted. 'I'm worried about Tansy, and I'm worried about causing the death of that small human, and we're not very good at worrying, are we?

'Great Nature, Fuchsia,' she exclaimed suddenly seeing a strange, horrified expression come over her husband's face suddenly. 'What's wrong?'

'Come on, May,' he said urgently. 'We have to go back.'

'But what is it?' she asked. 'You're frightening me.'

'I hope I'm wrong,' he said, putting his own hand over hers, and squeezing it tightly. 'I really hope I'm wrong, but I have a bad feeling. A very bad feeling. I think something is happening back at the fort.'

Chapter 5

Jules & Josephine

C ORNELIA WAS SURPRISED at the way Josephine kept moving. She was used by now to what it felt like when the toys quivered—a tiny shake that would make her feel tickly for a moment and produce a quick breeze—but what was unusual today was the way the movements came one after another.

The doll shook twice and there were two breezes, and then there were two more shakes and two more breezes, and all of this was distracting enough to make her less bothered about Puffy Pickenose for a while.

Her bedroom was full of toys, and their numbers were added to every birthday and Christmas, but privately she thought most of those unmoving objects pretty dull. They served a purpose, all right, when her school friends were still in Emeraldia, because her fashion-conscious classmates had a low opinion of toys that looked as home-made and eccentric and old-fashioned as the five moving toys did. So for the visits of those girls, she used to find it a comfort to be able to produce toys from the shelf of a shop, not wanting to seem unsophisticated or un-cool or anything in front of such discerning critics.

When she was on her own, however, it was a different story. Those five moving toys substituted for people or dogs whenever she felt a serious need for conversation; and now that all her friends and her grandparents were gone, she found herself talking to them a lot, even to Jules and Josephine, who were by no means obvious candidates for the role of confidant, looking back at her, as they did, with the coldest of eyes and the most indifferent of expressions.

Still, their boredom and possible wickedness were part of their charm for her, and sometimes when she looked at them, she almost felt as if she were getting a peep into a different, exotic, smoky and possibly naughty world. Anyway, like Tickles, Jules and Josephine made her laugh.

She felt lucky to be allowed to have them in her room at all because she knew they had not been intended as playthings, but had been hand-made a long time ago as a gift for an adult. When she was very small, they used to rest on a shelf in the kitchen, but from the time Cornelia was old enough to point, she had been pointing at them; and as soon as she could talk, she had been asking to hold them.

When she was three and got badly sick, her parents moved her from her own small bedroom to the bigger room they had been using as an office, and put the two dolls on a shelf over her bed where she could look at them all the time; and both Cornelia and the dolls had stayed in that big room ever since.

'But do be careful of them, Sweetie,' her mother warned her. 'They're very old and very special. They were made for your great-granduncle Finn a long time ago, and the woman who made them, Savannah Gray, became a famous artist after.'

Cornelia was particularly interested in one part of this information. 'You mean my great-granduncle used to play with dolls?' she asked.

'Not exactly,' her mother said, laughing. 'He wasn't a child when he got them. He was a young man. She made the dolls for him when the two of them were living in Paris.'

'What was he doing in Paris?' asked Cornelia. Paris had always sounded a very romantic place to her.

'He moved there in the 1920s. He wrote home to his brother that Savannah gave him the dolls because she didn't think he was doing the things he should over there.'

'But why did she give him a present if she thought he was doing something wrong?'

'Well, according to your great-granduncle, Savannah was a very serious woman, and when he went to Paris, he was very serious too, and I think he was also very angry and very bitter. He was young and he had just lost his wife and baby. They had just—well, they had died,' her mother said uncomfortably.

'But I think that after he was away from Emeraldia for a while, he changed a lot. The word was that he started spending all his time in nightclubs—particularly a place called The Silver Poodle, which was a very famous Paris nightspot then—and Savannah didn't have too high an opinion of that.'

'So why did she give him Jules and Josephine?' Cornelia asked, bewildered.

'They were two real people,' her mother explained: 'a man and woman Savannah and Finn knew who spent even more time in the Silver Poodle than your great-granduncle did. Apparently the dolls were perfect likenesses of the real Jules and Josephine, and the artist gave your great-granduncle the dolls as a reminder of what he might turn into if he didn't become serious again.'

'And did he?'

'He never had a chance,' her mother said sadly. 'He was murdered by an apache gang in Paris on the night Lindbergh's plane landed there. Lindbergh was the first person ever to fly from New York to Paris, and the streets were full of people celebrating that night. Poor Finn,' she added. 'He had very, very bad luck.'

'What's an apache gang?' Cornelia asked.

'It was a name given to some nasty criminals in Paris. They're not around any more, but the apache gangs were very dangerous in Paris in the 1920s. It's a confusing name if you see it in writing because the spelling is the same as for the American Apaches, which the American Apaches mustn't have liked too much, but the pronunciation is French—sort of like it was spelled a-POSH.'

'What happened to Savannah Gray?' Cornelia asked, fascinated.

'No one knows,' said her mother. 'That's part of her legend. She disappeared about the same time as your uncle was killed. It's one of the great mysteries of the art world, apparently. She only became famous after her disappearance.

'It was all so unfortunate,' her mother continued. 'Some people who knew the two of them in Paris were sure they were going to get married, but of course that never happened. Although your great-granduncle said in letters at the time that he didn't know if Savannah ever would marry him—that he didn't think he'd be able to measure up to her high standards.'

Cornelia thought this was the saddest, but most dramatic, story she had ever heard; and although she had been fascinated by Jules and Josephine all her life, she looked at them with a certain awe after she heard this story, and maintained an even more respectful distance in her relationship with them, never combing their hair, or adjusting their clothes, or anything like that; and she never even considered taking them to bed with her. None of which came as a special hardship to her either because, frankly, those dolls just did not invite familiarity.

They were very formal dolls in their own way, dressed in evening clothes of the 1920s. Jules was particularly immaculate in his black dinner jacket, black waistcoat, wing collar, tiny black bow tie, tiny gold cuff links, and very tiny studs that looked like tiny diamonds, and a white silk scarf. His hair was black and shiny and slicked down close to his head, and he wore a monocle and an expression of utter boredom.

Josephine looked just a little bit wilder. Her dress

was made of blue chiffon with little glass beads sewn all over it, and underneath this, she had a blue silk slip. She wore high-heeled shoes with straps, and with little diamond-like stones set into them, and shiny stockings made of silk with seams at the back.

Josephine's hair also was black and shiny and cut short, and with waves that framed her face and were inclined to fall forward over her right eye. Both her eyes were ringed with black shadow, and whereas Jules just looked bored, Josephine appeared to be both bored and very cross. Cornelia could never look at Josephine without wanting to giggle.

They were the most exotic of the toys that quivered all by themselves now and then. The small dog, Strudel, from the Christmas market in Vienna and the rag doll, Daisy, made by her great-grandmother were as charming and reassuring as Jules and Josephine were forbidding, and might almost have been considered orthodox toys if they never moved. Zanzibar, too was heavy on charm, but the little elephant from Africa had unusual eyes—so filled with pain that Cornelia thought they hardly belonged on a toy—as well as a general air of great solemnity. The woman artist who had made Jules and Josephine would have appreciated Zanzibar a lot, Cornelia suspected, studying him fondly, because Zanzibar looked as if he had very high standards and would never even think of going near a nightclub.

These were the five toys that, at present, were being given a full account by Cornelia of the appearance, character and general worth (or lack of it) of Puffy

Pickenose and the whole family Pickenose. She stopped talking for a moment only when she thought she heard a different noise outside—a machine that sounded even closer than the one that was knocking down the house.

'I don't like the sound of that at all,' she whispered to Zanzibar, who looked back at her sadly.

She went over to the window nervously and opened the curtains just a sliver, and immediately a groan of pure horror slipped out of her at what she saw. She had been shocked twice looking through a window in the last 24 hours, but what she saw this time shocked her most of all.

She wanted to run to her mother's room, but her mother had been crying, which was awful and strange and scary, and Cornelia didn't want to make that terrible situation even worse. So instead, she ran as quickly as she could down the stairs and out to where her father was sawing wood, and when she reached him, she found she could hardly recognise her own voice because the panic in it made it sound so different.

'Daddy, something awful's happening,' she said breathlessly. 'There's a big machine in the Ryans' field, and it's, it's…' She found it strange how difficult it was for her to get the words out, but finally she managed it. '…it's digging up the fairy fort.'

— *Chapter 6* —

The Fairy Forts

ER FATHER didn't hear at first over the noise of the chainsaw, and she went around to where he could see her. 'They're digging it up,' she repeated when he had turned off the motor. 'They're digging up the fairy fort over at the Ryans'.'

Quickly, her father put down the chainsaw and grabbed her hand, and then the two of them ran back into the house and up the stairs to her bedroom; and when they reached the window, Cornelia could hear him draw in his breath at the shock of what he saw outside. 'I don't believe it,' he said. 'I just don't believe it.'

He had been born in that house and had lived in it all his life, and until that day, what he had seen from its front windows had always been the same.

First there was the long, narrow front field which sloped down to a meandering stream; and beyond that, there was the long strip of wood which rose up steeply on the sloping ground at the other side of the stream.

The Ryans' property (he would never be able to think of it as anyone else's) was at the other side of the wood, and a well-worn path that started near a makeshift bridge made it easy to walk from one property to the other. Because of the trees, however, only a few tantalising glimpses of the Ryans' property could be seen from Cornelia's window, including the house chimneys, and certain areas of green pasture land, from which startled sheep and cattle that morning had been loaded unceremoniously into trucks and driven away.

Most clearly visible of all, however—because it was at the highest point of the Ryans' highest field—was their big fairy fort: a grassy mound with the outline of two ancient banks of earth around it.

It was an eye-catching feature, and all the more so because it was almost identical to a second fairy fort which was on the O'Haras' own land—their fort being located in the sloping field to the front of their house and off to the right as one looked out from Cornelia's window.

People who knew a lot about those ancient mounds, like Cornelia's teacher, or like her aunt who had written a book about them, called them by different names sometimes; but mostly people just called them fairy mounds or fairy forts because everyone knew that those little hills were where the fairies lived.

Although for some reason, not everyone liked to admit that any more; and Cornelia knew that there were two schools of thought now about the significance of fairies and fairy forts, one of which was altogether wrong and very boring, and based on the ridiculous modern idea that fairies might not even exist.

To Cornelia and Barry's infinite regret, their own parents were among the misguided who thought about fairies in this unsatisfactory way; or at any rate, they *said* they did. The brother and sister did notice that their parents were every bit as protective of their own fairy fort as their grandparents were, and never allowed it to be disturbed.

Also, Cornelia remembered a May Eve when she was much younger and she had wandered out unthinkingly towards the fairy fort looking for a missing ball, and her mother had come running after her, her face so white and frightened that Cornelia had never forgotten it, and warned her not to think of even going near the fort that night or the following day. 'But why not?' Cornelia had asked reasonably.

'Never mind why not,' he mother had answered, with unusual sharpness. 'Just don't go near it tonight or tomorrow. Do you promise?'

Cornelia had promised all right, but she felt bruised by the exchange until her grandmother told her the reason.

'You see, I told you she believed in the fairies, child. She just doesn't want to admit it, and that's why she seemed cross. She was worried about you, that's all. She knows as well as I do that May Eve is one night you have to stay away from the fairy world, because it's a night you could find yourself walking right into it. It's very nearly as dangerous as going near that mound on *Samhain*.' (That was what her grandmother called Halloween and she pronounced it to rhyme with 'now-in'.)

Cornelia and Barry remembered both of those episodes well, and each of them had come to the same conclusion. 'Gran is right,' is how Barry summed it up. 'They know the fairies are down there, but they don't want to admit it.'

Their grandparents, however, enjoyed talking about fairies, and seemed to know a lot about them. 'They don't know what troubles are,' said their grandmother, 'which makes their world seem very nice to humans, but they don't know what time is either, and that can cause problems, even thought the fairies don't mean it to. That's what your mother was worried about. She was afraid you might wander into their world, think it was a lovely place, and up staying there a hundred years even though you'd think you were there only an hour or two.'

'Listen, you'll be fine with the fairies,' her grandfather put in, 'so long as you don't interfere with what's theirs. That's why you never cut their trees or dig their forts. If you ever did—' her grandfather shook his head ominously. 'Well, the truth is, I don't know what would happen if you did that, and I don't want to find out either.'

All this knowledge raced through Cornelia's head when she saw the ugly machine take a great scoop of earth out of the fort, and made her heart beat so fast that she felt as if an engine were running out of control inside her. The machine dumped the fairy fort earth onto a truck and then returned to scoop up some more; and at that point, her father closed the curtains and told her not to look out any more.

'Daddy, the fairies will know that we're not the ones digging up their fort, won't they?' Cornelia asked worriedly. 'Granddad says—'

'Of course they'll know,' he said definitely, and for

once he made no attempt to imply that fairies could not think anything at all because fairies did not really exist. 'The fairies know as well as we do that the Lawful Guild and every one of those Pickenoses are nothing but trouble.'

After he left, Cornelia felt oddly lonely, and even a bit frightened. It had been bad enough seeing the Ryans' house being knocked down, but seeing their fairy fort being dug into bothered her in ways she didn't fully understand, almost as if the world were being controlled by different forces today than it had been yesterday.

After a few minutes, she went over to the bed and lay down on it, tucking Daisy and Strudel and Zanzibar under one arm; and just this once, she brought Josephine into bed with her, too, to cheer herself up, because, in happier times, even a single look at Josephine's unfriendly, forbidding face was enough to make her laugh. This time the doll had no effect, but after a while, Cornelia fell asleep. When she woke, the only light in the curtained room was coming from the fire that was still burning brightly.

She held Josephine up so that she could see her more clearly in the firelight and played gently for a while with the doll's beautiful, beaded dress; and for the first time in her life, she even touched Josephine's head gently to her cheek, and rubbed it up and down, as she was more in the habit of doing with Strudel or Daisy. 'I wish things were the way they were before, Josephine,' she whispered after a while.

'So do I, Kiddo,' she heard Josephine whisper back. 'So do I.'

—Chapter 7—

Homeless

INSIDE THE FAIRY FORT on the Ryans' land, preparations had been under way for some time for sudden evacuation, but nevertheless, when the big machine came and started to scoop away the roof from over their heads, there was widespread panic.

Some fairies fled immediately; some hung on until no trace of the fort remained. All of them were given shelter across the glen in King Thistle's fort, which was the mound in the field in front of Cornelia's house, where they were provided with warm, sweet drinks and wrapped in blankets by Thistle's very efficient emergency aid staff.

May and Fuchsia were with them, of course, but while most of their subjects could not stop themselves looking back across the glen at the site of their own vanished world, the king could not take his eyes off Cornelia's house, finding it hard to believe (and very glad none of his subjects knew) that he should now regard the survival of this mere human house as of greater significance than the destruction of his own kingdom.

'We mustn't panic,' he said to May perhaps half-a-dozen times. 'The house-knocking machine has gone away and it probably wouldn't have done that if it were going to knock down this house too, so we mustn't panic yet. And usually, the Lawful Guild drives the humans out before they knock down their houses, and these humans are still in there, so there's no need to panic.'

May hardly heard him, too disturbed by the misery she was seeing all around her.

'They find it hard to believe they're really homeless, don't they?' she said, distractedly. 'And if the machine destroys Thistle's kingdom as well—' Gratefully, the queen accepted the cup of sweet tea pressed into her hand by a solicitous nurse, fighting hard not to give way to the feeling of hopelessness growing inside her.

The truth was that fairies had just about run out of space in Emeraldia now that so many forts had been destroyed. The Terror had started over twenty great festival days ago (five years by a human calendar), and throughout that time, she and King Fuchsia had been taking in refugees from every part of Emeraldia as kingdom after kingdom had been destroyed. The legendary hospitality of May and Fuchsia had made their fort one of the most popular refuges; but as a result, it had got very, very crowded.

As far back as twelve festivals ago, they thought things had got about as bad as they could when they had been forced to knock down bedroom walls and create great open dormitories filled with rows and rows of bunk beds to accommodate all the new arrivals.

At first, just one narrow bed had been put over another, which was bad enough; but then a second had to be added above that, and then a third, and then a fourth, and then a fifth, as more and more traumatized and dispossessed refugees kept appearing from far and near. And finally, even that many sleeping places had not been enough, and they'd had to call in engineering fairies with calculators to work out the maximum safe number of these depressing beds that could be stacked on top of one another.

But even then, no one liked to talk about the crowding, because at the back of everyone's mind was the secret fear that they would run out of room entirely within the fort, and then no one was sure what would happen.

The fairies could not replace the forts that were lost. For them, the forts were the world, and were as irreplaceable to their existence as the sun and the oceans and the mountains were to humans; and now, their beautiful, happy ancient world, which had existed long before any human lived in Emeraldia, was rapidly being destroyed.

And it was not just their underground kingdoms that were being obliterated. Certain above-ground trees belonged entirely to fairies and were, in human terms, the equivalent of well established ancient inns, where fairies met one another when travelling. Until the Terror began, humans had respected these fairy trees and never even cut a branch from them. But lately—King Fuchsia shook his head just thinking about it—lately, fairy trees were vanishing as rapidly as the forts.

He found it hard to believe that he and May were homeless refugees themselves now, dependent on the charity of their good but solemn neighbour, Thistle, a much more serious and abstemious fairy than King Fuchsia, whose dinners rarely extended to more than ten or twelve courses, compared to the fifty courses that he and May were in the habit of presenting.

King Fuchsia took a drink of the sweet tea himself, and followed May's worried eyes, which now were focused on the lone hawthorn tree in the field in front of Cornelia's house (one of their traditional meeting trees) and at the fairy, Tansy, who, as usual, was sitting on a branch of it, looking intently at the humans' house.

'Hurry, Fuchsia,' May said urgently. 'Go talk to Tansy right now, and tell her what it is we need her to do. Just slip away quietly, and I'll talk to Thistle and make all the dining and dormitory arrangements.'

'Now?' said Fuchsia. 'Are you sure? Won't Thistle and our own fairies think it a bit odd if they see me in a tree talking to Tansy at a time like this?'

'They'll just think that Tansy has been badly affected by what's happened. Go ahead, Fuchsia. Quickly. And don't beat about the bush and worry her. Just tell her straight out how she's the only one who can do this for us, and she won't let us down.'

Chapter 8

The Foundling Fairy

TANSY WAS THE BIGGEST MYSTERY in the history of Emeraldia fairies. She was a foundling—the first and only foundling ever; and before she appeared, no one had believed there could be such a thing as a foundling fairy. She had come from nowhere, appearing one day outside May and Fuchsia's fort, unable or unwilling to tell the astonished fairies anything about her past.

King Fuchsia and Queen May were hospitable to every stranger, but on this mysterious, beautiful creature, whose eyes were full of pain and terror (unprecedented experiences for a fairy) they lavished real love.

After a while, Tansy became less nervous—at least, around Fuchsia and May—but no one ever found out anything about her background. Interestingly, when she first arrived, she spelled her name differently. Back then, she wrote it as '*Tänzī*'; but after just a short time in Fuchsia's fort, she changed the spelling to Tansy. None of the fairies understood the reason for this, but it added to her mystique.

She fascinated all the fairies and remained the subject of much speculation, because there really was something very different about her. She even looked different. She was just a little bit slimmer than other fairies, and a little

GALWAY COUNTY LIBRARIES

bit paler, and she lived in a world of her own. She was a very beautiful creature, and her unusual elegance might have intimidated the Emeraldia fairies a bit if she hadn't been so remarkably shy and nervous. Tansy dreaded attention, loved solitude, and, to the bewilderment of everyone in the kingdom, seemed to find humans more interesting than fairies.

This last quality was most confusing, because fairies in general paid very little attention to humans, unless fairies' self-interest was immediately threatened. A few did, but these tended to be academic-minded, eccentric fairies (badly dressed, usually, and in need of a haircut) who studied all types of mortal life.

In fact, there was a taboo about fairies having too much close contract with humans, although contact was allowed and enjoyed with other mortal creatures such as animals and birds. Humans were perceived as different from these, although a lot of fairies found it hard to understand why, as humans too were no more than insignificant, flawed creatures whose lives were hard and uncertain and, in fairies' terms, lasted for only a moment.

The only thing the fairies knew for sure about Tansy was that the mystery of her background had provided them with endless hours of pleasurable gossip and speculation. There were many colourful theories about her past, but the one which had the greatest backing was that she was a foreign fairy who had not grown wings.

Emeraldia fairies were the only fairies in the world who did not have wings and they transported themselves into the air by raising whirlwinds. If the popular theory about Tansy was correct, there was a thought that she might have been brought (or had run away by herself) to Emeraldia where she would not stand out for being wingless, but would be the same as everyone else.

What gave extra weight to this theory was that Tansy had been unable to raise whirlwinds at first, until Queen May had taken her in hand, and had worked with her privately until she could whirlwind well enough to get herself more or less where she wanted to go, although she never became skilful enough to gain speed or to keep a straight line.

However, Tansy was as good as any of them at mind-portation, which was the principal fairy mode of travel and used for journeys that were long or complex. When travelling by mind-portation, a fairy simply thought about where he or she wanted to go, and there he or she was; and so far as Fuchsia and May could see, Tansy had no problem with this.

She was a mystery all right, but an engaging one; and all the fairies respected—even though they could not understand—her very unusual need for solitude. So when the fort became so crowded that just about every fairy (except King Fuchsia and Queen May, of course) was sleeping in a bunk bed in a crowded dormitory, Tansy was allowed to keep a small cubicle of her own. None of the fairies grudged her this privilege. Tansy needed her privacy. They all knew that.

There were circumstances, however, in which Fuchsia and May only, to their great surprise, had seen Tansy relax and turn into the most exuberant and high-spirited fairy they had ever seen—a creature so different from the shy, nervous fairy they had come to know that, in talking privately about these occasions afterwards, they called her 'the other Tansy'; and it was because of what they had seen 'the other Tansy' do that Fuchsia had come here now to the hawthorn tree to talk to her in private.

In the present crisis, Tansy was even more jumpy and nervous than usual; and the king's unexpected arrival beside her on the tree gave her a particular fright.

'Oh dear,' she said anxiously, her mind leaping to the worst possible conclusion. 'Have you come to tell me there's no room for me in King Thistle's fort? If there isn't, it's all right really. I can—'

'No, no, no,' said Fuchsia quickly. 'In fact, so far as Thistle goes, it's just the opposite. He's made special arrangements for you and is giving you a little cubicle of your own, I believe, and he was very happy to do that. He's a good friend, Thistle, and that serious face of his shouldn't worry you. He looks a bit dour, I know, but that's only because he thinks the rest of us spend too much time thinking about food and clothes and parties and dancing instead of improving our minds, but at the back of it all, he's a very decent fairy, and anyone who's in trouble can always rely on him.

'No, the reason I've come to talk to you, Tansy, is because the queen and I need your help. We've been working on a plan that might help us all, but it involves the humans who live in that house, and that's why we need your help.

'Ah, Tansy, are you all right?' Fuchsia asked, as she stared at him wild-eyed. Her expression was so strange that he even wondered if he should fetch one of those tea-proffering nurses for her in case she was more shaken than he realised by the destruction of the fort. It could hardly be anything *he* had said that had induced such a dramatic change in her appearance—that her eyes glowed so fiercely they looked as if they could go on fire.

In fact, however, his words were entirely to blame, but for a reason that would have reassured the king if Tansy had not been so dumbfounded that she was unable to explain. The truth was that she had never heard such magical words before—well, not spoken to *her* anyway—and hearing them now amounted to nothing less than a fantasy come true.

Imagine—she had been asked for help by another fairy! And not just by any fairy, but by the great King Fuchsia himself. She was all too used to being an object of charity and pity, but this was the greatest compliment of her existence.

Fuchsia, unfortunately, had no inkling of any of this. He just had an uncomfortable feeling that what he was about to say would embarrass Tansy, and he did not relish that at all, particularly when she was looking so hot and bothered already. He took a deep breath, reminding himself of May's advice just to say what he had to say quickly and get this business over with.

'Right, well, you remember how I told in the past that it was wrong to go—well, you know, to get as close to humans as you have done?' he said hurriedly. 'And, you know, all things being equal, that would still be the right way of things, but of course we're in a special situation now—a battle for survival, in fact. The rulebook's been destroyed with the fort, you might say, and what we badly need now is someone who doesn't mind—well, you know what I mean—'

He was talking about the violation of an ancient and strict taboo, and that was why he was having so much trouble with his words. He was asking Tansy to do something with humans that Emeraldia fairies regarded as abnormal and wrong, and that he and May had told Tansy she must never do again, but now he was asking her to forget what they'd said because the survival of all of Emeraldia's fairies depended on it. (Yes, he knew he himself had engaged in that revolting manner with a human once, but the circumstances had been desperate on that occasion and left him no choice, and he still shivered in horror when he remembered the experience.)

Tansy turned away embarrassed, and Fuchsia, too, looked down at the ground, finding it hard to believe he was having to say these things. Still, he had to persevere. His Plan now was the only hope they had.

'You know what I mean, Tansy,' he added uncomfortably. 'You'll need to do what I saw you do before, and even more.'

Chapter 9

The House at Fairy's Leap

FUCHSIA had been working on this Plan for four human years, ever since his first visit to the human house when he had stumbled accidentally on the mysteries inside Cornelia's bedroom. Tansy, he discovered, had known about the strange phenomena in that bedroom even before he did, but had told no one. Fuchsia himself, when he learned about them, told only Queen May.

That momentous first visit had come about by pure chance. The morning had been an unusually fine one, and King Fuchsia happened to have wandered out for a sunny stroll in his invisible form.

It was the small terrier (then a young pup) that pulled him inside the house. The grey sheepdog had been stretched out asleep on the front step, but the white pup had been full of exuberance, expressing her general contentment with life and the world by running great, joyous figures-of-eight in the grass.

The sight of her had made Fuchsia laugh, and on impulse, he did something he had not done for a while: he went inside the little dog.

The power to possess animals and birds was something all fairies had, but Fuchsia had not used this power for a long time, because he had found that life as experienced by those mortal creatures was dull and often painful compared to the glorious existence of the fairies. Still, the degree of pleasure being expressed by this little animal made him curious to learn what might be the cause of it.

A tasty meal of left-over roast chicken just finished; the comfort of warm sun on sweet-smelling grass; the bliss of having been rubbed behind her ears and having had her tummy scratched by everyone who lived in the house that morning; and a well-formed plan to go upstairs and have a comfortable nap on Cornelia's bed just as soon as she had finished expressing to the world her satisfaction at a glorious morning in general and an excellent breakfast of chicken in particular—that, he learned, was the cause of the pup's exuberance.

Enjoying himself, Strudel decided to stay with her when she suddenly ended her figure-of-eight pattern and ran as fast as she could into the house, through the door at the back that led directly to the kitchen. Fuchsia started to laugh again at what he saw inside there.

Music was coming out of a machine (it was a CD player and the music was a rumba performed by a Latin American orchestra) and two humans (Cornelia's parents) were attempting to dance to it, and by the fairy's standards, doing a truly terrible job, although they were laughing so hard that he decided they were probably not concentrating on it as fully as they should.

Two older humans were sitting in front of the range watching them and they were laughing even harder than the people who were dancing.

'You're not going to get anywhere with him, Katie,' the older man said, wiping his eyes with the hilarity of it all. 'He never had a step in his leg.'

'Look, we'll just try to get the rhythm right anyway,' Cornelia's mother said as seriously as she could. 'This book says the rhythm is: slow—slowish quick—quickish quick; and we lift our bodies up slightly at the end of the second quick and we drop on the slow.'

At that point, the four humans all broke down laughing so hard they could do nothing at all. 'I wish we had a few more days to practice before the wedding,' Cornelia's mother said as soon as she could speak. 'All of the O'Donnells are such good dancers and we're going to be hopeless.'

Hopeless did not even begin to describe how bad they were, Fuchsia thought to himself. He would have liked to help, but he could hardly justify making himself visible before mortals just to show them a dance step. Still he did love to rumba, and he could see no harm in giving a little demonstration by other means.

'Well, will you look at that,' said Cornelia's grandfather suddenly. 'Look at the pup. She's dancing to the music.'

At the sight of this, everyone started laughing even harder. 'She's not just dancing to the music,' Cornelia's mother pointed out. 'She's dancing the "Right Top Turn". Look, she's crossing her right paws in front of her left paws.'

'And she's dropping on the slow and rising on the

quick,' Cornelia's grandmother added, and then the four of them started laughing helplessly again.

'Well, I think that decides it,' Cornelia's father said as soon as he was able to speak. 'Now that it's established that we can't dance as well as the dog, I think we ought to give up. We can send the dog to the wedding.'

Before Fuchsia could hear any more of this discussion, he heard a very faint rustle of paper that meant nothing at all to him but seemed to have great significance for the pup, who suddenly wanted to run upstairs.

Reluctantly, Fuchsia gave up his dance and went along with her as she tore out of the room and headed towards the stairs, taking in her shock as she slipped on the shiny flagstones in the hall, and her grumbles about how hard it was to get up the stairs, and her panic in case she would not reach the top of them in time when something so important was up there.

The childproof gate at the top was the final obstacle, and having squeezed herself between the slats, she tore down the hall and into a room where two very young humans were sitting at either side of a low table, and Fuchsia immediately understood the reason for her urgency.

The boy and girl (then aged five and four) had a small bar of chocolate, which they were in the process of dividing, and it was the sound of this being unwrapped that had caught the terrier's attention over all other noises. They started laughing when they saw her, and each of them gave her a piece of chocolate, the boy pointing out proudly to his sister, 'Tickles can hear a sweet being unwrapped from anywhere in the house.'

Already, Fuchsia was feeling more comfortable in this house than in any human dwelling he had ever been in. The laughter, the dancing, the love of food: it made him feel almost as if he were back at home in his own kingdom. And then, just to make the situation even more interesting, the children started to talk about fairies.

Or rather, the little girl did; the boy was concentrating on a pile of small coloured plastic pieces on the table out of which he was building a castle. The little girl was also working on the castle, but she was not as interested in it as the boy and she was doing most of the talking, and also much petting of Tickles, whom she had lifted on to her lap, and was holding there along with a small stuffed toy dog that she held tightly in her hand.

'The Emeraldia fairies don't have wings, you know,' she told the little boy. 'Fairies from outside Emeraldia have wings, but our fairies need to make their own whirlwinds to fly. Did you know that?'

'Everyone knows that,' the little boy said dismissively. 'That's how you know when fairies are around. When you feel the wind.'

Fuchsia listened to this discussion with interest from his position inside Tickles. The children's information was accurate as far as it went, but he wondered if they knew about mind-portation as well, which, of course, was the principal mode of fairy travel.

Before they could continue, however, he felt himself

jolted suddenly as Tickles snapped to attention at the sound of a machine being turned on downstairs. She jumped off Cornelia's lap and dashed over to the door that had closed behind her when she came in, pawing at it eagerly and wagging.

'Mommy's turned on the food mixer,' Cornelia explained to Barry, as she opened the door to let the pup out.

Quick as a flash, Fuchsia decided he did not want to leave that room just yet. He was interested in this discussion, and he thought it was a good thing for fairies to know the extent of common human knowledge about them.

However, to avoid the need to hover around in mid-air (and thereby create the give-away wind that he now realised the children knew about) he popped himself quickly out of Tickles and directly into the small stuffed dog the girl was holding in her hand.

It was a move made on the spur of the moment, and he would not have expected it to have any consequences, but he was wrong about this. Ultimately, in fact, it would prove to be the most important decision of his long existence.

—*Chapter 10*—

Strudel, Zanzibar & Daisy

THE BIGGEST SHOCK for Fuchsia came in the first second, because as soon as he went inside the stuffed dog, Cornelia's bedroom vanished. Quicker than even he could blink, the walls, the ceiling, the furniture, the children, and even the voices of the children had disappeared, and he was inside a wintry, outdoor world that smelled of cinnamon and pine trees and freshly baked cookies, and in which the people wore fur coats and spoke in German, which, perplexingly, was the language in which Fuchsia suddenly found himself thinking.

It was a nice world, but he had no idea how he had arrived in it, and experiencing for the first time in his existence a feeling that a mortal might call panic, he mind-ported himself back into the bedroom as quickly as he could, and began to breathe normally again only after he saw that nothing had changed and things were exactly as he had left them.

'Do you think that's a fairy breeze?' Cornelia asked, as she brushed away hair that had blown in front of her eyes.

'I don't know,' her brother said distractedly, his attention on the bright yellow tower he was adding to the multi-coloured plastic castle. 'Maybe.'

51

Well, this is something new, Fuchsia thought to himself, and his momentary panic was replaced by an unfamiliar sense of excitement. He had known much joy and comfort in his long life, but almost no mystery or adventure, and his trip inside the stuffed dog undoubtedly amounted to both.

Quickly, he smoothed down his hair and conjured for himself a sable overcoat and a black hat with a modestly rakish brim. Although he planned to remain invisible in this mystery world, he was not sure what rules applied in it; and if there was any chance he might be seen, he wanted to be certain he was appropriately dressed. Vanity had always been one of Fuchsia's small weaknesses.

'Well, here goes,' he murmured, and shot himself right back inside the dog.

Cornelia looked at Strudel with interest, and held the toy dog in front of her, again having to push back the hair that had blown in front of her eyes so that she could study him more closely. 'I think Strudel moved,' she said.

Barry said nothing, his full attention on the castle, to which he was adding a final turret.

Inside Strudel, Fuchsia could no longer hear anything being said in the bedroom. Instead, he was hearing carollers singing '*Stille Nacht, Heilige Nacht,*' and he was looking at a small merry-go-round of tiny live ponies, and at children waiting in line excitedly to get a ride on one.

He was surrounded by evergreen trees lit by what seemed to be thousands of small coloured lights and hung with primitive (no jewels and no gold, he noted sadly) but still pleasing decorations.

He whirlwinded around studying these cheerful baubles. They included lots of representations of a man in a red suit and white beard carrying bags of toys. There were shiny balls and bells; there were tiny toy bears and tiny train engines; there were images in every colour and size of beings with wings (foreign fairies, he thought at first, but on closer inspection, he could see that these were something different); there were tiny drums, tiny violins, tiny French horns, and tiny trumpets hung by tiny red ribbons.

Fuchsia had no idea where he was, but wherever he was, he loved it. It turned out that he was, in fact, invisible, so the dashing style of his sable coat and his rakish hat would not be appreciated here by anyone but himself, but he was glad of their warmth. Snow was falling and the air was bitingly crisp and cold; and thinking his feet and neck needed more cover, he decided to round off his winter outfit by conjuring up a cashmere scarf and fleece-lined boots and gloves. That is, he tried to conjure them, but when he did, nothing appeared.

Uneasy about this, he mind-ported himself back to the bedroom but relaxed again when he found he had no problem in conjuring up the wardrobe alterations there. So once more, he went back inside the dog, but this time he was even more careful to keep his wits about him, now that he knew he did not have the same powers inside this strange world as he had in the real world.

Most of the child humans were walking around with mugs of something hot and most of the adult humans were carrying glasses of something red, and almost everyone seemed to be eating something. The more Fuchsia saw of this world, the more he liked it. The aroma of baking overpowered his will entirely, and he decided no one would mind if he sampled a few cookies and a glass of that red drink; and to his delight, several couples started to dance a waltz in the square beside him.

The humans here were better at doing the waltz than the two people back in the kitchen were at doing the rumba, but they still were nowhere near his high standard. He was tempted briefly to go back for Queen May, who liked to dance as much as he did, and who would love this cheerful place; but then he hesitated.

Could he be sure it was safe for her to come here, he wondered? Or was there a chance this extraordinary world could close its portals and trap a fairy behind them? And how in Nature's name did it come to be here in the first place? —these were matters that required a bit of study.

He had made up his mind immediately that no fairy but May should hear about this world. He knew his fun-loving subjects only too well; if they heard about it, they would be flocking here as a holiday playground, and who knew what the effects or dangers of that might be?

All the same, finding such a jolly place was about the best surprise he'd ever had. He whirlwinded around a little, and saw even more dancing, only this time it was on ice. Humans, wearing boots with metal blades on them, were gliding over ice, holding hands and twirling to music; and straightaway, Fuchsia decided to re-create a copy of this ice-dancing arena back in his own kingdom, as a sort of a guilt present for all the fairies from whom he would be keeping this place a secret.

He was aware of one tantalising link between this world and the humans' world outside the toy dog that was familiar to him. The words he was hearing these beings saying most to one another were '*frohe Weihnachten*'; and as Fuchsia was now thinking in German (But why? Why was he thinking in that language?) he knew that these words were the equivalent of the humans in Emeraldia saying 'Happy Christmas' to one another; and Fuchsia applied himself with contentment to pondering an old mystery.

Since humans had first started celebrating Christmas, the fairies had been curious about it. It was the only holiday humans celebrated which made the fairies a bit envious. In all other respects, they felt sorry for humans and for their insignificant, short, and usually hard lives. In the opinion of fairies (for whom magic, joy, and eternity were the norm) the birth of a human was followed almost immediately by its death; and in between, there was nothing much but dullness.

Except for this Christmas business.

All the fairies popped their heads above ground on

Christmas Eve to get a feel of it. There was a magic in the air that night that was different from the magic of Midsummer Night or Halloween or May Eve. The magic of those great fairy festivals was connected to nature: to the earth, the streams, the trees and things the fairies understood. This Christmas Eve magic, however, was different. Its power source seemed to be from a different place; and although Fuchsia hated to admit it (even to himself) his experience was that it excluded fairies.

This thought made him remember that he was lingering longer than he should in an unknown world, and reluctantly, he decided he had better test once again his ability to leave it. So, just as he had done before, he visualised the bedroom and, yes, this time too, everything was all right. Out he popped, locating himself just over the table where the children were playing.

'He did it again,' Cornelia said suddenly, her hair blowing around her face. 'Strudel moved. He definitely moved.'

This time, Barry just grunted, but Cornelia stood up and took Strudel over to the window to look at him in better light. Fuchsia would have liked to take a close look at Strudel himself, but he decided it would be more discrete to do so when that now very curious human was not holding the toy in her hands, studying it from every angle, and looking particularly closely into the toy dog's little black eyes.

When it seemed the child was not going to let the toy out of her hands any time soon, he passed the time by taking a leisurely tour of the room. He looked out the window at his own fort at the other side of the glen, looked also at the closer fort of King Thistle, and saw many fairies from both forts stretched out on the grass and enjoying the sunny day.

Remaining at the window, he looked across at the other toys lined up on the bed; and then on a sudden impulse (and having grown in confidence following his third successful exit from the toy dog) he decided to see what would happen if he went inside another of them. The rag doll, Daisy, was the closest, and with a growing sense of excitement, he shot inside her first, and yes, the same extraordinary thing happened again.

One moment, Fuchsia was in the bedroom; the next, he was in a sunny meadow, in the middle of a group of people winching large, dome-shaped stacks of hay onto a hay float: a big, flat, timber structure on low wheels pulled by a large horse.

This time, he knew exactly where he was—the far south of Emeraldia—but this was old, familiar Emeraldia, before all the green fields were covered with concrete and tarmac and before the peace and sweetness of the countryside were destroyed by noisy, smelly, machines in which humans now seemed to spend all their time.

Three human children had just finished a picnic lunch, and as soon as the hay had been loaded onto the float, they hopped up excitedly behind it, and sat with their feet dangling over the back of the float as a man began to drive the horse through the fields towards the barns.

Fuchsia hopped up beside the children, and leaned back with a sense of deep contentment: sorry, yes, that he couldn't conjure up a cotton shirt and a straw hat; and sorrier still that May wasn't sitting here beside him in a summer dress; but nevertheless, loving every sound, smell and sight of this extraordinary experience, and lost in the memories this ride on a hay-float brought back.

He thought, not for the first time, what a great pity it was that humans had replaced horses with machines for doing their country jobs. From a fairy's point of view, the only result of this change was that, all at once, simple sources of joy had vanished, such as this most sublime pleasure of being transported slowly and bumpily behind a pile of sweet-smelling hay in the warm sunshine.

He would have enjoyed staying longer in this green and greatly-missed world, but he couldn't stop wondering now what might be lurking within the other toys he had seen in the bedroom. So far, he knew for sure, this house had provided him with more fun than anything he had before encountered above ground.

When he had mind-ported back to the bedroom, he saw that Barry was no longer there and Cornelia had fallen asleep on the bed holding on to both Strudel and a cloth elephant. Feeling freer to whirlwind about when she was asleep, Fuchsia shot confidently into a plastic doll with a pink dress and was surprised to find himself coming out the other side, having encountered nothing but plastic.

So not all the toys had a world inside them, he concluded; he hovered over them in the air, comparing Strudel and Daisy and the plastic doll, and formed a theory. He could see that Strudel and Daisy looked as if they had been made by someone who was not that much of an expert at making toys, whereas the plastic doll had no flaw or fault in it, and probably had been made by a machine.

He reached this conclusion surprisingly quickly because fairies had been making similar observations for some time in relation to hay and hedges and other countryside matters which were of importance to them. Before machines came into the countryside, every stack of hay was a different shape and hedgerows were not cut down almost to the ground in sharp lines that offended nature but were just nice, thorny collections of different trees and bushes that happened to be planted in a row.

The fairies were not big fans of machinery of any sort, and Fuchsia now had a strong impression that machine-created toys did not have a world within them, and hand-made toys did. He suspected that the personality, world and thinking of the person who made the toys, and the circumstances that led to each toy's creation, remained forever within it.

He looked carefully at the sad-eyed toy elephant, Zanzibar, which Cornelia had tucked under her arm as she slept, and he had no doubt that this imperfectly sewn little toy had been made by hand, so he decided to test his theory by shooting inside it.

He saw immediately that, yes, his theory was correct,

and once again he was in a separate world; but right away, he was sorry that he had ever even thought of going inside the elephant, because this was not a good world at all. Inside Zanzibar, he was forced to look at the most terrible scenes he had ever witnessed in his life.

He was surrounded by a cloud of dust and by elephants of every size screaming and running. To his amazement, he saw baby elephants with tears streaming from their eyes while terrible cracking noises exploded all around them. He saw huge adult elephants—some of them covered in blood and roaring in pain—trying to protect their young, while simultaneously trying to fight with and to run away from the cracking noises that came from guns held by a large number of male humans.

The humans were shooting from positions beside their driving machines, and they had lined up these machines behind a barrier they had constructed for the purpose of trapping the elephants in a small ravine.

Moving more quickly than he had ever done, Strudel shot out of Zanzibar and out the window, and got another big surprise when he almost crashed into Tansy who was travelling towards the window at that moment by means of her awkward whirlwind. Tansy, who never spoke until she was spoken to, made an exception this time when she saw Fuchsia's horrified expression. 'Oh, what happened?' she said. 'Has something happened?'

'Tansy, come away from there,' said Fuchsia, and guided her quickly to the fairies' own hawthorn tree, saying nothing for a few moments while he tried to steady himself, and while Tansy looked at him with wide, frightened eyes. Suddenly Tansy put her hands up to her face in horror.

'Oh, I know, I know,' she said miserably. 'I know what happened. You were inside the elephant,' she said, startling him. 'You were inside the elephant. Oh, I wish I'd known,' she added miserably. 'I wish I'd known. I could have warned you.'

— Chapter 11 —

The Silver Poodle Club

THE DAY HAD HELD SO many surprises for Fuchsia, he could barely take them all in. 'Tansy, do you mean to say you know about those toys?' he asked.

Tansy nodded guiltily. 'I go into the house a lot,' she said. 'I like it there.'

'I see,' said Fuchsia confusedly, as a thought suddenly struck him. 'Tansy, was it you…did you have anything to do with what's inside those toys?'

Tansy shook her head. 'No, I just found them. They're all very nice inside them, except the elephant. After I went inside him, I didn't go back to the room for a long time, but the elephant's the only one that's bad inside. The rest are lovely, and the mean-looking man and woman are—' She broke off, and surprised Fuchsia greatly by giggling. He had never seen Tansy giggle before. 'Well, I like them best. They're exciting.'

The longer this encounter went on, the more disoriented Fuchsia became, and also (in the face of Tansy's relaxed familiarity with the strange worlds inside that house) not a little embarrassed that he had been so frightened himself. Wasn't it lucky, he thought privately, that it was only the un-gossipy Tansy who had seen him whirlwinding in terror from that bedroom as fast as he could? Now, he was impatient to go back and see what else was in there.

'Which are the mean-looking man and woman?' he asked with interest. 'I'm not sure I remember them. I saw some pink things, but—'

'Usually they're on a shelf,' Tansy explained, 'but when the small mortal is having other small mortals to visit, her mother sometimes puts them away in a cupboard. Do you want me to show you?' she offered eagerly.

'Right now, if you're willing,' he said gratefully, and politely adjusted his own powerful whirlwind to Tansy's weaving, unsteady line. He followed her in through the open window of the bedroom, where Cornelia now was sitting up on the bed, having been awakened by a great shudder of Zanzibar, whose sad eyes and curled trunk she was studying very closely. Tansy went straight across the room into a pink wardrobe.

'There they are,' she said, giggling again.

Fuchsia looked appreciatively at the sour faces and distinctive clothing of Jules and Josephine—the male doll's beautifully tailored dinner jacket and the female doll's beaded dress and bobbed hair reminding him of some of the best parties he had ever attended.

'Which one do we go into?' he asked.

'Well, I usually go into her,' Tansy told him, but I don't think it matters really. They're nearly always together, so you end up in the same place.'

'You do what you usually do,' Fuchsia suggested, 'and I'll follow.'

So they both mind-ported inside Josephine, and

this time Fuchsia found himself in a crowded dark and smoky room reverberating with cheerful music and almost filled with tables at which very glamorous humans, dressed in much the same style as the two dolls themselves, were eating, drinking, laughing and talking loudly. There was a large dance floor, and this was teeming with couples dancing with wild vigour.

'Mother of Nature,' the king exclaimed enthusiastically. 'This is the best yet. A nightclub! And you know, Tansy,' he added, with a touch of awe in his voice, 'this is not just any nightclub. This is—'

Words failed Fuchsia for a moment as he surrendered himself to the dizzying exhilaration of a dedicated collector who has stumbled on a treasure rarer than he believed existed.

'It's very nice,' Tansy said helpfully.

'Nice!' he exclaimed, horrified. 'Tansy, this is not nice—this is *perfect*! In fact, what this is, Tansy,' he said seriously, and in a voice which mixed reverence with the didacticism of an authority speaking on a subject close to his heart, '*this* is a nightclub from the Golden Age of nightclubs.'

Being an acknowledged connoisseur in such matters, Fuchsia took in appreciatively the excellence of the jazz musicians, the bold decoration (cutting-edge for its period, he noted approvingly, which his practised eye judged to be the human year 1927) and the din created by those very well-dressed hundreds of humans talking, laughing and dancing.

'But our clothes are all wrong,' he said, finding the

two of them were disturbing the visual harmony of this world. 'Come on, we'll have to mind-port back to the house and change.'

They returned immediately to Cornelia's bedroom where Fuchsia conjured an outfit almost identical to that worn by Jules; and Tansy, to the king's surprise, transformed herself into a being of almost unrecognisable sophistication in a black dress with diamond straps and diamonds embroidered down the front in the pattern of a great and elaborate necklace; earrings so long they reached the middle of her neck; and a sleek, glossy bob.

'You know, we'll have to bring Queen May to see this world, whatever the risks,' Fuchsia said when they were back inside the doll. 'She was an exceptionally good Charleston dancer—the best in the whole kingdom,' he added with quiet pride.

Privately, Fuchsia thought he himself had danced a pretty mean Charleston too, and had greatly enjoyed doing so when it was in fashion; and he had been sorry that in the style-conscious fairy world, as much as in the human world, that joyous and liberating step and beat had been consigned to memory and to the odd masquerade party. The thought that he would be able to dance it again in its own era made him forget briefly his usual reserved caution and give Tansy a quick hug of gratitude for bringing him there.

'There's the head-waiter, Henri,' Tansy said, pointing to a heavy man in a tailcoat who was casting an unwelcoming eye towards a nervous young couple that had just come up the stairs and through the double entrance doors.

'Those people must be tourists,' she said, appraising the headwaiter's unfriendly expression, 'because Henri likes to be mean to tourists. He always puts them at tables in that back corner of the room, and he only puts people he knows at the good tables up near the dance floor. He's mean to new waiters too and takes their tips sometimes, but I make him give them back.'

'How do you do that?' Fuchsia asked curiously, but Tansy didn't hear him, having drifted away towards the dance floor. Her whirlwind, as always, was awkward, and caused such a breeze that it dislodged a feather from the headband of an older woman sitting at one of the tables, and several laughing men ran after it as it wafted around in the air just out of their reach.

Fuchsia was laughing with them, but then he stopped suddenly as he saw with astonishment what Tansy was doing next.

Having reached the dance floor, she looked around for a moment, and then—as if it were the most natural thing in the world to her—she shot inside a woman in a pink, fringed dress who was dancing on it.

The woman already had been performing a lively Charleston, but now she began to dance with a degree of wild, exuberant skill that made all the other dancers—including her own partner—stop to look at her, and then made the entire room applaud loudly as she followed a breathtakingly high kick with a backwards somersault, landing from it on a table, where she continued dancing the most high-spirited Charleston Fuchsia had ever seen.

Like everyone else in the room, Fuchsia could not take his eyes off the woman; but while the humans were applauding and cheering, Fuchsia was observing with an expression of pure dismay.

What Tansy was doing now was so terrible he could hardly believe what he was seeing. Fairies did not go inside human beings. They went inside birds and animals all the time, and that was the natural order of things, but it was unforgivable and entirely against nature to go inside a human being.

No Emeraldia fairy had ever done it. He knew that. There were the rumours about certain foreign fairies, of course, and as he watched Tansy now, he wondered what on earth was her background, and could some of the wilder gossip about her possibly be true.

But what was he to do? How was he to stop her unless he went inside that dancing human himself and how could he even contemplate doing something so horrible?

Then, all of a sudden, Tansy did a second backwards somersault—this time a double one—and landed on another table to wild applause, and then she followed that extravagant move by a triple somersault in the opposite direction that took her right over the heads of the flabbergasted but appreciative musicians and back to the middle of the dance floor.

Fuchsia decided then that he had no choice. Steeling himself, he went inside the dancing human, blocking his mind to everything he was hearing, seeing or feeling inside her and concentrating only on Tansy's giggling presence.

'Tansy, come out of there immediately,' he said fiercely. 'Don't say one word, just come out immediately.'

Startled, Tansy jumped out of the woman in the pink dress and Fuchsia followed close behind her. Glancing over his shoulder, he saw this woman, looking bemused at being the centre of so much attention, standing almost alone on the dance floor as just about everyone in the room, including the musicians, stood on their feet and applauded her.

'Really, Tansy,' said Fuchsia crossly, taking a firm hold of her arm so that she could do nothing else that he was not expecting, 'that's the worst thing I've ever seen a fairy do. You must never—'

He broke off suddenly, his eyes caught by the only two humans in the room who were not standing and applauding. They were a man and woman who looked strangely familiar to him, but as fairies are not good at recognising human faces, it took him a moment to think who they might be; but when it came to him at last, he stared at them in fascination.

Where he had seen these grim faces before, he realised, was in the child's bedroom. These two wicked-looking people, so detached from, and resentful of, the uproarious gaiety that now filled the room, were the models for the two dolls inside whose world he now was. He had come face to face with the real Jules and Josephine.

—*Chapter 12*—

The Guardian of the Soldiers' Fort

I F FUCHSIA WERE MORE HIMSELF—and not profoundly disoriented still because of what Tansy had done and because of what he himself had just been forced to do—he would have burst out laughing when he saw Jules and Josephine up close. For humans, they were surprisingly distinctive: their bored, harsh, lifeless expressions being fixed as immovably on their living faces as they were on the painted faces of the dolls modelled on the two of them.

'They look like a pair of party masks,' he said to Tansy, his fascination at the appearance of these two distracting him briefly from his shock at what Tansy had done (although not enough to make him loosen his hold on her arm). 'It's hard to believe they're living beings.'

The unhappy Tansy silently agreed, but was so shaken by what had happened that she did not want to risk saying anything, and certainly she did not think this was the moment to tell the king how she had played a joke on Josephine once just to see if she could surprise her into a change of expression, even for an instant.

She had taken possession of the headwaiter and got him accidentally to drop an ice cube down Josephine's dress. The joke hadn't worked out very well, however, because what happened was that Josephine had stood up and, without any movement of her facial features, and without saying a word, had tapped the lighted end of her cigarette onto the headwaiter's gleaming white shirt front.

Tansy didn't think she had actually burned the waiter, but she had certainly ruined his nice shirt and made the whole room smell of scorch. The headwaiter said a lot of nasty things then, but Josephine didn't say anything and didn't even look at him, but just sat down as if nothing had happened; and Jules seemed not to have noticed that anything had happened in the first place, having stared straight ahead the entire time.

The headwaiter told Jules and Josephine to leave, but they ignored him, and then Tansy heard rumours that the headwaiter tried to have them banned from coming back; but then she heard another rumour that Jules and Josephine had influential friends, and that was why the headwaiter didn't even dare to seat them at a really bad table the next night, which was what he always did when he was mad at someone, but he gave them their usual table near the dance floor, which was a great waste of a good table, Tansy thought.

Still, after that episode, Tansy lost all interest in Jules and Josephine, thinking them the two dullest humans in this world.

Fuchsia, however, could not take his eyes off them, and was curious to know who their companion was, as he had noticed that there was a third glass on the table, and a third chair, the occupant of which (along with everyone else in the room, except Jules and Josephine) had risen to his feet to applaud the bewildered but gratified woman in the pink dress, who now was being carried in triumph off the dance floor by some of her appreciative audience. When the applause finally ended, this man turned around and sat down again.

'Oh Mother of Nature,' Fuchsia exclaimed again, so surprised when he saw who this human was that, for the first time in his existence, he lost the power and control of his whirlwind, and fell from the air right into the real Josephine's lap, dragging the startled Tansy with him, and causing Josephine's face (to Tansy's further astonishment) to show something like real expression for the first time in many years, and to look as if she had experienced a tiny electric shock.

Fuchsia, however, had forgotten that Josephine even existed, and was looking in disbelief at the man in the threadbare dinner jacket who now was sitting across the table from them.

'Maybe I will,' he was saying in a tired voice to Jules and Josephine. 'Maybe I will go along with you to Longchamp after all next week.'

This was more than enough for Fuchsia. He had made a startled examination of this human, inside as well as out, so that he could identify him for certain, and now he recognised the voice as well. He was sure of that—absolutely sure.

This human—without any doubt—was The Traitor: the human the fairies hated more than any other who had ever lived in Emeraldia—more even than Lawful Guild members and Pickenoses.

The fairies also called him (when they were being polite) 'The Unforgivable One', although in private, they called him much nastier and less repeatable names because what he had done had such consequences for them. The fairies had depended on him, and he had betrayed them. Before that despicable act, they had called him 'The Guardian of the Soldiers' Fort', but his treachery had ensured that no human would ever have that title again, Fuchsia thought bitterly.

If Cornelia had been there, she would have been as surprised as Fuchsia to see this man. She would have recognised him, from old photographs, as her great-granduncle, Finn O'Hara: the man for whom the Jules and Josephine dolls had been made, and who had been murdered in Paris by the apache street gang.

She would have been even more surprised to learn that this dead relative of hers was believed by the fairies to be responsible for so much harm; and, in the light of recent events, she would have been especially worried if she'd known that the crime for which he was so hated by them was that he had left Emeraldia and allowed the fairy fort that had been on his land to be destroyed.

That momentous first sighting of Cornelia's great-granduncle by Fuchsia had happened four years earlier: four years before the Lawful Guild would take over the Ryans' place, and four years before that family would have to leave and before Fuchsia's own kingdom would be dug from the earth. Even back then, however, life in Emeraldia already had started to seem dangerous and bad.

Dozens of fairy forts already had been dug up, and fairies and humans alike (at least those humans who were not members of the Lawful Guild and who were not named Pickenose) could see that Emeraldia rapidly was changing beyond recognition, and many human families already had left the country.

And all that terror and evil was the fault of this unforgivable human now sitting across the table from him (with nothing more important on his traitorous mind, thought Fuchsia bitterly, than some excursion to a racetrack).

Fuchsia shot out of that doll, pulling Tansy with him, and out of Cornelia's bedroom as quickly as he could, and back to the fort. This was something he had to tell May about immediately.

'Listen, Tansy, I don't have time to explain things to you now, but you must not go inside humans ever again,' Fuchsia said quickly. 'Emeraldia fairies don't do

GALWAY COUNTY LIBRARIES

that, and it would be better if they didn't know that you did it, so don't say anything to anyone. Queen May will have a word with you, and she'll be able to explain all this to you better than I can.'

Tansy looked back at him so miserably that Fuchsia felt the need to reassure her.

'It's all right, Tansy, really. In fact, I can't tell you how grateful I am to you for bringing me into that doll, and I think you've done us a great service. The reason I pulled you out of there so quickly is not because of what you did, but because I saw something in that nightclub that I think might be very important indeed.'

He was not happy about having to abandon Tansy while she was in such a state; but what he had seen was of such significance that he knew he had to tell the Queen about it immediately.

'Sit down, May,' was all Fuchsia could say to her, as soon as he was back in the fort and had tracked her down to their private quarters. 'You are not going to believe what I have to tell you.'

—Chapter 13—

The Black Air from the Underworld

THE SOLDIERS' FORT had been an important fairy military installation in Emeraldia for over a thousand human years. It was headquarters for Emeraldia's first and only fairy regiment of soldiers, this regiment having been established to deal with a danger that, until the year 700 AD (recent history to fairies) no fairy believed existed.

Before then, it had been just a normal residential fort, under the reign of the much-loved and very easygoing Queen Honeysuckle. All of this had changed, however, when a great fault had opened up in the earth under it, and Black Air was seen to be seeping out.

Only fairies could see the Black Air. Humans could not. It would have been better, probably, if this were the other way around because Black Air could not infect fairies, but it could infect and change humans, and make them dangerous to fairies. And while fairies could see this change happening to humans, they could do nothing to stop it.

The connection of Cornelia's great-granduncle to the Soldiers' Fort was that it had been located on his land, which was land that had belonged to his ancestors over a millennium earlier when the Black Air crisis first developed. For the fairies, the ownership of that land by Cornelia's ancestors had proved to be the only bit of luck in a situation that posed a profound danger to them.

Because, unlike most humans, all of Cornelia's ancestors, including her great-granduncle, had been immune to Black Air. It had no effect on them at all—no power to infect them in a way that would make them do harm to the fairies' world.

It was for this reason the worried fairies had broken all precedent in 700 AD and taken a gamble with those humans that they had never taken with humans before: the fairies made contact with them. Specifically, Queen Honeysuckle and King Clover (whose fort on the nearby island of Inisure also had been affected by Black Air) made themselves visible and called to visit them.

Fairies from all the other forts in Emeraldia, unseen by the humans, were present watching that unprecedented meeting. King Fuchsia remembered the legendary encounter very well.

He remembered the smoky, dark, crowded room inside the round, thatched, windowless building which was the sort of house humans lived in at that time in Emeraldia. He remembered the sense of hospitality and friendliness in that house. He remembered how the humans had not been especially surprised to find the fairies on their doorstep, but had greeted them as valued neighbours they had been hoping to meet one day.

They had put a big plate of oatcakes, a great pot of honey, a bowl of buttermilk and a bowl of mead before the two visible fairies, and told Queen Honeysuckle and King Clover that they were the two most important and welcome visitors they ever had in the house.

Queen Honeysuckle did her best to explain to the humans the problem of Black Air.

Black Air was the air from the Place at the Bottom, which they called 'The Underworld'. This was a joyless, treeless place directly under Emeraldia that had been separated off from the fairy world when the planet was still new, at the end of a terrible war between Emeraldia's good and bad fairies.

The power of the two sets of fairies had been evenly balanced in that war, and neither side had been able to defeat the other. Finally, however, a truce had been agreed between them.

It was decided that the good fairies (who loved trees, flowers, rippling water, and laughter) would have the part of Emeraldia that was right up at the top, where they would live so close to the surface that the roofs of their kingdoms would be visible all over it as mounds.

The bad fairies, on the other hand, who fed on cruelty and hated nature, would have the hard, ugly, dark, and smelly Underworld that was deep under that green surface. Both sides saw this as a permanent arrangement, and as a mark of their new independence, the Underworld beings even changed their name: they would no longer be called 'fairies' but 'Spirits of the Underworld'.

An unbroken period of peace followed. Life for the fairies in Emeraldia changed very little over the subsequent millennia, although they noted small variations in the environment around them, such as the arrival of humans.

Gradually humans spread from the main island of Emeraldia to some of the small islands around it, such as to the beautiful little island of Inisure, which once (many millennia earlier when it was still attached to the mainland of Emeraldia by a narrow, stony landbridge) had been inhabited by fairies of King Clover's kingdom, but then had to be abandoned by them after the landbridge disappeared under water.

When humans began travelling to and from this island by boat, King Clover was able to travel with them and to repossess his long-deserted kingdom; and because of its exciting location, and because fairies could reach it only by humans' boats, he decided to open up his kingdom as the first ever fairies' adventure-holiday resort.

Then one day, the whole island of Inisure shook a little, and one of the visiting fairies saw Black Air rising out of a crack that had formed on the ground. This caused much concern, and without delay, an ambassador fairy carrying a white flag went down to the Underworld to speak to the Spirits that were in charge there, and to find out if they were attempting to re-start the war.

The Chief Spirit of the Underworld, Chief Fungus, kept the fairy ambassador waiting a long time ('can't let a fairy think he's as important as we are,' he said to his muscular wife, Redeévil). Then he told the ambassador sullenly that the fairies were over-reacting as usual, and that all that had happened was that the Spirits were doing a bit of tunnelling to expand their territory (typical, thought the ambassador fairy—those unpleasant Spirits had never been able to stop themselves spreading into the territory of others) and this must have caused a few cracks in the earth.

'If they bother you, seal them up,' Chief Fungus said sourly. 'Although knowing you fairies, you'll probably write us a long letter about them first. You always make a great fuss over nothing.'

Relieved, the ambassador returned to the surface, but when he reached it, he found Inisure almost unrecognisable. To his amazement, he saw that all the fairy trees had been cut down and their roots removed and the humans were busy breaking stones and spreading them over the earth where the roots had been.

The fairies—residents and holiday-makers alike— were in a panic, standing around in large groups and looking on helplessly as the humans behaved in that strange and unprecedented way.

The ambassador fairy found it hard to believe that the humans he was seeing now were the same as the ones who had been there before. To his eyes, they looked so different that he had to ask King Clover if new humans had arrived while he was down below, and the shaken king said, no, they were the same humans, but he could see why the ambassador had asked because he couldn't recognise them himself, their appearance had changed so much. The change had happened the instant these humans came into contact with the Black Air.

A human observer—used to identifying other humans by physical matters such as differences in faces or height or hair colour—would have been puzzled by this discussion, because none of these physical characteristics had changed at all (unless you counted the humans' facial expression, which undoubtedly had grown duller and more calculating).

Fairies, however, not being made of flesh, paid little attention to the differences between one physical human body and another, as all humans looked pretty much alike on the outside.

On the other hand, because they were creatures of the supernatural, fairies were able to recognise big differences between the spirit of one human and the spirit of another, and could see clearly the spirit of every human as a visible mass inside him or her.

They had noted that the colour of the spirit in humans varied from snowy white to a very dark grey; and in size, the spirit varied from the size of a watermelon to the size of a chestnut. It happened that the spirits of the Inisure humans generally were medium-sized (about the size of an apple) and just a slight bit grey; but now the ambassador hardly recognised them.

Their spirits had blackened and hardened and shrunk to the size of a raisin; and when the ambassador fairy looked at them, he felt as if he were looking at the Spirits of the Underworld.

The situation quickly got much worse. Having covered with stones the places where the trees had grown, the humans looked dissatisfied and as if they felt that something more was needed. One of them took up the implement which at that time was the equivalent of the modern shovel, and started to dig away at the edge of the fairy fort.

The fairies could do nothing except look on in helpless horror as other affected humans joined him and dug and dug as if they were possessed, which, of course, they were in a way.

This was a disaster the fairies could not have planned for, because they had never imagined it could happen. There was only one bit of good news that day, and this was brought by fairies who had watched the cloud of Black Air as it drifted out to sea. These fairies reported that, as the cloud floated over sea air, they saw it lose its blackness and power.

This was not entirely a surprise (the fairies themselves, and the Spirits of the Underworld, also lost their power over the sea) but it was greatly reassuring. It meant the separate land mass of Emeraldia would not be threatened by that leak in Inisure, even if the fairies were unable to seal it. None of this was much comfort to poor King Clover, however, who this time had lost his kingdom forever.

Other panic-stricken fairies, however, soon arrived at Inisure on the next boat from Emeraldia bringing the worst news of all. The underground tunnelling had caused a second leak in Emeraldia itself, they reported, right under the fort of Queen Honeysuckle. A small cloud had escaped and had affected immediately some humans called Pickenose who had been lurking in an area of woodland nearby, trying to work out how best to steal a goat that was tethered not far from the fort.

Those Pickenose humans already had been notable to the local fairies for the smallness and darkness of their spirits. When they breathed in the Black Air, however, their spirits became even harder and smaller, and turned so black in colour that they became nearly invisible; and just like the humans in Inisure, the first thing they did after that happened was to start cutting down the trees on top of Queen Honeysuckle's fort.

Then, however, something unexpected happened. Other humans ran towards the Pickenoses, shouting at them to stop and to get off their land; and although these shouting humans walked right through the cloud of Black Air, they were not affected by it at all.

These humans were Cornelia's ancestors and their spirits were remarkably large (close to the size of a watermelon) and very pale in colour, and the Black Air had no effect on those large, white masses.

These white-spirited humans seemed to be unaware of anything happening inside them, but the fairies knew they were watching a battle. They saw the Black Air concentrating around the watermelon-sized masses of whiteness inside the humans, getting blacker and blacker at the edge of each mass it tried to penetrate; and only when it failed to get inside any of them did it gradually move on.

The watching fairies then seized their opportunity to blow the Black Air away. Using all the power of their whirlwinds, they drove the cloud up in the air and towards the sea, keeping it well above the height where it could touch humans. Only when they had seen it fade away to nothing over the ocean did the fairies return finally to Queen Honeysuckle's fort.

The fairies knew they were very lucky indeed that this mainland leak had developed right under a fort, because the powers of the fort were so great that they would be able to seal the leak completely by concentrating and directing those powers at it.

It was for this reason that they established the first ever fairy military garrison there, with soldiers on constant watch in case any Black Air did escape; and, if that happened, the soldiers on duty would whirlwind it out over the ocean immediately.

As a priority, however, they had to make sure the fort itself was protected from any interference or damage by humans. That was why they enlisted the aid of Cornelia's ancestors and explained to them, at that historic and unprecedented meeting, that they needed their help with a big problem.

Chapter 14

Rubies & Emeralds

A T FIRST, communication had been tricky. The fairies had tried to explain to the family about the ancient war between the fairies and the Spirits of the Underworld, and about the badness of those Spirits, and about the way in which humans were affected and made dangerous to fairies by Black Air.

The assembled humans, young and old, heard them out with great politeness, but the more observant fairies thought that maybe the family did not really understand the significance of what was being said; and they also suspected that the fairies—unused to this sort of dialogue—were doing a poor job of explaining themselves. Still, none of that made any difference: those humans wanted to help the fairies, no questions asked.

'I give you my word, little lady, my family will always protect that fort,' Cornelia's distant ancestor had assured Queen Honeysuckle, in the language the humans in Emeraldia spoke back then. 'I don't understand everything you're saying about that Air problem, but it doesn't matter. We would have protected your fort for you anyway. But if you're saying it needs special protection, we'll give it special protection. Don't you worry a bit about that.'

After speaking to them, the fairies felt as reassured as

they could be. Everyone who attended the meeting said they could almost feel the affection those people had for the fairies, although a few of the more pessimistic fairies pointed out that humans' lives were very short, and that even though the humans they had spoken to could be relied on entirely, they had no way of knowing if their descendants could be trusted.

'I believe they can be,' Queen Honeysuckle told the assembled fairies. 'I've watched generations of that family come and go, and they've always been respectful of fairies, and the spirits in that family have always been very big and very white. There's no reason to expect that any of that will change.'

'I think we ought to pay them for their trouble,' King Riverbank suggested. 'We're asking them to do a job for us, and we ought to make it a formal arrangement. We ought to give them a retainer.'

'I think that's a very good idea,' Queen Honeysuckle agreed, as did all the other assembled fairies. 'I think we ought to give them gold and emeralds and rubies. Humans can't make their own gold and emeralds and rubies, and they seem to like them a lot.'

'Do we give them loose gold and emeralds and rubies,' King Thistle asked, 'or do we give them made up in some way?'

'We'll give them as jewelry,' Queen Honeysuckle said definitely. 'We'll give them a necklace with twenty strands of gold and five hundred rubies and five hundred emeralds, and two bracelets of solid gold with fifty rubies and fifty emeralds set into each of them.'

All the fairies agreed that this sounded an excellent plan, but because they did have a certain amount of knowledge about humans and their weaknesses, they decided they would present the jewelry in a plain timber box so that other humans would be less likely to know what was inside it and want it for themselves.

So when the humans woke up the next morning, the first thing they saw was this box just beside the place where they lit their fire. The fairies kept themselves invisible at first, and they were both surprised and gratified when they heard what the female human said when she saw the box.

'Will you look at that?' she said. 'The fairies have left us something.'

'How do you know it's the fairies?' a child asked excitedly.

'Who else would have left a grand box like that? And it's very nice of them, although I wouldn't want those lovely people to be thinking that they have to give us something to mind their fort for them. But what a grand present it is. Won't it make a lovely seat by the fire?'

At that point, Queen Honeysuckle made herself visible, and the humans greeted her as if she were an old friend, and offered her a bowl of buttermilk.

Queen Honeysuckle politely accepted the buttermilk, and then suggested that the humans should look inside the box.

'You mean there's more?' the woman said, as the children eagerly opened the clasp and lifted the lid and revealed the dazzling jewelry. The family gasped when they saw it, and looked down at it, almost in fear.

'We could never take a present like that from you,' the woman said. 'It's too much. It's far too much. But oh how beautiful it all is. I never dreamed I'd ever see anything like it in my life.'

The Queen had to persuade them to keep the jewelry. 'It's very good of you, Queen,' a very old man said. 'But people can be greedy about such things. It might attract robbers.'

'No one need ever know about it except you,' Queen Honeysuckle pointed out. 'I'll make you a secret place where you can keep it.' And just like that, although the family couldn't see it at first, she created a small, secret room behind the wall; and then the box disappeared.

'There. Your house is just a little bit bigger now, but nobody will notice the difference. Do you see that timber peg? Just twist that three times to the left, once to the right, seven times to the left again, and then pull, and you'll be in the room.'

The woman's husband did this and the children jumped up and down in excitement as the wall opened and revealed the box behind it.

'Ye're decent people, Queen,' the woman's husband said. 'And you and all the fairies can be sure we'll never let you down. Nobody will ever touch that fort of yours while any member of this family is alive.'

In the centuries that followed, the fairies helped those humans (the Guardian family, as they referred to them) in ways the humans knew nothing about. The fairies could not influence mortal behaviour very much, but they did have the power of a few tricks and curses that could affect humans, and over the bad centuries that followed in Emeraldia, they used these for the benefit of that family. When other families were being put off their land, that family was never disturbed. When other families starved to death, that family always had food.

Fuchsia was not even sure why everything had changed with the last Guardian. All he knew for sure was that he had taken the jewels and left Emeraldia, and shortly afterwards, the Lawful Guild—headed at that time by Primus Pickenose—took over and destroyed the Soldiers' Fort.

Black Air had been leaking out of the ground in vast quantities ever since; and although the fairies had kept large numbers of soldiers on duty to whirlwind away to sea as much of it as they could, so much of that terrible Air was escaping through the great leak created by the destruction of the Soldiers' Fort that their efforts no longer had any effect, and most humans in Emeraldia had been affected by it, including every member of the large and horrible Pickenose family and every member of the Lawful Guild.

That unforgivable abandonment of the Soldiers' Fort by the last Guardian had been the start of the current, terrible situation. Fuchsia was very angry with the man he had seen in that unfamiliar world inside that wicked-looking doll. And yet, at the same time, deep inside his fairy mind, he had felt a small stirring of hope at the sight of that treacherous human—the first he had felt in a long time.

Chapter 15

Walter

CORNELIA LAY VERY STILL for a moment, and then she held Josephine out in front of her and looked at her closely. After a few seconds of this, she stood up and turned on all the lights and looked around the room carefully, wondering if Barry was hiding somewhere, playing a trick on her; but there was no sign of him anywhere.

She had not been dreaming either. Just to make sure she was awake, she carried out the usual tests: she blinked hard, jumped up and down and pinched herself; and having done all this, she was left in no doubt: she was awake all right. She was awake and she had heard Josephine talk to her. Josephine had called her 'Kiddo'. She was sure of it.

'Come on, Josephine,' she begged in a thrilled whisper. 'Say something else.' Excitedly, she straightened Josephine's dress, tidied back her hair and told her that she had always believed she was the best-dressed doll in the whole world. 'Please, Josephine,' she urged coaxingly. 'Just say one more word. Any word at all.'

From the mantelpiece, three fairies were watching this with a certain satisfaction. They had come directly to Cornelia's bedroom after Tansy had told King Fuchsia that not only would she help him with his Plan but, please, could they get going on it immediately.

All three fairies felt helpless and uncomfortable looking at Cornelia, whose deep unhappiness filled the room when they first came in; and when she rubbed Josephine to her cheek and said she wished things were the way they were before, May decided to try to comfort the small human by having the doll respond to her in a manner appropriate to a habituée of the Silver Poodle Club. 'So do I, Kiddo,' Josephine had said. 'So do I.'

The few words did perk up Cornelia so satisfactorily that Josephine probably would have said more, if events hadn't intervened.

Cornelia's bedroom door opened suddenly, and Barry and the two dogs came running in. 'Neely, a car is coming up the drive,' Barry announced breathlessly, 'and Puffy Pickenose and her crazy cousin and that smelly Walter are in it. I think they're going to come into the house.'

─◇─

'Oh, don't let *Walter* in the house!' Cornelia said urgently. 'It would be horrible if he touched anything, and she'll let him bite us.'

Walter was Puffy Pickenose's dog: a small, black-haired creature of some breed no one could recognise, and an animal that made most people shiver just to look at him.

Even Cornelia and Barry, both of whom had the highest opinion of dogs, thought Walter was the most revolting creature they had ever seen.

Partly, this was because of his face, which was oddly humanoid, and might have belonged to some as-yet-undiscovered evil breed of monkey. It was round in shape, almost hairless, and was strangely flat except for the turned-up nose. It was further distinguished by his tiny, vicious eyes and long, sharp teeth.

He looked most disturbing of all when he was out walking with his mistress, as the bond between the two of them was very strong, and Walter always ensured that his horrible little turned-up nose was somewhere between Puffy's legs. ('Yuk,' said non-Pickenoses when they saw them together.)

Worst of all, however, Walter bit people—all the time—and the police would do nothing about it. Just a few months ago, he had bitten a little girl.

'He's a Pickenose dog,' the sergeant said tiredly to the girl's mother, when she made a complaint.

'But he's dangerous,' she said. 'My little girl could have been—'

'You don't have to tell me,' the sergeant said nervously, looking over his shoulder, 'but as I say, he's a Pickenose dog, so—'

'Look, I'm making a formal complaint,' said the now very angry woman.

'Ma'am, he's not only a Pickenose dog,' the sergeant told her, 'he's a Horse-Bottom-Wig Wearer's dog; if you make a complaint about that dog, you're the one who's going to end up in jail, and me along with you for taking the complaint.'

'I don't even know what a Horse-Bottom-Wig Wearer

is,' said the indignant woman, who had just moved to Emeraldia from Connecticut, 'and I thought they were called the Lawful Guild.'

'They're a different bunch,' said the sergeant tiredly. 'They wear different clothes. The Horse-Bottom-Wig Wearers are the ones with the funny costumes who do the talking in the courts, like that Puffy Pickenose. The Lawful Guild are the boyos that sit in the court and tell the talking lawyers what to say, but say nothing themselves except in their own sound-proofed offices, and most of them are Pickenoses, including that crazy cousin of hers, Pompeous. Honestly, ma'am, you don't want to make that complaint.'

The sergeant dropped his voice to a confidential whisper. 'I'll tell you what it's like, ma'am, because you're new here, and you wouldn't know. You take that Puffy Pickenose herself—lately she's even taken to stealing things from people's houses, and all we can do is let her at it. She steals pictures, she steals statues, she steals vases, she's stolen every Christmas wreath in Emeraldia, and nobody can figure where she stashes them or what she wants them for. She'd need a warehouse now to store everything she's stolen.

'And as for that Walter dog of hers, you know I've had twenty people here in the last month with bandages on their legs after that Walter bit them, and some of them said she set the dog on them, and any time that Pompeous fellow saw it happen, he nearly burst his sides laughing but—' The sergeant broke off, shook his head, and when he resumed, sounded even more tired than before. 'Honestly, Ma'am, you really don't want to make that complaint.'

═══◇═══

Now, that woman had moved back to Connecticut and the sergeant had gone to Australia, and no one went to the police for anything any more because everyone knew that the few members of the police who were left were just spies or agents for the Lawful Guild.

As for the dog, Walter, Cornelia could hardly bring herself to believe that horrible creature might at any moment be coming into their house. All of a sudden, however, as she heard a loud noise from the floor below, and Freddy and Tickles tore down the stairs, she knew he had come in. She and Barry ran after the dogs, Cornelia still holding on tightly to Josephine. Their mother, her face white as chalk, ran after Cornelia and Barry. Three fascinated fairies brought up the rear.

Before they reached the kitchen, they heard loud noises coming from it. They heard what sounded like a dog fight, they heard their father shouting, then they heard a loud guffaw ('that's Puffy', Cornelia whispered) and then they heard a loud maniacal laugh ('that's Pompeous', she added nervously) and they heard one or two words spoken by Puffy; and at the sound of her voice ('that woman's voice makes my skin crawl,' said their mother; 'it's like the voice of an Underground creature,' said May) they all shuddered.

In the kitchen, they found the three dogs circling one another, all of them with their teeth bared; but to

Cornelia's frightened eyes, Walter's long dirty teeth looked a far more dangerous weapon than the normal-sized teeth of poor Freddy and Tickles.

Pompeous was laughing all the time, although Cornelia could not tell if that awful madman was laughing at the dogs or at her father or just at something he was hearing inside his own head. Her father was holding a piece of paper in his hand, and telling Puffy that it meant nothing and that he was going to tear it up.

Pompeous laughed more loudly then, and Puffy's lips, which curved downwards rather than upwards, curved down a little farther, which was what happened when she smiled.

'They're very ugly looking, aren't they?' Tansy whispered.

'They're the ugliest two mortals I've ever seen,' May whispered back.

Their opinion probably was affected by the fairies' way of viewing mortals, which looked at the spirit rather than the body. But even to other human eyes, these two did look exceptionally repulsive.

To most people, Pompeous just looked mad. He was tall and thin with blond, curly hair that tended to stick up in the air, and his eyes appeared to be all of one colour, as if the black circle in the middle had dilated to fill the entire eyeball. Nobody ever looked closely enough to check, however, because Pompeous was a starer.

If anyone ever met his eyes, he stared at them as if his eyes had become fixed to that person by a magnet and he could never look any other way. So people learned very quickly: never look directly at Pompeous Potty-Pickenose XIII.

Puffy was just the opposite. She would never look straight at anyone who was not a Pickenose, and always looked in another direction when someone spoke to her. As Cornelia's father spoke to her now, she was looking at the door to the outside, and Cornelia noticed that a crack had appeared in the timber of that door since the last time she had seen it, almost certainly made by Puffy when she came into the kitchen.

Puffy was very rough on doors. Rather than just turning a knob, she always gave a great push; and very often, she succeeded in forcing doors open by this method, but it never did much good to the doors.

In build, she was the opposite of Pompeous, being as short and stout as he was tall and thin, and she had a very heavy walk. 'The only thing good I can say about that woman,' Mrs Ryan had said once, 'is that you can always hear her coming. It's like the sound of a large machine approaching.'

What the fairies noticed most about Puffy, however, was the appearance of her spirit, which was jet black and so tiny that it was hardly visible.

'Do you think they're still fully human?' May asked.

'Hard to say,' Fuchsia admitted, looking at them. 'Both of them spend all their time in the Guild Headquarters, and the Black Air is nearly denser in that place now than in the Underworld itself, so maybe they're merging some way. But, Mother of Nature, they're repulsive-looking aren't they, both of them?'

'That paper gives you three months to leave this house,' Puffy was saying to Cornelia's father, in that voice that made May and every other being in the room (except Pompeous and Walter) shiver. 'That's a very generous amount of time.

'You must have your furniture out in advance, of course, because our people will need room for their desks and equipment. We won't be demolishing the house immediately because we plan to use it as a site-hut for the factory we'll be building in the field at the front.'

'You have no right—' Cornelia's father began furiously.

'But of course we do,' Puffy said softly, as Pompeous laughed loudly. 'You have been served with a compulsory purchase order. You can appeal it of course, but no one has ever won an appeal so I'm not sure if you really want to bother, and the State will require a payment of €10,000 a day from you while you're waiting for the appeal to be heard. And then, of course, there will be the costs if you lose, which are usually about four million euro.'

'That's crazy,' said Cornelia's father. 'You—'

'Look, I'm being very patient with you,' Puffy said in that blood-chilling voice. 'I'm trying to help you, but you make it very difficult for me because you don't listen. That's your problem, Sir, you don't listen. My time is valuable, and I've been very generous in giving you so much of it, but I may have to add up the cost of the time you have wasted so far, and ensure that you're forced to pay for it. You—'

Puffy broke off suddenly as her sideways-turned eyes landed on the doll, Josephine, which Cornelia was clutching tightly to her chest. Puffy darted quickly to grab it, and Cornelia screamed and held on to Josephine so tightly that, for the first time since the doll had been made, a few beads fell off Josephine's dress.

Cornelia's mother let go of Barry's hand for a moment, and she and Barry both held on tightly to Cornelia and the doll, and her father ran over and tried to pull Puffy away.

'I want that,' Puffy said viciously. 'Give that to me, or you'll be very sorry.'

'Don't touch Josephine. Don't touch Josephine,' Cornelia screamed fiercely.

'You must be mad,' her father said even more fiercely. 'Get your hands away from that child, or—'

'Oh, I've had enough of this,' said May furiously. She paused just long enough to conjure herself a scuba diver's outfit, and then went straight into the dog Walter. Immediately, Walter turned away from Tickles and Freddy, bounded over to Puffy and sank his teeth into her bottom.

Puffy screamed and jumped back from Cornelia and Josephine, and then Walter seemed to sink his long, yellow teeth even more deeply than before.

All the humans looking on were too astonished to do or say anything, except Pompeous, who laughed even more loudly. Tansy and Fuchsia were laughing uncontollably, while Puffy screamed and tried with no success to push Walter off her.

'Aren't you going to go after her?' Cornelia's mother said to Pompeous, as Puffy went running from the house with Walter still attached to her.

Pompeous stopped laughing when she said this and began to stare at her, and then Cornelia's father told him to get out of the house.

Only when Freddy and Tickles (taken over by Fuchsia and Tansy) went towards him growling savagely, however, did he take his one-coloured eyes off Cornelia's mother and turn to leave, and his ferocious escort then accompanied him as far as the gate, at which point Fuchsia and Tansy left the two dogs. May, however, stayed longer with Walter, happily escorting Puffy about a mile down the road, and then exiting Walter with some reluctance.

'That was the most fun I've had in ages,' she said, laughing, when she finally came back. 'I'm glad I thought of the scuba gear though. That creature stank inside as much as outside.'

'Why do you suppose she wanted the doll,' Fuchsia asked worriedly. 'Do you think she knows what's in it?'

'I don't think that's the reason,' Tansy said guiltily. I think she just wanted the doll because it had shiny, pretty clothes. You see, I put a Beauty Spell on her.'

Fuchsia stiffened a little when he heard this. He was not comfortable at the idea of Tansy casting spells on humans without his knowledge. Queen May, however, who was much less of a stickler than her husband about Fairy Deportment, was not bothered at all.

'Clever you, Tansy,' she said, laughing. 'Not everyone

can cast a successful Beauty Spell, but you obviously did.'

Although fairies rarely interfered with humans, they had the ability to annoy them when they were provoked, including by spells that would deprive humans of the four gifts of life that gave the greatest pleasure to fairies: these were the joy of taking part in a banquet with others; the pleasures of dance and of laughter; and the enjoyment of objects of beauty.

These gifts were valued more by fairies than by humans, but nonetheless, the effect of these spells was more bothersome to humans than might be expected, and often it drove the victim to do very odd things to get the better of the spell.

A Beauty Spell meant that anything pretty or beautiful would fall apart in the hands of the affected human; so that after a while, even humans who cared very little about pretty things (such as Puffy Pickenose) would feel a sense of desperation about making even the briefest contact with objects that were not entirely ugly before their touch would cause them to disintegrate.

In the case of Puffy Pickenose it had driven her to stealing paintings, vases, china figurines, most of the Christmas wreaths in Emeraldia, and to try to steal the eye-catching doll, Josephine.

'Maybe you should lift the Beauty Spell now, though,' May suggested, 'because we couldn't do without this doll, and she might try to steal it again. But there's no harm in leaving the other spells,' she added quickly, before her more proper husband might suggest that all the spells should be lifted. 'With any luck, they might be causing Puffy some bother we know nothing about, and I, for one,' she added, looking significantly at Fuchsia, 'think that would be a very good thing. I mean, look at what she's done to these poor mortals.'

In fact, Cornelia's family and their dogs did look a most pathetic sight. Cornelia was sitting on her mother's lap and they were clinging on tightly to one another. Her father was sitting at the table, his head resting on his hands; and Barry, like Freddy and Tickles, was just looking frightened and bewildered.

'There's nothing we can do, is there,' Barry said in a scared voice. 'I didn't understand last night why the Ryans just ran away like they did, but now I do.'

'We definitely won't wait any longer,' Fuchsia said, when he heard this. 'We'll make contact with the two young humans as soon as they're on their own, and see if we can do the test run with the boy and that elephant straight away. If the boy survives, there's no reason we shouldn't get going on the Plan immediately.'

Tansy looked frightened when he said this, and May looked at him disapprovingly. 'I know we have no choice,' she said, 'but I don't think you should be so cold about it. I don't think you should say things like, "if the boy survives".'

'Well, it's the only chance we have and it's the only chance they have. If it works, we'll all be saved, but the first time anything is done, there's a risk. All we can do is go about this business in the most practical way we can.'

—Chapter 16—

First Contact

IF IT WEREN'T FOR MAY, the family would not even have had dinner on that awful day. Cornelia's mother put in the oven a dish of lasagne she had taken from the freezer, but then she forgot about it and it burned.

'Well, this, at least, I can fix,' said the queen; and just before the black and smoking disaster was discovered, she conjured a fresh one made to the recipe of the Hotel Eden in Rome and got it into the oven just in time. After this succulent dish was served, May beamed at Barry when he told his mother that this lasagne was much better than her last one and that she should make it that way all the time.

Barry, however, and Tickles were the only ones who even noticed the food that night. The rest of the family found it hard to eat at all, and after the meal, were inclined to sit around dully clinging on to one another.

Inside Josephine, Fuchsia was growing impatient. 'Don't these humans ever go to bed?' he asked half-a-dozen times.

Finally, however, the family did go upstairs and the king quickly conjured the noise of mice scampering and a cat meowing behind a skirting board in the kitchen to draw the attention of the two dogs (that suspicious sheepdog in particular) and to keep them from following Cornelia to her room.

As the moment was imminent when the Plan was about to be tested, all the fairies started to get nervous.

'Fuchsia, I'm going to make the first approach,' May said categorically. 'I think I know what to say to her.'

Tansy observed that the fire in the bedroom had gone out, and said Cornelia might feel more comfortable if they re-lit it.

'Yes, that's much better,' May agreed as the room suddenly became warm, and then added distractedly: 'You made this a fairy fireplace, didn't you, Tansy?'

Tansy flushed guiltily. 'Well, she was sick when she was small, and the room was very cold.'

'Oh, don't be embarrassed,' May said quickly. 'I think it was a wonderful idea. Mortal fires are so dull. They produce no heat and you can't see anything in them.'

When Cornelia turned around, she was surprised to see the fire burning brightly, but she felt too dulled to think much about it. She sat down in front of it, all right, but that was only because she didn't have the energy to put on her nightdress and go to bed. She wondered vaguely why the dogs had not come up with her as usual, but mostly she did no thinking at all. She was feeling rather than thinking, and all that she was feeling was a deep sense of hopelessness and misery.

The three fairies looked at one another. 'Now?' said May.

'Now,' said Fuchsia nodding.

May squeezed both Tansy's and Fuchsia's hands and then cleared her throat delicately and called out softly: 'Cornelia, do you mind if I talk to you for a moment?'

Cornelia jumped in fright when she heard the voice, and then stared wide-eyed when she discovered that she had been joined suddenly by the most beautiful creature she had ever seen, sitting beside her on the arm of the wing chair.

'Are you a ghost?' she gasped.

May laughed. 'No, Cornelia, I'm a fairy,' she said gaily. 'I'm your neighbour from the other side of the glen. I've known you for years. My name is May.'

Cornelia put her hand over her mouth, certain she knew why the fairy had come. 'We had nothing to do with digging up your fort,' she said frightened. 'Honestly. We'd never, ever do harm to a fairy fort. It was the Lawful Guild that did it, and we hate the Lawful Guild.'

'Of course you do,' May said approvingly. 'And I know you wouldn't harm a fairy fort, and I know the Lawful Guild and those terrible Pickenoses are trying to make you and your family homeless too, aren't they?'

'Yes, they are,' said Cornelia, relaxing now as she discovered how well-informed this beautiful fairy was, who had such a nice smile. 'And do you know something else? They say they're going to build a factory in our front field and turn this house into a hut, but we can't stop them, although we honestly and truly would if we could. But even the police can't stop the Pickenoses, not even when their creepy dog bites people.

'Oh, I beg your pardon,' Cornelia added suddenly, remembering her mother's firm instructions about offering hospitality to guests. 'Would you like a glass of chocolate milk or juice or anything? Or some fudge?'

'Not just at the moment, thank you,' said May, although she was pleased to be asked. Indeed, she was much impressed generally at the way this small human was dealing with a visit from a fairy—with the same uncomplicated ease as her distant ancestors. 'But it's nice of you to offer.'

'I always hoped I'd see a fairy some day,' Cornelia said earnestly. 'But I never thought you'd be so beautiful. And I never really thought you'd be dressed like Josephine, and have hair like hers and everything; although of course your dress is much, much more beautiful than Josephine's. It's the most beautiful dress I've ever seen.'

'Why, thank you,' said May, liking this human more all the time. 'I designed it to wear when I go inside Josephine. I don't suppose you'd have guessed that a fairy was popping in and out of your doll, would you?'

Cornelia thought for a minute. 'Well, actually...' she said slowly, putting two and two together even as she spoke, '...do you pop in and out of Strudel and Daisy and Zanzibar and Jules as well?' she asked. 'Is that why they move sometimes and make my hair blow around?' She looked even more curiously at the fairy then. 'You know, Josephine spoke to me today. But maybe that was you, too, was it?'

'Aren't you smart!' said May laughing. 'And I'm sure I do go into those other toys, although I didn't know their names until now. My husband goes into them too occasionally, and so does another fairy, who is a very good friend of yours, although though you don't know her. She even gave you a fairy fire.'

'A fairy fire?' repeated Cornelia, and giggled then as she looked at the fire and saw an exotic picture of herself in it wearing bobbed hair and the same dress, shoes and long earrings as this beautiful fairy. 'Is that why you see pictures in it?' she asked excitedly.

May nodded. 'You see whatever you're thinking about,' she said, 'so long as it's something you want to see. And it keeps your room as warm as toast, too, doesn't it?'

Cornelia didn't say anything for a moment. It wasn't often that she was rendered speechless, but on this occasion, it had happened. The thrill of everything she was hearing and seeing was almost too much for her to absorb. So many mysteries were being solved at once and with explanations more satisfactory than she would have dared imagine.

'My father keeps measuring this fireplace all the time to see why it's so much better than any of the other fireplaces in the house and why he hardly ever needs to put wood in it,' she confided to May, 'and my mother's always talking about how she can see pictures in it.

They're going to be so surprised when I tell them it was a fairy that made it so good.'

'I think you and that other fairy could become great friends,' May told her then, sidestepping for the moment the awkward subject of parents. 'Do you think you'd like to meet her?'

Speechless again, Cornelia nodded.

A moment later, another dazzling creature was standing in the room, this one looking even more excited than Cornelia.

'Hello, Cornelia,' Tansy said, giggling.

At first Cornelia was too awe-struck to answer, unable to do anything except stare open-mouthed at this extraordinary vision.

She had thought May the most beautiful creature she had ever seen, but Tansy was—well, Cornelia wouldn't have thought it possible, but Tansy was even more beautiful. She also looked younger than May—hardly much older than some of the girls in the senior school. Like May, her hair, too, was arranged in a style that reminded Cornelia of Josephine's, and she had long, wonderful earrings, and her dress—

'I'll bet you like my dress,' said Tansy gaily, spinning around to show it off. 'It's a present from Queen May.'

The dress was almost blindingly beautiful. May had found a method of cutting diamonds which was far more complex than any other fairy had been able to manage, and she had covered this dress with fringe made from millions of these extraordinary diamonds, each of them so tiny that it was hardly bigger than a grain of sand, and the dress moved, glittered and sparkled as if it were alive. 'You're going to be doing something very important for us inside that doll,' May had said when she presented it to Tansy. 'We have to have you looking your best.'

'It's a gorgeous dress,' said Cornelia sincerely, hardly able to take her eyes off it and the fairy wearing it. 'Please, would you both mind terribly waiting here for just a minute please while I bring my parents and my brother in to meet you?' she asked then, her face a deep, hot pink from the unrelieved excitement. 'They're feeling very bad at the moment, and they'll feel a lot better if they can meet you, and I can tell them about why the toys move and about the fire and everything.'

'Right,' said Fuchsia to himself from the mantelpiece. 'Here's the tricky bit. Come on, May. You're doing great. Just keep it up and manoeuvre out of this one.'

'Well, I'd love to meet your parents someday,' said May guiltily, 'but fairies are not really allowed to appear to adults. Not unless we get a great many forms signed and stamped, and get consents from the Governing Board of Fairies,' she continued smoothly, as both Tansy and Fuchsia stared at her in astonishment.

'In fact, we'd have to go away from here immediately if adults saw us. So it would be much better, for the moment, if you didn't mention anything about me to your parents until we can fill out those forms and get them authorised. We might not be allowed to see you ever again if the Governing Board thought we'd seen an adult without a stamped consent document.'

'Oh, really, May,' thought Fuchsia, not knowing whether to be impressed or shocked at this newly discovered ability of his wife to lie so fluently.

'You have wonderful toys,' May continued quickly, as Cornelia's face filled with disappointment. 'We fairies have been around forever, you know, but we've never seen toys like yours. Especially Jules and Josephine.'

'They were people my great-granduncle knew,' Cornelia explained distractedly, wondering how long all that stuff about forms would take. 'They weren't supposed to be very nice, but I think they make very nice dolls because they have lovely clothes and they look mean and cross instead of smiling and stupid, which is unusual in dolls, don't you think?'

'Very unusual,' May agreed. 'But if you want to see truly nasty faces, you ought to look at the real Jules and Josephine. They look even meaner than the dolls.'

'You mean you've seen the real Jules and Josephine?' Cornelia asked eagerly, as distracted from her disappointment as May could have wished. 'Wow. They must be really old now. Do they still live in Paris?'

'I honestly don't know. I only met them in the 1920s, when they looked just like the dolls.'

'You didn't by any chance meet my great-granduncle as well, did you?' Cornelia asked eagerly. 'That's when he knew Jules and Josephine. In the 1920s. His name was Finn O'Hara. He had the same name as my brother—

Finbarr—only he was called Finn for short, and we call my brother Barry. I'll show you his picture.'

Quickly, Cornelia ran over to a bookcase and brought back an album of her favourite pictures. 'That's my great-granduncle,' she said, pointing to a man sitting around a table with a lot of laughing people, although her great-granduncle was not laughing. 'My grandfather says I look like him, and that Finn had blue eyes and black curly hair, just like I do. And that was the woman who made Jules and Josephine,' she continued, pointing to a woman sitting just beside him, whose dark hair was cut into a severe bob. 'Her name is Savannah Gray, and she was a famous artist, but she disappeared and no one knows what happened to her. Her paintings sell for loads and loads of money now, my father says.'

'Yes, I've seen your great-granduncle,' May said carefully, trying not to let anger creep into her voice at the sight of this man. 'I saw him in a Paris nightclub with Jules and Josephine.'

'He was murdered, you know. By apaches. They were a gang of bad people in Paris in the 1920s.'

'Yes, I know,' said May slowly, buying time to think about what she would say next, but before she could say anything at all, Tansy startled everyone by jumping up and down in impatience.

'Can't we just tell her?' she said urgently. 'Please. Everyone in this house is so unhappy and we're in a terrible way and she can make everything all right. Please, can't we just tell her?'

Chapter 17

The African Job

SITTING INVISIBLE on the mantelpiece, Fuchsia put his hand over his eyes. 'Oh, Tansy,' he groaned. 'Just control yourself for a minute, can't you. Don't spoil everything.'

Even May, who never looked at Tansy with anything but indulgence, looked exasperated for a moment when she said this.

'We have to explain things to Cornelia first,' she said quietly. 'Remember, she doesn't even know what her toys are like inside.'

Then all four heads, visible and invisible, swung around quickly as the door to Cornelia's room, which had been open, suddenly closed; and a wide-eyed Barry stood just inside it.

'What do you mean Cornelia can make everything all right?' he asked Tansy. 'I've been listening, and I heard what you said. Are you trying to do something with my sister?'

'Barry, don't talk so loud,' Cornelia said quickly. 'You'll get the fairies into trouble. Mommy and Daddy will hear, and the fairies can't be seen by adults without permission.'

'We're here to help your sister, Barry,' May said

kindly. 'We're here to help all of you because we think you're in a lot of trouble.'

'But why do you say Cornelia has to do something?' he asked suspiciously. 'She's only eight years old. You should be asking me to do something if there's something to be done. And what do her toys have to do with it?'

'It's complicated to explain,' May said calmly. 'But I could show you if you like. Do you see that sad-looking elephant?' she asked, pointing to Zanzibar.

'He was made in Africa,' Cornelia said quickly, wanting to change the subject before Barry made the fairies angry. 'We bought him at a stall at the farm show from a woman who was trying to make money for an elephant orphanage there.'

'Well, if you could go inside Zanzibar, as a fairy can, you'd see something you wouldn't like at all. You'd see his parents and his aunts and his cousins and his big sisters getting killed and Zanzibar being made an orphan. Inside Zanzibar, the massacre of his family is going on all the time. Can you understand why he looks so sad?'

Cornelia looked in fright at Zanzibar then. She had no trouble believing May, because she had been wondering for a long time how any stuffed toy could communicate as much sadness as Zanzibar did.

Barry, however, was more sceptical, and he went over and picked up the elephant.

'That doesn't make sense,' he said. 'There's just stuffing inside him.'

'I can show you if you want,' May said. 'Would you like to see?'

Cornelia looked away quickly—not wanting to say no to a fairy, but not wanting to say yes either. Barry, however, said he wanted to see.

'In fact,' said May smoothly, 'I could do more than show you. If you were willing to help, I think we could stop that massacre and save Zanzibar's family. It's something we've thought about doing for a while, but we need a human to help. You'd find that interesting, wouldn't you?' she said, glancing at the mantelpiece.

Fuchsia beamed back at her. 'This is working out perfectly,' he thought. 'She couldn't have handled it better.'

What May had set up, without seeming to do anything except respond to Barry's scepticism, was the trial run which was the final step needed before the real Plan could get under way.

The scheme Fuchsia was devising was unlike anything that had ever been done before, and he had no idea if the intimate co-operation between fairies and humans on which it depended would be successful or if it would end in disaster. That was why it was of great significance that he could experiment with the boy and the toy elephant before he launched the real mission, which depended on Jules and Josephine and Cornelia.

And there was a second advantage as well to using Barry instead of Cornelia. From his observations of these two small humans, he had noticed that the boy was a natural risk-taker, which the girl most certainly was not; and he had no doubt the boy would be much less cautious about going on a venture into the unknown than the girl.

May had criticised him for being unfeeling in regarding Barry as sacrificial, if necessary; but, as Fuchsia saw it, the future of all Emeraldia was at stake, and he had to be practical. If sacrifices had to be made, they had to be made. He just had to make sure those sacrifices did not include Cornelia and Jules and Josephine, without whom his Plan would come to nothing.

What happened to Barry and Zanzibar would tell him a lot. Fuchsia would find out if a human's mind and spirit could be carried inside one of those toys by a fairy (by Tansy, of course—no Emeraldia fairy could bear such close contact with a human); and once they were inside the toy, he would find out if Tansy and the accompanying human spirit would be able to influence events in that world.

And very importantly, could the fairy and the human spirit come back undamaged? And even if the human spirit came back intact, could it then be re-joined with its human body, or would the two parts remain forever separate?

These were big unknowns, and this was going to be a very important and interesting experiment, but Fuchsia could not believe how smoothly things were going so far.

'Tansy can take you inside Zanzibar if you like,' May said casually to Barry. 'My husband can go with you as well, and between the three of you, you might be able to stop the massacre before Zanzibar's mother is killed. Do you think you'd like to see Africa and save Zanzibar's family?' she said sweetly to Barry.

'Wow, cool,' said Barry. 'Would I?'

'Barry can't go into a massacre,' Cornelia protested. 'He might get killed.'

'He'll be perfectly all right,' said May, hiding her own worries about what might happen, which were nearly equal to Cornelia's. 'In fact, why don't I call my husband now, because he understands these things very well and he'll be able to make sure that Barry...gets the most out of the experience.'

Without waiting for her call, Fuchsia appeared suddenly before them; and just as Cornelia had thought May and Tansy were the most beautiful female creatures she had ever seen, now she thought Fuchsia was a dazzlingly handsome man.

Perhaps it added to her impression that Fuchsia, ever conscious of the correct clothing for an occasion, had appeared dressed in a safari outfit such as Cornelia had never seen before except in movies; in fact, Fuchsia's outfit was so perfect in all its detail, at once so well suited to the hardest conditions and yet so exquisitely cut and fitted, that it made the ones she had seen in the movies seem second-rate beside it.

'How do you do,' said Fuchsia politely to Cornelia, making a small, formal bow. 'Barry, are you ready?' he asked, not wanting to allow Cornelia any more time to worry about what was happening. 'The sooner this young elephant gets his mother back, the better.'

'What do I do?' asked Barry eagerly.

'Just lie down on the bed and close your eyes,' May said softly. 'Tansy will do the rest.'

All of a sudden, Cornelia was very frightened, and thought about running as fast as she could to her parents' room to see if they could stop what was happening. Seeing the way she was looking at the door, May smiled reassuringly and said in a soft whisper:

'Cornelia, we really can save you and your family from having to leave this house. I know we're asking you to take a lot on faith, but remember, we did give you a magic fire just because we wanted to do something nice for you, and now we want to do something nice for you again.'

Cornelia just did not have it in her to distrust or disoblige this beautiful fairy, so she stayed where she was and sat wide-eyed while Tansy—now also wearing safari clothes—disappeared briefly into Barry. The fairy reappeared a second later, and all the time Barry remained motionless on the bed with his eyes closed. Cornelia could not stop herself running over to check that he was breathing, and when she found that he was, she was reassured a little.

'Don't talk to him or try to wake him,' May called out quickly, afraid that if Cornelia found that she could not wake him, she would forget every other consideration and run straight to her parents, and then everything would be lost.

So Cornelia said nothing, but she did sit beside her brother and hold his hand.

What Cornelia had not seen was that, when Tansy came out of Barry, she had carried with her the white (to the fairies' eyes) mass that the fairies called his soul, and which incorporated everything that made Barry a thinking, feeling being.

His heart was still beating and he was breathing normally, and to May's great relief, this was what Cornelia thought important; but in fact, the body lying there on the bed was no longer Barry—just the casing that held the spiritual part of him, which was all the fairies really recognised, and this spirit was now being carried away by Tansy.

Fuchsia and May could hardly bear to look at Tansy when she re-emerged holding Barry's spirit by the hand, because they found this closeness of human and fairy so unnatural and contrary to an ancient and strict code. Both of them had to keep reminding themselves that these were desperate times and this was a desperate measure.

'Okay, Barry,' Fuchsia said to the part of the boy that Tansy was holding, and that was now looking back at himself in bewilderment lying on the bed. 'Here we go.'

Cornelia put a hand on Zanzibar when he said this, and as Tansy and Fuchsia disappeared, she felt the elephant give a great quiver. At the same moment, inside Zanzibar, Barry shouted in horror at the bloody spectacle that was in front of his eyes, and at the roars of agony and fear coming from the herd of elephants as they were hit by a fusillade of bullets from which they had no escape.

All he wanted to do was go back, but then he heard Fuchsia say to him reassuringly: 'Don't worry. We're going to stop all of this right now.

'Tansy, you find the leader of the men doing the shooting,' Fuchsia ordered, 'and I'm going to produce a sand-storm.'

One moment, Barry was looking at the heart-breaking sight of a group of elephants roaring in panic as bullets were fired into them from men standing beside trucks drawn in a circle around a ravine, and the next moment, he seemed to be one of those men, holding a gun in his hands; and he could hear Tansy saying to him that he could lift the gun in the air and stop shooting, and he did.

A moment later, everyone stopped shooting because the air suddenly was full of sand, and no one could see any more, and most of the poachers even put down their guns so that they could pull handkerchiefs over their eyes and noses.

Fuchsia, who had one of the most powerful whirlwinds in Emeraldia, was making more use of it now than he had ever done before, and was enjoying himself thoroughly; and although he knew nothing about such things, he would have been gratified to learn that the freak sandstorm he produced was so severe that it caused an alert to be issued by several weather-monitoring stations, and emergency warnings to be issued to aircraft to stay away from the area.

'Use that radio, and order everyone to abandon their

trucks and walk back to the camp,' Tansy instructed Barry.

'What camp? Anyway, I don't know how to use the radio.'

'I'll make the man handle the controls for you,' Tansy responded. 'Just do it.'

'But how can they go anywhere when they can't see where they're going?'

'That's their problem,' Tansy said fiercely. 'Just give the order.'

'Leave your vehicles and walk back to the camp immediately,' Barry ordered imperiously, his voice sounding deep and dangerous as it emerged from the mouth of the leader of the gang of poachers. 'I said immediately.'

'Now use the radio again and give a general alert that ivory poachers are shooting elephants here,' Tansy ordered, following Fuchsia's instructions precisely.

'Emergency,' said Barry, now enjoying himself hugely, 'Emergency. Emergency. Ivory poachers are shooting elephants in the area of the sandstorm. Emergency. Poachers are shooting elephants in the area of the sandstorm.'

He was not sure if the words he was using were entirely the correct ones, but he didn't much care. In his wildest dreams, he had never imagined himself having total power over a large group of brutish men with guns, and he was happy to be able to prolong that pleasurable, if disorienting, state of affairs by any improvisation necessary.

'Can I give some other order?' he asked Tansy, just as Fuchsia materialised suddenly in the truck beside them.

'Go back now, Tansy,' Fuchsia ordered sharply. 'Quick. Go back immediately while the poachers are still here and before the toy—'

An instant later, Cornelia saw Fuchsia and Tansy reappear in the bedroom, and then she saw Barry open his eyes and look around the bedroom with a stupefied expression that quickly became a huge grin.

'Wow, Neely,' he said excitedly. 'Wow. You've never seen anything like it in your life. We—' But then he broke off suddenly as Cornelia gave a distressed gasp.

'Zanzibar,' she cried out. 'Zanzibar just vanished.'

May clapped her hands, and Fuchsia, his smart safari outfit now covered with sand, looked triumphant.

'But that's wonderful,' May said, as Cornelia stared in shock at the place where Zanzibar had been. 'That means the poachers have been arrested or have run away. It means Barry saved Zanzibar's mother. His mother wasn't shot by the poachers and Zanzibar was never made an orphan and there was no stall at the farm show selling Zanzibar to you because there was no elephant orphanage.'

'Barry changed history,' Fuchsia said triumphantly. 'Well done, Barry!'

'With Tansy's help, of course,' May pointed out, as Tansy—now back in her dazzling dress—cleared her throat and sat beside Barry on the bed.

'Neely, that was the coolest thing I've ever done in my life,' Barry said elatedly. 'I was inside this big guy and he was holding a huge gun, but he couldn't use the gun because I made him point it in the air and stop shooting and then I ordered all these big guys with guns to stop shooting, and they did. And I called for help for the elephants on this big guy's radio and he couldn't do anything about it, and wow, Neely, you just should have been there.

'Hey, can we do it again?' he asked May and Fuchsia enthusiastically. 'Or something like it, anyway?'

'Of course, we can,' said May, who had to resist an urge to hug him, as she saw that his excitement had made Cornelia look less fearful for a moment. 'Although it will have to be your sister's turn the next time.

'Fuchsia, you really ought to get rid of that safari outfit now,' she added, turning to her husband. 'You're getting sand all over Cornelia's bedroom.'

Fuchsia bowed apologetically, and in a flash, was wearing an immaculate ensemble of white tie and tails, and the sand was in a neat pile in Cornelia's waste-paper basket. 'You're right, as usual, May. Anyway, this outfit is more in the spirit of where Tansy is going next.'

—*Chapter 18*—

The Lawful Guild

'So, what do you think?' May said, turning towards Cornelia. 'Do you think you'd like to see what's inside Josephine?'

'It's wonderful in there,' Tansy said excitedly. 'There's music and dancing and most of the humans in there just want to have fun all the time. Except for your great-granduncle, of course. He's very serious. And Jules and Josephine, who are *very* sour.'

'Have you met my great-granduncle too?' Cornelia asked eagerly.

'Two or three times,' Tansy told her. 'He was sitting with Jules and Josephine in the nightclub, but he wasn't enjoying himself at all, but then he never is. He's the only one inside Jules and Josephine—apart from Jules and Josephine themselves, of course, who look cross all the time—who never has any fun.

'He's very careless about his clothes,' she went on, shaking her head with disapproval, 'and he hardly ever dances, which is a pity, I think, because most of the people in there dance all the time. Even when they're driving in motorcars, they stop the car and wind up a gramophone and dance at the side of the road. Almost everyone inside Josephine dances every day except your uncle. Do you think he never learned to dance?'

'Well, how could my great-granduncle have had fun when he was in Paris?' Barry said quickly, coming to the defence of his namesake. 'After all, he was just out of jail, and his wife and his baby had been murdered.'

The three fairies were as startled as Cornelia when they heard this.

'Murdered?' Cornelia repeated wide-eyed. 'Mommy just told me they had died. And I don't know why you say he was in jail,' she added indignantly. 'Our great-granduncle couldn't have been in jail.'

'Well, he was. And I know Mom didn't tell you. She didn't tell me either,' Barry admitted. 'But one night I heard her and Dad and Gran and Granddad talking about him, and that's when I heard about him having been in jail. And while he was in jail, his house burned down and his wife and baby were killed in the fire, and according to Granddad, nobody believed that fire was just an accident.'

Fuchsia and May looked at one another. They knew, of course, that the house had burned down, and they knew the Guardian himself had been murdered in Paris, but they had never heard any of the rest of this before.

'But why was he in jail?' Cornelia asked.

'Oh, he hadn't done anything. Primus Pickenose put in jail a load of people he didn't like back in the 1920s, and they had to leave the country as soon as they got out, but Finn hadn't done anything. Primus just wanted to get his hands on Soldiers' Fort.'

Soldiers' Fort was the name of a townland a few miles from the O'Haras' farm, and it was where Primus

Pickenose had built Pickenose Palace—the biggest and ugliest house in Emeraldia—and where the Lawful Guild had built its terrible headquarters: a huge building that no one liked to enter who wasn't a member of the Lawful Guild or a Pickenose. After dark, no one liked even to go by it; and older people, like her grandparents, used to look away and cross themselves when they went past it.

Her aunt and uncle used to call it the Hellfire Club because it reminded them of a building in which the devil was supposed to have appeared, but most people found it hard to say why they were so frightened by it. It just made them shiver and feel a sense of horror for some reason they couldn't explain.

'But what did our great-granduncle have to do with Soldiers' Fort?' Cornelia asked.

'He owned it. That was where his house was that burned down, and where his wife and baby died in the fire. You'd never have guessed that, would you—that Finn used to live exactly where Pickenose Palace is now, and right beside the Lawful Guild Headquarters?

'The only reason I found out,' he explained cheerfully, 'is that I was in the pantry that night sneaking a bit of cake when Mom and Dad and Gran and Granddad came into the kitchen and they all started talking about it.'

'Did they know you heard them?' Cornelia asked.

Barry shook his head. 'No. But I had to stay there for hours till they were all gone to bed.

'What they were talking about mainly,' he continued, to the most appreciative audience he had ever enjoyed, 'was the extra room. They said the house that burned down had been almost exactly the same as our house here, only it had one extra room. And the really weird thing was that the extra room survived the fire. Nobody but Finn had known about the extra room, and nobody could find a way into it until he got out of jail, but Finn got into it no bother.

'There was nothing in it, though, but a real old box, and he took that with him when he left the country. Then, even weirder, when Primus Pickenose was having his house built right where Finn's old house had been, Granddad said they weren't able to knock down that one room so it still exists somewhere inside it.'

'Did they burn the house down just to kill his wife and baby?' Cornelia asked in a frightened voice.

'According to Granddad, Primus and the Lawful Guild wanted Soldiers' Fort really badly for some reason, and they figured that was the only way they could get Finn to leave it. Granddad says they could have got their hands on half the country without much bother at that time, but Soldiers' Fort was the only place they really wanted.

'And they didn't even buy it,' he added indignantly. 'They just waited until Finn had been gone for twelve years, and then they took it over. They said they'd been occupying it for so long they'd got some sort of right over it.

'But then what happened was that everyone in the family got really mad at this, because they had been expecting all the time that Finn would come back from wherever he was some day, and it was only after the Lawful Guild and the Pickenoses had taken over Soldiers' Fort, and the Lawful Guild started building their Headquarters, and the Pickenoses started building Pickenose Palace right where Finn's house had been, that the family tried really hard to find him and hired someone in Paris to track him down.

'That was when they discovered that he'd been murdered a long time before, but the Paris police hadn't known who he was, and that's why they hadn't told the family about it. But it sounded like Gran and Granddad were really mad both at the guy who'd found out all this and at the Paris police too because of something they said about Finn, but I don't know what it was because all they'd say was that they didn't believe it, and that everybody'd always had a good opinion of Finn.'

It was hard to say which of his listeners was the most shocked at hearing this story. Cornelia was ashen-faced, and May and Fuchsia were thinking guiltily how wrong they had been to blame the last Guardian for the destruction of Soldiers' Fort, when it had been the fairies' own fault really. They should have kept a better eye on him so they would have known about his problems and could have helped him while he still was in a position to keep the fort safe.

'Well done, Barry, hiding in the pantry,' Fuchsia said stoutly. 'That's important information you learned, and we might never have heard it any other way.'

'Cornelia, would you like to change history, too?' May asked her suddenly, not wanting to lose any more

GALWAY COUNTY LIBRARIES

time. 'Would you like to let Tansy take you inside Josephine so that you could travel back in time and see the wonderful world that's in there and have a chance to change this world?'

The proposition was a bit more than Cornelia wanted to hear, and she looked down at Josephine and tweaked the hem of the doll's beaded dress so that she wouldn't have to meet any of the fairies' eyes. 'I don't think my Mommy and Daddy would let me,' she said finally. 'They won't even let me cycle into town by myself.'

'No, they probably wouldn't let you if they knew,' May agreed. 'But if you were willing to do it secretly, you could do wonderful things. You could save your family and save the fairies and you could save your great-granduncle from being murdered, just like Barry saved Zanzibar's family from being murdered. You could do more for Emeraldia than any other single person has ever done.

'Wouldn't you like that, Cornelia?' she said in her most coaxing voice. 'You can just about save the world, you know. Wouldn't you like that a lot?'

Chapter 19

The Recruit

'I COULD DO ALL THAT,' Barry volunteered eagerly. 'Cornelia's too young to time-travel by herself, but I could do it.'

'It would be handy if you could,' Fuchsia said truthfully, 'but there's a reason why Cornelia is the only human who can do this job. It's to do with—'

He hesitated, however, as Barry looked at him with growing excitement. He had formed a high opinion of this obliging young human, and didn't want to give him the true reason if there was any chance it might hurt his feelings. He found it hard to make up a different explanation, however, and wished May could take over for him—or at least whisper some story or other in his ear—since she had proved so imaginative at that kind of thing.

Stalling for time, he coughed once or twice, cleared his throat, and then begged pardon politely, as he racked his brain to remember what it was he had heard a long-haired professor fairy say once in the course of a very boring lecture at King Thistle's fort.

That interminable speech (arranged by his high-minded neighbour as after-dinner *'entertainment'*, but failing so badly in this aim that Fuchsia had dozed off twice before it was over, although he was pretty sure no one but May had noticed because she had been quick to jab him awake each time) had covered the topic of the more eccentric human beliefs.

Now he felt a sudden rush of gratitude to the earnest Thistle for the strange human lore that had been communicated to him in his intervals of wakefulness during that endless evening.

'Well, it's to do with the position of the stars when she was born,' he said finally. 'You see, that's why you were the right one to go to Africa and Cornelia is the right one to go to Paris. It's because of the stars.'

May and Tansy avoided looking at one another when he said this, both of them afraid they would start to laugh, and Tansy, in particular, finding it hard to believe that the very correct and upright King Fuchsia would come up with such a colourful lie. Still, they were glad to see that the brother and sister accepted his story without question, Barry's face filling with disappointment because he couldn't go, and Cornelia's filling with dread because she might have to.

The true explanation was less dramatic but also, Fuchsia suspected, capable of being misunderstood, which was why he didn't want to go into it. It was based on observations he had made when he was mind-porting in and out of Cornelia's toys, and had to do with the different personalities of the brother and sister.

He had noticed that Barry concentrated hard on what he was doing at a particular time and tended to ignore everything else, whereas Cornelia missed little that was going on around her, and was a surprisingly shrewd interpreter of events for one so young. He knew this because she also talked a lot more than Barry, discussing and analysing people and events with any being or thing which happened to be in her presence, even though very often this was just the dogs or her toys.

Fuchsia was pretty sure that most fairies would not be able to communicate satisfactorily with most humans. Humans and fairies viewed the world so differently one from the other that they might as well be talking in different languages most of the time. Even with other fairies, Tansy had problems expressing exactly what she meant, and Fuchsia suspected she would have worse problems still with humans; and for this Plan to work, effective communication could easily prove to be the keystone, without which the entire elaborate edifice he had devised could collapse.

That was why Cornelia had the edge on Barry for his present purpose. The brother and sister were equally smart, and Barry was more fearless and adventurous, but he lacked Cornelia's exceptional ability for judging what other humans were thinking, and at adjusting her conversation accordingly.

But why say all that? No, much better to stick to the ridiculous explanation he had already given, and which the young humans appeared to have accepted fully, although it did not suit either of them.

'I could go with her then,' Barry pleaded. 'I could help her.'

'Only one can go at a time,' May told him, wishing as much as Fuchsia that the eager little boy could go instead of the terrified little girl, who was now avoiding eye contact with them and sinking ever more deeply into the chair.

'You have no idea of the difference you could make,' Fuchsia told Cornelia. 'If you can go back in time and save Finn from being murdered, the Pickenoses and the Lawful Guild wouldn't bother you any more, and we'll have our fort back again.'

'How could saving Finn do all that?' she asked in a tiny voice. 'I'd like it, of course, if I could stop him being murdered, but I don't really think I'd be able to stop a gang of apaches killing someone.'

'Of course you could,' Tansy said eagerly. 'I'd be with you.'

'But I don't really understand,' said Cornelia stubbornly, determined she would never again so much as look at those stupid stars that had landed her in this mess. 'How could my great-granduncle have stopped the Lawful Guild and the Pickenoses from doing stuff?'

'He wouldn't have had to do anything,' said Fuchsia, 'except come back to Soldiers' Fort to live. We had a very important fort there that protected the whole of Emeraldia, and all he had to do was to stop other humans from destroying it.'

'What's the big deal about Soldiers' Fort?' Barry asked curiously, remembering now with pleasurable excitement the shiver of horror he always felt when he went past it.

'Right under the fort,' Fuchsia explained, 'well, where the fort *used* to be, there's a big crack in the earth and it goes right down to the Underworld where our old enemies live. We used to call them bad fairies when they lived among us, but now they call themselves the Spirits of the Underworld, and believe me, they're a bad lot. Very evil indeed.'

This was a more dramatic answer than even Barry would have liked. 'Wow,' he said finally. 'Do they come up through the crack?'

'No,' said Fuchsia. 'but they might as well, because what does come up is something that makes humans nearly as bad as they are. It's the air those Underworld Spirits breathe and it's full of their evil.'

'We call it Black Air,' said May, 'because that's what it looks like to us. We know humans can't see it, but we're surprised your scientists haven't detected it, because it's very powerful. If a human spirit has no resistance to evil—and most don't, unfortunately—the Black Air will infect it and change it. The Black Air is what made the Lawful Guild and the Pickenoses so powerful.'

'But how?' asked Barry, who could see how bad fairies would be a problem, but this air stuff—

'It made their souls smaller and blacker than anyone else's,' Tansy explained brightly, 'so they're the meanest and the greediest and the bossiest. Other black-souled humans look up to humans that are meaner and greedier and bossier than they are, so they think the Pickenoses are the best.'

'Unfortunately for us fairies,' said Fuchsia, 'the places where we live are the places the black-souled humans hate most of all. It's some instinct that comes to them when they breathe the air that our old enemies breathe. They hate anything that's green and growing, but if a landscape has a hint of magic in it as well, they want to dig it up instantly and replace it with stone or something that feels like stone, which is all there is in the Underworld; and they become obsessed—absolutely obsessed—about making our streams as smelly and dirty as the Underworld streams.'

'Lawful Guild people really like the Black Air,' said Tansy. 'That's why they built their Headquarters right on top of the earth-crack.'

'The air in that building,' said May, in a voice so filled with horror that both Barry and Cornelia felt the hairs stand up on the back of their necks, 'is almost the same as the air in the Underworld. We call their Central Hall the Black Hall because we can hardly see in there. Very few humans who pass through that Hall have any visible soul left when they come out again—all they have is a tiny, black spot.'

'Your great-granduncle wasn't affected by the Black Air at all,' Fuchsia told them. 'Neither are the two of you nor anyone in your family. We can see inside you more clearly than we can see what's outside you, so that's how we know.

'So long as our fort was there, the earth-crack down to the Underworld did no harm. In fact, the fairy soldiers that were based in that fort made sure that your ancestors were breathing the purest air in Emeraldia with no contaminant of any kind in it. But since the fort was destroyed, so much Black Air has been coming out that we can't control it any more, and most humans are infected.'

The brother and sister stole a glance at one another, each of them suitably impressed, but also wondering if the other actually understood any of this.

'It's a bit weird,' Barry said finally, speaking for them both. 'I mean, how it made the Guild and the Pickenoses so powerful and everything. Maybe we could just take your word for all that stuff.'

'It's just evil in a physical form,' May said simply. 'Almost like a virus, really. As it spreads, it creates more bad humans, and it causes the ones who are already bad to become even worse, and then good humans aren't safe any more, which is what's happening now in Emeraldia. Wouldn't you like to be the one who puts an end to that, Cornelia?'

What Cornelia would have liked was to be able to get out of this room right now and run down to her parents' room and tell them everything, and then her mother and father could tell the fairies that they wouldn't let her go anywhere and then she personally wouldn't have to say no to the fairies and disappoint them; but these beautiful creatures had told her they'd get into trouble if she did this because they weren't licensed to talk to adults or something, so she tried hard to push this unworthy thought out of her mind before they could see it, since they were able to see inside her and everything.

She also didn't want them to see just how much she wished they would stop telling her that she personally could save Emeraldia. She wasn't at all like her brother in wanting adventure. Danger and excitement were by no means Cornelia's cup of cocoa. What Cornelia liked was playing with the dogs, watching her DVDs, reading her books while curled up in a chair in front of the fire, exploring their own small, safe woods, and having picnics down by the stream in the summer.

'Oh, please,' said Tansy, as if she really could read Cornelia's thoughts. 'It's so snug and comfy here, and none of us will ever have a place as snug and comfy as this again unless you save Finn.'

May and Fuchsia looked at one another in surprise. Tansy, of all fairies, had found the magic words for persuading this particular human to do what they wanted. 'Snug and comfy'—those words counted with Cornelia. They could see how her expression changed when she heard them.

In fact, Cornelia still was scared out of her wits at the idea of abandoning her body and taking on a gang of murderers, but she did find herself thinking for the first time that maybe even that gruesome prospect would be less scary than the alternative, which Tansy had summed up so succinctly. After all, how could anything be worse than facing a future in which every day for the rest of her life would be as depressing and frightening and Pickenose-filled as yesterday and today had been?

'Well, *maybe* I could do it,' she said in a small, uncertain voice—relenting, but still worried about committing herself unequivocally. 'I mean, I really would like to save Finn, and I would like it if people could just go on living here, and my grandparents could come back and everything, and everyone wasn't so cross and worried as they are all the time now. So *maybe* I could do it.'

—Chapter 20—

The Jewel Thieves

'IT WILL BE FUN,' said Tansy gaily. 'And remember, I'll be taking care of you,' she added, somersaulting backwards, and then forwards, over the wing chair in her exuberance at the prospect, 'so you have nothing to worry about at all.'

Fuchsia closed his eyes for an instant, but May could not help smiling. This was 'the other Tansy'—the impetuous, gay, unpredictable, dancing fairy she became when she was inside Jules and Josephine. 'It might be important,' Fuchsia said tentatively, trying without success to catch Tansy's excited eye, 'not to do anything that would attract too much attention to yourself when you're in there.'

'Oh, no,' Tansy agreed whole-heartedly, now doing ballet leaps around the chair. 'We'll find Finn and tell him he has to come back and no one else will have any idea at all that we're there.'

Fuchsia had his doubts, but decided to turn his attention to Cornelia before she lost courage again.

'All you have to do,' he told her, 'is to make contact with Finn, by any means, or through any person, you think necessary, and tell him who you are and make sure he believes you, and say whatever you have to say to get him to come back to Soldiers' Fort.

'Don't take no for an answer,' he continued, as Cornelia stared at him wide-eyed. 'Finn has to come back to Emeraldia, and when he does, you tell him he should come to our fort and leave a note on it tied to a stone addressed to Queen May and King Fuchsia, and to say in the note that Soldiers' Fort is in danger and that he wants us to go there to talk to him.'

'Okay,' said Cornelia weakly, unsure how she would ever be able to carry out these instructions, and trying once again to think of an excuse that might get her out of this terrible situation.

'Can we go in right now?' asked Tansy eagerly.

'Whenever Cornelia is ready,' May said.

'Ready!' thought Cornelia to herself. 'Ready!' As if she would ever be *ready* to take on a gang of apaches— she just wasn't being given any real choice.

As the dreaded moment approached, her anxiety about her long-term future grew smaller, and her terror about the immediate unknown grew bigger, but she was too embarrassed to say that out loud. All she could do was look furtively in the direction of the fairies as she let this subversive thinking have its way in her mind, because they had said they could see inside her, so maybe if they saw what her real thoughts were, one of them would give her a last-minute reprieve; but all they did was smile at her.

Sighing, she decided she had no hope of overcoming the force of will in *this* room, and she more or less gave up at that point and lay down on the bed.

'No, stop it,' said Barry suddenly, seeing his sister's

frightened face. 'Cornelia's too scared. She can't go in there.'

His sister looked at him gratefully, and for a few seconds, thought she was saved; but then something interesting happened. As is often the case when someone else recognises a problem and sympathises, the problem shrinks; and as a consequence of Barry's intervention on her behalf, Cornelia suddenly felt a bit less afraid than before.

'It's okay, Barry,' she said, putting together the bravest voice she could manage. 'You came back okay from Zanzibar, so I'll probably come back okay from Josephine. I think I'd better just do it,' she added, closing her eyes again, and listening to her heart thump, and wondering if she would ever see her brother again.

This time, it was Barry's turn to watch as Tansy disappeared briefly, reappeared, and then vanished; and it was Cornelia's turn to look down at herself lying in the bed, but only for one disoriented instant.

Then, quicker than the blink of an eye, her cosy bedroom with her toys and Barry (his face white and panic-stricken in the glimpse she got of him) and her big chair and her fireplace had vanished, and she was in an adult world of the night: a dark, smoky room in which her ears were almost overwhelmed by the music of a jazz band combined with the din of hundreds of people laughing and talking.

She found it hard to remember at first that she was invisible, and was expecting every instant that one of the many cross-looking waiters who were rushing around and holding trays high in the air with one hand would order her to leave. Everything was so different, and things were happening so fast, that she felt as if she were on a strange and very novel amusement-park ride, flitting effortlessly, silently and at speed over a world of hundreds of laughing, talking and dancing people dressed like Jules and Josephine.

Then Tansy came to a sudden stop; and when Cornelia looked down nervously to see why, she saw something so exciting that she forgot to be frightened any more and even started to giggle. What happened was that she had caught her first glimpse of the real Josephine.

'Oh, look at her, Tansy,' she said, thrilled. 'Look at her. She looks just like the doll,' she added, giggling so hard that she was barely able to talk. 'Only worse.'

Cornelia was describing just the expression on Josephine's face when she said 'worse', because in other respects, Josephine looked very smart indeed. On this night, she was dressed in a white satin dress and a diamond necklace, and her sometimes-wayward hair was controlled to the highest demands of fashion, almost glued to her head in large glossy waves. Her eyes, however, had no more expression than two pieces of burnt coal, and the lifeless harshness of her voice startled Cornelia when she heard it first.

'I didn't come to this place to enjoy your company,' she whispered roughly to Jules. 'Why isn't Finn here yet?'

Jules turned a tired, monocled eye in the direction of Josephine, and gave the appearance for a moment that he was thinking; but then he shrugged, and looked back at the dance floor.

Cornelia giggled again. 'Jules is even more like his doll than Josephine. Oh, I wish my great-granduncle would hurry so I can see him,' she whispered excitedly. 'He's probably exactly like his photograph, too, isn't he?'

'Turn away if you like,' the real Josephine then hissed to Jules, 'but there's no point in bothering with this jewel robbery at all if Finn isn't in on it.'

'Keep your voice down,' Jules replied, in a bored drawl. 'We're going to get those jewels and Finn will be there when we need him. I don't have any doubt about that.'

This was by no means the sort of conversation Cornelia had expected to hear. 'What are they talking about?' she asked indignantly. 'They're making it sound like Finn is some sort of jewel thief.'

Tansy was as bewildered as Cornelia. 'I don't know,' she said. 'I never hang around Jules and Josephine because they're so boring. I haven't heard any of this before.'

'Finn doesn't even have a costume planned,' Josephine continued in her flat, angry voice. 'He can't really be planning to go in that worn-out dinner jacket. He'll stand out a mile.'

'Doesn't care much about clothes, Finn,' replied Jules. 'Much less about costume balls. I'd say he hates having to go down there, but he knows there's something in it for him.'

'Are you sure he's booked on the *Train Bleu* with everyone else?' Josephine asked.

'Arranged it for him myself,' said Jules. 'He has his ticket.'

After that, the couple fell into their usual silence, and Cornelia became even more agitated. 'You don't think they're talking about a real jewel robbery, do you?' she asked in a tiny voice.

'It sounds like it,' said Tansy unworriedly. 'Anyway, I have an idea. Do you see that man sitting over there?'

Cornelia followed her point, and looked at a man with blond hair and glasses sitting at a table by himself.

'He's a gossip columnist,' Tansy explained. 'He's not a nice man at all. In fact, he's even meaner than the headwaiter, but he knows everything about parties and things. We'll get someone to ask him some questions, and then maybe we'll know what they're talking about.'

They flitted around the room while Tansy cast an appraising eye over some of the most glamorous of the patrons, and then suddenly they were inside a beautiful young woman sitting at the table just beside that of the gossip columnist. Driven by Tansy, and to the great surprise of everyone else at her table, the young woman stood up suddenly and moved to the columnist's table.

'Well, this is a pleasant surprise,' the columnist said in a voice almost as harsh as Josephine's.

'I wanted to ask you about a ball,' the young woman said. 'I think it's a costume ball and I think people are going to it on the *Train Bleu*. Do you know anything about it?'

'What's your angle?' the columnist said. 'Everyone knows about Ella Manchester's ball.'

'Well, I don't,' the young woman said, 'and everyone else is talking about it, and I want to know all the details, and I thought you would be the person who would know most about it.'

'You came to the right man all right,' the columnist acknowledged, softening a little at the flattery. 'It's the biggest costume do Ella's given yet, and there's going to be a charity display the next day of all the jewels the guests were wearing at it. You can bet that all the most valuable jewels in Europe will be there because everybody's going to be showing off the best sparklers they have.

'The police and the insurance companies hate Ella for it because it's going to mean the priciest security operation of the decade, but they can't make Ella change her mind. The *Train Bleu* won't be carrying anyone else except people going to that ball. It's been booked out for months. How could a looker like you not know all about that shindig?'

'Thank you very much,' the young woman said politely, and returned to her own table, where Tansy and Cornelia left her. Glancing down, they saw the woman shake her head and look around the table in bewilderment as her even more bewildered companions looked back at her. 'Can you tell me what I just did?' she asked, and then she and all the people at the table began to laugh uproariously.

'Finn would have much more fun sitting with those

people than with Jules and Josephine,' Cornelia said regretfully. 'Tansy, you don't think he's really become a jewel thief, do you?'

'Well, frankly, it doesn't matter whether he has or not,' said Tansy practically, 'so long as we can stop him from being murdered and he comes back to Soldiers' Fort.'

To Cornelia, however, it mattered a lot, and she could hardly bear the thought that this romantic relative of hers, who already had been made to suffer so much by the Lawful Guild and by the Pickenoses, had become a thief as well.

'Something's up,' Tansy said then, becoming aware of an uproar near the entrance door to the club. Waiters went running towards it, and then Cornelia saw one of the waiters being flung against a table, which fell over, toppling bottles, full glasses of drink, and plates of food over the well-dressed patrons who were sitting around it.

'Oh, no, it's apaches!' said the same young woman through whom Tansy had spoken to the gossip columnist.

Chapter 21

Apaches!

THERE WERE SIX OF THEM in all—three men and three women. The men had scarred, rough-looking faces and wore caps and eye-catching scarves, and one of them had an earring. The three women also wore scarves and their eyes were even colder than Josephine's. They walked towards the dance floor, from which all the dancing couples fled as they saw them coming.

The band had stopped playing, but started up again hurriedly after the man who appeared to be the leader of this gang of apaches said roughly: 'Are you going to play, or do we get rid of you and bring in our own musicians? You know what we want to hear.'

'Cornelia, this is wonderful,' Tansy whispered in excitement. 'They're going to do an apache dance.'

'They're going to do what?' said Cornelia startled, looking at the six thugs. 'I thought they came here to rob people or something. You mean they came here to dance?'

'It's their own dance,' Tansy explained. 'It's like a street fight. The gangs were given the name apaches after a big street fight they had among themselves—which was very unfair, I think, to the real Apaches—and they like to act out that fight in a dance.'

Not all of the gang danced. One man and one woman took over the dance floor while the others watched, and at first Cornelia found it hard to believe she was looking at a dance rather than a fight.

The man appeared to be throwing the woman around very roughly, but then the woman would come back to him and be thrown around again; and once or twice, the woman threatened the man with a knife, and he would seem to twist it out of her hands and then throw her around some more and pull her by the hair; but nevertheless, this extraordinary spectacle did seem to be just a dance, and not a real struggle between the two of them.

Many of the people in the club had stood up, intending to leave; but what was happening on the dance floor was so dramatic that not one person was able to take his or her eyes off it, not even the indifferent Jules and Josephine.

'Now this is really going to be fun,' said Tansy, and before Cornelia knew what was happening, the two of them were inside the dancing apache woman and spinning across the dance floor, having been flung from one side of it to the other by that terrible, smelly apache man. As Tansy giggled inside her, the bewildered apache woman (transporting a dumbfounded Cornelia) cart-wheeled back to the apache man, lifted him over her head, spun him around several times, and flung him across the dance floor with so much force that his dazed body skidded well beyond it, knocking down two tables laden with food and drink, and sending startled patrons scattering in all directions.

For a moment, the apache man was too dazed to move, but then his face took on a furious expression, and the even more bewildered apache woman experienced real terror as she saw the man pull a knife from his pocket and get to his feet. Then the woman felt herself somersaulting right over her dancing partner, and kicking the knife out of his hands with her strapped high-heeled shoe as she went.

The two non-dancing apache men then started coming towards the woman, and seeing them, Tansy quickly left her and went inside her dance partner, who had been staring in bewilderment at his right hand from which the knife had been kicked. Under Tansy's giggling control, however, this man leapt back into action with renewed vigour, and grabbed an arm of each of the two apache men before they reached the woman.

He pulled them to the middle of the dance floor, and there he began to spin around so quickly that his two fellow gang members were flying sideways through the air and were visible to the room only as a blur, although to most people in the room, they were not visible at all because nearly all the patrons had dropped down to the floor under the tables, afraid the dancer would let go, and the two apaches would come flying like missiles through the nightclub.

As the dancing apache man finally slowed down his spin, a stupefied Cornelia saw the three apache women trying to run from the club. Before they could reach the door, however, the police arrived, blowing their whistles and being applauded by the patrons as they ran across the big room towards the dance floor.

'Um, Tansy, do you think we can get out of this man now?' Cornelia asked in a faint voice.

Giggling uncontrollably, Tansy obliged, just as two policemen grabbed the bewildered apache man by the arms. As the gang was led from the room, the patrons loudly cheered and applauded the two dancers. Fifty or a hundred people seemed to be shouting at once: 'Best apache dance I've ever seen!'

'One thing I'll say for this place,' one young man was saying to his companions at the table over which Cornelia and Tansy were hovering, 'you never know what you're going to see on the dance floor. Do you remember the night Eleanor did the wild Charleston and somersaulted from table to table but could never remember afterwards how she did it? Well, that dance was good, but this one was even better.'

'Maybe we won't mention anything about the apache dance to Fuchsia,' Tansy said guiltily when she heard this. 'You know how he said not to do anything conspicuous, and there's a chance he might think the apache dance was a teeny-weeny bit conspicuous.'

'I just wish Finn were here,' said the disoriented Cornelia, even more worried now about her unfortunate relation since she had seen an actual apache gang. 'How are we going to save him if we can't find him?'

'Oh, we'll find him all right,' said Tansy confidently. 'I've been coming into Josephine for quite some time, you know, so I'm pretty good at finding my way around Paris; and even if he's gone somewhere else, we'll track him down.'

'You don't really think he's a jewel thief, do you, Tansy?' Cornelia asked in a tiny voice.

'It's hard to know any other reason he'd have for spending time around Jules and Josephine,' Tansy said disinterestedly. 'But I still don't see how it matters one way or the other to us if he is robbing jewels here in France so long as we can get him to go back to Emeraldia. Anyway, we're not going to find out any more tonight because the police are making them close the club early. We'd better just go back now and tell May and Fuchsia what we found out.'

—*Chapter 22*—

A Trip to the Woods

BACK IN HER BEDROOM, Cornelia opened her eyes and found Barry lying asleep on the bed beside her. May and Fuchsia were gone, but they had left the fire burning brightly, and the familiar room with its small pink bed, and pink-and-white striped wallpaper with tiny pink flowers, looked even more inviting and snug than usual. Tansy whirlwinded out the window immediately, saying she expected May and Fuchsia would be waiting for her and wanting to hear everything.

'Barry, wake up,' Cornelia said, shaking him. 'You won't believe the things that happened.'

Barry groaned when Cornelia told him what Jules and Josephine said about a jewel robbery, not because he was shocked or worried about Finn, as Cornelia was, but because of the excitement he was missing; and he groaned even more loudly when she told him about the apache gang and what Tansy had done to them.

'I really wish you could come too,' Cornelia said sincerely. 'Because, you know, it is very interesting in there, and not as scary as I expected. Barry, what time is it anyway?' she asked, as a feeling of great sleepiness swept over her suddenly.

'Five o'clock. Lucky you don't have school tomorrow, isn't it?'

Cornelia thought it was very lucky because she had never been so tired in her life. She slept until lunchtime, and when she came downstairs, her mother looked at her anxiously for a moment.

'Are you feeling all right, Sweetie?' she asked. 'I went in earlier to wake you because I thought you and Barry and I would go down to the woods today and pick holly, but you were in such a deep sleep, I was afraid you might be sick.'

Cornelia said she was fine, and proved it by tackling her lunch of homemade sausage and mashed potatoes and cabbage with the appetite of someone making up for missing her usual hearty breakfast. When they had finished the meal, her mother instructed both Cornelia and Barry to put on caps and scarves and gloves and several layers of woollies under their old jackets, and she put a flask of hot chocolate and three cups in a knapsack, saying they were going to be out for the rest of the day.

'Because we have serious holly-picking to do,' she explained, 'since today is a whole new start to Christmas, and that's official. We're going to make two new wreaths, we're going to wire them to the front and back doors so that no one can pull them off, and whatever else happens from now on, nothing is going to stop us having a sensational Christmas.'

Something about her tone made her children look at her alertly, both of them sensing there was more on her mind than she was letting on. What they were hearing was less like her 'proposing-a-fun-outing voice' and more like her 'final-word voice'—the one she reserved for when she was going against the wishes of her children, but was not to be questioned, as when she wouldn't let Barry take the computer to his bedroom, or let Cornelia read at the dining table—although that voice was unexpected in these circumstances, as she knew neither of them was going to object to a holly-picking expedition. Cornelia suspected their mother didn't feel nearly as cheerful as she was trying to let on.

'Just in case this is our last Christmas ever here,' she continued '—and remember, we never mention that possibility in front of Daddy—we have to make sure we do this place proud. I'm sorry there won't be many presents, but we'll have plenty of goodies to eat, and at least the holly and ivy are free, and we're going to hang so much of them that every room in this house is going to look like the fairies have taken possession of it.

'But I want a solemn promise from both of you,' she went on, surprised at the way Barry and Cornelia both had jumped at those last few cheerful words of hers, 'that you're not going to let a single thought about the Pickenoses or the Lawful Guild enter your heads between now and the sixth of January. Okay?

'Well?' she persisted, as the brother and sister avoided her eyes, both of them reluctant liars, and both of them knowing they would be unable to think of anything else. 'We all agree on that, don't we?'

Without waiting for an answer, she took out of a

drawer the large canvas bags they used every year to gather holly, and when Freddy and Tickles saw these, they began to bark exuberantly and jump all over her before racing one another excitedly to the door to jump and paw at it.

'Now, no more long faces,' she pleaded. 'Cheer up, for heaven's sake,' she said, 'or you'll depress the dogs.'

The weather could not have been better for the outing. The day was bright and dry and windless, and so cold that the frost was still on the grass. The walk to the woods was easy and quick because it was downhill all the way, and within the woods, they found more berries on the holly than Cornelia ever remembered finding before. They had their hot chocolate sitting on a log, and after they finished it, they decided to hunt around the ground for fir and pine cones as well.

Cornelia felt so much happier than she had in days that she started humming without even noticing, and after a minute or two, her mother looked at her curiously. 'That's a nice tune,' she said. 'It's sort of like a tango, but not quite a tango. Where did you learn it?'

'Oh, I just heard it somewhere,' she said vaguely, remembering suddenly that it was the music to which the apaches had danced.

'You and I will have to learn to tango, Cornelia. I've always wanted to. I don't think I could ever get your father to learn, but I'd say you'd enjoy it.'

There were so many cones on the ground that they did not stop gathering them until darkness fell, but as this was December, that happened early, at about four o'clock. As they crossed the stream going back, her mother started singing *Good King Wenceslaus*, and Barry and Cornelia joined in with great gusto. Then, all of a sudden, the dogs ran barking towards the house, and the three of them stopped singing and looked at one another. When they had gone a little farther, Cornelia felt her stomach tighten up nervously as she saw they were not alone in the field.

About a dozen strange men had assembled there and were doing frightening things in the area of their fairy fort, sticking pegs into the ground and taking measures and looking through machines to work out levels.

Puffy Pickenose and Pompeous Potty-Pickenose XIII were there as well, and so was Cornelia's father, arguing heatedly with them. 'You're trespassing,' her father was saying. 'You're trespassing, and I'm telling you to get off this property.'

Pompeous, typically, was saying nothing in reply, just staring back at him without blinking, and Puffy, as usual, was looking sideways and doing all the talking.

'I cannot go on being patient with you and helping you forever,' Puffy was saying, 'and letting you waste even more of my valuable time with this nonsense. You act like you still have some rights over this property, and you keep persisting in this stupidity because you refuse to consult a member of the Lawful Guild for proper advice. Any Lawful Guild member would have advised you to be off this property long before this, but you're determined to continue with this nonsensical time-wasting.

'I don't know if you have any capacity at all for understanding, but if you do, you might try to understand now that I'm instructing you to stop harassing the workmen in this field. If they refuse to work because you are harassing them, you will have to pay for their wages and compensation for the time lost.'

Her sideways-looking eyes then landed on the group coming from the woods with their three canvas bags. 'And you must take nothing from the property. If you've taken anything from the woods, you're taking goods that do not belong to you. If you try to keep possession of them, that will be theft, and you'll be liable to imprisonment. You must hand those bags you're carrying over to our workmen immediately, and if they turn out to contain things you've taken from the woods, I'm going to see that charges are brought against you for that.'

'You're mad as a hatter,' Cornelia's father said heatedly. 'You and Pompeous both. I don't know which one of you is crazier than the other.'

'Hey, I see you didn't bring Walter with you today,' Barry put in. 'So you got him off you eventually, did you?'

'Criminal charges will certainly be brought against you,' she said. 'A lot of people have tried to steal things from the properties they used to live in before they left, and we've had to introduce very strict legislation to deal with that. You could be facing five to ten years in jail.'

'What are those men doing measuring our fairy fort?' Cornelia asked near to panic.

The two Pickenoses ignored her, but one of the workmen heard the question. 'We're building a big factory here, little girl. We're seeing now how much ground levelling we'll have to do for that.'

Silently, Cornelia's mother put her bag of holly down on the ground. 'Barry, Cornelia, you leave your bags as well,' she said then. 'We're going back to the house now and we're not discussing anything more with these people.'

Hearing this, Pompeous shifted his stare from her father to her mother, and Barry and Cornelia each grabbed one of her hands quickly.

'Come on, Danny,' her mother said quietly to her husband. 'I want you to come back to the house with us.'

'Kate, I can't—' her father began.

'Danny, please. I want to get the children away from here, and I want you to come with us.'

Reluctantly, her father came with them, and when they got back to the house, her parents sat down silently at the kitchen table. Cornelia and Barry, however, ran straight upstairs and breathed a great sigh of relief when they found Tansy waiting in Cornelia's bedroom, although the day's developments had made the fairy even more agitated than the brother and sister.

'It's terrible inside the fort,' she said. 'Everyone's ready for emergency evacuation, but the fairies from our fort won't be able to stay together any more when King Thistle's fort is destroyed. We're going to have to be divided up between forts all over Emeraldia, in any place where there's a small amount of space left. Do you know if they're planning to dig it up straight away? Oh, poor May and Fuchsia. I want to help them so badly, but I don't know if there's time now.'

'We don't know when they're going to dig it up,' said Cornelia, 'but I'm really scared too. Can we go to Paris right now and look for Finn?'

'Oh, yes, immediately,' Tansy agreed eagerly. 'Immediately, right now. May and Fuchsia told me I'm to take responsibility here and I'm to be very sensible because, the way things are, they can't leave the fort any more because everyone is too frightened, and there was some very mean gossip that they had found some refuge of their own and abandoned everyone, which I thought was very unfair, because everyone knows that May and Fuchsia would never do anything like that, but no one back there is thinking very rationally at the moment, I must say.'

'But if you go now, Neely, Mom or Dad might come in and find you lying in the bed,' Barry pointed out. 'What do I say if they do?' he asked.

'Just say I'm asleep.'

'Yeah, but Mom will want you to come down to dinner.'

'Oh, you think of something, Barry. They're so worried about everything, it will probably be easier to fool them than usual. Anyway, maybe we'll even be back before dinner. Come on, Tansy,' Cornelia said, lying down on the bed. 'Let's go right this instant.'

—Chapter 23—

The Concierge at the Ritz

A MOMENT LATER, she was back in the now-familiar world of the nightclub. Jules and Josephine were at their usual table, Josephine tonight dressed in a blue beaded dress, very like the one on her doll. The room was even noisier than usual and many people were wearing masks and costumes, as nearly half the tables had been taken over for a boisterous masquerade party; but once again, there was no sign of Finn.

'You know, he's very frustrating,' Cornelia grumbled, exasperated by her elusive relation. 'Do you know what I think we should do, Tansy? I think we should try to find that artist, Savannah Gray, who made the dolls. She knew Finn really well, and she might be able to tell us where he is. But how do you think we can find her?'

'The concierge at the Ritz,' Tansy answered promptly.

'What's that?' Cornelia asked.

'It's a man who works at the Ritz Hotel who finds out things for people and gets tickets for them and stuff like that; and everyone who comes to the Silver Poodle Club says that if there's anything you can't find in Paris, the concierge at the Ritz can locate it for you. That's what they all say. They tip him, I think, but I'm sure we'll be able to do that.'

'Then let's go ask him right now,' Cornelia said

urgently. 'If we could find out before it's dinner time at home, it would be much less complicated.'

An instant later, they were inside a young man in white tie and tails, and sporting a mask, who had been hurrying up the stairs to the noisy party, pulling behind him an unwilling fox terrier on a leash. Under Tansy's guidance, he now spun around and hurried down the stairs again, retracing his steps so quickly that he found his own car and chauffeur had not yet driven away. *'Place Vendôme,'* he said to the chauffeur, *'à l'Hôtel Ritz.'*

Cornelia was delighted at first that Tansy had decided to go inside a person with a dog, but when they were in the car, she started to worry about this dog. His name was *'Frites'* according to the medal hanging from his collar, and Cornelia thought she had never before seen such an aggrieved animal. She began to have some doubts then about Tansy's choice, finding it hard not to be suspicious of someone whose own dog disliked him so much that he would snarl at his owner non-stop. She wondered if he was mean to the dog. At the very least, it was clear that he didn't pet him enough.

She had the power to control the young man, of course, and she would have liked to use it to make him cuddle and hug the furry little animal right now to make up for past failures and possible sins, but she didn't quite dare, because it seemed to her there was a good chance the young man might have his hand bitten off him if he put it anywhere near that very cross dog. So instead, she restricted herself to having him just talk nicely to the fox terrier, drifting now and again into the affectionate baby-talk she sometimes used with Freddy and Tickles when they were agitated about an upcoming event, such as a bath or a visit to the vet.

In a soft voice, the young man told the snarling dog he was 'wovely widdle woggie' and 'a furry-wurry wumpkin' and a 'sweetsie-weetsie Fritsie' and—in tribute to his breed—that he was the best 'widdle foxy-woxy-woodle'; and although these endearments did not move the fox terrier at all, they undoubtedly impressed the chauffeur, causing him to pull shut the glass screen between the front and the back, and to mutter under his breath something about 'imbeciles' and 'too much money' and 'didn't fight in the Great War for this' and 'revolution'.

When they reached the hotel, the young man hurried into the lobby pulling the unappeased dog behind him, and went directly to a desk, behind which an attentive-looking man in a tailcoat was standing.

'I need the address of an artist, Jacques,' the young man said urgently. 'I need it straight away. Her name is Savannah Gray and she's a young American woman. It's a real emergency, Jacques.' To Cornelia's surprise, the young man then took out his wallet and removed a large number of notes from it, which he handed to Jacques. 'Nobody else but you could find out so quickly, Jacques, but I'm sure you'll have no problem at all.'

Just for an instant, Cornelia was shocked to see how freely Tansy made use of the money of a complete stranger, and then guiltily relieved. Her parents would disapprove, of course, but those two sticklers were in a different world at the moment, and even they would surely understand that Finn's chances of being saved were bound to be improved by the fairy's open-mindedness about such matters.

Jacques, too, proved most open-minded, and gave the impression that it was an everyday matter for him to be asked for assistance by a masked man in white tie and tails attached to a disgruntled dog that was snarling without pause and making a mighty effort to free himself, first by trying to pull his head through his  collar and then by trying to chew through his leash.

'Just have a seat in the bar, Sir,' Jacques said tranquilly. 'There is no gallery owner in Paris I cannot contact, and I have no doubt that one of them will know where your artist lives. And if that method should fail, I have other means. Just make yourself comfortable, Sir, and as soon as I have the information, I'll bring it in to you.

'And I'm sure the barman would be glad to provide a bowl of water for your dog,' he added, as the frustrated terrier changed tactics, and taking a brief rest from its attempts to chew its way to freedom, decided instead to clamour for it, and commenced the loudest howl Cornelia had ever heard. 'That often settles them down.'

The young man took the last free seat at the crowded bar counter and ordered orange juice as the fox terrier tried to bite his leg.

'You know, I think I'll have an orange juice as well,' the man next to him said in an American accent.

'An orange juice, Mr. Fitzgerald?' the barman asked in surprise.

'I have work to finish tonight,' the American said. 'Yes, an orange juice.'

'Cornelia, this is a huge piece of luck,' Tansy whispered to her eagerly. 'Do you know who that is? It's Scott Fitzgerald, the writer.'

Cornelia had never heard of Scott Fitzgerald, but she assumed he must be someone very important because of the awe in Tansy's voice.

'This could make everything much easier. You see, I was thinking that, even when we find Savannah Gray, she may not want to tell us where Finn lives because she might worry about giving out his address to some stranger. But I'm sure she'd give his address to Scott Fitzgerald if he asked for it. Oh, I wish that concierge would hurry up.'

In fact, the concierge proved himself very worthy of the tip he had been given, and he arrived back with the artist's address written on a card after only about ten minutes. 'It was not hard to find,' he said modestly. 'She's having an exhibition in a week's time, and there's a lot of interest in it. Are you going there to buy one of her paintings?'

'Yes, that's it exactly,' the young man answered, putting down the card on the counter. 'Thank you, Jacques.'

As soon as the concierge left the room, Tansy and Cornelia left the young man, and went inside Scott Fitzgerald, who picked up the card with the address. They watched as the man whose body they had just left looked around him in a daze, studied in bewilderment the glass of orange juice in his hand, and after a moment asked the barman: 'François, when did I come in here?'

'Not long ago,' the barman answered. 'That's your first drink.'

'And I ordered this?' the young man asked, shaking his head as if trying to clear it, and then looking at his watch. 'I was supposed to be back at Bella Chase's party at the Silver Poodle Club half an hour ago. Wonder what brought me here? And why would I have brought this dog with me?' he asked, looking first at the leash in his hand and then at the fox terrier who bared his teeth, growled and tried to bite the young man again.

'Taking him for a walk, perhaps?' suggested François.

'Lord no,' said the young man. 'Not this brute. I only have him for Bella's scavenger hunt. A fox terrier was on her list, and this fellow happened to be tied in front of a house I was passing. Bit of luck, that was, although

I had the devil of a time getting him into the car. Doesn't seem to go much for strangers,' he explained, as the kidnap victim made yet another lunge at his leg.

Paying for his drink, the young man seemed surprised for a moment by the small number of banknotes left in his wallet, but then shrugged and got to his feet. 'Anyway, mustn't keep Bella waiting,' he said unworriedly, as he headed on his way with an awkward, dragging gait, the terrier's jaw now being clasped around his right shoe.

'How much of his money did you take?' Cornelia asked, interested.

'I have no idea,' Tansy answered. 'They were just bits of paper, but I've noticed that it often produces good results for humans when they hand over several of them. I'd have taken all of them if I'd known he'd stolen the dog.'

Scott Fitzgerald picked up the card on which the concierge had written Savannah Gray's address, and left the hotel.

'Do you want a taxi, Mr Fitzgerald?' the doorman asked him.

He nodded. 'Yes. For Montparnasse.'

—*Chapter 24*—

Savannah Gray

To Cornelia, the taxi ride seemed to take forever, although the driver, to be fair, drove as fast and as wildly as anyone in a hurry could wish, blowing his horn and shouting insults out the window at whatever he judged to be an obstacle to his progress, which broad category included anything on the street that either breathed or moved: pedestrians waiting to cross; cars foolishly slowing at corners; cyclists, of which there were many; horses pulling carts; men in overalls pulling carts; dogs; pigeons; other taxis; even a traffic policeman.

'*Rue Vavin,*' the driver announced at last, stopping the car with a great screech of brakes.

Scott Fitzgerald pulled out his wallet and put a bill into the driver's outstretched hand, and when the hand remained outstretched, slowly added another bill and then a third, at which point the driver withdrew his hand, wished the writer a cheery good night, and drove off, blowing his horn as he did. 'I didn't want to spend any more of Scott Fitzgerald's money than necessary,' Tansy explained. 'But I think that probably worked out all right, didn't it?'

Scott Fitzgerald knocked on the door of another concierge, this time not a grand personage in a tailcoat like Jacques at the Ritz, but a cross-looking elderly woman with very red-coloured hair and a cat on a leash. 'Well?' she said in a surly voice. 'What do you want?'

'I'm looking for Savannah Gray,' he answered.

'What do you want with her?'

'I'm thinking of buying one of her paintings.'

'Well, all right then,' she conceded grudgingly. 'Top floor.' Scott Fitzgerald took out his wallet again, and handed her some coins.

He was tired by the time he reached the fifth floor, all of which was taken up by just one big room with a large skylight. The door of this was open, and inside it, a tall, slim young woman dressed in a cap and several cardigans was standing at an easel, and working on a painting of another, very elegant, young woman in a ballet costume who was shivering with the cold. He knocked on the open door several times, and both women looked around.

'Who are you?' the artist asked, startled.

'I'm sorry to disturb you,' he said politely. 'Are you Savannah Gray?'

'Yes,' the woman answered. 'Oh, you're American, too, aren't you?'

'Yes. My name is Scott Fitzgerald.'

'My God, you are Scott Fitzgerald,' the artist said, surprised. 'What on earth brings you here? Oh, do come in,' she added. 'I'm sorry it's so cold. Nobody expected a cold snap at this time of year, and I haven't been able to buy fuel since March. The cost of it, you know. It's very hard on poor Claudette,' she explained, looking sympathetically at her ballerina model, 'but this painting has to be finished before her big night. She's going to be dancing the lead in *Swan Lake* when it opens at the *Opéra*, you know. You're not by any chance here to buy a painting, are you?' she asked, as Claudette took the opportunity to pull a thick blanket around herself briefly and put her feet on top of a hot-water bottle that was beside her.

'I'd like to buy one soon,' he said, 'but tonight, I was hoping you could give me the address of someone who's a friend of yours. Finn O'Hara.'

'You know Finn?' she said surprised. 'He's a big fan of yours, but he never said he knew you.'

'We have mutual acquaintances,' he said. 'He goes to the Silver Poodle Club a lot.'

'Oh, I see,' Savannah Gray said tiredly, and then she looked at him with a hint of suspicion. 'Your mutual acquaintances aren't that Jules and Josephine couple, are they?'

He shook his head. 'No. I know some of the musicians.'

Tansy was the best liar she'd ever heard, Cornelia thought, giggling privately. She herself had no capacity for lying, but obviously it was an invaluable skill in their present situation, and she would have rated their chances of saving Finn much lower if Tansy suffered from her limitations in that area.

'Oh, I see,' said Savannah, relaxing a little. 'I've only been there twice, but I did think the musicians were awfully good. They were the only interesting people there. But why do you want Finn's address? I don't mean to be rude, it's just that—'

'Oh, that's quite all right,' he said smoothly. 'He's going down to Monte Carlo in a few days, and I just wanted to give him the address of some people I know down there.'

'Finn's going to Monte Carlo?' she said, astonished. 'Why on earth is Finn going to Monte Carlo? He never said a word to me about it.'

'I think he has some business there.'

'Oh, I see,' she said, as if this made some sense to her. 'Maybe he's had some word of a job. I know he's had a terrible time trying to get work in Paris. I thought maybe that was why he spent so much time with that scary Jules and Josephine, in case they could give him work.' She hesitated a minute. 'Well, anyway, I'm sure I can give *you* his address, Mr Fitzgerald. It's at the *Rue Jacob* end of the *Rue Saint-Benoît*. This is the number,' she added, handing him a bit of paper. 'I should warn you, you'll find his flat even colder than mine. At least, I have a heater that I can light now and then, when I have the money for the fuel. He doesn't even own one, and his window's broken.'

Scott Fitzgerald thanked her politely and said good night, and then said good night just as politely to the surly concierge who opened her door to look at him as he left the building. He picked up a taxi close to *La Coupole*, and gave the driver Finn's address. This driver drove just as fast and with as much blowing of his horn as the previous one, and he delivered them to *Rue Saint-Benoît* in only a few minutes, and was paid by the same method as they had used with the last driver.

This time, because they might be meeting Finn in less than a minute, Cornelia was feeling excited and nervous as they approached yet another grumpy concierge. Their conversation with her was very similar to the one they had just had with Savannah Gray's concierge, except this time when Scott Fitzgerald was asked why he wanted to see Finn, he said that he wanted to offer him a job.

'Oh, well in that case...' the woman said, visibly softening, '...he's on the top floor.' Scott Fitzgerald took out his wallet, and gave this concierge some coins as well, and when her hand remained extended, he pulled out a banknote and laid that on top of them.

On this second climb, Scott Fitzgerald (who was not the fittest man in Paris) was very tired indeed when he reached the top floor; and having reached it, to make matters worse, he found the door locked. He knocked repeatedly, but no one answered.

'We have to get in,' Cornelia said agitatedly. 'We have to get in. Maybe Finn is lying in there dead or something.'

'Oh, don't worry,' Tansy said easily. 'We'll just kick in the door.'

A second later, Scott Fitzgerald stepped back, and put his foot to the door with such force that it flew open immediately, and indeed, very nearly came off its hinges.

They looked into a cold and almost empty room. There was a camp bed, a small table, a broken chair, a towel hanging on the window as a curtain, and very little else. A few items of clothing, including a very worn dinner jacket, were hanging from nails on the wall.

On the table was a ticket for the *Calais-Méditerranée Express.*

'That's the real name of the train,' Tansy said, 'but everybody just calls it the *Train Bleu* or the *Blue Train* because the carriages are all painted blue. Although some people call it the Millionaires' Train, because it costs so much to travel on it.'

'This ticket is for tomorrow night,' Cornelia said when Scott Fitzgerald picked it up. 'You know, Tansy, I think he probably is a jewel thief,' she said miserably. 'He obviously has no money at all, and yet somehow he's got a ticket for that millionaires' train to go to some big ball that rich people are going to. We just have to stop him. I don't want Finn to be a criminal.'

'Well, at least we know where he'll be tomorrow night,' Tansy said practically. 'If he's on the train, he can't escape us. We'll make contact with him there.'

'I wonder what he'll think when he finds his door kicked open.' Cornelia said uneasily. 'He might think poor Mr Fitzgerald did it, and be mad at him.'

'Well, when we find him, we can explain,' the fairy said guiltily. 'Although I think we'd better get Scott Fitzgerald back to the Ritz now,' she added, looking even more guiltily down at his right foot which he'd used to kick in the door. 'He's been very helpful, hasn't he?'

Chapter 25

The Home Front

THIS TIME, as she returned to her bedroom, Cornelia's quick, and always surprising, view of her own body from above was partly hidden by Freddy and Tickles, who were sitting on the bed and looking down at her. When she opened her eyes, both dogs reacted by barking, squirming, wagging their tails, trying to lick her every place she could be licked, and then, in Tickles' case, running ecstatic figures-of-eight around the room. They made so much noise that Cornelia's father came to the door.

'Everything all right in here?' he asked tiredly.

'It's just Cornelia and the dogs,' answered Barry, who was sitting in the wing chair. 'They're playing.'

'Well, good night then,' he said, closing the door after him.

'Poor Daddy looks terrible, doesn't he?' Cornelia said.

'Yeah. And Mom looks even worse.'

'Tansy must have gone back to the fort,' Cornelia said, looking around the room. 'Is it dinner time yet?'

'It was dinner time ages ago, but I took care of everything,' Barry reported, pleased with himself. 'Mom was looking really miserable and like she didn't want to have to cook anything, so I offered to make sandwiches for everyone, and she thought that was great, and then

I asked if I could bring ours up here, and she and Dad thought that was even better because they were trying to come up with some excuse to get me out of the room so they could talk. But never mind that stuff, Neely. Did you find Finn?'

Cornelia told him everything that happened, although this took a surprisingly long time because of the zeal with which the dogs were squirming over her, and because Barry had so many questions to ask.

'I thought Savannah Gray was very nice,' Cornelia told him. 'It's a pity Finn had to become a jewel-thief instead of marrying her. Although I suppose he might not have been able to come back to Emeraldia if he married her, so that mightn't have worked out anyway, but I'd really like it if he did. Oh, I don't know,' she sighed, rubbing Freddy's tummy and scratching Tickles behind the ear. 'It's all very complicated, isn't it?'

'I just hope Mom and Dad don't start noticing when you're in Josephine,' Barry said, 'because the dogs know something's wrong. I mean, they went sort of crazy when they saw you lying there, like they knew you weren't just asleep. When I tried to pull them off you, they started barking, so I had to let them keep trying to wake you because I didn't want anyone coming up here.

'They wouldn't even eat,' he said, uncovering a very hearty sandwich, an apple, and a glass of milk. 'Not even Tickles. This food is for you by the way.'

Cornelia shared her enormous sandwich with Barry and the two dogs, all of whom, she suspected, had been through a worse time that night than she had; and when she finished eating, she was glad to go to bed. Like everyone else in the house, she was worried about what the following day would bring; and as expected, it did not bring anything good, but at least it did not bring Puffy Pickenose or Pompeous Potty-Pickenose XIII, so everyone agreed it could have been worse.

Once again, strange men came and swarmed all over their front field and put pegs into the ground and did mysterious things with tape and coloured poles and telescope-type things and made human and fairy alike feel scared all the time as they watched them, but they dug nothing up, which was what everyone had worried about most.

'Maybe they don't dare to do anything until they see us gone,' her father suggested. 'Maybe what they're doing now is trying to bully us to make us go sooner.'

'It's working too,' Barry whispered to Cornelia, as their father was walking away. 'I saw Mom throwing away a load of stuff this morning, and she was packing other stuff into cardboard boxes.'

Cornelia could hardly wait until nighttime, and when Tansy was later than usual, she came close to panic. Just in time, they remembered to put the dogs out of the room, before Tansy came in the window.

'It's really awful in the fort,' Tansy reported. 'Two other forts have been dug up today over in the west and King Thistle has taken in more refugees, and it's so crowded in his fort now, we have to take turns sleeping. Every bed is used by three different fairies at different times.'

'Oh, come on then, Tansy, let's hurry,' Cornelia said anxiously, jumping up on the bed. 'I don't think we should waste a minute.'

—*Chapter 26*—

Le Train Bleu

A S SOON AS THEY WERE BACK in the doll, they found, as they expected, that Jules and Josephine tonight were not at their usual table in the nightclub, but were inside a bustling train station.

'This is the *Gare de Lyon*,' Tansy whispered knowledgeably, 'and that's the platform for the *Blue Train*,' she added, pointing to an area thronged with fashionably dressed travellers, trailed by porters struggling under the weight of great towers of leather cases.

The *Blue Train* itself was distracting Cornelia, because it was unlike anything else she had seen before. In Emeraldia, trains just had seats, and often they were so crowded that there were more people standing up in them than sitting down; but this train had nothing but beautiful little rooms, each of them for only one or two people. 'This is the carriage Finn is in,' Tansy said, coming to a halt. 'Berth no. 7,' she added, having memorised the information on his ticket.

At the entrance to this carriage was a man in uniform who was taking tickets. At present, he was talking sympathetically to an elderly man and woman, both of whom were wearing old and moth-eaten fur coats that reached nearly to their ankles. 'Yes, I know Your

Highness,' he was saying. 'The two of you sharing a double compartment, that is very difficult, but—'

'Difficult!' exclaimed the woman. 'It is impossible. One of us sleeping in an upper berth! And we would not even have our own washroom.'

'Before the revolution, we always had an entire carriage,' the man protested. 'Surely you can give us at least two compartments.'

'I am so sorry,' the man in the uniform said politely. 'This particular train has been booked out for months. But I will inform the dining car that you are travelling so that you will be sure of getting the best service when you go in for dinner.'

Not pleased, the fur-coated man (a former Russian prince) boarded the train and led his equally indignant wife ('Does he really know who we are?' she kept repeating. 'Do these awful little people think they can do anything now?') into the compartment beside Finn's, which remained unoccupied still.

Boarding just behind them were an Englishwoman and her daughter who had two interconnecting compartments, nos. 12 & 13, farther down the corridor.

'I'm so glad you were able to lose all that weight at Baden-Baden,' the older woman said, having settled herself on one of the sofas and watching her daughter take off her coat. 'It doesn't matter how much money your father has, or how many jewels you wear, if a shift dress doesn't hang on you properly. Still, with your new dress size, and wearing these diamonds,' she added, patting a large box on the seat beside her, 'you're going to be in plenty demand at the party tomorrow night.'

Listening in the doorway, Cornelia and Tansy giggled, and on their way back to Finn's compartment, stopped again outside compartments 10 & 11, which a young American couple had turned into a home from home. A portable record player was softly playing a jazz record, and beside this, they had set up a portable cocktail set. 'We don't have ice,' the young woman pointed out.

'The attendant said he's going to bring some,' her husband answered. 'He'll probably be too busy until everyone's boarded, but I gave him a decent tip and he knows the Buchanans will be stopping by, so I'd say he'll do his best to bring it as soon as he can.'

'Do you think we're safe leaving my jewels here when we go for dinner?' the young woman asked then.

'Lord no,' the man said definitely. 'I'll carry them in my pocket. I'd say there won't be a jacket in that dining car tonight that hangs correctly, all of them will have their pockets so bulging with jewels for safe-keeping.'

'Come on. Let's go back to Finn's compartment,' Cornelia said nervously. 'I don't like the way everyone is talking so much about jewels.'

They waited impatiently in the empty compartment, listening to laughing, chatting people walking by outside in the corridor. They flitted restlessly between the armchair and the long sofa, blind to the prettiness of the intricate inlaid designs in the shiny timber walls, but searching all the time for a familiar face as they looked out the window at the handsomely dressed people on the platform who were waiting to board: the men in fedora hats, and the women in slim coats and long scarves and cloche hats that came down over their foreheads.

They got a surprise when a discreet door in the side wall of the compartment, just beside the armchair, opened suddenly, and the fur-coated Russian woman came through it. This door led to a washroom, and they found they could see right past this washroom into the Russians' own compartment, through a second open door. 'This compartment's empty,' she called back loudly to the fur-coated man. 'Go and tell the conductor to give it to us.'

'He should have done that in the first place,' said the fur-coated man crossly, as he pulled down their window blind. 'Still, close that door now because I need to check something in my lining, and we can't take a chance that someone might come in.'

'That's what she meant when she said they'd have to share a washroom,' said Tansy giggling. 'Poor Finn.'

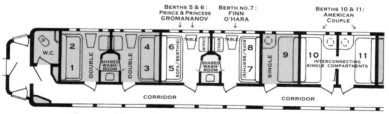

PLAN OF FINN'S SLEEPING CAR ON THE BLUE TRAIN

After a while, it seemed that there were no more people to get on board and Cornelia started to panic. 'I don't think he's coming, Tansy, and the train is starting to move. Should we jump off it while it's still in the station?'

And then the compartment door opened, and a tired-looking man with a small battered case and a raincoat from which several buttons were missing came in and sat down. He flung the case beside him on the seat, resting his elbows on his knees and his face in his hands, and looked so tired and unhappy that Cornelia would have thrown her arms around him if she had her body with her.

Tansy was prepared to try to talk to him immediately, but Cornelia held her back for a moment, feeling a little overawed by this meeting. Then there was a knock on the door of his compartment, and a fat man wearing a pale suit came inside. He closed the door carefully behind him. He was a good deal older than Finn, and he spoke very quietly in an American accent.

'Well, have you found out who hired them?'

'Some American,' Finn answered. 'His name is Omera, but that's all I know. Jules and Josephine wouldn't tell me anything more, but whoever he is, they're scared to death of him. They're more frightened of this Mr Omera than they are of getting arrested. They're not happy about going ahead with the robbery tomorrow night, because they think it's badly planned, and they think there's a good chance they'll get caught, but because this Mr Omera has arranged for them to do it, they're going to go ahead with it anyway.'

'I see,' the man said quietly. 'Well, that explains a lot. I have heard of Omera before, all right, but like you, I haven't been able to get any more information than that. No one's ever seen him or knows where he is or even knows where he's based, and that's part of his success. He hires people through agents, and everyone is more afraid of him because they can't find out anything about him. Jules and Josephine don't have any doubts you're with them on this robbery, do they?'

'Oh, they don't doubt that at all,' Finn reassured him. 'They think I'm some kind of famous thief, and they're depending on me to pull off this stunt because they don't believe they could do it by themselves. So far as that goes, I agree with them. Even with a dozen people working with them, I don't think they could pull it off. You can tell the insurance company they don't have much to worry about, because there's no way those two are going to get away with any jewels.'

'You're sure of that?'

'It would be a miracle if they do. They have inside help, all right, from the servants and some police, but they plan to carry out the robbery while the party's in full swing, and with all the secret security, that's an insane plan. They're sure to be caught.'

'Good work,' the American man said. 'I told the company they'd be glad they hired you as a detective, instead of using one of the usual people. The guys who normally do this work are all known to the professional thieves, and Jules and Josephine would have seen through them immediately and guessed they were detectives, but obviously they don't suspect you at all.'

'Oh, Tansy, did you hear, did you hear?' Cornelia said excitedly. 'Finn's a detective, not a thief. He's a real detective. Did you ever hear anything so wonderful?'

'It was almost too easy,' Finn said tiredly.

'Well, you know how it works,' the man said. 'We know how to plant rumours when it helps us, and obviously, the rumours about you were believed. If you learn anything more, you can give me a hint over dinner. Use the word "George" so I'll know you have something to tell me, and I'll call in here afterwards.'

'We can talk to him now,' Cornelia said contentedly as the unknown man left. 'Isn't this the most wonderful thing that's ever happened. Finn's a particularly perfect detective who uses code words and everything. Come on, let's hurry, Tansy, please. Let's talk to him right this second.'

'I think I'd like to follow that man first,' Tansy said suspiciously. 'I didn't like him. He's small and black inside and he talks funny. Like his voice isn't connected to the rest of him.'

Reluctantly, Cornelia let herself be taken from Finn's compartment, and they accompanied the unknown man through two carriages. In the third, he stopped for a while, looking out the window while a number of passengers walked past him, and when he was alone in the corridor at last, he knocked on a compartment door. The door was opened by Jules, who looked at the man without recognition. 'What is it?' he asked. 'You're in the wrong compartment,' he added curtly, about to close the door.

'Shanghai,' the fat man said.

Jules turned pale on hearing this, and opened the door quickly.

'What did I tell you?' said Tansy smugly. 'I knew that man couldn't be trusted. Now we know he has a code word with Jules and Josephine as well.'

—Chapter 27—

Mr Omera

TANSY AND CORNELIA followed the man in, and saw Josephine in the interconnecting compartment, stretched out on the sofa smoking a cigarette in a very long holder. She appeared to have heard what the man said because she looked even more frightened than Jules.

'He sent you?' Josephine asked in her harsh voice. 'Mr Omera sent you? Why? Is there a change of plan?'

'It will seem to you that there is,' he said. 'But, in fact, I'm just going to tell you now for the first time what the plan really is.'

'Have you told Finn yet?' Josephine asked.

'No, Finn doesn't need to know. Finn has only one part to play in the robbery tonight, and it's not one he needs advance knowledge for. Finn's job—though he doesn't know it, of course—is to be informed on to the police as the perpetrator of tonight's robbery. That will give the two of you time to get well away with the jewels.'

Quickly, Tansy tightened her hold on Cornelia as she felt the human's shocked spirit seem to shrink and hop at the same time.

'What do you mean tonight's robbery?' Jules asked, looking back at the man. 'You mean tomorrow night's robbery?'

'No, tonight's. You'll be taking jewels from a compartment on the train tonight after everyone's gone to bed. There was never a plan to take jewels at the party. That was just a decoy—a story made up to make sure nothing about the real plan leaked out in advance.'

Cornelia gasped and she and Tansy both glared furiously at the unknown fat man.

'But why aren't we using Finn?' Josephine asked. I thought he was the great expert in robbing jewels. We were told that he'd already stolen the most valuable jewels in the world.'

'Finn's never stolen anything. Finn thinks he's an honest detective working for an insurance company. No, Finn just happens to be the *owner* of the most valuable jewels in the world. He owns a necklace and bracelets containing several hundred rubies and emeralds—all of them more perfect than any others that exist in the world—and Mr Omera wants those jewels very badly. That's why he recruited Finn for this operation.

'We had to go to a lot of trouble and expense to convince Finn that I'm a reputable insurance company employee and he's doing an honest job,' the man continued, 'but this is going to be the most profitable operation in Mr Omera's career; and as you know, that's saying quite a lot. Mr Omera already owns many of the legendary treasures of the world, but those jewels of Finn's will be the prize of his collection.'

It is not easy to feel it when a fairy goes stiff with surprise, but for once, Cornelia did physically feel Tansy's shock, which seemed to be as great as her own.

'But Finn doesn't have jewels,' Cornelia said. 'He doesn't have anything at all. Don't you think this is all some terrible mistake?' she added pleadingly. 'That awful man has him mixed up with someone else. Finn doesn't even have enough money to buy a raincoat with all its buttons.'

'You mean we're going to rob Finn tonight?' Josephine asked. 'But if it's Finn's own jewels that we're robbing, how are the police going to blame Finn for that?'

'We're not going to rob Finn at all,' the man answered. 'We'd have no hope of getting the jewels from him that way. Finn is going to give us the jewels, because he won't be able to face what will happen if he doesn't.'

Tansy closed her eyes and drew on all her reserves of willpower, almost overcome for a moment by a strong inclination to throw this fat man out the window.

'Well, this all sounds like a very big change of plan,' Josephine said impatiently. 'So, who are we supposed to rob tonight? You'd better hurry up and tell us.'

'The Gromananovs,' he answered. 'You'll be robbing the Gromananov jewels.'

'Never heard of them,' said Jules tonelessly.

'I'd be surprised if you had,' the man said in a bored voice. 'They were thought to have disappeared ten years ago during the Russian revolution. Confiscated by the government, it was believed. But in fact they were brought to Paris, hidden in the linings of two very old and very shabby fur coats.'

Cornelia gasped again. 'I think he must be talking about that grumpy old couple we saw getting on the train,' she whispered. 'The ones in the compartment next to Finn's who were complaining that they didn't get an entire carriage to themselves any more.'

'How do you know these jewels are on the train?' Josephine asked.

'A few days ago, an agent of Mr Omera made contact with the prince and princess,' the man explained, 'and was able to convince them that the greatest opportunity for selling jewels this century would arise during and after this party in Monte Carlo. He told them that the principal jewel dealers of Europe would be there—which is perfectly true—and that there would be great competition for the Gromananov jewels—also true—and they would be able to auction them in total secrecy.

'The secrecy,' he continued, 'would be important to the Gromananovs because a lot of other family members claim rights to the jewels, but the prince and princess want the profits all to themselves. And the profits they expect would be very fat ones indeed because their jewels were the most prized collection in Russia, next to the czars'.'

'So what compartment are they in?' Josephine asked.

'The one that has a washroom connecting with Finn's.'

'You see,' whispered Cornelia. 'I told you it was those grumpy people.'

'And that was arranged?' Josephine asked.

'Of course it was, although neither Finn nor the prince and princess have any idea they were given those compartments for a special reason. The train has been booked out for many months, but Mr Omera arranged that a cancellation would be made as soon as the prince and princess asked to make a reservation.'

'Are you listening to all this?' Cornelia whispered frantically, wondering how Tansy was managing to stay so silent.

'Better not talk for a while,' Tansy warned her. 'We have to hear what they're planning so we can stop them.'

'Finn will get off the train as soon as it stops at Lyon shortly before 2.00 in the morning—' the man began.

'Finn's getting off at Lyon?' Josephine interrupted in her harsh voice. 'He didn't say anything to us about that.'

'He'll get off the train the moment it stops at Lyon because he will just have received an urgent telegram from someone who means a great deal to him, and he will be getting on the first train back to Paris,' the man replied. 'When you see that he has got off with his suitcase, you will go into his compartment, and you'll bring these with you.' He reached up and lifted down two objects from the overhead shelf.

'The portable gramophone and the portable cocktail set,' said Josephine as she looked at them. 'So it was you who had them put there. Why do we need to take those? And do you have keys to them? They're both locked.'

'Both of them have had their interiors removed, and are now just empty cases. You're going to hide the Gromananov jewels in them, but if anyone sees you carrying them, it will just look like you're going to or coming from a small private party.

'You will go into the Gromananovs' compartment through the washroom they share with Finn. It is likely they will have locked their own door to the washroom, but here is a *Wagons-Lits* conductor's master key,' he said, taking an object out of his breast pocket and handing it to Jules. 'And here are the keys to the two cases. And you'll also have this with you,' he added, pulling a small bottle from another pocket. 'Chloroform.'

'Oh, the old chloroform method,' said Jules comfortably. 'I see it all now.'

'Chloroform's a gas for putting people to sleep,' Tansy whispered to Cornelia. 'They must plan to make the Russians unconscious before they rob them.'

'You will need to enter quietly and use the chloroform quickly. I think you will find the Russians already so deeply asleep that you will hardly need the chloroform, but you must use it anyway. I have arranged that Finn and I will be seated at the same table as the Russians at dinner, and I'll drop a sleeping drug into the glass of Cognac that I'll offer them just before they retire. And the Gromananovs will certainly accept the Cognac because they always accept anything that's offered to them for free.

'You'll find the jewels still concealed within their fur coats,' he continued, 'sewn into an extra lining. You'll take them all and conceal them in the gramophone and cocktail set cases. At Marseilles, you will get off the train, and your own driver will be waiting for you. You will give the jewels to him.

'Then,' he continued, 'the two of you will be driven to

Cherbourg, where you will board the *Aquitania*, bound
for New York in the morning, carrying these false
passports.' He handed the couple two documents. 'I have
an additional job for you to do on board the *Aquitania*,
and the driver will give you your instructions.'

'It sounds all right,' Josephine said grudgingly, 'but
how do you know for sure that Finn will leave the train
at Lyon and won't come back on board?'

'I know because the message Finn will receive just
before the train stops there will appear to be from
Savannah Gray, a person who means a great deal to him,
and she will say that an emergency has arisen and ask
him to telephone a certain number and to get back to
Paris by morning.'

'Is this Savannah Gray in on it too?' Josephine asked.

'No, not at all. Savannah Gray is Mr Omera's secret
weapon for forcing Finn to give him the jewels. You see
Savannah Gray,' he explained coldly, 'was kidnapped
this evening in Paris, and in the morning she is going
to be brought secretly on board the *Aquitania*. When
Finn makes that telephone call, a man will tell him that
if he does not return to Paris on the first train and hand
over the jewels within three days, Savannah Gray will
be killed, thrown overboard from the ocean liner.

'You will not be involved in her killing,' the man
continued, as Tansy and Cornelia struggled with a
state of fear and shock so great they could barely keep
listening to him, 'and you will not even know where
she is. However, if everything goes well, and we get the
jewels, and Mr Omera decides she is not to be killed,

then you will be told where to find her and you will be responsible for her in New York.'

'What about these jewels that Finn owns,' Josephine asked. 'How can he hand them over to Mr Omera if he's in jail?'

'Why do they keep talking about Finn having jewels?' Cornelia whispered frantically. 'They are so stupid. Anyone can see that Finn is much too poor to own jewels.'

'Don't talk now,' said Tansy urgently. 'Don't say anything more at the moment. I'll explain later.'

'Finn will not be arrested immediately. Mr Omera will see to that. The police will be convinced that Finn is part of a great criminal organization, and he will lead them to its Mr Big if they keep him under observation instead.'

'Can't say I go for any of this,' said Jules doubtfully. 'Too risky. Finn may go to the police himself about this Savannah Gray and spill the beans on all of us. And even if he doesn't, the police are not going to hold off that long before they bring him in, and he'll spill the beans then.'

'Mr Omera doesn't take risks,' said the fat man complacently. 'Finn is not going to go to the police about Savannah Gray, because he will be told she will be killed immediately if he does, and Finn is not going to let that happen. If my information is correct, and I find it usually is, Finn would do things to save her that he wouldn't do to save himself. Secondly, the police will never get their hands on Finn—not alive anyway—

because as soon as Finn hands over the jewels, he's going to be killed.

'He will be found murdered in the street in Paris with some small piece of jewelry from the Gromananov collection in his pocket, and also a bottle of chloroform with a label that will link him beyond doubt to the criminal gang of which he's supposed to be a member.

'You see, at every stage of this operation,' the man continued, 'Mr Omera understands the value of a decoy. Because of what they'll find on Finn's body, the police will never link Mr Omera to the Gromananov robbery. And of course, with Finn dead, Mr Omera will be left in peaceful possession of Finn's jewels.

'Such a fine criminal mind that man has,' he added in a voice filled with admiration. 'I've never met one better.'

'Okay, now we go back to Finn's compartment,' said Tansy grimly.

'It would be better if he could see you,' Cornelia said worriedly as they made their way along the swaying corridor filled with people on their way to the dining car. 'Will he be able to see you?'

'We're about to find out,' Tansy answered, shooting inside one of these passengers for a moment to produce a knock on Finn's compartment and then shooting out of him again as the passenger continued on his way. 'You know, Cornelia, I've never had anyone depend on me before for anything, and now all the fairies and humans in Emeraldia are depending on me for everything. I'm so nervous, I—' And then she broke off suddenly as the compartment door opened.

Chapter 28

Finn

FINN LOOKED MILDLY SURPRISED at finding no one at the door when he answered the knock, but he also looked too depressed to spend any time thinking about it. He glanced tiredly along the corridor in both directions, then closed the door and sat down again near the window.

'Do it now,' Cornelia urged. 'Go on, Tansy, please. Do it now.'

Nothing happened for a few seconds, and then Cornelia heard Tansy clearing her throat gently. Finn seemed to hear it too because he opened his eyes quickly, and his look of depressed exhaustion was replaced by one of startled disbelief. 'What in the—' He blinked hard once or twice, and then surprised Cornelia by saying: 'You're a fairy, aren't you?'

'Yes, I am,' Tansy told him nervously. 'My name is Tansy.'

'Are you from Emeraldia?' he asked, surprising Cornelia again.

She had not expected that Finn would accept the idea of a fairy appearing in front of him in such a matter-of-fact manner. She knew that if her parents were in the situation that Finn was in now, they would act very differently and tell one another they were dreaming or start looking for hidden electrical devices or something.

But then she remembered that Finn was much older than even her grandparents were, and her grandparents always had talked about fairies with as much familiarity as if they were distant cousins, and Finn seemed to think that way about them too—all of which was very lucky for her and Tansy, she thought. If Finn had been born later on, after adults became embarrassed and silly about fairies, the two of them would have an even harder job ahead of them than they did now.

Tansy confirmed that she was from Emeraldia, and then Finn surprised both Cornelia and the fairy by asking: 'There's no trouble back there, is there? About Soldiers' Fort, I mean. Nothing's happened, has it?'

'Oh, yes,' said Tansy, without hesitation. 'Terrible things have happened all over Emeraldia. The fairy forts are almost all gone and humans who aren't members of the Guild, or Pickenoses, are not being allowed to live there anymore.'

It seemed to Cornelia that Finn almost shrank visibly in size when he heard this. 'But it's only been a couple of years,' he said miserably. 'I thought I had some time.'

'No, you've no time at all,' she said definitely. 'Although now, of course, we have a new problem because—'

'What about Soldier's Fort itself?' he interrupted. 'Is it all right?'

'Well, the Lawful Guild dug that up, of course. And they built their headquarters on it, and the Pickenoses built a big ugly house where your house was.'

'They what?' he asked frantically.

'You're telling him too fast, Tansy,' said Cornelia, who was becoming worried at Finn's panic. 'You're telling him much too fast. He doesn't understand that we live in the future and that he does still have time.'

'Well, maybe you should be talking to him then,' Tansy said in a harassed voice. 'I'm doing my best.'

'Is there another fairy with you?' Finn asked in surprise.

'Oh, I forgot,' Tansy answered. 'She can't speak except through a human body.'

Finn looked at Tansy suspiciously. 'What's going on here?'

'Tell him I'm with you,' Cornelia said agitatedly. 'Tell him I'm with you.'

'I'm not alone,' Tansy explained nervously, trying hard to keep her composure in this unprecedented situation, 'but it's not another fairy who's with me. It's your great-grandniece. I'm holding her hand,' she added, holding Cornelia's spirit out in front of her, 'only you can't see her of course, although if we had another human in here, you could hear her because she can talk through another human. Do you want me to get another human?'

'What the blazes is this?' Finn asked angrily. 'What kind of being are you?'

This could not be going worse. All the feelings of failure and inadequacy Tansy ever had experienced in her long existence came rushing back at her now. Here she was, doing the most important job she had ever been given, and already she was making an absolute mess of it. She was tempted for a moment to abandon it entirely, and to flee from Josephine and go back to King Thistle's fort, but what would she tell them when she got there? For that matter, maybe King Thistle's fort would not even be there when she got back, and maybe all the forts would be gone, and it would be her fault because everyone was relying on her, and she was the only one who could save the fairies from—oh, she did not even know what she would be saving them from, she thought, looking around the compartment wild-eyed, and wondering how in the world she had got herself into this mess anyway.

'Poor Tansy,' thought Cornelia, wishing she could do something to help. 'And poor Finn,' she thought, as she saw how this powerful, heroic great-granduncle of her imagination now had taken on the appearance of a crumpled, heart-broken victim, which was sort of the way her parents were starting to look as well.

As Cornelia looked back and forth between the two of them, the bewildered fairy reminded her of the way Barry looked sometimes when, for one reason or another, he was at cross-purposes with someone, and had no idea why the other person was not understanding him. Like Tansy, her brother found it easier to do things than to talk about them, and he often had the same sort of problems in explaining himself that Tansy was having now. Seeing how upset both of them were, Cornelia even began to worry that this stupid misunderstanding between the fairy and her great-granduncle might sabotage their entire mission.

GALWAY COUNTY LIBRARIES

'It's all right, Tansy,' she said soothingly. 'Just tell him that you made a mistake, and that he does have time. Why don't you tell him that you get mixed up about stuff to do with time because you're a fairy? My grandparents say that fairies don't understand time at all, and Finn would know that too.

'Well, tell him something,' she persisted when Tansy did not respond, but looked at her even more wild-eyed.

'Cornelia says I should tell you that I get mixed up about stuff to do with time because I'm a fairy.'

'Tell him he still has time to save Emeraldia,' Cornelia continued urgently. 'Tell him he still has time to do that because we've come from the future. That's the most important thing of all to tell him.'

'Cornelia also says I should tell you that you still have time. We just have to stop you from being murdered by the apaches,' Tansy added, using her own initiative. 'Only now we also have to stop Savannah Gray from being brought to Mr Omera on the *Aquitania* because he wants the necklace and bracelets of rubies and emeralds we gave your family a long time ago.'

'What?' shouted Cornelia and Finn simultaneously, each one of them as shocked as the other.

In that moment, the situation became too much for Tansy. If she were mortal, she thought she would have liked to die right there on the spot, so that she would never again say the wrong thing and make a bad situation worse, but this was a fate not available to fairies. Instead, she escaped from the mess as best she could by making herself invisible again.

Finn leapt up and opened the door. 'Go into him quick,' Cornelia said urgently. 'Or else he might go looking for that fat man and start fighting with him or something.'

Tansy sighed and followed him out to the corridor where she went inside him, causing Finn immediately to return to the compartment and close the door behind him. 'Tansy, does Finn actually have a necklace and bracelets of rubies and emeralds?' Cornelia asked bewildered. 'I don't understand how he can because Finn is awfully poor, and his clothes are all worn out, and he lives in that awful room with the broken window, and he wouldn't be working for that awful man if he owned a load of emeralds and rubies.'

'I knew he did have jewels,' Tansy said. 'I didn't know whether he still had them or not, and I suppose it's surprising he didn't sell them when he needed the money so badly. They're jewels that were given to his family—your family—a long time ago by the fairies, but we had no idea if Finn still owned them, or if they had been lost. But it's probably true that, in human terms, they would be very valuable. They include hundreds and hundreds of rubies and emeralds, and humans seem to get very excited over rubies and emeralds.'

'But how would Mr Omera have known about them?' Cornelia wondered.

'I don't know,' Tansy said. 'Maybe someone in your

family talked about them sometime. Maybe long before Finn was born.'

'I don't think anyone in my family knows about them now. I know my parents don't know about any fairy jewels, because my parents don't even believe that fairies exist. Oh, just wait until I tell Barry about the jewels,' Cornelia said excitedly, forgetting all her worries for a moment at the thought of how astonished his expression would be. 'I'd really love to tell my parents too, but I suppose May and Fuchsia would get in trouble for breaking the law if I did that. But of course I shouldn't even be thinking about the rubies and emeralds,' she added guiltily. 'Not until we save both Finn and Savannah Gray.'

'If we can save Savannah Gray,' Tansy said uncertainly. 'If she's on a ship going out to sea—'

'Oh, of course we can,' Cornelia said without any doubt whatever. 'But you know what, I think we ought to ask that man in the uniform who wouldn't give the grumpy couple a carriage to themselves for some paper to write on. Even if I can't talk to Finn, I could get him to write what I wanted, couldn't I?'

Tansy thought this was a very good idea, so under her guidance, Finn walked out into the corridor, putting out his hand to balance himself as the train made a sharp turn, and located the attendant in another compartment where he was converting the daytime sofa that stretched along the length of it into a cosy bed for the night, dressed with crisp white linen and a woolly blanket.

Finn asked for some writing paper, and the man went away and returned with several sheets. 'You know, they have been serving dinner in the dining car for about half-an-hour now, Mr O'Hara.'

'Yes, I'll be going down there in a few minutes,' Finn replied, under Tansy's guidance. 'But I want to get this letter written first.'

'Now I should be able to make things perfectly clear,' Cornelia said contentedly, when Finn had returned to the compartment and seated himself in front of the shelf-table beside the window. He laid the paper on this and then searched through his pockets for a pen, and when he had found it, Cornelia concentrated hard on composing the longest letter she had ever written to anyone.

Chapter 29

The Letter

'*Dear Great-Granduncle Finn,*' she began. '*My name is Cornelia O'Hara, and I'm eight years old. I was born a very long time after you left Emeraldia. I live at Fairy's Leap, where your brother lived, who was my great-grandfather. As you know about fairies, you will find this situation much easier to understand than my parents would, who do not believe in fairies at all.*

'*I am sure it must seem very odd to you that Tansy and I could be inside you just now and controlling what you say and do so that you are writing this letter, but we have been inside many people so far and it has not harmed any of them, except maybe Scott Fitzgerald might have bruised his foot a little when he kicked open your door, but Tansy does not think so, and says your door was not very good anyway and really did not have to be kicked very hard.*

'*You probably also wonder how we came back in time, but that really was very easy. You may remember the dolls Jules and Josephine which Savannah Gray made for you and which you sent back to Emeraldia and which I now have in my bedroom. The fairies discovered that when they went into Jules and Josephine, they went back to this time, and they are able to take a human spirit with them if they want to, and they took me so that I could talk to* you, *except that I won't really be able to talk to you except through another human.*

'The reason we came back is to warn you that you are in Great Danger and to save you from it and to ask you please to return to Emeraldia and protect Soldiers' Fort because the Lawful Guild moved in and dug it up when you did not come back, and because of that, very many bad things have happened. At the time we are in now though, Soldiers' Fort is still all right, and there still is time for you to come back and save it and stop all the bad things happening.

'The man you were talking to in here today is a very bad man and works for Mr Omera and he has arranged that you will get off the train when it stops at Lyon and you will go back to Paris, but something very bad will happen to you there. Also the police will think that you stole jewels from the old Russian man and woman with fur coats who are in the compartment next to yours, although it will be Jules and Josephine who will steal the jewels and hide them in things that are called a portable gramophone and a portable cocktail set.

'Another really bad thing, as you have already heard from Tansy, is that he has had Savannah Gray kidnapped to make you give him the emeralds and rubies in order to save her. She is to be handed over to Mr Omera when the ship reaches New York, if she has not already been thrown overboard by then, which would be terrible, but you do not have to worry about that at all because Tansy will be able to find Savannah Gray first before anything like that happens to her.

'I think Savannah Gray is very nice, and I think she will be very glad to hear that the reason you spent so much time at the Silver Poodle Club with Jules and Josephine is because you are a detective and not because you like them. She doesn't like Jules and Josephine at all, and she doesn't like the Silver Poodle Club either, except she thinks the musicians are nice. She also likes Scott Fitzgerald, and she told us where you lived because she thought she was talking to him. Tansy likes Scott Fitzgerald too, and she spent as little of his money as she could on taxi drivers and things.

'It has been very nice to meet you. I wish I could tell my parents all about you, but I can't because the fairies would get in trouble if I did, but I am allowed to tell my brother Barry everything, and he is working very hard back at home to make sure that no one disturbs Tansy and me before we have saved you, even though he would much rather be in here with us, and he would love to meet real jewel robbers.

'I have to end this letter now because Tansy says we don't have all that much time before the train gets to Lyon, and I also think it will save a lot of time if Tansy can talk to you directly, because she is very smart and knows lots and lots of things about ~~consierjes~~ concierges and apaches and stuff like that, and she knew right away that the man you were talking to in here was a bad man, so will you please be especially nice to her because she is working very hard to try to make everything all right, and I think she gets upset if people are cross with her.

  Yours truly,
  Cornelia Mary O'Hara

'After he's read that, I'm sure it will be all right for you to make yourself visible to him again, Tansy,' Cornelia said confidently, 'and maybe you will try very hard not to get upset at anything he says, because everyone's being very mean to him and that always makes people grouchy.'

Tansy went out of Finn then, but as soon as she was gone, he let the letter drop on the table without looking at it, and jumped up quickly in order to try again to leave the compartment; and for the second time, Tansy quickly shot into him.

'I didn't think he'd do that,' Cornelia said, flattened. 'How do we get him to read it?'

'Maybe we should write a notice in really big print saying "*READ THE LETTER ON THE TABLE BEFORE YOU GO OUT THE DOOR,*" and then we could chain the door and hang the notice from the chain,' Tansy suggested.

So Finn sat down and wrote himself that instruction, adding, at Cornelia's initiative, a giant '*SOS*' at the top of it, hung this notice from one of the fixings of the door chain and sat down again. Then, for the second time, Tansy went out of his body, and for the second time, Finn went directly to the door, but this time his attention was caught by the notice; and looking back in bewilderment at the table and at the letter lying on it, he sat down and started to read.

—Chapter 30—

The Dining Car

WHEN FINN HAD FINISHED reading the letter, he looked around the compartment as if waiting for Tansy to appear, and after a few seconds, she did. 'Can you save Savannah?' he asked her. 'Can you get her away from them?'

This was a question she really did not want to be asked, but his voice now was so businesslike that she reacted in a businesslike way herself. 'If we can reach her before the ship goes to sea, it will be easy,' she answered calmly, 'but if the ship has sailed, I'm not sure. Over the sea, I have less power. I don't think I can whirlwind very well over the sea, and that's the only way I can travel in this world. Mind-portation doesn't work at all.'

'I see,' said Finn, and to Cornelia's amazement, he looked as if he really did. People as old as Finn seemed to know everything about fairies.

'We'll get off the train when it stops at Dijon,' he said. 'It stops there well before midnight. We'll get on the first train going back to Paris tonight, and then we'll get the boat train from Paris to Cherbourg, and if we haven't found Savannah before the ship sails, I'll go on board the *Aquitania* as well. We'll deal with Mr Malo-Alto over dinner.'

'Is that the man who was talking to you here in your compartment?' Tansy asked.

'That's him. I'm due to meet him in the dining car in a few minutes.'

'He's having dinner with the Russian couple as well,' Tansy told Finn. 'He plans to drop a sleeping drug into something they're drinking so that it will be easier for Jules and Josephine to make them unconscious with chloroform later.'

Finn took this information in his stride. 'Well, maybe we can make use of that,' he said after thinking a moment. 'Could you could arrange for him to drop that sleeping drug into his own drink instead?' he asked.

Cornelia and Tansy both thought this was an excellent idea, and Tansy even did a little twirl in excitement at the prospect. 'Oh, yes,' she said eagerly.

'Maybe now would be a good time to warn him about the apaches,' Cornelia said in a whisper, forgetting for a moment that Finn couldn't hear her.

'It's probably as well you're sailing on the *Aquitania*,' Tansy said calmly. 'It will mean you won't be in Paris on May 21st, and that's very important. It's to do with the reason you never came back to Emeraldia and the reason Cornelia and I are here now. You are due to be murdered by a gang of apaches in the *Place de l'Opéra* on May 21st, the night Lindbergh arrives in Paris. You must stop that happening.'

'Well, I'll do my best,' he said, and surprised them by laughing. 'But who's this Lindbergh? Is he an associate of Omera?'

'No,' said Tansy, who was so relaxed by now that she was even able to smile herself. 'He's an aviator. He doesn't have anything to do with this. But it's very serious. You must make sure you're not murdered.'

'I'll make sure of that all right,' he said, laughing again, 'but it's Savannah I'm worried about. All I care about right now is getting her away from those people. None of this business has anything to do with her. After we find her, I'll stay away from Paris for a while. You can rest easy about that. I'll probably take a boat directly back to Emeraldia.'

'The fairies will help you protect Soldiers' Fort,' Tansy told him. 'King Fuchsia and Queen May say they're very sorry they didn't help you before. They didn't know about the bad things that were happening to you.'

'I beg your pardon, Tansy,' Cornelia said in some embarrassment. 'I know this is not important at all, but Barry is going to be asking me all about it. Does Finn really and truly have rubies and emeralds?'

Tansy cleared her throat again. 'Cornelia has a question. She never heard of the rubies and emeralds before, and she was wondering if you really have them. She says she knows it's not important, but her brother will be surprised too and he'll be asking her all about them.'

'Believe it or not, yes, I do,' said Finn laughing, 'and Cornelia can tell her brother that, as rubies and emeralds go, there's supposed to be nothing like them in the world. With any luck, the two of them will see them one day,' he added as he got to his feet. 'But now let's go have some dinner.'

When they reached the dining car, an impressive man, dressed a bit like the headwaiter at the Silver Poodle Club, greeted them. He seemed to know who Finn was without even asking, and showed him to a table at which Mr Malo-Alto was seated opposite the Prince and Princess Gromananov.

The prince and princess and Finn all looked out of place in the elegant dining car. Everyone else looked as if they had stepped out of a fashion magazine, but the prince and princess were wearing their heavy old fur coats with the holes in them, and Finn's jacket was shiny with wear, and threads were visible at the collar and cuffs where the fabric had been worn away. The prince and princess, not noticing at all how odd their own moth-eaten outdoor coats appeared in this immaculate evening dining car, looked at Finn disapprovingly, and seemed to be trying to catch the headwaiter's eye, as if they hoped he might be persuaded to seat Finn at another table.

'Finn, this is the Prince and Princess Gromananov,' Mr Malo-Alto said, making the introductions. 'Your Highnesses, this is Mr Finn O'Hara, a business associate of mine.'

'How do you do?' said Finn politely.

The prince and princess gave the smallest of nods, just as a waiter set down in front of them and in front of

Mr Malo-Alto plates with bowls that were coated with ice, and that contained some black stuff which Cornelia did not recognise.

'At least the *Wagons-Lits* company still gets good caviar,' the princess said haughtily. 'Of course they carry passengers now that they would not have carried ten years ago,' she said, looking significantly at Finn's worn cuffs, 'but then, since the revolution, nothing has been the same.'

Tansy looked fiercely at the princess when she said this, disliking her more all the time, and feeling even sorrier for Finn, who she felt had enough problems already without having to listen to insults from this rude woman as well. She was tempted to go inside the Russian and make her throw her jewel-laden fur coat out the window, knowing that the greedy princess almost certainly would throw herself out the window after it; but as this excellent scheme might interfere with Finn's plan, she decided to content herself with a lesser revenge.

Giggling, she shot inside the princess, and as the Russian started to lift a spoon of caviar towards her mouth, Tansy made her arm give a jerk so sudden and violent that the round black fish eggs flew up in the air and landed with a splatter all over the princess's unsmiling face and carefully dressed hair. The princess made an angry, sputtering noise, and several waiters came running in consternation, carrying large white napkins.

'You got some on my coat,' the prince said in

annoyance. 'What am I going to do now? It's going to smell of fish forever.'

Tansy shot out of the princess then and inside Mr Malo-Alto. Mr Malo-Alto dipped his small silver spoon into his own caviar and flicked it at the princess, spewing more caviar over her face and over the front of her coat.

'I am so sorry, Your Highness,' Mr Malo-Alto said in genuine consternation. 'I seemed to lose control of my hand for a moment. Please let me help you,' he said, starting to stand up.

'I think you must be mad,' the princess said, just as Tansy shot back into her. She dipped her spoon into her own caviar again, and this time she flicked it so as to cover Mr Malo-Alto with the black fish eggs.

By now, all the waiters in the dining car were surrounding their table, and the other diners were ignoring their own meals and were looking only at the princess and Mr Malo-Alto.

'I want these people to be taken away,' the Princess said imperiously, waving her hand at Finn as well as at Mr Malo-Alto. Finn only smiled when she said this, but Tansy was even more offended on Finn's behalf. She went back into the princess again, and this time the princess lifted up the bowl holding the caviar and emptied it on top of her own head.

'Oh, please, Your Highness,' said the headwaiter unhappily. 'I don't understand. Is this all a great joke?'

By now, Tansy was enjoying herself so much she just could not stop. As Cornelia too giggled helplessly, the fairy shot inside the prince who then picked up his own bowl of caviar and emptied it over his own head, and followed this by picking up Mr Malo-Alto's bowl of caviar and emptying it over the headwaiter's sleek black hair.

'Take all this caviar away,' the headwaiter ordered furiously, as the other waiters frantically tried to clean the fish eggs from their cranky boss's head and face and from his impeccable white linen. 'And I must ask the three of you to leave,' he said to the prince and princess and Mr Malo-Alto.

'The code of the *Compagnie Internationale des Wagons-Lits* is that the passenger is always right,' he continued in a most superior voice, 'but I do not believe that code extends to a situation such as this. You may play jokes on one another if you wish, but you may not play jokes on the headwaiter of the *Calais-Méditerranée Express*. Please leave this dining car,' he said impatiently. 'All three of you.'

The prince straightened his shoulders and looked directly ahead. 'I…' said the prince, 'am the Prince…' and he listed a great many long names which Cornelia could not understand at all, '…and I am going nowhere until after I have dined. Now please take away this man,' he said, indicating Mr Malo-Alto, 'and this man as well,' he added pointing to Finn, 'and please serve the soup.'

'You know, I think I'd feel safer if you didn't bring hot soup to this table,' Finn said amiably to the headwaiter. 'It's hard to know where it might end up. But I'd be glad if you brought another bottle of that wine.'

Tansy remembered suddenly, as Finn had hoped she would, that her job was to drop sleeping medicine into Mr Malo-Alto's glass. She shot back inside him, and immediately he began to search all his pockets, and found in his inside jacket pocket a small brown package that instructed: *'Take one sachet before bedtime.'*

'Three sachets then,' said Tansy to herself, and Mr Malo-Alto began emptying them into his own glass. He had emptied two and was about to empty the third when Finn's hand reached over suddenly and rested on Mr Malo-Alto's.

'I'd say two of those are enough,' he said.

Tansy took the hint, and reluctantly put the third sachet back in its packing.

'I think I'll skip the caviar and the soup, and just have the turbot and the lamb,' Finn said to the waiter.

Tansy remained inside Mr Malo-Alto who said to the waiter: 'I'll skip all the courses, please, except dessert,' he said. 'And I'll have two portions, of that, please, and also two glasses of chocolate milk. And please bring some chocolates, as well, and—' And then to Cornelia's great disappointment, before he could even finish giving this wonderful order, Mr Malo-Alto's head dropped down on the table and emitted a great snore; and no one in the dining care was left in any doubt. Mr Malo-Alto had fallen asleep.

— *Chapter 31* —

A Change at Dijon

To the surprise of Tansy and Cornelia, both the Gromananovs and Finn continued to tuck into the braised turbot and the leg of lamb *en croûte* with gusto even after Mr Malo-Alto had been carried out unconscious from the dining car by a sulky kitchen assistant and a very indignant, caviar-spattered waiter, both of whom were saying things under their breath about this fat, non-tipping American that would have made Cornelia's mother hold her hands over her ears if she had been with her and if she could have understood them.

Finn was eating as much as he could because he did not know where he would find his next meal or how he would pay for it, and he wanted to make sure he had all the strength and energy he needed to get to Cherbourg and to find Savannah. The prince and princess, on the other hand, just wanted to be sure they got the full value out of a meal which they were told had been paid for in advance by a friend, even though they had enough jewels concealed in their smelly fur coats to buy many millions of meals, and they had to eat this one while their hair and their clothing smelled of fish.

They were already feeling very cheated in relation to

the caviar, because the waiters—in spite of impassioned and angry requests of the prince and princess—refused to bring them any more to replace what they had thrown on their heads, and then refused to bring them the steaming turtle soup; so they were resolute about extracting every rouble's worth out of the remaining five courses.

'You know, I can't say it would bother me a lot if Jules and Josephine did rob those greedy royals,' Finn said to Tansy and Cornelia when they were back in his compartment. 'If this Mr Omera didn't plan to land the blame on me for it, I think I'd help them out.'

'We know the code word,' Tansy said. 'So all we have to do is say "Shanghai" and then Jules and Josephine will do whatever we want. In fact I think it would be best if I go find them straightaway,' she continued eagerly, 'and give them lots of orders.'

Back in the dining car, most of the passengers, including Jules and Josephine, were still sitting having coffee and brandy and liqueurs; and on each table now was a plate of delicious-looking little *petits fours* that made Cornelia think wistfully about being in her own body for a few minutes.

The headwaiter had seated Jules and Josephine at the same table as the English woman with the daughter who had been on a diet regime in Baden-Baden (the daughter had finished the entire plate of *petits fours* and was asking the waiter for another, Cornelia noticed enviously) and Cornelia was surprised that Tansy did not go inside one of those two women, but instead continued on to a table near the other end of the dining car, and went into Prince Gromananov.

'Excuse me a moment,' the prince said to the princess, and then he stood up and walked over to Jules and Josephine.

'I wonder if I could have a word with you,' the prince said with unusual politeness, causing the mother and daughter to look up in real terror and to put their hands protectively over their cups of hot coffee. Jules and Josephine, however, did not bother looking up at all. 'It's about Shanghai,' the prince said.

Jules and Josephine looked up quickly then, and their eyes showed more expression than Cornelia would have thought possible, a mix of surprise, fear and greed transforming their faces for an instant when they heard this word. The two of them stood up quickly without saying anything, and Jules led the way out of the dining car and into the corridor of the adjacent sleeping car.

'All the plans have been changed,' the prince said. 'The new instruction from Mr Omera is that you will get off the train at Dijon, and hire a fast car and driver to take you and Finn back to Paris as quickly as possible.'

Cornelia looked admiringly at Tansy for coming up with that ingenuous solution. She herself had been worrying quietly about how Finn would be able to pay for a train ticket back to Paris and was afraid that Tansy would have to steal money again from some innocent passer-by.

'You will act towards Finn exactly as you did before, except you will give him all the cash you have in your possession. Mr Omera has a very important job for Finn to do tonight, and he will need money to carry it out. You will be paid back, naturally, in due course.'

'I've never known Mr Omera to change his plans this often,' Josephine said suspiciously. 'There's something a bit fishy about all this, and I'm not just talking about the smell,' she added, her nose curling up distastefully at the lumps of caviar now dried and matted on the prince's hair and on his ancient fur coat.

'All that's happened so far has just been a test,' the prince said smoothly. 'Mr Omera needs to be sure that he can rely on people to follow orders, whatever they are. Don't forget to give Finn the money,' he added, and then he turned away immediately and returned to the dining car.

'That was good thinking, Tansy,' Finn said gratefully when she described the arrangements. 'I was wondering what I'd do for money. You think of everything, don't you?'

Embarrassed, Tansy did not answer him, because she knew that this was praise she did not deserve. From the time she had heard that Savannah Gray was to be taken on board a ship, Tansy had been worrying nearly all the time about the problems that lay ahead to which she could see no solution, but she had not wanted to say anything about these concerns to Finn or Cornelia, both of whom now were relying on her; and she knew that Cornelia, in particular, just took it as a certainty that, because she was a fairy, she would be able to find and rescue Savannah Gray from the *Aquitania*.

Tansy, however, did not know if she would be able to help or rescue anyone on a ship, and she was especially worried about taking Cornelia with her on an ocean crossing that would last at least six days in each direction.

She had no worries about Cornelia's safety so long as their visits inside the doll were short enough for the child's spirit to return to her own body every day; but if a human's body were to be separated from its spirit for a much longer time, Tansy did not know what might happen to it.

Cornelia had to eat, after all, and then there was the problem that Cornelia's parents were certain to notice and get worried if Cornelia stayed asleep for day after day, and they might even be frightened enough to take her away from her house to one of those places where humans take their sick, and where no one would understand what was the matter with her, and where someone might even do the small human harm by trying to treat her for a sickness she did not have.

What worried her most of all, however, was her own ignorance of what powers she would retain when she was over the sea.

Like all fairies, both winged and wingless, Tansy was a creature of the land, and her source of strength was the land itself along with the fresh-water streams and lakes that run through it. Even foreign fairies, who had wings, could not fly over the sea, as the power to use those wings came from the land.

The native Emeraldia fairies, who had strong and

very controllable whirlwinds, did venture out over sea occasionally for a certain distance when there was a good reason to do so (most significantly, to whirlwind away the Black Air) but they did not feel safe going for more than a few hundred feet.

That was why the foreign fairies and Emeraldia fairies had never mixed, and knew only as much about one another as they learned from individual adventurers (or spies?) from each side. Both groups of fairies did make use of human ships for travel, but only for short journeys, so far as Tansy knew. Sea travel was always a calculated risk. (That was why King Clover had branded his kingdom on the island of Inisure, before it was destroyed, as an 'adventure holiday destination', knowing its appeal would be to excitement-loving fairies who would enjoy the minor danger of the half-mile journey to the island dependent on human boat.)

Tansy's only personal experience of sea travel was the relatively short journey from a continental port to Emeraldia, arranged by a heroic secret band of winged fairies who had smuggled her there, at great risk to themselves, because they knew it was the only place in the world where it was normal for fairies not to have wings.

She remembered vividly how the fear of the sea had mixed with the fear of pursuit on that short journey which had lasted less than a day in human time, and how none of her escorting fairies had relaxed for even an instant until they were off the boat.

The ship on which Savannah Gray was a prisoner,

however, would be on the ocean for nearly a week in human time, and it would take another week to come back again, and Tansy did not know if a fairy could survive such a prolonged separation from land. Equally frightening was her uncertainty about whether or not Cornelia's body could survive separate from its spirit for so long.

'As soon as the car and driver have been arranged,' she told Finn in a voice that she had to fight to keep calm, 'I'm going to mind-port back to Emeraldia to talk to Queen May and King Fuchsia, but I should be back before the car reaches Paris. There's some information I need,' she added vaguely.

Jules and Josephine, too, were uneasy at the turn of events, and were looking even crosser than usual when they got off the train. They met Finn on the platform and studied him with more sour suspicion than before, but nevertheless, they handed over to him a large amount of money and hired a fast car with a driver exactly as they had been instructed to do.

'Very queer business all of this,' Jules said shortly, keeping his eye on the fat roll of money disappearing into Finn's pocket. 'Never came across anything like it.'

Finn shrugged. 'It's a high-stakes operation, I suppose. Shanghai and all of that,' he added cryptically, and was relieved to see the suspicion in Josephine's cold eyes replaced once again by fear and unease when she heard that word.

Jules and Josephine then sat into the back of the car, while Finn said something quietly to the driver and handed him a banknote. Immediately the driver moved over to the passenger seat and Finn sat at the wheel.

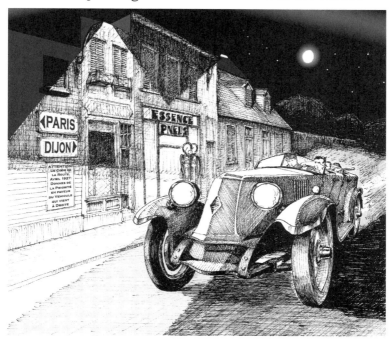

Tansy watched the car roar off into the night, and then mind-ported herself and Cornelia back to Cornelia's bedroom, which was a lot more crowded on this occasion than she would have liked it to be. Both of Cornelia's parents were there, the dogs were there, and Barry was sitting on the window seat, looking guilty and uneasy.

Tansy did not like this situation much, and if those unwelcome visitors stayed, she would have to get rid of them before taking Cornelia away again, but for the moment, she had a much more serious worry on her mind.

Chapter 32

A Worldly Fairy

THE INSTANT CORNELIA opened her eyes, the room exploded with noise and activity, her parents cheering and hugging her, and the two dogs barking and wagging and landing ecstatic licks wherever they could. Barry remained at the window, keeping a guilty, watchful eye on all this activity.

Tansy whirlwinded out the window over Barry's head, and went straight back to King Thistle's fort. When she got there, she found so many new refugees had arrived in the short time she had been away that she could barely squeeze inside.

'Can you tell me where King Fuchsia and Queen May are, please,' she said to the first fairy she recognised, who happened to be gentle little Primrose, the librarian from King Fuchsia's fort.

Primrose looked sadly at Tansy over the top of her half-glasses. (Not that she needed to wear those glasses, because her vision was exceptionally good, even by the very high standards of fairy eyes. However, she was as image-conscious as any other fairy; and together with her long cardigans and comfortable shoes, she felt the eyeglasses were part of an appropriate uniform for a librarian.)

Primrose told Tansy where she would find the king

and queen, and then warned her: 'But don't even think of trying to whirlwind there, Tansy. None of us can get around inside the fort by whirlwinds now. There just isn't room. Everyone has to mind-port all the time, and even then, there are still crashes happening all over the fort, whenever too many of us decide to go to the same place at the same time. It's got so bad that timetables are being drawn up specifying certain times when each fairy is allowed to move.'

She dropped her voice then, and added discreetly: 'Tansy, my dear, if you happen to have found a nice place outside the fort where you can rest quietly and peacefully, then you just stay there and make sure no one else finds out where it is. It's very difficult in here now, Tansy,' she said tiredly. 'Very difficult.'

Tansy thanked Primrose; and following her directions, she found May and Fuchsia in the room that once had been King Thistle's own bedroom, but now had been turned into an office for all the royal fairies. At present, every one of those royal fairies was in that room, trying to work out the timetables for mind-portation that Primrose had told her about.

As soon as she saw Tansy, May knew by her worried look that a new problem had arisen. She whispered something to Fuchsia, and then (conscious that every eye in the room was fixed curiously on her) stood up saying she'd have to excuse herself very briefly, and led Tansy out of the room with a careful show of nonchalance.

'What's the matter?' May whispered worriedly as soon as they were out of hearing.

Quickly, Tansy explained how Savannah Gray had been kidnapped and was to be hidden somewhere on the *Aquitania* and brought to New York, and about how she was worried about having to travel all the way to New York and back by ship if she didn't find Savannah before the ship left the harbour, and about what might happen to Cornelia if her spirit were separated from her body for that long.

'Well, it would be wonderful, of course, if you could find her before the ship sails,' Queen May said, 'but I do agree with you, Tansy, we can't rely on that happening. No, we must make arrangements about the human; but Fuchsia and I have been thinking about that a great deal, and I believe we've come up with a solution to the problem. We think there is a way her body can be fed and can exercise every human day.

'It's not a pleasant way, I have to say,' she continued in a resigned voice, 'at least not for Fuchsia and me; but then pleasantness or unpleasantness is not something that matters very much at the moment. It's what we must do.'

'What are you going to do?' asked Tansy uneasily.

'Well, you understand how you find it perfectly natural to go inside humans, Tansy, but Fuchsia and I don't at all. Indeed, we find it most unnatural, although we know we can do it when we have to. Well, now I'm afraid the time has come when we have to, although believe me, it will be the most unpleasant task of our entire existence.

'First we'll have to go inside Barry and take out his

spirit,' May said shuddering. 'And then we'll have to go inside Cornelia and deposit her brother's spirit inside her body for a time every human day, and that will allow Barry to eat and exercise for Cornelia during that time.

'Oh, don't worry, my dear,' she added reassuringly, seeing Tansy's uneasy face. 'It will be hard on Fuchsia and me, but it shouldn't badly affect the children at all.

'What bothers me much more,' May continued worriedly, 'is what our own fairies will think when they see one or the other of us disappearing so often from the fort. They have an idea now that Fuchsia and I are working on some Plan to try to improve the situation, but we were foolish really to have given them any hint of it because they haven't stopped pestering us since to know the details, and they're frustrated when we can't tell them. We both know how resourceful and really very sneaky they can be when their curiosity is roused, so we have to make sure, somehow, that nothing draws their attention to that house. We cannot have some curious fairy disturbing you while you're inside that doll, Tansy.'

'There may be another problem as well,' Tansy said then, although disliking having to add to the queen's worries. 'With the small human's parents, I mean. They were in the bedroom when I came back, which I didn't like at all, because it means they've seen the small human when they couldn't wake her, and I think they might think she's sick when they can't wake her, and that would be very bad because humans do funny things when other humans are sick. Sometimes they even take them away to big, dirty buildings full of beds which they build just for sick humans, and they leave them there.'

May nodded. 'Well, Fuchsia already thought of that, and he had a very good idea. I don't know if it will work or not, but at least it should help.

'According to Fuchsia,' she explained, 'humans are inclined to believe the things they read in newspapers, so he changed the front page of the newspapers which the humans read around here and he added a story about an epidemic of a sickness that causes children to sleep for most of the time, but which is not serious and which usually goes away within what humans call a month without doing any permanent damage.

'Fuchsia wrote it himself,' May added with a hint of pride in her voice, 'and put in so much detail that I almost believed it myself. He said the illness had started in Asia and spread quickly throughout continental Europe, and already had affected tens of thousands of children, but all of them had recovered completely. He also put the same information on a thing that's called the Internet, so I think there's a reasonable chance humans may just believe it.'

'King Fuchsia's terribly smart,' Tansy said admiringly; and feeling reassured on this point, she then felt safe to raise the matter that had been uppermost on her mind since she had first heard about Savannah Gray being kidnapped.

'Have you heard of any fairies crossing an ocean before?' she asked, trying hard to keep the fear out of her voice so that May would not guess how worried she was about the prospect of this unprecedented expedition. 'I was asking just because I was wondering if you've ever heard of any fairies who have survived for so long being so far away from land?'

'Oh, you'll be fine so long as you're on the ship,' May said reassuringly. 'You may not be as strong as when you're over land, but those ships are made from things that are part of the land—tons and tons of things from the land—so the *Aquitania* itself should provide you with enough power. Just don't attempt to leave it.

'Anyway,' she added, 'there may be one big advantage in the crossing taking so long. That is, if I understand these human dates correctly. Am I right in thinking that, inside the doll, the date is now the 12th of May?'

Tansy nodded. 'Although it may already be the 13th,' she said cautiously, 'because it was nearly midnight when I left. That's how it works in human time.'

'Well, I've been reading about the *Aquitania*, and I happen to know it will take six human days to get you to New York. That means that Finn has no chance of being in Paris on May 21st, the night he was murdered. He'll either be in America, or else he'll have boarded another ship that has just started the crossing back to Europe.'

'But what if I haven't found her before we reach New York?' Tansy asked. 'Do I have to stay in America then and look for her?'

'You'll have to judge the situation for yourself, Tansy,' May told her. 'I know we're asking something of you that's very hard, but you have great abilities, and you'll be well able to cope.

'And as well,' she added, a tone of wistfulness in her voice, 'you're very worldly, Tansy, which I wish I were, so you'll know what to do much better than I would in a new situation where you don't really know what rules apply.

'I know you've never wanted to talk about your background,' May continued, dropping her voice to a confidential whisper, 'but I've always had this idea that you're from the middle of Europe, and I know that fairies from the continent are much more sophisticated than we are here in Emeraldia.

'They look down on us, of course, because we don't have wings and they also think we're very green and rustic here, and they may well be right about that; but that's only because life has been so easy and safe for us since the truce with the Spirits of the Underworld, and we've had to think about nothing except how to enjoy ourselves.

'Over there, because the bad fairies are still mixed with the good fairies, we hear the stories of how they're fighting all the time, which would not be nice and comfortable at all, and I wouldn't like it; but on the other hand, there's nothing that exercises your brain as much as coming up against evil and needing to get the better of it, and I suspect that's what you had to do before you came to us, my poor Tansy. I feel it was terrible for you, but I also feel it made you quick and smart and ingenious, and gave you an instinct for danger. In fact, what I really think now is that fate sent you to us so that you could save us when we needed to be saved.

'Anyway,' said May more brightly, as she saw how Tansy appeared to be even more weighed down by this description of the trust that was being placed in her, 'you'll probably find Savannah Gray on the first day out and after that you'll have the time of your life.

'You'll find, I believe, that humans used to act very like fairies when they were on those old ocean liners. All they thought about was what they were going to wear, who they were going to dance with, and what silly party game they'd play next. You just make the best of the experience, Tansy, and when everything's back to normal again, you're going to find that you're the envy of every fairy in the kingdom because of all your travels and adventures.'

This great pep talk given to her by May did fill Tansy with resolve, and she decided she could regard it as a good omen for the mission when she returned to the bedroom and found that neither Cornelia's parents nor the dogs were in the room, but just Cornelia and Barry, Cornelia having finished a hearty meal of chicken and mashed potatoes and ice cream, and her mother, for the first time, not having uttered a word of reproach when she carefully left to one side the single Brussels sprout and the puree of carrots and parsnips.

'Come on quickly,' Tansy said to Cornelia, 'while Finn is still in the car with Jules and Josephine.'

Cornelia would have given anything for another few minutes at home, and could not get out of her mind how frightened and worried her parents looked when she first opened her eyes. Her mother had insisted on bringing her a meal right there in the bed, and had banished the dogs from the room for a few minutes because their excitement when Cornelia woke up was so extreme that she thought Cornelia would not be able to eat anything. She had gone downstairs now only to get second helpings of ice cream both for her and for Barry, and her father had gone out to collect some wood to put on her fire.

Cornelia did not want even to think about how her parents would feel when they came back to find she wasn't awake any more, and she was having the unpleasant experience of feeling both sorry for herself and guilty at the same time, because it was scary to think of having to go to New York without Barry and her parents and maybe having to stay away from them for weeks while all the time her parents were going to think she was almost dead; and then, to make matters worse, just at the last instant, when it was too late to do anything about it, she remembered that she had forgotten to tell Barry about Finn's rubies and emeralds.

Not that this was so important, she supposed, but the regret of it added to her sense of general unease as she watched her snug bedroom float away below her, and she started back to the tumultuous world of 1927 once again.

Chapter 33

Primrose

'Oh, no, Barry, she's not asleep again, is she?' his mother said unhappily as soon as she came into the room. She had come up as quickly as she could from the kitchen with two re-filled dishes of ice cream, but found, as she had dreaded, that she had been away too long. Cornelia's eyes were closed, and she had fallen once more into that strange, unnatural sleep which was so deep that nothing would wake her from it. 'This is terrible,' she groaned, handing both dishes of ice cream to Barry before settling herself again beside Cornelia on the bed.

'I wouldn't worry, Mom,' Barry said uncomfortably. 'She's just sleeping. Remember you said when you read the article in the newspaper that you weren't going to worry about it. It's just a bug that kids everywhere had. She'll get over it.'

'Yes, I know I said that,' his mother agreed miserably, 'but I really thought that when she woke, she'd stay awake. It was wonderful when she opened her eyes, wasn't it? She seemed so perky and hungry and full of chat for a little while.'

'Remember the newspaper said that loads of kids everywhere had got this sleeping sickness but all of them were fine when they got over it. And I read the same thing on the Internet, so it must be true.'

'It's hard to believe there's not even a doctor we can call on anymore,' his mother said, smoothing Cornelia's hair as she spoke. Imagine, every single doctor around here gone now except that terrible Dr Purulent-Pickenose, and I wouldn't let him within a mile of Cornelia.'

'She doesn't need a doctor,' Barry said determinedly. 'The newspaper says so.'

'I wish Dr Kavanagh hadn't left,' his mother said sadly. 'And Dr Logan. And Dr Murray. You know, Barry, I wouldn't say this to your father because it would upset him so much, but I can't help thinking it would be one advantage of moving to France straight away. At least we could get a doctor for Cornelia there.'

'Oh, no, Mom,' Barry said horrified. 'That would be terrible. We couldn't leave now. Not while Cornelia is— while she's sleeping. I mean Cornelia would drop dead if she woke up and found herself anywhere except this bedroom.'

'I know, Barry. I hate thinking about it myself, but I'm so worried at seeing her like this and not even being able to ask anyone about it.'

'We just can't go now, Mom.' Barry said desperately. 'Please, promise me you won't even think about that any more.'

Cornelia's mother stood up and walked over to the window, from where she looked down at a large number of men in helmets, doing the same peculiar and useless work they had been doing every day recently. Mysterious lines of tape were stretched in all directions, and by now the men had stuck so many marker posts into the ground around the fairy fort that the family could not even count them.

'Just look at them down there, Barry. Every day, there are more of them. They have no right to come on to the property without our permission, and yet the law won't stop them because the Lawful Guild wants them here. We know the only reason they come is to make us feel powerless and scared, and obviously they're doing a good job of that. But now I'm worried that maybe it's because of so much intimidation that Cornelia's got sick.

'That's what I keep thinking about all the time now. I can't look at Cornelia lying there on the bed and not wonder if we're being very foolish in trying to fight a force as powerful and evil as the Guild.'

His mother frightened Barry a lot with these words and with her air of deep worry and unhappiness, but he was not the only being in the bedroom to whom she had caused alarm. The fairy Primrose, sitting invisibly on top of the big wardrobe in the far corner, had listened to this talk with great interest and with growing concern.

This was the librarian fairy from whom Tansy had asked directions on her quick visit to the fort; and although the few words exchanged between Tansy and Primrose at that time had been insignificant, the encounter nevertheless had made a deep impression on Primrose because Tansy had changed so much. Usually Tansy was dreamy and shy, but in that brief meeting, she had been as alert and as confident as any fairy in Emeraldia.

Primrose (who had the reputation of being the smartest, as well as the most silently observant, fairy in the kingdom) had a fairy's natural curiosity about such a transformation, so she decided to follow Tansy to Cornelia's house, keeping a cautious distance behind the other fairy so that she would not be seen; but by the time she reached the house, Tansy had disappeared entirely, having already mind-ported into Josephine. And then Primrose grew very curious indeed.

Even before that encounter, however, the sharp-eyed Primrose had been quietly keeping an eye on the comings and goings of Fuchsia, May and Tansy between the house and the fort for some time, and had wondered if something was going on. She had chosen an old haunt of Tansy's as her observation post: a branch of the lone hawthorn tree in the field in front of Cornelia's house (the fairies' own meeting tree) which now had been defaced by a chalk mark to show the men in helmets that it was a tree to be cut down as soon as possible.

Primrose had been very surprised to find that this tree had been abandoned by Tansy; and in fact it was this discovery, combined with the number of times she had seen May and Fuchsia and Tansy go into that house together, and the serious, purposeful expressions of the three of them as they came and went, that first made her believe that May and Fuchsia and Tansy must be up to something interesting.

With a degree of self-control that almost no other

fairy could have managed, Primrose had refrained from gossiping with other fairies about this intriguing situation.

She had no doubt that these mysterious comings and goings were connected to the hints May and Fuchsia had dropped that they were working on a Plan that might yet save them all; and because the librarian understood better than anyone the incurably chatty and curious temperament of fairies, she thought it proved what a sensible king and queen they were that they should operate in total secrecy in these desperate times.

Now, however, she decided she had to talk to them, to report what she had observed, and what she had heard the human woman just say. She sensed that this human woman proposed to take all the humans who lived in that house out of Emeraldia as soon as she could; and Primrose had a suspicion that this might not suit the king and queen at present.

Heroically, Primrose made up her mind to suppress her own natural curiosity and not to ask May and Fuchsia a single question about what they were planning. These were desperate times in which every fairy was obliged to play her part, and if the information she could give to the king and queen could be of any use to them, she was going to make sure they had it—no questions asked.

She hurried back to the fort, and found May and Fuchsia still at the same meeting, still tussling with the other kings and queens over the mind-portation schedules. Just as when Tansy had appeared, the watchful May could see that Primrose now wanted to talk to her;

and for the second time, she slipped as discreetly as she could out of that troublesome meeting.

Primrose wasted no time. 'I don't want to beat about the bush, May,' she began. 'I think that you and Fuchsia and Tansy are doing something in that human house that you don't want any of us to know about, and I'm sure that's for a very good reason; but I just wanted to warn you that if what you're planning depends in any way on the humans who are living in that house, you may need to do something pretty quickly to stop them moving away.'

Primrose recounted then the conversation she had heard between Barry and his mother, and she also told May how the frequent royal visits to the house had caught her own attention, and how she occasionally had felt the need to create distractions to stop any other fairy from becoming aware of them.

'What would we do without you, Primrose?' May said warmly. 'I always thought you were the smartest fairy in Emeraldia, and now I'm sure of it. Well, I won't go into any more details just yet, but I can tell you that you're perfectly correct about that family of humans and how important it is that they stay in that house. But tell me what you think we should do. I can see you have an idea already.'

'Horseflies,' Primrose replied succinctly.

Chapter 34

Horseflies in December

'HORSEFLIES,' May repeated thoughtfully. 'What an interesting idea,' she said then. 'I think I see exactly what you have in mind. If we could use horseflies to drive away the men, the family probably would feel less intimidated. But the weather is cold now. Where would we find horseflies?'

'Well, do you remember the family that used to live near King Yew's fort before it was destroyed? They had stables and a big glasshouse, just beside Willow Lake. So, as soon as the men started working in the field, I started looking for horseflies, and I found thousands of them in that deserted glasshouse. It's flooded and warm and it's like an incubator specially built for them.'

'And you can get them over here?' May asked, and then quickly answered her own question. 'But of course you can. You did it before, didn't you? In fact, you did it for the Guardian and his family, I remember, back when the sheriff was coming to evict them from their little house and to tear down the lintel of it, as they were doing to all the poor humans' houses back then; and you made sure that the sheriff and his men couldn't get near the Guardian's house because of all the horseflies, didn't you? Oh, Primrose, you are so clever. When are we going to arrange it? Can you do it as soon as possible?'

'Of course,' said Primrose. 'The sooner the better. I'll just bring a certain ration of horseflies—maybe forty or fifty per man—in case we need to repeat this every day for a while. I'll make sure the insects go for the area around the eyes. That used to do the trick with that terrible sheriff and his men. If they send in replacement men with protective clothing, I'll add fleas into the mix as well.'

'We are so lucky to have you, Primrose. I don't think there's another fairy in Emeraldia who can herd fleas as well as horseflies, but it's never caused you a bit of bother, has it?'

'It's all to do with practice,' Primrose said modestly. 'I don't know why I hadn't thought of making use of insects before this, because they always worked so well in the past. I've got so absent-minded, haven't I May?'

'You've always been absent-minded, my dear,' May said fondly, 'but that's just because you're so intelligent. Brainy fairies are always a bit absent-minded.

'This is going to be fun,' the queen added eagerly, 'and fun is just what we need now—some good entertainment to make us all laugh. Do you remember when we used to laugh all the time? It seems so long ago now, doesn't it? I'll go inside and ask King Thistle to make a general announcement. I think everyone will want to be watching when you bring back the horseflies. But just before that, Primrose, could you keep watch and make sure that no one is looking while I make one quick visit inside that house?'

'Of course,' said Primrose. 'Now is a very good time if you go quickly.'

May was hoping to find Barry alone, and she was in luck. He had gone back to his own room, and was moodily bouncing a ball off a wall. 'Hey, listen—' he began when he saw her.

'Not now, Barry,' May said quickly. 'I'm in a great hurry. But I want you to keep watch at your window and be ready to call your parents to look out as well. I think, for a change, you're going to see something out that window that will make you feel a lot better.'

Before Barry could say a word, she was gone again. 'All right, Primrose,' she said when she came back. 'I'll just go inside now and tell King Thistle.'

Every fairy in King Thistle's kingdom (refugee and resident alike) came outside to look at the spectacle. They were in less high spirits than they usually would have been for such an event because recent hard times had left them all a bit depressed, but a few fairies did what they could to make the show more interesting.

The fairy Turf, for instance, organised a competition to see which fairy could guess most correctly the order in which the men would be driven from the field, but this produced less entertainment than expected because most of the fairies complained that they could not tell one helmet-wearing human from another. 'All their spirits are the same colour,' the fairy Hedge pointed out regretfully. 'Small and black, every one of them. And they're all wearing those white helmets and yellow jackets, so you can't even tell them apart by their clothes.'

In any event, when Primrose returned with her great cloud of insects, it would have been hard to tell the order in which the men left the field, even if each of them had been wearing a number on his back, because they crashed into and stumbled over one another so much as they tried to escape or swat away the horseflies that were biting every inch of their faces and hands. The men ran around in circles at first, and then galloped from the field in one large group, making a great deal of noise as they went.

'A bit too quick, wasn't it?' Fuchsia said after all the men had disappeared through the gate.

'Reminds me of the *Tour de France* when it came here,' Turf agreed. 'A lot of waiting and build-up, and then the bikes just flashed by.'

Still, even if the fairies were disappointed at the short length of time the spectacle lasted, the three humans and two dogs who were watching from the window of the house had no complaint at all about what they saw. The two dogs barked excitedly as the men ran, and Barry and his parents just looked on in wide-eyed gratification.

'They looked almost like horseflies, those things attacking them,' Barry's father said in surprise. 'I never remember seeing horseflies in December before.'

Even Barry's mother smiled, which was something neither he nor his father had seen her do since Cornelia had fallen into her deep sleep. 'Cornelia would say the fairies did it,' she said, making Barry squirm uneasily.

'So would her grandparents,' said her husband. 'And to be honest, I don't know if I'd even argue the point with them at the moment. If I could think of a better explanation, I'd give it; but right now, I'm just not able to think of one.'

—Chapter 35—

The Cloche Hats

THE MOTORCAR WAS HALFWAY TO PARIS by the time Tansy and Cornelia returned, and they were surprised to see that Finn was still driving it. Jules, Josephine and the hired chauffeur all were asleep and snoring noisily.

Tansy made herself visible to Finn for an instant, and immediately he stopped the car and got out. 'Just stretching my legs,' he said unnecessarily to the three snoring passengers.

'Well,' he asked Tansy, when he had walked a distance away from they car. 'Any problems? Will you be coming on the *Aquitania?*'

Tansy confirmed that she would, but then asked immediately: 'Did you get enough money from Jules and Josephine to buy a ticket?' This question was at the top of her mind because she needed to know if she would have to make other humans give him extra money as soon as they reached Paris.

Finn took the roll of cash out of his pocket and started to count it, and when he was finished, he whistled. 'There's more than 75,000 francs here. Well, at least that solves one problem,' he added in a relieved voice. 'I can buy a first-class ticket with this. I was wondering how I could search for Savannah in first and second class if I only had a third-class ticket, but I don't have to worry about that now.'

'Then you'll have to get new clothes,' Tansy said firmly, looking at the threadbare cuffs of his shirt and jacket. 'A first-class stateroom will cost you a lot of money, so will you have enough left over to buy clothes? And will you have enough time in Paris to buy them before we get on the train?'

'I don't think any of that is worth worrying about,' Finn said uneasily.

'I've spent a lot of time at the Silver Poodle Club,' Tansy told him. I hear things. You'll stand out in first class if your clothes are shabby and people will say mean things about you afterwards in the Silver Poodle Club. And you'll need cash for tips as well,' she added knowledgeably. I've heard lots of conversations among Americans who had just come over on the *Aquitania* or the *Berengaria* or the *Paris*, and all of them said they spent nearly as much on tips as on their tickets.'

'Ask Finn why he has to drive the car while the chauffeur's sleeping,' said Cornelia disapprovingly. The exhausted, unhappy look of her great-granduncle had bothered her from the moment she first laid eyes on him, and he looked particularly worn-out now at the prospect of having to go shopping for clothes before he could rescue Savannah.

'The chauffeur wouldn't have driven fast enough,' Finn explained. 'I don't want to take any chance of missing the boat train.'

In fact, Finn was in such a hurry to get to the city that

he drove more wildly, and directed more bad words at other cars that got in his way, than any driver Cornelia had ever seen—even more than the taxi drivers in Paris. He blew his horn all the time and overtook all the other cars on the road, and Cornelia thought the journey would never end, although in fact, it took less time than any previous motor journey between Dijon and Paris.

When they reached the capital, Jules and Josephine were left off at their apartment, and the chauffeur was allowed to return to his seat behind the wheel where he waited while Finn bought his boat ticket. When Tansy reminded him again, however, of all the clothes he would need for the trip, Cornelia was afraid there would be real trouble between the fairy and Finn, because Finn kept refusing even to talk about clothes and Tansy was determined that he could not board the *Aquitania* until he had bought some.

When Tansy saw that Finn was paying no attention to her whatever on this most serious subject, matters came to a head. She muttered impatiently, 'Oh, for Nature's sake,' took possession of him, and brought him straight to a men's clothing shop, where the now transformed Finn delighted the manager by telling him that he needed a complete wardrobe for a six-day ocean crossing as a matter of great urgency, and then he delighted the shop's messenger boy by handing him a wad of money, telling him to keep one bill for himself, and to go to the nearby luggage shop and to buy and bring back to him three new leather suitcases and a leather dressing case.

As controlled by Tansy, Finn was unrecognisable to

Cornelia. He agreed sincerely with the tailor that yes, indeed, it was nothing less than a tragedy that he did not have time for the usual fittings, and yes he would need evening clothes, of course, and also three lounge suits, one for morning, one for afternoon, and one for the first and last nights out, plus a sports coat and a blazer and yes, he would take two pairs of those very full Oxford trousers, plus shirts and collars, three pairs of silk pyjamas, a silk dressing gown, four pairs of shoes, a dozen pairs of silk socks, a rakish steamer cap, a new fedora hat and all incidentals please, and he would pay in cash.

It was a mistake for Tansy, who wanted Finn to be wearing his new clothes when he boarded the ship, that the last outfit she had him try on was the blazer and a pair of very eye-catching and baggy Oxford trousers. She herself was so delighted with the fashionable look of this outfit that she departed Finn's body, with great confidence, while he was still in the shop.

Unfortunately, however, the moment Finn saw his own reflection, he stared at it in horror, declared to the startled salesmen that he looked like a sailor in a musical comedy, and insisted on putting back on the threadbare old jacket and trousers he had been wearing when he came in, cramming the clothes he had just bought into the new suitcases.

'This human couldn't be more troublesome,' Tansy said to Cornelia in frustration. 'He's making it very hard for me to save him.'

'Oh, don't get mad at him, Tansy,' Cornelia pleaded,

sensing trouble between these two determined personalities. 'Finn just isn't smart about clothes the way you are.'

Finn and Tansy still were barely speaking to one another when they boarded the boat train, and the journey from Paris to Cherbourg turned out to be even more nerve-racking for Cornelia than the drive from Dijon to Paris had been.

Her two companions, both of them in a bad temper, went up and down the full length of the train again and again, looking closely at every passenger. Most of the women wore fashionable hats shaped like close-fitting helmets that hugged their heads and had brims that came down to cover much of their faces; and in the case of the women who were sitting farthest away from the aisle and looking out at the countryside, Finn was able to check their identity only by leaning over other passengers and peering under their stylish hats, but he made several women jump when he did this, and several men asked him nastily what he thought he was doing.

Worst of all, when he saw a woman in a smart black hat and a silver fox cape who, from behind, looked exactly like Savannah, in his excitement, he reached over the man sitting beside her and lifted her hat right off, causing both that man and the man sitting across from her to jump up and try to hit him.

'It's because of your clothes,' Tansy said smugly, after the conductor grabbed Finn by the arm and forced him to return to his seat, and warned him that he would have him removed from the train if he disturbed even one more woman passenger. 'If you were wearing your new clothes, I'm sure he'd treat you more politely. Anyway, you'd better just stay where you are now, and I'll check out the rest of the passengers by myself.'

'I think that Finn likes Savannah Gray a lot,' Cornelia said, as she and Tansy were flitting through the carriages. 'Do you think now that we're saving him from being murdered that she and Finn might get married?'

'Maybe that would cause too many problems,' said Tansy practically. 'If she's becoming an important artist, she might not want to live in Soldiers' Fort. And Finn just has to live in Soldiers' Fort.'

'But it would be nice, wouldn't it?' said Cornelia wistfully. 'Then they'd be neighbours, and I could—' But then she broke off, remembering suddenly the time difference between her own world and this one. 'Oh, that's awful,' she said unhappily, having reached the natural conclusion of her own thought. 'They might be dead before I'm even born.'

'She might be dead already,' Tansy said impatiently. She was still in a bad temper, and now she was bored with the tedious chore of inspecting so many almost identical (to her) human females, every one of their faces half-covered by those fashionable helmet-like hats.

'Oh no, she couldn't be,' Cornelia said, shocked.

'Well, there's no reason to think she is, but we'd better keep our minds on just finding her.'

Cornelia decided to say nothing more, because she thought that both Tansy and Finn were getting too short-tempered for comfort, and she just hoped they would find Savannah quickly before everyone fell out completely.

After she had finished scrutinising all the passengers, Tansy had a look into the baggage compartment, but Cornelia took fright when she saw how many trunks there were, thinking that Savannah could be in any one of them. 'Well, we won't worry too much about baggage,' Tansy said reassuringly. 'They can hardly have concealed her in a trunk if they wanted to get her there alive, and we know they did want her alive.'

Cornelia felt as relieved as Finn did when the train finally reached Cherbourg, although Tansy, she thought, became even more anxious. Finn was first off the train, and Cornelia had assumed that Tansy would follow immediately behind him, but instead, the fairy was inclined to dawdle, particularly when she learned that they would not be boarding directly on to the big ship with the four tall funnels that they could see out on the ocean, but would have to travel out to it on a small boat called a tender.

Cornelia got the impression that Tansy really did not want to go aboard this tender. She let all the other passengers board first and, only at the last second, just as the gangplank was being drawn up, did she close her eyes and whirlwind crookedly aboard.

Having achieved this, however, she then began to act more like herself, flitting around the deck of the tender and looking at the face of every passenger on it. She did not find Savannah, however, and neither did Finn, who had resumed his search with such determination that Cornelia noticed people starting to whisper to one another about him because of the peculiar way he was acting around women and their hats.

Cornelia's spirit sighed to itself tiredly. She was already thinking how scary it was to have to go to New York without her family if they didn't find Savannah immediately, and it seemed even worse now, when Tansy and Finn were cross with one another, and she always felt tense and knotted up inside when people around her were cross. If only they could find Savannah straight away and could go back to shore on this little boat, things wouldn't be so bad; but if they didn't find her, and if Tansy and Finn stayed fighting with one another all the way across the ocean—

Her spirit sighed again, just thinking about that awful possibility. If they didn't, she had a suspicion it was going to be a very long six days.

—Chapter 36—

The Aquitania

FINN WAS THE FIRST PERSON off the tender, having pushed himself right to the front of the crowd of passengers waiting to board the big ship. 'Come on, Tansy,' Cornelia urged, as they started to lose sight of him. 'We have to stay with him.'

Tansy was slow to approach the gangplank, and then looked so reluctant to cross it that Cornelia was reminded of a nervous farm animal being forced up a ramp on to a trailer, and she felt compelled to give her some encouragement.

'It's all right, Tansy,' she said soothingly, as the fairy made her slow, awkward way across the short platform of metal and wood that joined the small tender and the great liner. 'It's all right, you can do it,' she said again and again, until finally they were on board the *Aquitania*, at which point she became too surprised to say anything at all for a while, because it didn't seem to her then they were even on a ship any more, but rather inside some great mansion with fireplaces and everything.

Finn already had got directions to his cabin and had walked away so quickly that the white-jacketed man who was preparing to show him the way had lost sight of him, and Tansy had to put everything she had into her whirlwind in order to catch up. When they reached the stateroom, they discovered Finn would be sharing it with another passenger who had boarded in Southampton—a much older man than Finn, whom both Cornelia and Tansy disliked at first sight: Tansy because he had a small black soul, and Cornelia because he looked so like a picture of a wicked gremlin in a book she had at home, and even a bit like Walter the dog.

This man didn't have horns, of course, or long yellow teeth, but he had the same tiny eyes and turned-up nose of both of them, and he had deep frown marks on his forehead as a result of his features being set permanently in an expression of annoyance. The man was sitting at the dressing table writing a letter when Finn came in, and he looked up angrily at the interruption, his frown marks growing even deeper when he saw the steward deposit Finn's cases in the room.

'Are you sure you have the right cabin?' the man asked crossly. 'I was guaranteed that I would have this stateroom to myself.'

Finn glanced at his ticket. 'Sorry,' he said. 'I only bought this ticket a few hours ago. They said the boat was full up. But this is the correct stateroom, all right. Which bed are you using?'

'No, this is a mistake,' the man said angrily, looking so significantly at Finn's down-at-heel shoes and threadbare jacket cuffs, that Cornelia began to wonder if there was anyone at all in this world who was not obsessed about the condition of other people's clothes. She worried even more about the long ocean crossing that lay ahead of them all. It was bad enough that Finn and Tansy were cross with one another, but now this gremlin-Walter-man was going to be making trouble as well.

'Are you sure you're even in the right class?' the man asked unpleasantly. 'I'm Archibald Durham, Managing Director of Mayberry Mackintoshes and Bimble Woolly Jumpers. This is my fiftieth crossing with this company, and I have never had to share a stateroom before.'

'Well, there's not much point in talking to me about it,' Finn replied, impatient at having to waste time listening to this man when he wanted to start searching the ship for Savannah. 'Anyway, I don't expect to be spending too much time in here.'

'Well, don't unpack anything yet,' Mr Durham said testily. 'Not until I've spoken to someone about this.'

If Mr Durham had been able to see Tansy, and noted how the look in her eye changed as she listened to him, he might well have started to worry.

The fairy took seriously her responsibility to protect Finn, and in her style-conscious mind, this included protecting him from insults about his appearance as well as saving his life, which was why she had got so cross with him about his refusal to wear his nice new clothes.

Mr Durham had picked an especially bad time to be rude to her charge. The strain and unnaturalness of being away from land, and of being surrounded on every side by power-draining ocean, was taking a heavy toll on the fairy. She couldn't stop worrying all the time in case she would find herself unable to protect Finn and

Cornelia—let alone to find Savannah—in such a hostile environment, and this sense of potential powerlessness was making her very bad-tempered indeed.

On the short journey across the gangplank, she found her whirlwind hard to control, and she had experienced briefly the horrible feeling that if she had let her concentration slip at all, she might easily have been swept away.

On board the liner itself, which was a world of timber and potted palms and marble and many tons of other materials all taken from the land, she had felt more like herself again, just as May had promised she would. All the same, however, this was an untested environment, and the unfamiliar sense of not being able to rely on her own abilities at a time when every creature in the world—fairy and human alike—seemed to be depending on her had created a boiling-over stew of worry and frustration inside her that she thought would make her explode if she could not vent it on someone; and if she could test out her powers just a little at the same time, well that would be good too.

In all those circumstances, this arrogant Mr Durham, looking with such disdain at the preoccupied Finn, was an irresistible target for her.

First she would get this stupid man off the ship, she decided, so that he *could* not waste her or Finn's time any more over the next six days, and then she would feel better; and having resolved on this plan, she shot inside him immediately. Mr Durham had remained sitting at the dressing table, but as soon as Tansy went inside him, he stood up at once, and said, 'I'm getting off this ship.'

Finn, who had found a copy of the passenger list and was reading it with great concentration, appeared not even to have heard him. 'Princess Carlotta of Modonia,' he muttered. 'That doesn't make any sense.'

Tansy paid no more attention to Finn than Finn was paying to her or to his disdainful cabin mate. If Tansy had known where this unpleasant man's coat was, she would have had him get it; but as she didn't know, Mr Durham just walked out of the stateroom wearing his shirt, his sleeveless Fair Isle jumper, and his plus-fours. At the last second, Tansy spotted his steamer cap hanging from a hook on the back of the door, and he put this on his head. Finn, his mind elsewhere, did not even look up.

'Could you direct me to the Purser's Office, please?' Mr Durham asked the first steward he met in the corridor.

At every stage of this adventure, Tansy found she was grateful for the worldly knowledge she had picked up in her many pleasurable sessions of eavesdropping at the Silver Poodle Club. She knew just what the sophisticated passenger had to do after boarding a ship: waste no time and tip as heavily as necessary to secure a dining table in the location of choice (unless of course one had been invited to sit at the Captain's table, but not many of the Silver Poodle Club patrons had been) and a deck chair on the correct side (port side, going to New York); and if one wanted to change the accommodation one had been given, one went immediately to the Purser's Office. Those were points on which everyone in the Silver Poodle Club agreed.

'I want to leave the ship,' the man told the purser. 'I want to get back on the tender while that's still possible. Will you please have my luggage put into storage for me when the ship reaches New York?'

'Is there a problem, Mr Durham?' the purser asked worriedly.

'No, I have simply changed my plans,' replied Mr Durham, 'but I wish to leave immediately.'

Mr Durham then turned away and walked as quickly as he could to the place where they had embarked and where the gangplank was just about to be removed. 'Wait, please,' said Mr Durham, and walked across the gangplank.

Tansy then found herself in a bit of dilemma. She knew that if she left Mr Durham before the gangplank was lifted, Mr Durham would go back on board the ship, and Tansy really did not want to see Mr Durham ever again. On the other hand, if she waited until after the gangplank was lifted, she would have to get back on board the liner without the comfort of knowing that something that came from the land—even that thin gangplank—was separating her from the hostile, power-draining sea.

Still, there were times when a fairy's temper and pent-up tension (and her secret need to know the worst) could get the better of her judgement, and this, it seemed, was one of those times. Having decided to get rid of Mr Durham, she knew that he would annoy her twice as much if she took fright now and she let him back on board.

In the world of fairies—of Emeraldia fairies, anyway—Tansy had what humans would describe as 'a short fuse'.

As for Cornelia, she knew nothing about Tansy's fears of being away from land and travelling over the sea, and she was not sure why Tansy was doing what she was doing, but she did know that she would be glad to see the last of Mr Durham. Not only did he remind her of the bad fairy in her book—and, even more disturbingly, of Walter—but she also was tired of people who thought they could be mean to Finn just because his clothes were old, and the trip to New York was going to be scary enough without a gremlin-Walter-man to worry about.

They had only a few minutes to wait before the gangplank was lifted. When only about ten feet separated the great liner and the small boat heading back to Cherbourg, Tansy left Mr Durham and then she concentrated with every scrap of her being on getting back on board that big ship. She fixed her eyes on the rails of the *Aquitania*, allowed herself to think about nothing else, and whirlwinded as if her existence depended on it, which maybe it did.

To Tansy's great horror, however, she found that her whirlwind had no power or direction, and the more she concentrated on getting to the ship, the more she and Cornelia drifted away from it.

Cornelia was surprised to find that they were moving in the opposite direction from the liner at first, and she would have liked to ask why, but she had a strong sense that Tansy was not in a mood to be asked anything at all. Tansy herself was almost overtaken by panic when she saw the ship sailing away from them, and she was too worried even to be amused when she heard (over all the noise being made by the two ships and by the ocean itself) the great ruckus Mr Durham suddenly started making on the tender.

'Three men are holding down Mr Durham,' Cornelia reported to her. 'Tansy, don't you think we ought to go back to the ship now?' she added tentatively, as the *Aquitania* drifted farther and farther into the distance.

'Okay,' thought Tansy to herself. 'This has to be possible.' She tried to remember all the instructions May had given her when she was teaching her how to whirlwind, and she remembered how the one word May kept repeating to her all the time was 'relax'.

'Don't think about it so much, Tansy,' May used to say. 'Just do it. It's like dancing. Do you think you'd be able to dance at all if you thought about every step?'

Tansy remembered this advice and fought down her own panic by trying to imagine herself on the dance floor of the Silver Poodle Club, just doing a tango from one end of it to the other. Cornelia then became even more worried as Tansy's movements suddenly became jerky and without any apparent direction. They went forwards a bit and then they suddenly went backwards, and then they went from side to side, and all the time, the big ship was going farther and farther away from them.

Tansy tried to forget where she was and hummed

to herself the tune the band in the Silver Poodle Club had played for the apache dancers. Then she began to picture herself doing an apache dance in which she had to pursue her partner across a giant stage, relentlessly following him, perhaps carrying a knife, and doing a few cartwheels just to add a certain distinction to the performance.

'Tansy, is anything wrong?' Cornelia asked nervously, as she felt herself going head over heels at great speed.

'Shh,' said Tansy impatiently. 'I'm dancing. I'm dancing over water, and that's special dancing.'

Cornelia fought down her own panic by reminding herself that Tansy was a fairy and could do anything, and sometimes she just chose to do things that were very odd, but nevertheless, they always worked out in the end, and, of course, Tansy did love to dance.

'I am doing the most dramatic apache dance ever seen in Paris,' Tansy said to herself. 'I am doing a dance so extraordinary that a special dance-floor has been laid for me in the biggest nightclub ever built in the world, and thousands and millions of humans and fairies are rising together to applaud me and—'

And then, for an instant, Tansy didn't know where she was, because she was upside down and it was hard to tell whether she or Cornelia was feeling the more disoriented. But in fact, May's good advice to her—'just relax and remember how you feel when you dance'—had done the trick. What had happened was that, with a final, great cartwheel, and imagining herself about to land from above on her astonished imaginary partner in the most spectacular apache dance ever performed anywhere in the world, Tansy had succeeded in landing the two of them—head first but perfectly intact—back on the deck of the *Aquitania*.

'Are you finished dancing over water now?' Cornelia asked in a trembling voice. 'I don't think I like doing that very much.'

'I don't either,' Tansy agreed. 'And we're not going to do it any more. No matter what happens, we're not going to move an inch away from this ship from now on until it reaches New York.'

Chapter 37

Princess Carlotta of Modonia

WHEN THEY GOT BACK to the stateroom, neither Tansy nor Cornelia was surprised to find that Finn already had left it. The door was open, and the room was occupied only by a steward who was unpacking Finn's new suitcases.

Tansy, shaken still by the brief, strange experience of finding herself almost without powers, was glad of the chance to compose herself while the man finished his work. Then Cornelia called her attention to the copy of the passenger list which Finn had thrown down on the table, remembering how his attention had been caught by one particular name.

'Some Princess something,' Cornelia said. 'He seemed to think it funny that the name of some Princess something was on it.'

Tansy began to read through the names. 'Princess Carlotta of Modonia,' she said after a while. 'That was the name, wasn't it? Well, I suppose we should start with her. That means we go to the Purser's Office again and we see what stateroom she's in.'

They learned that she was in the Royal Suite and that she had four attendants travelling with her. Tansy and Cornelia lost their way a few times trying to find this suite, and ended up walking through some of the biggest and grandest rooms Cornelia had ever seen, with great domes and marble columns and wonderful paintings everywhere, not only hanging on the walls but even painted right on to some of the ceilings.

If it weren't for the noise of the engines, and the sight of people putting out their hands now and then to balance themselves against a wall or a chair as the ship gave a gentle roll, Cornelia would have found it very hard to remember that she was on a ship at all. If she weren't with Tansy, she would have been a bit intimidated by all this grandeur, because these rooms really were very formal and very posh.

Tansy was inclined to dawdle wherever she found people dancing, and groups of people were dancing in all sorts of places. They were dancing to the music of a small band in a gigantic, columned room at the top of the ship; they were dancing to the music of a pianist in one corner of another great room which had a fireplace that made Cornelia think wistfully of home for a while; and the jolliest group of all was dancing to a portable record player at one end of the boat deck.

'That last dance was the black bottom,' Tansy said knowledgeably. 'It's all the fashion now, and people are starting to dance it more than the Charleston, which is a pity really. You know,' she added confidentially, 'Queen May says she doesn't think she's very sophisticated, but I think she's really very smart about the human world. She told me that on ocean liners, humans used to have as much fun as if they were fairies, and they are having fun here, aren't they?' she said, looking wistfully at the cheerful group of dancers.

'We have to hurry,' Cornelia said, trying to urge her on. 'We have to find Savannah first, and then you can dance, too, if you want to.'

They made use of a steward to get themselves inside the Royal Suite, and this time, Cornelia felt sorry for the human whose body Tansy had taken over because it seemed like they might be getting him into trouble with the princess and her mean attendants. These included two footmen wearing powdered wigs and velvet knee breeches, one of whom had a great scar on his cheek and the other had the biggest moustache Cornelia had ever seen. Both of them jumped up angrily when the steward entered the room.

'You had specific orders from the Chief Steward not to come in here unless we asked for you,' said the scarred footman in a very harsh voice. 'You wuz told the princess had her skin removed as part of a beauty treatment, and she don't want to see no one until it grows back.'

'I beg your pardon,' the steward said politely. 'A passenger who was walking by reported a cry for help coming from in here. Perhaps the passenger was mistaken?'

The two footmen looked at one another and then the one with the moustache walked over quickly to a door of another room and opened it just enough to slip inside. After a few seconds, he reappeared. 'The passenger didn't hear nothing,' he said. 'Now get out.'

'I do beg your pardon,' the steward said again, even more politely. 'The ship makes so many creaks and groans that passengers who are sailing for the first time often mistake those noises for voices. That's probably what the passenger heard. Shall I just go in and check that there's nothing wrong in the princess's room that might cause a strange noise that would disturb her?'

The two footmen jumped in front of the steward then. 'Get out,' the scarred footman barked. 'No one asked you to come in here. Get out.'

'Yes, of course, Sir,' the steward said politely. Then he bowed slightly and left the room. Out in the passageway, Tansy left him immediately, and the steward was left standing in front of the door and looking back at it with puzzlement. Tansy and Cornelia hovered just above him, and they too were looking back at the door, only they were looking at it with deep suspicion. However, even Cornelia said nothing for a moment, because both of them were just too surprised by what had happened.

'I think we ought to go find Finn,' Tansy said after a while. 'I'd like to know why he's so interested in this princess.'

'Those men acted like they were hiding something,' Cornelia observed. 'But why would a real, live princess want to hide someone like Savannah? Kidnappers and burglars hide people—not princesses.'

'Finn knows something,' Tansy said. 'We'll ask him.'

Finding Finn, however, was easier said than done. They searched the lounges, smoking rooms and dining rooms of the three classes, but found him in none of them. They searched the baggage compartment where thousands of leather and brass trunks were stored five and six layers high; they even searched the stores, where the food for the week's voyage was kept, looking behind all the mountains of kegs and boxes, and even peering behind the long, scary lines of animal carcasses hanging from hooks.

Feeling worried and discouraged, they returned to the stateroom, and both of them could tell immediately that Finn had not returned to it. 'Tansy, you don't think, do you,' said Cornelia worriedly, 'that the princess and those men did something to Finn as well as to Savannah?'

'They will be so sorry if they did,' Tansy said fiercely. 'I think it's time we went back to that suite, and this time, we're not going to bother with the steward, we'll just go in through the vent, although it's not so easy to get through very small spaces in this world, so hang on tight.'

This was good advice, and Cornelia clung on for all she was worth as Tansy gritted her teeth and squeezed and squeezed and squeezed her way through the tiny horizontal vents in the door. Once again, they were back in the vestibule of the royal suite and this time, they found the footman with the moustache settled comfortably on the damask-covered sofa, holding a cigar in one hand and a glass of some amber liquid in the other.

It took every bit of self-control Tansy possessed to pass by him without making him empty his drink on his head and eat his cigar, but she did so because she wanted to get into the Princess's bedroom before any alarm was raised.

She squeezed through a second horizontal vent, and then she and Cornelia were inside the bedroom and they were looking at a very strange sight: a person lying on the bed and bandaged from head to toe, with what looked to be a breathing tube coming out of the head area, and being watched over by the scarred footman, who was sitting just beside the bed, and had a gun resting on his lap. Like the other footman in the adjacent room, he too was holding a cigar in one hand and drinking a glass with amber liquid in it with the other.

'Tansy, do you think that might not really be the princess at all,' whispered Cornelia indignantly. 'Do you think it might be Savannah or Finn?'

'I'm absolutely certain it's Savannah or Finn,' Tansy whispered back ferociously, 'and these men are going to be sorry they were ever born. But first we're going to get this man to unwrap that person, and find out who it is.'

'If it is the princess under there with no skin, what will we do?' Cornelia whispered.

'Put the bandages back,' Tansy answered impatiently.

Without wasting any more time, Tansy shot inside the footman, who immediately put out his cigar and laid down his glass, and threw his gun out the porthole. Then he took a pair of nail scissors from the dressing table and carefully cut through a few layers of bandage, before starting to unwrap the rest. Cornelia felt so nervous watching that she was glad she didn't have her heart with her, and when the face that finally emerged turned out not only to have skin on it, but to be that of Savannah Gray, she couldn't stop herself giving a sharp yelp of relief.

Savannah gazed up dozily at them, and looked particularly confused when the scarred footman in the velvet knee breeches said to her: 'Oh, good. We've found you. Right, I'll just throw a blanket over you now and turn off the lights so that other footman won't know we've found you while I take care of something.'

'Um, Tansy, I think you need to tell her a bit more,' said Cornelia, observing Savannah's look of dazed perplexity. 'Maybe you could tell her that you're here to help her and that Finn sent you.'

'Oh yes,' the footman told Savannah. 'Finn sent me, and I'm here to help you.'

'I beg your pardon,' said Savannah, her voice slurred but fierce. 'You don't really expect me to believe that, do you? I *saw* what you did to Finn when he found me. You chloroformed him and then you put a bandage around *his* head and then you lied to the steward and said Finn worked for the Princess and had got so sick that he had to be taken off the liner and put on the pilot boat and brought back to France.'

'What?' shouted the footman, as a panic-stricken Cornelia and Tansy both spoke through him at once. 'You mean Finn's not on the *Aquitania* any more?'

'You said he wasn't,' said a bewildered Savannah. 'You said you were having him brought back to Paris.'

'This is awful,' Cornelia said in a panic. 'If they've taken Finn back to Paris, we have to go back there too.'

'Don't say anything and don't leave this room,' the footman barked at Savannah. 'Someone will come back to get you out of here.'

The footman closed the bedroom door behind him and then went back to the vestibule of the suite. 'Where's Finn now?' he asked the other footman, who had stretched out on the sofa and still had a glass in his hand.

'Halfway back to Paris, I guess. When they have him in Paris, they'll get what they want out of him.'

The scarred footman then lifted the footman with the moustache off the couch and punched him in the jaw so hard that his wig went flying across the room. Then he hit him a second time, threw him into a closet, and locked him inside it.

Cornelia's panic at the thought of Finn having been taken off the boat increased with every second, but Tansy's mood was so fierce that she hardly dared speak to the fairy. The footman walked towards the centre of the boat and asked the first person in uniform he passed where he would find the Master at Arms, and said that he needed to see him on an urgent matter.

'Who's the Master at Arms?' Cornelia whispered bravely.

'He's the person in charge of security on the ship,' Tansy growled in reply.

A very solicitous steward, making many polite enquiries about the health of the Princess (all of which the footman ignored) escorted him to the timber-panelled quarters of the Master at Arms; and this officer stood up politely when the footman came in, and held out his hand to him.

The footman did not shake it but instead said to the officer: 'This is the worst-run ship I've every sailed on, and I have never met such incompetent or ugly looking officers. You yourself,' he told the Master at Arms (who happened to have a very prominent nose) 'look like a seasick rhinoceros. I will now demonstrate what I intend to do to every officer on this ship.' The footman then clenched his fist and punched the Master at Arms in the jaw just as hard as he had punched the other footman back in the Royal Suite. The officer fell back against the table and chairs, which flew around the room with a great clatter.

Almost immediately, the door from the passageway opened, and a junior officer came in to see what had caused the noise, and what happened then was that the footman punched the junior officer in the jaw as well. Then a third officer came in and the footman punched him even harder than he had punched the other two.

By that time, the other two officers had risen to their feet and Tansy allowed the footman to be restrained by these two for a short while, although she was ready to fling both of them across the room if they didn't say what she wanted. 'Get some help and take this man to the brig,' the Master at Arms ordered fiercely. 'And be sure he stays there for the rest of the crossing.'

This was all Tansy wanted to hear, and immediately then, she left the footman and headed back to the Royal Suite; and not for the first time, Cornelia thought how lucky she was that Tansy was on her side and not on the side of Mr Omera, because Tansy really was very scary indeed when she was cross, and Cornelia had never seen Tansy as cross as she was right now.

Back in the Royal Suite, they ignored the loud knocking and kicking coming from inside the closet, and Tansy went directly into the bedroom and inside Savannah. Savannah had opened the bedroom door just a crack, and was looking with interest across at the closet from where all the noise was coming, and appeared to be thinking of trying to make her escape. As soon as Tansy was inside her, however, she left the suite immediately, and then walked very quickly down the long corridors to Finn's empty stateroom.

She closed and locked the door, and sat down on the sofa under the portholes, and then Tansy left her.

—*Chapter 38*—

A Letter to Savannah

'YOU'LL HAVE TO MAKE YOURSELF VISIBLE and talk to her,' Cornelia whispered nervously, hoping that Tansy, in her present mood, would not do or say anything that would frighten Savannah into trying to escape from the stateroom.

Cornelia need not have worried, however, because when Savannah found herself suddenly in a strange room with no idea of how she got there, she was strengthened in her conviction that she was having the strangest dream of her life. She knew she had been drugged by her kidnappers to make her sleep, and she had formed the conclusion that the strange things that seemed to be happening to her now were hallucinations brought on by those sleeping powders. What other explanation could there be, after all?

However when a beautiful figure in an exquisite dress and breathtaking dangling earrings appeared in front of her, she formed another theory.

'Have I died?' she asked. 'Although I never imagined an angel would be as fashionable as you are. That is the most beautiful dress I've ever seen. If I were alive, I'd ask you who designed it.'

'I'm not an angel,' Tansy said. 'I'm a fairy. I came to rescue Finn, but I'm afraid I may have failed and all the fairies in Emeraldia will be lost now because they were depending on me. We've rescued you, of course, but you don't really make any difference to the fairies. And Queen May designed my dress.'

Savannah blinked hard a few times. That did not sound much like her idea of how an angel would talk, which was good, really, because it probably meant she was still alive; but was this a dream, a hallucination, or could this stylish creature really be one of the fairies that Finn talked about as if he believed they really existed?

Cornelia coughed discreetly. 'Tansy, maybe I ought to write a letter to Savannah the same as I did to Finn. And I've been doing a lot of thinking, Tansy, and I think we can still save Finn. I was thinking that you could go inside the captain and make him bring the boat back to France so we can find Finn again.'

Tansy had wondered about this herself, but she doubted her ability to achieve something so sensational. First of all, she thought she would not have the navigational knowledge to control the captain usefully; and secondly she suspected that the captain might well end up being thrown into the brig himself beside the scarred footman if he single-handedly tried to turn the boat around and take it back to France.

Still, she thought the idea of the letter was a good one, and she was glad of the chance to be able to take a rest from this complicated talking-to-humans while Cornelia made use of Savannah to write her letter.

Savannah walked over to a dressing table, and on top of it found some writing paper left there by Mr Durham headed '*On Board the R.M.S. Aquitania*' and a pen. She sat down at the table and started to write.

Cornelia remembered the trouble they'd had in getting Finn to read the letter she'd written to him, so this time, she wrote in big print on the top of it: '*SOS—READ THIS LETTER—URGENT.*' Then she wrote:

'*Dear Miss Savannah Gray,*

'*My name is Cornelia O'Hara and I am Finn's great-grandniece and I live in the future when things have got very bad in Emeraldia and everyone who is nice, which includes fairies as well as humans, may have to leave it. We are on this boat because Finn wanted to rescue you, and Tansy and I were trying to rescue Finn because it is very important that he not be m hurt in Paris after Lindbergh arrives there and that he comes back to Emeraldia immediately to protect Soldiers' Fort. Very bad things have happened in Emeraldia because Finn did not stay in Soldiers' Fort, and it is very important that we get him to go back there. It would be very nice if you came with him. Soldiers' Fort is not exciting like Paris is, but Tansy would bring you back to Paris any time you wanted if you didn't mind leaving your body behind and coming back through the Silver Poodle Club. I am sure you would not mind at all when you got used to fairies and how they do things. Finn was used to fairies, so he wasn't even surprised when he saw Tansy, although I think it surprised him that I was there too but he couldn't see me.*

'*Tansy and I were able to get here through the doll, Josephine, which you made and which is a very wonderful doll. We could also have got here through Jules, but we usually use Josephine.*

Oh yes, we met you once before, although you did not see us,
when Scott Fitzgerald came into your apartment and you were
painting the beautiful ballerina who is to dance in Swan Lake.
Tansy was able to rescue you today from the two men with
the funny wigs who were pretending that you were Princess
Carlotta all bandaged up because she is very smart and very
strong, so I am sure she will be able to rescue Finn, although
it would be much better of course if he were here with us now,
and then Tansy wouldn't have to turn the boat around so that
we can get back to Paris before Lindbergh does. Tansy will be
able to explain everything to you when you get to know her.
Thank you very much for making Jules and Josephine.
   Yours truly,
   Cornelia Mary O'Hara (age 8)'

As soon as Cornelia signed her name, Tansy left
Savannah, and then they waited to see if she would put
the letter down without noticing it and try to leave the
room as Finn did. Savannah, however, saw the letter
immediately, and seemed to be fascinated by it. She
read it twice, laughing now and then; and when she
had finished, she looked around the room and then she
delighted the two beings watching her by calling out
softly: 'Tansy? Cornelia?'

Tansy made herself visible immediately. 'I'm sorry
you can't see Cornelia as well,' she said regretfully,
although in a calmer voice than she had used all day.
'When she says anything though, I can tell you.'

'Well thank you both for rescuing me,' Savannah said.
'And thank you for the letter, Cornelia. I never imagined
I'd receive such an interesting letter from a little poppet

from the future. But tell me why have people gone to so much trouble to kidnap Finn and me? Neither of us has a bean.'

'Finn has jewels,' Tansy answered. 'The fairies gave them to his family a long time ago. They're just rubies and emeralds, but humans seem to value those things a lot.'

'Finn has rubies and emeralds!' Savannah repeated laughing. 'Well, I'd never have guessed. And given to him by the fairies! Are they the most wonderful rubies and emeralds in the world?'

'Humans think they are,' said Tansy. 'That's why Finn was tricked by jewel thieves. He thought he was working for an insurance company, but he was really working for a very bad man called Mr Omera, who's a jewel thief. Everyone is afraid of Mr Omera but no one ever sees him. Jules and Josephine work for Mr Omera, and they're jewel thieves too; and those two men who were pretending that you were Princess Carlotta, they're also working for Mr Omera.'

'Jules and Josephine are jewel thieves?' said Savannah fascinated. 'So that's why Finn was spending so much time at the Silver Poodle Club.'

'Do you know if there's a real Princess Carlotta?' Tansy asked, passing on Cornelia's question.

'There used to be,' said Savannah, laughing, 'but Finn heard at the nightclub that she'd died six months ago after setting a world record for false insurance claims. That was why he came to her suite straightaway and knew it was me wrapped up in a bandage, but then those awful men discovered him.' She shook her head in puzzlement then. 'But it was one of those dreadful men who let me go in the end. Why did he do that?'

'He didn't let you go,' Tansy said fiercely. 'That was me. That footman is in the brig now. But the purser said there were four people on the ship who are supposed to be working for the princess so some of them might try to kidnap you again, but they won't be able to because I'm going to stay with you all the time, although I really wish I could go back to Paris and find Finn.'

'But if you're a fairy, can't you just flash yourself back to Paris?'

Tansy shook here head miserably, and suddenly felt a great urge to confide in this calm, and apparently very open-minded, human. 'This is not my real world or time, and I don't have that much power here. But even in my own world, I don't have a lot of power over the sea. I don't have the power to get back to land unless I'm carried there on a boat, and I don't think I can get this boat to turn around and go back to France; and if I can't do that, I don't see how we can get to Paris at the same time as Lindbergh so that we can save Finn.'

'Is Finn in serious danger?' Savannah asked worriedly.

'Yes he is,' Tansy said. 'He will be attacked in the *Place de l'Opéra* after Lindbergh arrives in Paris. There will be celebrating in the street after Lindbergh's arrival and then an apache gang will appear and they'll—attack Finn. We thought we could get Finn out of Paris before it happened, but now we don't even know where he is.'

'Who's Lindbergh?' Savannah asked, bewildered.

'Oh, he's very famous. He'll fly all by himself non-stop from New York to Paris and he'll be a very big hero. He'll arrive in Paris on the night of May 21st.'

'My goodness,' said Savannah impressed. 'But can't we warn the Paris police that there's an apache plot to murder a man in the *Place de l'Opéra* on that night?'

'I don't know if the police would believe us,' Tansy said. 'But if I can't get back there, that may be all we'll be able to do. Do you have friends in Paris who could help him?'

'Yes, I do,' said Savannah. 'In fact, Claudette, the girl you saw modelling for me, spends all her time around the *Place de l'Opéra* and she knows everyone. She even introduced Finn and me. Her mother is from Emeraldia, and she was the only person Finn knew in Paris when he first arrived. I'm sure she could arrange for people to be on the lookout around the *Place de l'Opéra* that night.'

Tansy sighed, and whirlwinded distractedly back and forth across the room. 'You really are the most elegantly dressed creature I've ever seen,' Savannah said smiling at her. 'I never imagined fairies would be so fashionable. You look as if you just stepped out of one of the couturier houses on the Right Bank. Only much more perfect of course.'

There was a knock on the door then, and all three beings in the stateroom jumped.

—*Chapter 39*—

The Great Æneas

'Q UICK, HIDE IN THE BATHROOM!' Tansy said to Savannah. 'We don't want Mr Omera to know where you are.'

In the event, however, it was only the steward who was at the door, and not finding anyone in the stateroom, he went away again. His visit, however, caused Savannah to think about a different problem.

'You know, what if the ship's officers don't believe me when I tell them what happened? I mean, here I am without a ticket or even a passport, and they may think I was just making up a story when I say I was kidnapped and smuggled on board. If this Mr Omera really has agents everywhere, he probably already has some other woman wrapped up in bandages, and those *footmen* (Savannah's nose curled in distaste as she said the word) will be able to convince the crew that it really is Princess Carlotta they have in the Royal Suite.

'Oh my word,' she gasped, putting her hand over her mouth, 'I might be put in the brig as a stowaway for the rest of the trip and not even be able to send telegrams asking people to help Finn.'

'You could always pretend to be Finn,' Tansy suggested. 'His raincoat is in the closet, and he kept his passport and ticket in the inside pocket.'

Savannah looked, and found not only his passport and ticket, but also what was left over from the great roll of banknotes given to him by Jules. She looked at it in disbelief. 'How did Finn get all this money?'

'Oh, that was easy. I made Jules give it to him. You'll find it very handy, I think. Humans are much nicer to other humans who have money.'

Savannah put the wad of bills back in the pocket, and opened Finn's passport. 'Aeneas Finbarr O'Hara,' she read. 'I always found it hard to believe his first name was Aeneas.'

'He has another name?' said Tansy eagerly. 'Then that solves the only problem. The people in the Royal Suite might be suspicious if they heard there was a Finn O'Hara on board, but an Aeneas will fool them. They're not very smart.'

'It's worth thinking about, I suppose,' said Savannah. 'Only passing for a man mightn't be that easy. What would I wear?'

'Finn has very nice new clothes,' Tansy pointed out proudly. 'They would be big for you, of course, but you could adjust them. You could explain that you were an artist, so nobody would be surprised if you look a little unusual. I don't think he made any table reservation though, so you'd have to do something about that. He hasn't made a deck chair reservation either,' she added, going through a mental checklist of shipboard priorities.

Savannah tried on one of Finn's new lounge suits, and wet and combed back her short hair.

'I'll need a sewing kit and an iron,' she told Tansy. 'Do you think you could get them?'

Tansy went out and a few minutes later, a stewardess came in and wordlessly deposited a sewing basket and an iron on the table. Tansy stayed inside the stewardess until the woman was settled at her station again, and then she came back to find Savannah making darts, tucks and hems in Finn's clothes with great speed and ability.

'You're very good at that,' Tansy said admiringly.

'I haven't been able to afford new clothes since I've been in Paris,' Savannah explained. 'I've become pretty good at altering other people's castaways.'

When she was finished, the suit looked as if it had been made for this slim and delicate-looking young man, but his shoes were much too big. None of them could think what to do about this until Cornelia remembered that all of Mr Durham's shoes were still in his wardrobe; and as luck would have it, Mr Durham had very small feet and a large selection of shoes and socks, so this problem was solved most satisfactorily.

Savannah topped off her outfit with Finn's new steamer cap, but seemed dissatisfied with the effect. 'He has a fedora as well,' Tansy said, 'but I don't think—'

'Perfect', said Savannah, who re-shaped the brim and crown of the fedora as best she could with such steam as was produced by a hot iron on very wet towels. 'And yes, I know it's not the thing for wearing on a liner,' she said soothingly to Tansy, 'but remember Aeneas is an artist, and nothing shouts "artist" to the world in general as much as a big, floppy hat.

'Maybe I could also use one of Mr Durham's ties,' she said, loosening the one she had just knotted. 'The ties you picked for Finn are all in such good taste, and this get-up might benefit from something a bit showier. Well, what do you think?' she asked laughing, as she sat down for a moment, and crossed one leg over the other. 'They're not going to think I'm a stowaway in this posey outfit, are they?'

'I think we ought to go for a walk now,' Tansy suggested, the fairy having her own ideas about how to add to Savannah's credibility. 'If we walk five times around the promenade deck, that's a mile,' she added informatively. 'And they may still be serving tea in the main lounge.'

Savannah's appearance was so unusual that a lot of eyes did follow her as she walked around the deck, but she carried herself with such assurance that the curiosity she excited was not critical. Everyone wanted to know who was this slender young man with such a delicate complexion and such a very odd hat.

Tansy, meanwhile, was studying the human faces they were passing, trying to find one of the celebrities whose names she had seen on the passenger list. It was on their second turn around the promenade deck that she had her first sighting of one, and she shot inside him immediately. Everyone nearby then turned to look as Charlie Chaplin jumped up from his deck chair to throw his arms around this object of general curiosity.

'Aeneas!' he exclaimed. 'It's so good to see you again. I booked on this ship because I heard you were sailing on it. We'll meet later and we'll discuss the portrait I commissioned.'

'I'll look forward to that,' said the startled Savannah. 'It's good to see you again too.'

Tansy stayed inside Charlie Chaplain until he was settled in his deck chair again and had a chance to answer the questions of the people sitting to either side of him about who that very unusually dressed young man was.

'Oh, that's the great Aeneas,' said Charlie Chaplin. 'But I shouldn't be telling you that really. He's an important painter, but a total recluse. In fact, I'll have to drop him a note now to reassure him that I won't say another word to him in public for the rest of the trip. He doesn't like people even to know his last name.'

'I see,' said the woman on his right. 'Of course, with that hat, I knew he had to be something in the artistic line, only I thought he might be a dancer. He has a particularly graceful walk for a man, doesn't he?'

From the Promenade Deck they went to the great lounge, where tea still was being served and a tea dance was in progress. As Savannah made her way towards an empty table, Tansy could hardly believe her luck when she spotted a deeply tanned, elegant woman in a long cardigan and a pleated skirt, and she shot inside her without hesitation. Then Coco Chanel leapt to her feet as enthusiastically as Charlie Chaplin had done and hugged and kissed Savannah.

'Aeneas, my dear, forgive me for speaking to you, but it's been so long. Of course I won't disturb you again during the crossing, but you must promise to call to see me when we're both back in Paris. If you'd just run your eye over my next season's collection, I can't tell you how grateful I'd be.'

'Oh, yes, of course,' Savannah replied, looking in real awe at the famous dress designer.

Again, Tansy stayed inside Coco Chanel for several minutes after she rejoined her companions. 'But you never allow yourself to be influenced by anyone,' the startled woman sitting next to the designer said. 'Who is that man?'

'Oh, that's Aeneas. But for heaven's sake, don't tell anyone that you saw me talking to him. He's obsessive about his privacy and it was a bit gauche of me, but I couldn't resist when I saw him.'

'Is that a new style in men's jackets he's wearing?' the same woman asked curiously. 'It's quite different, isn't it? Less padded than usual at the shoulders and very tight at the waist? I don't know if it would suit everyone, but it looks good on him. Isn't he lucky he can stay that slim when he likes his food so much?'

In fact, Savannah was famished, and was grateful that Tansy did not see another celebrity until she had finished her tea. She kept beckoning back the waiter for second and third helpings of sandwiches, scones and pastries (a large number of which, Cornelia noted with interest, disappeared discreetly into Tansy); and by the time she finally felt full enough to say 'no thank you' to a replenished tray of pastries offered, the waiter had concluded that this polite but odd young man had the biggest appetite he'd ever come across. As Savannah was about to rise from the table, an elderly man with a beard then stopped for a moment, bowed politely, and said, 'It's very nice to see you again, Aeneas.'

'It's very nice to see you again, too,' Savannah answered, wondering who this person was.

'Good afternoon, Dr Freud,' said the waiter with the pastries, and then Sigmund Freud bowed politely again and continued on his way.

By the time Savannah left the lounge, everyone on the ship wanted to make the acquaintance of the great and mysterious Aeneas, and when they returned to the stateroom, Tansy was not at all surprised to find an envelope waiting for them. It was an invitation to Mr Aeneas O'Hara to sit at the Captain's Table. Savannah read it and hooted with laughter, and Tansy just looked smug.

'Now you don't have to worry at all about being thrown in the brig,' the fairy told her. 'Isn't it lucky that I learned so much about humans at the Silver Poodle Club?'

—*Chapter 40*—

The Telegrams

SAVANNAH SENT A POLITE REPLY to the invitation to sit at the Captain's table. She thanked the Captain for the honour, but explained that Aeneas had been advised that he needed rest and solitude, and would be forced to take his meals in his stateroom.

Savannah hardly slept at all that night, and when she did drop off briefly, she had a nightmare of being stuffed in a coffin by two men in powdered wigs, and she woke in a sweat of terror. Quickly she felt at her face to see if it was still wrapped up in bandages, and was relieved to find that it was not.

Nonetheless, lying there in this strange room and terrified after her nightmare, she didn't trust herself to know what was real or not. The bit about the fairy, for instance. Had she really been rescued and turned into a shipboard celebrity by a fairy? She badly wanted that memory to be real, but how could it be, for heaven's sake?

Then she heard a long, sad sigh, and turned to see Tansy sitting in mid-air in front of a porthole, looking through it unhappily as its curtains blew around her in the breeze caused by her own whirlwind. Savannah blinked a few times, but the vision was still there. After a few seconds, she remembered the letter Cornelia had written, and she reached over quickly and was glad to be reassured that this was no dream; there was certainly a letter on the bedside table, and it felt every bit as real and yet as inexplicable as these very expensive and unfamiliar silk pyjamas she was wearing.

She breathed a sigh of relief as she concluded that, against all the odds, she was indeed sharing the cabin with a fairy, although unfortunately that fairy looked even more worried and frightened than she did herself.

The ship was passing noisily through a small storm, and that made both of them nervous. Savannah remembered wistfully how, when she had made the crossing in the other direction from America to Europe years earlier, she had grown to love the sound of a ship in rough seas: the mixture of great creaking noises that would get louder and louder as the ship rose or fell in the water and then slowly would fade away to nothing before the whole cycle started up again, with always in the background, the constant vibrating hum of the engines.

On that carefree voyage, she'd been in much less grand accommodation, in a tiny stateroom down in third class shared with three others, but with an easy mind focused on nothing except the achievement of a shipboard romance. She might reasonably have worried about how far her scholarship money would go in Paris or if her school French would be understood, but she never did. The only problem that ever kept her awake at night was the snoring of the woman in the bunk below.

Now she was travelling in splendour, but she would

have given anything to be off this ship. After all, she had been smuggled on to it wrapped up like a mummy on the orders of some gangster in America to whom she was to be handed over when they reached New York, and most of those cruel people who had kidnapped her were still free and might easily track her down to this grand stateroom. So every time the ship rolled and creaked, she wondered if the noises were hiding the sound of footsteps and if those dangerous people might burst into her cabin at any moment.

What was really preying on her mind though was Finn and what might happen to him. She herself had a fairy bodyguard after all (listen to that, a fairy bodyguard!—how could any of this be real?) but that bodyguard's primary concern was Finn, and it was unsettling to Savannah that this magical being was so fearful on Finn's behalf that she was reduced to sitting in mid-air and sighing loudly because she could do nothing to help him.

Savannah spent the rest of that long night planning the telegrams they would send the next day. She kept trying to convince herself that the police in Paris would take them seriously, and that they would easily stop a crime when they knew where and when it was to be committed. At the back of her mind, however, she suspected the police would think the telegrams had come from a crazy person and throw them away. Mostly, however, she just thought the night would never end.

When she finally dropped off, she was awakened after what seemed a few minutes by Tansy hissing in her ear:

'You should hide in the bathroom quick, the steward's coming with your breakfast.'

For some reason, the minor indignity of having to run from a steward until she had her disguise in place made Savannah feel a bit less pessimistic—taking action apparently being better for the spirit than lying in bed. The daylight too, made the situation seem less hopeless, and the hearty breakfast also helped.

'I don't know how you persuaded Finn to buy all these glamorous clothes,' she told the gratified Tansy as she polished off her kippers and eggs in bed, now wearing his exotic new dressing gown as well. 'You gave him no choice, I suppose?'

'None at all,' Tansy admitted. 'He was very unreasonable. I think he doesn't even like clothes. You should cut off all the labels, by the way,' she added knowledgeably, 'and try to make everything look like it's been worn once before you reach New York. That's what all the Americans in the Silver Poodle Club do when they've done a lot of shopping in Paris. If you don't, the customs men in New York make you pay a lot of money.'

'Are you a typical fairy?' Savannah asked fascinated. 'In storybooks, Emeraldia fairies are supposed to be creatures of the countryside. Do all of you wear such fashionable clothes, and know about smuggling designer wear through customs, and how to get invited to the Captain's table?'

'We all like clothes,' Tansy answered, 'but I'm not sure about the other things. I think you have to spend time at the Silver Poodle Club to learn things like that, and King Fuchsia and Queen May and I are the only ones who go there.'

'I'm going to give Finn a shock by asking him to bring me there sometime,' Savannah told her. 'I had no idea how lacking I was in worldly knowledge until I met you, and that club obviously is the place to pick some up.'

Immediately after breakfast, Savannah put on again the suit she had altered for herself the day before, and the three of them headed out to find the ship's wireless operator, who was on a break and having tea and biscuits when Aeneas came in on him. Tansy shot inside the operator, and immediately he sent a telegram to the head of the Paris police, warning him that there was to be a serious attack on a man by a gang of apaches on the night of May 21st in the *Place de l'Opéra*, and that it was of international importance that this be prevented.

The operator then sent telegrams to the President of France and the Mayor of Paris and to the administrator of the Paris *Opéra* saying the same things, and then he sent half a dozen telegrams to friends of Savannah, including Claudette.

'Now, who else has influence in Paris that we might wire?' Savannah said thoughtfully.

'Josephine Baker,' Tansy said immediately. 'Everyone at the Silver Poodle Club says that she's the most important person in Paris now.'

So the operator sent a telegram to Josephine Baker as well, and then Tansy, Savannah and Cornelia went to find the ship's photographer. Tansy was wondering would she go into him, but Savannah said she didn't think they'd be able to use his equipment, so Aeneas just had his photograph taken in the normal way, having told the photographer that he needed a passport photo immediately as part of a collage he was working on.

'Savannah's very good at lying too, isn't she?' Cornelia whispered admiringly to Tansy.

They waited impatiently until this was developed, and then Savannah herself replaced the photograph on Finn's passport with this new photograph of herself, as Cornelia and Tansy watched her handiwork admiringly.

'To think I used to be critical of Finn just because he spent so much time around Jules and Josephine,' Savannah said, laughing, 'and I didn't even know then that the two of them were thieves; and now here I am doing things that are serious crimes, and it's not costing me a thought.'

'I think Savannah's really smart,' Cornelia said to Tansy when the passport was finished. 'When we save Finn, I really, really want him to marry Savannah. She'll be able to deal with that old Guild and the Pickenoses and everything, and Soldiers' Fort will always be safe if she's there.'

Tansy then wanted to check inside the Royal Suite, but she was afraid to leave Savannah on her own.

'No, it's all right,' said Savannah reassuringly. 'The ship has a library. I can wait there. None of the gang members I saw has ever been inside a library.'

So Tansy took a chance, leaving Savannah sitting close

to the librarian, and in possession of a very large art book which she instructed her to hold up in front of her face if she heard or saw anything suspicious. Then she herself went as quickly as she could to the Royal Suite, which she entered again through the narrow vent in the door. Once again, they found two men in the vestibule. The footman with the moustache was still there, and now he had the company of a very fat man with a red nose. Both of them were wearing the knee breeches and powdered wigs, and neither of them seemed to care much for the wigs.

'I think there's fleas in them,' one of the men said. 'My head itches all the time since I put it on.'

'Well, the word from the boss is that, if we take them off now, we might as well take our heads off with them. He said it's bad enough Frankie went mad and let the dame go and started slugging everyone in a uniform, but he don't want none of the ship's geezers getting suspicious about the princess, so everything has to be done by the book. Full dress uniform, and don't let no one in that bedroom.'

Tansy hurtled herself towards the bedroom and rocketed into it through the vent; and inside it, they found an older man in a tweed suit, and a woman smoking a cigarette through a long holder who reminded them both of Josephine. They seemed to have stumbled on an argument between these two unfamiliar people. There was a roll of bandage on the bedside table and the woman was looking at it.

'I'll put it on before someone comes in, but I'm not

going to lie here all day with it on,' she said determinedly. 'Mr Omera is not going to know one way or the other unless you tell him, and if you want to go spilling the beans on me, you just remember that there are a few choice things I could tell him myself about the way you've been doing things.'

'Oh come on, Margie,' the man wheedled. 'I'm not telling Mr Omera anything about you, but you know he's going to make big trouble for all of us if the crew smells anything phoney about this princess. You saw Mr Omera's telegram. If you don't think I decoded it right, you do it yourself, and you'll see he's pretty mad. He thinks his whole operation may be at risk now that Frankie's in the brig and that artist broad got away. That's why Mr Omera wants the ship searched from top to bottom for her, and when she's found, he wants her thrown overboard as soon as no one's looking.'

Tansy waited to hear no more, but returned as quickly as she could to Savannah, and brought her back to the stateroom.

'Maybe I should have gone straight to the captain and told him everything as soon as you found me,' Savannah said when Tansy told her what she had heard. 'But I know he wouldn't have believed me. It would seem like a story I'd made up to get away with being a stowaway and I'd probably have ended up in the brig myself.'

'We could write him a letter,' Cornelia suggested.

'That's not a bad idea,' Savannah said thoughtfully, when Tansy reported the suggestion. 'An anonymous letter. After all, one person from the Royal Suite is already in the brig, so the crew may already have suspicions about that bunch. And even if the captain doesn't entirely believe the letter, he still won't be able to ignore the possibility that he has a gang of jewel thieves and would-be murderers on board. We'll tell him the real princess died six months ago. Maybe we'll be lucky and they'll all end up in the brig.

'And in the meantime,' Savannah added, having cheered herself with this line of thought, 'I'm going to ask the steward how I can get hold of painting materials on this ship. I want to do a painting of you in that beautiful dress and those sensational earrings, Tansy, to give as a present to Finn. You wouldn't mind sitting for me, would you?' she asked, and was answered by seeing the look of worry vanish briefly from the fairy's face as Tansy straightened her shoulders, tweaked her bobbed hair, and twirled around a few times to see herself from all sides in the mirror. 'Unless I've caught you on canvas, I suspect I'm going to be doubting for the rest of my life that any of this was real.'

— *Chapter 41* —

Nijinsky's Return

I
F THEY HAD NOT BEEN SO WORRIED about Finn and
fearful of what might be happening to him,
Savannah and Cornelia both would have enjoyed
the rest of the crossing.

Savannah got her painting materials, and spent long,
satisfactory sessions trying to capture the most elusive
and interesting subject who had ever modelled for her.
She was so taken up by the project that she was glad
to be able to give all her time to it and to take quiet,
if enormous, meals in her stateroom, helped in their
consumption by Tansy, who intrigued both Savannah
and Cornelia by the amount of food she could make
quietly disappear, although they never really saw her
eating it.

Savannah did leave the stateroom every afternoon
to go for tea in the great Palladian lounge, and there
she continued to impress the waiters by her capacity
(assisted again by the sweet-toothed Tansy) for more or
less vacuuming up the great trays of pastries offered to
her; and, having altered Finn's new dinner jacket to fit
her, she wandered out every night just before midnight
for a buffet supper.

She took walks on the boat deck and the promenade
deck, and both she and Cornelia enjoyed these, but

Tansy (notwithstanding her excellent appetite) was unhappy all the time, a combination of guilt and fear making her an edgy companion. She was on guard every second during the walks on deck, always expecting one of Mr Omera's men to rise up suddenly from a deck chair or jump out from a lifeboat.

To try to cheer her up, Savannah played an occasional game of shuffleboard, allowing Tansy to control her, and of course, the much-talked-about Aeneas always won those games. She even entered the potato sack race for Tansy's amusement, although this was about the last thing she felt like doing; and Aeneas not only won this race, but afterwards did a lap of victory in his potato sack around the promenade deck, completing the circuit in 23 seconds to thunderous applause.

'Olympic medal winners have run around this deck and taken almost twice as long,' an officer told Savannah admiringly when Aeneas had finished. 'To do it in 23 seconds while hopping in a potato sack is a truly extraordinary achievement. When the captain hears about it, I believe he will want to have a plaque made and hung here on the deck to commemorate it forever.'

This cheered Tansy so much that Savannah agreed to take part in the tug-of-war that was being organised immediately afterwards. As the two sides were choosing teams, neither side much wanted to select this foppish-looking little man with the girlish voice and tightly waisted jacket for its team, however remarkably fast he was at hopping in a potato sack; but of course, the side that ended up with the deceptive Aeneas (he was the last man chosen) won handsomely, pulling the other team not just over the line, but right to the end of the deck, in one effortless jerk of the rope.

Savannah felt most sorry for Tansy when they had to pass other passengers dancing, and this happened very often. It was, after all, 1927, and everywhere on the ship, people were dancing morning, afternoon, and night.

On the decks, portable record players provided music twenty-four hours a day for impromptu dance parties. Inside, musicians played for tea dances in the afternoon, and played again after dinner until the small hours of the morning; and everywhere the rise and fall of the ship seemed to add to the good humour of the dancers, as one moment they struggled to dance uphill and the next moment had to fight to keep their balance as the dance floor fell away in front of them.

Then the ship's newsletter announced that a masquerade competition was to be held, and Savannah saw an opportunity for Tansy to indulge herself in a way that might snap her out of her guilt-induced moroseness.

'How would you feel about dancing yourself tonight, Tansy?' she asked her. 'Dancing as no one has danced before?'

Tansy's eyes lit up at the prospect.

'I was thinking you might give a ballet exhibition?' Savannah continued bravely, her body still feeling the aches of her potato sack triumph. 'Poor Aeneas could enter this masquerade competition—anonymously—as Nijinsky.'

'Who's Nijinsky?' Cornelia asked.

'He did this,' said Tansy eagerly, and she leapt as high in the air as the ceiling would allow and paused in mid-leap.

'That's it exactly,' said Savannah. 'Most people think he was the greatest dancer ever,' she explained for Cornelia's benefit. 'He's retired now, but he was very famous for his great leaps, and especially because he appeared to be able to stop in mid-air.'

Keeping in the spirit, Tansy back-flipped exuberantly around the room, pausing in the middle of each flip. 'Have you been to many ballets?' Savannah asked her, interested.

'Oh, yes. Not so much in Emeraldia, of course, because the Emeraldia Ballet Company is not very good; but the Russian Ballet has visited Emeraldia twice, and every fairy in Emeraldia went to see them. They were very good.'

'And I will be safe if you do the choreography, will I?' Savannah asked. 'I don't think Nijinsky did back flips. Just leaps. And remember you'll be inside a body that's already a bit worn out from setting a record hopping around the deck, so make sure it lands gently, won't you? And I'd say just to circle the lounge once would be enough of a performance. Twice would be the absolute maximum.'

Savannah sacrificed a pair of Finn's silk pyjamas to make up a copy of the costume Nijinsky had worn in *The Faun*, using ink to draw the pattern on it. She made painted ear tips of *papier maché* and got toupee glue from the barber to fix these in position, and darkened her eyes and painted her lips dramatically with make-up borrowed (with Tansy's help) from the ship's beautician. When she was finished, Tansy and Cornelia agreed that it was a wonderful disguise and that no one at all would recognise her in it.

The lounge was full for the masquerade competition, and Tansy, seeing how many spectators there were, could hardly contain herself to wait her turn. When finally Nijinksy was announced, neither she nor the large audience was disappointed.

The dancer in the painted silk pyjamas and *papier maché* ears leapt around the floor as no human ever had leapt before, pausing one, two, three, four, even five seconds in mid-leap. Savannah wanted to tell the fairy she was overdoing it a bit, but she did not have the heart because she could tell that Tansy, while she was dancing, had nothing else on her mind—no guilt, no fear, no Mr Omera, no worries about the future of the fairies, nor even about Finn or Cornelia.

The audience could not have been more appreciative. Even before Nijinsky had completed a single circuit of the room, all of the passengers were on their feet clapping. A few wondered if wires could be involved, but even as they spoke, they could see that this was impossible and that there could be no wires. A few even wondered if it could be the great dancer himself who had recovered his health and was performing again better than ever.

As Savannah had expected, Tansy did a second triumphal circuit to the loudest cheering Savannah ever had heard, and then, following instructions, made a formal bow and exited the lounge immediately, not even waiting for the announcement that the anonymous entrant, 'Nijinsky', had won first prize.

As Savannah had hoped, the experience did cheer up Tansy and she was less on edge for the rest of the crossing. It was only when the ship reached New York and they had got through the last challenge of passport

GALWAY COUNTY LIBRARIES

control and were standing in the Customs hall under the letter 'O' waiting for Finn's suitcases to be unloaded from the boat, that her fierce mood returned. What provoked her was the sight of a group of beefy men looking at them.

'They're just longshoremen. They're here to move luggage,' Savannah whispered, afraid Tansy's nervousness might cause her to throw the whole lot of them into the water.

Still, as they waited in that noisy, crowded, bustling hall, all three of them became very jumpy. Strangers were coming and going in every direction, and sometimes brushing against them; and apart from worrying about their own safety, now that they were off the boat, Savannah, Tansy and Cornelia all were more conscious of the size of the ocean that separated them from Finn, and of the immediate and certain danger that faced him, about which they could do nothing whatever.

They were confused about where they should go and what their plan of action should be, they were terrified for Finn, and they were entirely helpless; and by the time the customs man had finished looking through Finn's suitcases and drawn a chalk mark on them, it was hard to say which of the three of them was in the greatest state of panic and bewilderment about what they were going to do next.

—Chapter 42—

Elder

BOTH BARRY AND HIS PARENTS now were spending nearly all their time in Cornelia's room, his parents rarely taking their eyes off Cornelia, and Barry rarely taking his eyes off Josephine, hoping against hope that he would see the magic quiver that would mean this awful interlude was at an end.

Barry was having a very uncomfortable time. He was not greatly worried about the length of time Cornelia was missing because he had known where she was going and how long she would be away, but he was getting very worried about his parents' reactions to her condition. His mother, he noticed, had packed two suitcases full of Cornelia's things, so that she could be moved, if necessary, at a moment's notice.

He was worried too about Puffy Pickenose and Pompeous Potty-Pickenose XIII, who were becoming more and more troublesome.

Most of all, however, he was worried that he might not be playing his own part well enough.

Just as they had promised, May and Fuchsia came regularly to take Barry's spirit out of him and put it into Cornelia. Physically, this kept Cornelia in good health, but its effect on everyone else was traumatic. Her parents were bewildered that, in those magical moments when she opened her eyes and talked and walked around the room and wanted to eat, she just did not sound like herself any more. 'She almost sounds like Barry,' his mother said worriedly. 'She didn't even call me Mommy. She called me Mom.'

Even worse for his mother, when she tried to discuss this with Barry at the time she first noticed it, she couldn't do so because he had fallen into the same frightening condition as Cornelia: that horrible deep, untouchable sleep.

So Barry tried hard to remember what Cornelia sounded like, but Barry had always thought Cornelia just sounded like Cornelia. He knew she talked a lot, but he'd never paid any attention to the particular words she used. Now, he wished he had, and he became so worried about saying the wrong thing that, when he was inside Cornelia, he said hardly anything at all, and this worried his mother even more.

'She must be feeling terrible to have gone so silent,' she said unhappily. 'Even when she had that awful sickness when she was three, she talked all the time.'

May and Fuchsia and Primrose were having a hard time too. They had set up a rigid schedule for themselves, going into the house three times a day to take Barry's spirit out of his body and put it into Cornelia's; and for beings who had no understanding of time and whose living accommodation was shared with countless very curious fairies, trying to keep to this schedule was an exhausting undertaking.

For the first time in their ancient existence, May

and Fuchsia became conscious of the sun as a clock and a taskmaster, rather than just a source of pleasure, although they depended on the brainy Primrose to guide them through this mysterious state of affairs.

'Humans can't see in the dark,' Primrose explained, 'and I think that's why they have this thing they call a day. The world looks very different to humans depending on whether the sun is visible or not, and for the most part, humans sleep at times when the sun is out of sight, and they eat and work at times when it's visible. Some animals do that too, although a lot of them do the opposite.

'Now I've researched the subject, and it's usual for humans to eat something while the sun is visible in that part of the sky,' she said pointing east, 'and then again when it's in the centre part of the sky, and then again,' she added pointing west, 'just after it disappears in that direction. I know that you two are far too busy to be trying to see where the sun is all the time, so I'm going to keep an eye on it for you, and I'll call you when you're needed. I'll be above ground anyway keeping guard on the house.

'And speaking of keeping guard,' she added seriously, 'I have a proposal to make, and you can see what you think about it. This is a delicate matter and you may think what I'm proposing is too big a risk, but I'm going to put it to you anyway. I'm going to suggest that you take one more fairy into your confidence.'

'Oh, I don't know, Primrose—' Fuchsia began.

'Well, let me just explain,' Primrose insisted, in the

soft but attention-commanding voice by which she used to ensure that no fairy ever spoke loudly twice in her greatly missed library.

'You see, now that the two of you are going in and out of that house so often, I'm worried there's more and more chance that you'll be noticed, and I've been thinking that we might have a better chance of keeping the project secret if someone were posted permanently at that house who would discourage any fairy from looking at it at all.'

'But who?' Fuchsia asked worriedly, not able offhand to think of any fairy, other than Primrose, who was entirely discreet and able to control the love of gossip that was part of fairy nature. 'Do you have someone in mind?'

'Elder,' she replied.

'Ah,' said May.

'Yes, I see what you mean,' said Fuchsia.

Elder was a most unusual fairy. Almost all fairies have lively personalities and a love of chat. Not Elder, however. Elder communicated in grunts mostly, reserving words for when he wanted a particular item of food or drink, and then using only the name of the item he wanted, never bothering to add a please or thank you to it.

When the crowding in the forts became so severe that the fairies had to give up their own bedrooms and sleep in dormitories in great tiers of bunks, Elder was the only non-royal fairy, apart from Tansy, who was allowed keep a room to himself. Tansy was allowed to keep a room out of compassion. Elder was allowed to keep a room because no other fairy wanted to share a room with him. As well as being uncommunicative, he also was stubborn, a very rare trait in fairies whose temperaments usually were excitable and light-hearted.

'I believe that keeping silent about a subject will not tax Elder at all,' said Primrose. 'And although he is not a fairy whose company anyone seeks, he is a loyal subject to both of you, and if you ask him to keep a secret, he'll find it much easier to do so than not.

'Between the three of us,' she continued in a confidential whisper, 'we know that all the other fairies in the fort cannot stop themselves dropping hints and tantalising little clues whenever they have the smallest titbit of interesting information that no other fairy has, but the last thing Elder would want is put himself in a situation in which other fairies are asking him questions.'

'And of course, if Elder locates himself at the house all the time, no other fairy will want to go near it,' May added. 'That's what you're really thinking, isn't it Primrose? Fuchsia, haven't I always said that Primrose is the cleverest fairy in Emeraldia?'

'Very good thinking, Primrose,' agreed Fuchsia. And what you say about his loyalty is perfectly true. We can depend on him for anything except small talk, and there is no doubt we will be much safer in having a fairy on duty up at that house all the time in case some emergency arises. Excellent thinking, Primrose. Excellent thinking.'

Without wasting any time, Fuchsia sought out Elder in order to brief him. Fuchsia had wanted May to brief him, but May insisted Fuchsia do it.

'No, really, Darling, I just couldn't,' May insisted, when Fuchsia was saying that he had an important meeting scheduled with King Thistle and that she was so much better at those things anyway. 'I've never been able to hold a conversation with Elder. You know that. And I have tried. No, Darling, you'll just have to take care of this one.'

The briefing took some time. That was just the way Elder was. When he got an idea into his head, it stayed there forever and could not be dislodged, but getting it in there in the first place was always hard work. First of all, Fuchsia made clear to him that everything he was being told was to remain a secret forever. Elder had no problem about this. 'I'm no gabber,' he reminded Fuchsia needlessly.

Then Fuchsia told him that what he and May and Tansy were doing in that house was very important and might save the fairies, but it was of the greatest importance that no other fairy, except Primrose, find out that they were doing anything there at all. Also, the humans and their possessions in that house were to be protected at all costs. The Pickenoses should not be allowed to disturb or break anything in the house or to take anything out of it; and on no account should they be allowed to intimidate the family into leaving it.

Fuchsia suspected that Elder might be short of ideas of his own about how to deal with an emergency if it arose, so he described what happened in the kitchen the day that Puffy had tried to grab the human child's doll, and how Queen May had thought quickly of going inside Puffy's dog and having the dog attach himself to Puffy.

It took a few moments for the details of this story to sink into Elder's brain and then slowly, to Fuchsia's astonishment, he began to laugh. Fuchsia had never heard Elder laugh before. And then there was a second first. 'You can count on me, King,' said Elder, using six words at the one time.

Elder always had been a one-word-at-a-time fairy—three-words-at-a-time at most—and Fuchsia was duly impressed to hear him come out with a sentence of this length, and impressed again to hear him come out with a second: 'I'll go up there right now.'

May was even more surprised when Fuchsia reported this to her. 'That's interesting,' she said. 'It's interesting how a fairy can change just by getting responsibility. It's been very noticeable with Tansy. Primrose and I both have noticed how she's become a much happier and more confident creature because of the job we've given her. Maybe the same thing will happen to Elder. Maybe this experience will give him a whole new purpose in life.'

—Chapter 43—

The Wearers of Horse-Bottom Wigs

ELDER'S services were called on sooner than anyone expected. This was because Puffy Pickenose and Pompeous Potty-Pickenose XIII were feeling frustrated. Both of them were used to getting their way quickly, but this was not happening in their dealings with Cornelia's family.

They had expected the O'Haras to be gone by this. They had served a notice that allowed the family three months before they had to leave, but both Puffy and Pompeous had been certain the O'Haras would go much sooner than that, especially when they had taken over the family's front field and brought in a lot of men to make very noisy and visible preparations for the factory that was to be built there.

When those men refused to return to that particular field after being driven away by horseflies every day for a week, and then finding that they had become infested with fleas as well, Puffy and Pompeous became irritable.

They hated the O'Haras a lot because they were the only people in a long time who had been able to cause them any trouble. With all the other families whose properties they had taken away, there had been a short period of outraged, vocal, but entirely futile resistance, and then they were gone. Pompeous never had to stare down any of those unimportant people twice.

Now Pompeous and Puffy had run out of patience entirely with the O'Haras. They did not see why they should have to be annoyed by them anymore, and they wanted them gone immediately. So Puffy had made an application to the Emeraldia Courts, asking her uncle, Judge Prosy Pickenose for a document to serve on the O'Haras, ordering them to vacate the property Fairy's Leap in 48 hours.

Puffy had to wait longer than she would have liked to get this Order, because she had irritated the Emeraldia judges lately for reasons that would have given Tansy a good deal of pleasure if only she had known. These reasons were the Laughter Spell and the Feasting Spell that Tansy had put on Puffy at the same time as she had put on the Beauty Spell, and which May had surmised (when she advised Tansy to lift only the Beauty Spell) might be causing trouble for Puffy in ways that none of them knew about.

In fact, they were causing Puffy great problems. As a member of the Wearers of Horse-Bottom-Wigs Society (the full name of which was the Wearers of Horse-Bottom-Wigs, Diners, and Snuff-Takers Society) Puffy had a great many responsibilities and duties, including— most importantly—attendance at The Dinners.

All the judges and talking lawyers were obliged to attend The Dinners, even the retired ones; and indeed, because the retired Horse-Bottom-Wig Wearers had been to more Dinners than the practising Horse-

Bottom-Wig Wearers, they had a position of particular eminence at these Dinners, and had been bestowed with the august title of Belchers. It was obligatory for more junior talking lawyers, who had been to fewer Dinners, to bow to The Belchers.

Unfortunately for Puffy, however, Tansy's Feasting Spell meant that she could no longer eat in company, but could only eat alone; and her inability to eat at these important Dinners meant that she was in real danger of being struck out of the profession altogether and no longer even being allowed to wear a Horse-Bottom-Wig. (In fact, if her name weren't Pickenose, this would already have happened, the other disgruntled Horse-Bottom-Wig Wearers muttered among themselves.)

To make matters worse, Tansy's Laughter Spell meant that Puffy could not laugh (although she could still emit her loud guffaw, which, being unconnected to mirth, was not affected by the Spell). This did not bother her at all in her personal life, but that Laughter Spell was proving to be a real problem in her work.

When a judge made a joke, however unfunny, it was taken for granted that all the wig-wearing lawyers, of which Puffy was one, would laugh.

Puffy, however, was not able to do this now; and as a consequence, even her father, Judge Punitive Pickenose and her brother, Judge Prat Pickenose, were finding her annoying when she appeared in front of them, particularly as she tried to compensate for her inability to laugh with more frequent explosive guffaws that made everyone turn to look at Puffy, even at times when a judge might be in mid-oratorical flourish and the rightful object of every eye in the court.

At least her uncle, Judge Prosy Pickenose, was so fond of listening to the sound of his own voice that he was hardly aware of what anyone else in the room was doing, so he was the only judge that Puffy dared to appear in front of now, and she had to wait for a day when he was sitting to ask for the Order against the O'Haras, and she also had to make sure that her muscular cousin, Parmesan Pickenose, who was Chief Enforcer of the Lawful Guild, would be sitting in the room just behind the judge that day and able to speak into the judge's hidden earpiece.

Parmesan Pickenose did this in any court case which affected the Lawful Guild, because the Guild knew that to keep control of Emeraldia, it needed to have complete control over the judges and the Courts, and it was Parmesan's job to make sure it kept this control and that no judge ever thought about stepping out of line.

(Although, it should be pointed out that Parmesan was not her cousin's real name. His correct name was Pusillanimous; but because he had been controlling all the decisions in the Courts for a while, people first started calling him The Big Cheese; and from this had grown the nickname Parmesan; and eventually, no one even remembered that he had any other name.)

The O'Hara case, being small and unimportant, would not, in the usual course of events, have got Parmesan's personal attention, but he could never refuse anything to his lively cousin, Pruella; and Parmesan's personal attendance at the other end of the earpiece would ensure that Judge Prosy did everything that Puffy wanted.

The judge did talk for an hour or two first, of course, because Prosy Pickenose just could not stop himself talking; but as he spent all this time saying insulting things about Cornelia's family, neither Puffy not Pompeous minded the wait at all, and indeed Pompeous enjoyed the judge's words so much that he laughed until he couldn't catch his breath, and the Lawful Guild member sitting next to him even felt it necessary to give him a slap on the back so that he would start breathing again.

'I must commend you for the extreme patience you've shown to the O'Haras,' the judge said indulgently to Puffy, 'but you've probably learned from this experience that you just cannot help some people. They have no other purpose in life except to waste the valuable time of busy people like you and me with a lot of foolish nonsense, and they never listen.'

He went on to describe the O'Haras as criminals and liars and schemers and subversives, and at the point at which he said loudly, 'such people are a burden on any State,' his fingers twitched wistfully at the black handkerchief for putting over his head that he was not allowed to use yet (not until the new Constitution drafted by the Guild came into force the following year, at which time he would at long last be able to deal with enemies of the Guild, such as the O'Haras, in the only way that was truly satisfactory).

As his mind drifted to those wonderful days ahead,

he lost the direction of his speech for a moment until a loud guffaw from dear niece Pruella and an impatient whisper from Parmesan to 'hurry up, I want to go to lunch,' recalled him to the task in hand, and then he made the Order that the O'Haras were to be gone from the property Fairy's Leap in 48 hours.

Pompeous and Puffy came to serve this dreaded Notice on Cornelia's parents only minutes after Elder took up his guard position under Cornelia's window. Usually, they did not do such jobs personally, it being more common for them to use the services of their detective cousin, the multi-scarred Miss Peeping Pickenose, who liked to look through windows and who—under the guise of serving Notices and Summonses—had been given the privilege of peeping into the bedrooms and other private spaces of every enemy of the Lawful Guild in Emeraldia.

Unfortunately for Miss Peeping Picknose, however, in the course of her much-enjoyed work, she had lost the asset—useful to every detective—of being inconspicuous, as Peeping had so often been pushed off ladders by outraged householders who had discovered her looking in on their upstairs bedrooms that gradually she had taken on the appearance of a legendary pirate, having lost her right eye (the socket of which was now covered by a black eye patch) and part of her right ear, and having gained a large bump on her left shoulder that bore an uncanny resemblance to a small, ugly parrot.

The O'Hara case was special, however, so Puffy and Pompeous disappointed Peeping by insisting on serving this Notice themselves, and they brought with them two unsmiling, bulky men carrying large measuring tapes and clipboards. Walter the dog, as always, was staying as close as he could to Puffy, keeping his ugly, hairless face resolutely between her legs as she walked, although on this visit, he was wearing the muzzle with which he had recently been fitted.

'We're here to survey the house,' Puffy had announced,

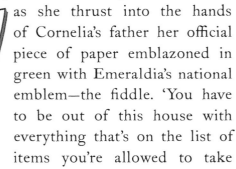

as she thrust into the hands of Cornelia's father her official piece of paper emblazoned in green with Emeraldia's national emblem—the fiddle. 'You have to be out of this house with everything that's on the list of items you're allowed to take with you in 48 hours. We'll be coming back then with the sheriff to make sure you're gone.

'If you're still here, any items remaining in the house will be appropriated, and you'll be fined €10,000 a day. Meanwhile, these men are here to measure all the rooms and to catalogue the fireplaces and the other fittings that we'll be taking out, and if you cause them any delay or interfere with them at all, you'll be charged for their time.'

'You can't do this,' Cornelia's father said, but without the conviction that he would have had even a week or two earlier. The truth was that he knew now these two could do whatever they wanted. 'We have two sick children in this house, and no one can go into their rooms.'

As soon as he said this, his wife wished he hadn't. Pompeous just stared at him; but Puffy's mouth moved in the way Cornelia's mother dreaded. She was reminded of the way the dogs salivated at the sound or smell of food being prepared: Puffy seemed to salivate in the same way at the prospect of a new act of cruelty.

'We'll start in the children's bedrooms,' she said to the two bulky men, both of whom looked a bit uncomfortable at this order. 'The girl's bedroom first.'

Elder was listening to all of this, his slow brain doing its best to process what he was hearing, and he tried hard to think of what he should do. He didn't like those two Pickenose humans with the tiny black souls, but he didn't know what to do about them just yet. His instructions were to protect the family who lived in the house (and their possessions) at all costs, but he was not certain at what point he'd be expected to intervene.

Did pushing a piece of paper into the hands of the human man who lived in the house count, or should he just keep watching until they tried to harm the people, or at least to take away some possession of theirs? He wished King Fuchsia were here now to give him more specific instructions.

For the moment, he decided he'd better just keep watch, and he followed the six humans up the stairs, the two tired-looking humans who lived there, and the four others, including that female human who seemed to have no soul at all and who was followed closely by that strange animal that was trying to walk between her legs. Elder noted regretfully that this ugly animal had a piece of leather tied around its mouth, so he wouldn't be able to do the same thing as Queen May had done, but he'd have to think of something else he could do, so he would.

Cornelia's mother rushed ahead of them into her daughter's bedroom, finding it hard to believe that all of this was real. What was happening now was worse than any nightmare she'd ever had in her life. She sat on the edge of the bed with Barry, so that the two of them formed a barrier between Cornelia and the rest of the room; and behind them, Freddy and Tickles had positioned themselves protectively over Cornelia, both of them growling and with their teeth bared.

Typically, this caused Puffy to direct all her attention to that bed, and for the second time, her eye landed on the doll, Josephine.

Although Puffy was no longer under the power of the Beauty Spell, she did remember that the family had got very worried and excited when she tried to take this doll before, so she just could not stop herself reaching out to take it again.

Curiously, Puffy did not remember what the consequence for herself had been the last time she had tried to take Josephine from Cornelia. In Puffy's mind, events got re-written in accordance with the way she wished they had turned out, so she remembered herself always as coming out the winner from every encounter. It was one reason why Puffy was such a formidable enemy. She never took fright when she lost and therefore feared she might lose again, because she remembered herself every time as having won. What others might have viewed at the time as a great personal rout, she remembered in her own mind as a great personal victory.

The only reason she had put a muzzle on Walter, she told Pompeous (and as she told this lie, she herself actually believed it) was to make sure that he wouldn't bite the two men who were accompanying them because he was so protective of her. As she reached for the doll, she looked at him approvingly as he put his two front paws up on the bed and snarled at Tickles and Freddy.

Barry got a terrible fright when he saw that Puffy was trying to take Josephine again, and decided immediately that he would risk going over to the window to shout for a fairy to come and help them. In case one came, he decided to provide a weapon, and he reached down heroically to unfasten Walter's muzzle, as revolted by the prospect of having to touch this unnatural dog as he was frightened of being bitten. In fact, he certainly would have been bitten if Freddy had not seen the danger and lunged pre-emptively at Walter's neck, drawing his fire just long enough for Barry to get the clasp undone.

Barry's timing could not have been better. Elder, observing the dog's jaw being freed, was in position to go into Walter immediately, which he did with a great sense of relief because he was having no luck at thinking up an alternative plan of his own; so before anyone knew what was happening, once again Walter had sunk his long yellow teeth into Puffy's bottom.

—Chapter 44—

Job Satisfaction

PUFFY SCREAMED and tried to knock Walter away, and the two bulky men tried to help her. Once again, Pompeous threw back his head and laughed loudly; and once again, Cornelia's parents could only stare at this scene, flabbergasted. The truth is that, no matter how many times one has seen a dog jump up and sink its long yellow teeth into its owner's bottom and keep them there, the spectacle never ceases to be very surprising.

Elder had been so preoccupied when he first came into the bedroom, and then was enjoying himself so much once he was inside Walter, that he had not even noticed that there was another fairy in the bedroom: Primrose, who had come in and perched on top of the wardrobe as soon as she saw these horrible humans enter the house.

Primrose had been observing the Pickenoses, and struggling fiercely with herself about what she should do next. She knew she could take just one action that would be effective, but she found the idea of it unnatural and repellent, and she hesitated.

When she saw what Elder had done, however, and saw the very amusing situation he had created, she decided to overcome her own feelings of revulsion, and play her part as well in dealing with these odious humans. It was unnatural and disgusting, but just this once, she would do it: she would force herself to go inside a human, specifically that horrible laughing lunatic Pompeous.

She cringed as she went into him, and for the first few moments, she could do nothing more than shudder at the disgusting situation in which she found herself. 'Oh, pull yourself together, Fairy,' she told herself resolutely over and over until she had recovered her composure enough to start controlling this human creature.

Pompeous continued to laugh, loudly and maniacally, but as he was doing so, Primrose caused him to take hold of the two heavy-muscled men who were trying to pull Walter away from Puffy, and to knock their heads together twice. Those two hefty men responded as quickly and effectively as Primrose could have wished, one of them hitting Pompeous in the stomach so hard that his false teeth fell out on the floor, and the other hitting him in the jaw. 'You're even crazier than everyone says,' one of the men said.

'We're sorry about this ma'am,' the other man said to Cornelia's mother, as the two of them prepared to leave the house. 'But you know how it is these days. If you don't work for the Pickenoses, you don't work.'

Puffy ran from the bedroom then, Walter hanging from her bottom, and Pompeous followed behind, now bent over double, holding his stomach with one hand and his false teeth with the other.

'Sometimes I think I dream the things that happen when Puffy comes into the house,' Cornelia's mother said.

'This Notice means business, though,' said Cornelia's father, looking grimly at the piece of paper in his hand with the green fiddle at the top of it. 'You know, I hate to say it Katie,' he said, in a voice so emotionless and dead that it sounded as if another person were speaking, 'but this really is it. There isn't a thing in the world we can do now except get the kids away to where the Lawful Guild and the Picknoses and the Courts can't do them any more harm. As you said yourself, at least we'll be able to get the two of them to a doctor once we're out of Emeraldia.'

Primrose listened to every word these humans were saying, feeling sorry for them, but worrying even more about Fuchsia and May, and whether it might have fatal consequences for the scheme—whatever it might be— that they were trying to put into effect if these humans suddenly went away.

Elder, on the other hand, was oblivious of the scene he had left behind, and had settled in with great satisfaction to the job he was performing. When May had gone inside Walter, she had stayed only as long as she had to, but then May did not possess Elder's stubborn temperament. The harder Puffy tried to get Walter off her, the more firmly Elder clung on. He saw no reason to do anything different. This job suited him.

The only vet left in Emeraldia, Dr Pawson Pickenose, came to see Walter after a few hours, and injected him with a tranquilizer to make him sleep. The dog's body went limp, but to his astonishment, Walter's teeth stayed as firmly embedded as ever in Puffy.

'I can see no other course except to put the dog to sleep permanently and then you can have a surgeon remove his teeth from you,' the vet said.

Sadly, Elder knew that he could not let matters come to this. Fairies did not kill other creatures or cause them to be killed, so he decided to leave Walter then, and for a few seconds, Puffy was in the happy situation of having no dog attached to her bottom.

Dr Pawson Pickenose, however, was the proud owner of a pack of hounds, and one or two of these beasts accompanied him everywhere. On this occasion, he had brought his prize hound, Dermot, with him; and it seemed to Elder that Dermot could serve his purpose just as well as Walter had done. So Elder went into Dermot and then Dermot leaped up from the floor mat on which he had been dozing and sank his gold-medal-winning teeth into Puffy's bottom.

Puffy screamed more loudly than she had ever done, and Dr Pawson Pickenose now had a problem. It would not have bothered him much to put down that unnatural creature, Walter, but nothing in the world would make him put down Dermot.

'Do something!' Puffy screamed.

Unwillingly, Dr Pawson Pickenose injected his prize hound with a tranquilizer drug, but the effect of this drug on Dermot was the same as it had been on Walter.

The dog went limp everywhere except for his jaw, which stayed firmly attached to Puffy.

'Do something else!' Puffy screamed again.

Dr Pawson Pickenose scratched his head. 'Well, I don't know,' he said reluctantly. 'Look at it this way. A dog is bound to get tired eventually in that position. Maybe you should just ignore him until he lets go.'

'Ignore him?' Puffy screamed indignantly. 'How do I ignore a dog whose teeth are stuck in my bottom?'

'Well, make sure you don't harm him,' the vet said, looking worriedly at his prize dog. 'Dermot's a valuable animal.'

Elder settled in to stay with this job forever, if need be. He remembered, of course, that he had a second job as well, that of guarding the family's house, but a fairy could be in only one place at a time, after all; and if a fairy were given two jobs, any sensible fairy would stick to the job he could do best. And Elder was very good at this job. He had no doubt at all about that.

So it was only Primrose who looked on mournfully as Cornelia's father started to load box after box into a farm trailer and a horsebox. He telephoned a moving company to remove the family's large furniture, but all the moving firms were so busy now because of the great number of families that needed to leave the country in a hurry that none of them could promise to have a truck at the property until the last hour before the 48-hour deadline was up.

Up in Cornelia's bedroom, Barry tucked Josephine

under his sister's arm and he himself held on to Jules. Even if the worst happened, and the family was forced to leave the house, the most important thing, he decided, was that the dolls and Cornelia should be together. He made up his mind that he was not going to let himself sleep for one minute until his sister came back. He settled down with Freddy and Tickles at the foot of her bed for the unhappiest and most frightening vigil of his life.

—*Chapter 45*—

The Stowaways

ORNELIA, SAVANNAH AND TANSY were looking back at the great steel side of the docked *Aquitania* a bit wistfully when suddenly Cornelia saw something that made them all feel much better.

'Look, Tansy,' she said, pointing at the third-class gangplank. 'Isn't that Frankie—the footman you had put in the brig?'

As the three of them watched, two police officers led Frankie (who had discarded his wig although he was still dressed in the same velvet knee breeches) down a gangplank and put him into a large police van. A few seconds later, a dozen more policemen came out of the ship, bringing with them in handcuffs the rest of Savannah's kidnappers: the three other men and the woman called Margie who had been occupying the Royal Suite.

'There's the Master-at-Arms,' said Tansy, pointing to a uniformed man with a bruised face, who was overseeing this arrest with a big smile.

Savannah, too, could not stop herself smiling broadly as the entire gang was shoved into the van; but as it was driving off, her attention was caught by a young boy who was coming through the Customs Hall selling newspapers, and shouting: 'Flyin' Fool delayed by weather.'

Savannah stopped him and bought a newspaper, the front page of which was filled with stories about a competition with a prize of $25,000 for the first airplane which would cross the Atlantic non-stop from New York to Paris, and about the pilots of three airplanes who were vying with one another to be the first to make that very hazardous journey, and who were waiting for a chance to take off from New York when the weather cleared.

'You know, it's a pity I don't know the wrong sort of people here in New York,' Savannah said reading it. 'If I did, I could make a lot of money by placing a bet that Lindbergh would win the competition and would arrive in Paris on the 21st.'

'You all right, Sir?' asked a Customs man, who was wondering why this most unusual-looking young man was talking to himself.

'That's how we could get to Paris in time to save Finn,' Cornelia said suddenly. 'We could fly there with that Mr Lindbergh. We could explain to him how it's a great emergency and about Soldiers' Fort and everything, and I'm sure he wouldn't mind bringing us in the plane with him then. Not when he knew how important it was.'

Savannah smiled at the Customs man who continued to look at her, and walked over to a telephone booth, where she picked up a receiver and pretended to talk into it.

'Cornelia, that's a brilliant idea,' she said, when Tansy

318 The Secret of Jules and Josephine

passed on Cornelia's suggestion. 'Only I don't think we should come right out and ask him to take you. He… well, I don't think he'd really understand.'

'We could write him a letter,' Cornelia suggested.

'Well, I think in this case, even a letter might be unwise,' Savannah said. 'But the idea of you and Tansy going with him is an inspiration. It means the two of you would be certain to get there on time. But what you'll have to do is to slip on board his plane as stowaways. That's the practical thing to do. Just stay invisible, and say nothing.'

'You will do it won't you, Tansy?' Cornelia asked, as the fairy remained silent. 'We know Lindbergh reaches Paris before Finn gets attacked, and he doesn't take off until tomorrow.'

Tansy was slow to answer. For an instant, she had felt a surge of hope at the idea, but as she thought about it longer, this was replaced by fear. The fear, however, was not for herself, but for Cornelia. So far as her personal safety was concerned, Tansy was willing to take any risk now to justify the faith May and Fuchsia had put in her that she, and she alone, could save the fairies.

But Tansy had never heard of any fairy travelling in an airplane before, and she had serious worries about what might happen to her in such a hostile environment—so high up in the sky that she would be totally removed from the support system of the earth, and flying over thousands of miles of strength-sapping ocean as well, for goodness' sake. And if anything happened to her, Cornelia's spirit might be separated from her body for a very long time, or maybe even forever. That was the risk that frightened Tansy the most, but she could not bring herself to say it out loud.

'Do you know what Lindbergh's plane is made of?' Tansy asked.

'Canvas, timber and a bit of metal, I suppose,' said Savannah. 'Oh, yes, and piano wire probably. I think that's what planes are usually made of.'

'Would it be just a single layer of canvas?' asked Tansy uneasily.

'I really don't know,' said Savannah. 'Would that make a difference?'

Tansy had no idea if it would or not. 'I don't think a fairy has ever flown in an airplane before,' she said. 'If I didn't have Cornelia with me, I'd just take the risk and not worry about it. But I don't know if I'll have any powers up there.'

Neither Savannah nor Cornelia was able to take Tansy's fears seriously. Tansy had admitted to them how worried she'd been that she would have no power when she was on the *Aquitania*, and yet they had seen her leaping through the air while she was on that ship, and she'd had strength enough to knock huge men senseless. Tansy was just a worrier, they both thought. That was her biggest problem.

'Why don't we go out to look at the airplane?' Savannah suggested. 'It says here in the paper that it's called the *Spirit of St. Louis* and it's out at Curtiss Field in Long Island and that Lindbergh is staying nearby at a place called the Garden City Hotel. We could take a taxi out there and I could see if they have a room and then we'll go out to the airfield and you can inspect the plane, Tansy.'

'Want to see Lindbergh, eh?' said the taxi driver, when Savannah told him where she wanted to go. 'Well, take a good look at him, because I don't think anyone's going to see him again after he takes off. A single engine and flying by himself? He'll never make it. Those other pilots have more sense. A plane with two engines and two men to fly it. That's the only way anyone will make it across the Atlantic.'

So many journalists were interested in the flight that they had filled all the hotel rooms, but the receptionist allowed Savannah to leave Finn's suitcases in the lobby, and then the three of them went off to the airfield. Savannah was not permitted to go near Lindbergh's plane, but Tansy and Cornelia had a good look at it.

'It's very small,' Cornelia pointed out. 'And you can't see out the front. How can he fly when he can't see where he's going?'

This did not bother Tansy much, who would have been happier if the plane had no windows at all. She did not like the look of the window openings at the sides, unable to stop herself thinking that, if she did become powerless up in the air, she and Cornelia could be just blown out through them.

'He's never going to make it,' a passing airfield worker said, looking at the plane and shaking his head.

'Not a chance in the world,' his companion agreed.

'Even if the engine doesn't fail, no one could stay awake for that long.'

As the three of them walked around, they heard more and more of this kind of talk, and in fact, they did not hear a single person say that he or she thought Lindbergh would make it to Paris. Interestingly, the more of this pessimistic but misguided talk Tansy overheard, the more she was inclined to suppress her own well-founded fears and take the risk of going up in that small airplane.

It was too easy, she decided, to believe a thing was impossible just because it had never been done before. It might even turn out that she herself would become famous for being the first fairy ever to fly non-stop from New York to Paris, but she did not let that splendid consideration influence her much. Rather she thought about the grim and certain alternative if she did not go, and did not reach Paris in time to save Finn: power forever for the terrible Lawful Guild, and an unknown and possibly very grim future for Emeraldia's fairies and for Cornelia and her family.

'All right,' said Tansy. 'We'll chance it.'

'You're going to make it, Tansy,' said Savannah with conviction. 'You're going to save Finn,' she added in a strained voice. 'You have to save Finn.'

The rest of the day was full of tension. At least they had the advantage, which Lindbergh himself did not have, of knowing that he would take off the following morning, but Tansy remained nervous; and a nervous

Tansy, as Savannah and Cornelia already knew, was an unrelaxing being to be around.

When they got back to the hotel where they had left Finn's cases, and Savannah again used the trick of going into a telephone booth and speaking into a receiver in order to talk to Tansy and Cornelia, one of the many newspaper reporters crowding the lobby impatiently tried to take the receiver from her. A second later, that impatient reporter was surprised to find himself somersaulting backwards across the lobby and into the hotel's kitchen, where he stuffed a large raw potato into his mouth.

When another reporter tried to push ahead of Savannah when she was waiting in line for a taxi, he found himself instead stealing a delivery boy's bicycle and riding it as fast as he could into a nearby muddy pond, while the furious delivery boy ran shouting after him. No, Tansy was not a restful fairy to be around when she was nervous.

The next morning, Savannah joined the crowd of spectators at Roosevelt Field who had come there after the news had spread that the *Spirit of St. Louis* had been towed there from Curtiss Field and that Lindbergh was going to take off for Paris that morning. Savannah already had said good-bye to her two companions (trying hard to hide how bereft she felt at having to stay behind); and a worried Tansy and an excited Cornelia then got on board the small plane ahead of the flyer, having fitted themselves into the small space remaining around the simple wicker chair, which was the pilot's seat.

When Lindbergh finally appeared, he was offered a kitten by one of the excited spectators to take with him to Paris as a mascot, but to Cornelia's great disappointment, he refused.

After the aviator had taken his place on the wicker chair, a man on the ground at the front of the plane started the propeller turning, and another man twisted something else, and the *Spirit of St. Louis* started to make a lot of noise and jerked a bit, but it didn't go anywhere because of things on the ground blocking its wheels.

After what seemed to Tansy and Cornelia like a very long wait, Lindbergh finally put on his helmet and goggles and put cotton wool in his ears, and men took away those things from in front of the wheels, and then more men went under the wings to push the plane along the runway until it would go by itself.

To the surprise of its two passengers, however, and to the consternation, it seemed, of its pilot, the plane, which was carrying a great weight of gasoline, acted as if it were so overloaded that it did not want to leave the ground. It went up and down, and then up and down again; and then to Cornelia's horror, when they did take off, they flew so low at first that they almost hit a tractor in a field; and a moment later, worst of all, it seemed like they were going to crash straight into some telephone wires. Tansy whirlwinded for all she was worth, not sure whether this would help them to go higher or not, but at any rate, the plane did just barely clear the telephone wires.

For the first hour or so, while the airplane was still flying over land, Tansy was able to relax a little. Being so far above ground, her powers were not as great as they were when she was in contact with the earth, but they were not so much lessened that she worried about them. Then, between Massachusetts and Nova Scotia, they were over the Atlantic Ocean, and to Tansy's great horror, she felt herself grow noticeably weaker.

To keep herself alert, she tried to concentrate on what Lindbergh was doing, because he was keeping himself very busy, twiddling with knobs and switches on the instrument panel in front of him, making notes on a paper with a pen, and then giving instructions to himself out loud, as if, like Tansy, he too was having trouble staying alert. Listening to him, they learned that he had been up all the night before, so that he'd been awake for 24 hours before he'd even started his journey to Europe.

Tansy got back some of her strength while they were flying over Nova Scotia, but felt so drained and feeble as they crossed a second short expanse of ocean on the way to Newfoundland that she concluded there and then that she had no hope of surviving the long flight over the fullness of the Atlantic. Over the very last point of the American continent, at St. John's in Newfoundland, Lindbergh brought the plane down so low that it almost touched the buildings.

During that descent, as they got nearer and nearer to

the wonderful, strength-giving earth and trees, Tansy quickly recovered; and for a moment, she felt she almost had her full strength back. Immediately, while she still could, she decided that she had to get Cornelia out of that plane.

If she did not do it there and then, over that last piece of land, she thought there was a very good chance that Cornelia's spirit would end up separated forever from her body, carried away from Tansy's powerless hands somewhere out over that power-draining, hostile ocean.

Feeling worried and guilty, she prepared to whirlwind out through one of the windows at the side of the plane, but then, to her horror, she discovered that she had left her jump just a moment too late.

Looking down, she saw that the wretched plane was travelling so quickly that it had left the precious land behind once again, and now there was nothing below it but sea.

She remembered all too well what had happened to her before when she had tried to get back on board the *Aquitania* from the tender, and she knew she would have no hope at all of whirlwinding the two of them safely back to shore from this great height.

It was a very bad moment for Tansy. She felt stupid and useless and powerless and terrified. The debilitating effect of flying high in an airplane was greater than she had expected; and realistically, she now believed that the chances of the two of them staying safely in this horrible machine until they reached the other side of the Atlantic were very small.

—*Chapter 46*—

Not a Hallucination

CORNELIA TRIED TO CHEER UP TANSY, sensing that the fairy was very worried. 'You know, we flew to Italy last year on a holiday,' she said chattily, 'and I didn't like being on that airplane at all because it made my ears sore and it was crowded and everyone was grumpy and we had to stand in line for ages and ages before we could even get on it, and then when we were coming home, we had to wait even longer at the airport in Rome, and then we all had to sit apart from one another, and my mother said she'd never travel by airplane again in her life. But this is fun.'

Tansy hardly heard her, worrying more all the time about the open windows, and preoccupied with trying to wedge the two of them into a secure position behind the wicker seat.

After a while, Cornelia gave up trying to chat; and before long, she—like the pilot—was surprised by sudden nightfall, which brought with it complete darkness and a disorienting sense of isolation, as a dense fog hid entirely the light of the stars.

Tansy was almost unaware of the darkness, but the consequences of it for her were terrible, because the pilot had to climb higher and higher in the sky to be able to see the stars above the fog; and as he did, Tansy found to her horror that she was drifting in and out of consciousness. She wedged Cornelia tight beneath her, and tried to concentrate as hard as she could in the moments when she was fully lucid.

After a while, the moon came out, and now and then, the fog lessened, and in those intervals, Cornelia was startled to see the ocean filled with what appeared to be great mountains.

'They're icebergs,' said Tansy, gathering up all her remaining energy to make her voice seem normal. 'You should probably take a good look at them,' she added. 'They say that, by the time you're an adult, most icebergs will be melted.'

'Melted?' said Lindbergh.

Startled, Tansy turned her half-conscious eyes towards the aviator, and then Cornelia said in a surprised, excited voice: 'Tansy, you're visible.'

'Why did you say that about the icebergs?' he asked. 'Why should they melt?'

Tansy could not believe what had happened. She had lost the power to make herself invisible. This had never happened before and she had never heard of it happening to any other fairy.

Now, she really was frightened. Her barely conscious brain also worried in case the surprise of seeing her might cause the pilot to lose his concentration and to do something that would put them all in danger, but in this respect, she had no cause for worry. The aviator accepted her sudden appearance with no more excitement than he would accord a minor change in the weather, and seemed surprised only by what she had said.

'I'm sure this is not a hallucination,' he said to himself when she didn't answer. 'I'm perfectly certain I'm talking to a female being here in the cockpit. But I don't believe she weighs anything, so she shouldn't affect flight time or fuel consumption.'

'Talk to him Tansy,' urged Cornelia, as the pilot, in an effort to stay awake, brought his plane so close to the ocean that spray would splash on his face through the side window opening. 'Tell him who you are, and that we're not bad stowaways or anything, but we have to save Finn.'

'I'm not a hallucination,' Tansy confirmed to Lindbergh in a faint voice. 'Usually, you couldn't see me at all, but I'm not feeling very good at the moment.'

'You sound a bit weak all right,' the aviator agreed. 'But why did you say that about icebergs melting?'

'That's what's going to happen,' Tansy said dozily. 'But I don't think I should be talking about it.'

'I don't get it,' he persisted. 'I'm just trying to think of what could happen that would be so powerful it would make the icebergs melt. Will there be a big meteor hit or what? Or a volcano eruption?'

'Humans will cause it. They'll do things that will make the air around the earth different so the weather will be changed. They'll cut down forests and build factories and have too many cars and airplanes, and—'

'Too many airplanes?' he said, startled.

'A lot of places will get hotter and stormier but some places, like Emeraldia, might get cold because the Gulf Stream won't flow to it any more.'

'Tansy, tell him why we're on his plane,' Cornelia pleaded.

'There's another being here as well,' Tansy told him, 'but I don't think you can see her. She's worried because we didn't ask permission to come with you. We would have, of course, if we knew you'd be able to see us.'

'Don't worry about that. I'm just glad of the company, you being weightless and all. Who are you anyway?'

'My name is Tansy. I'm a fairy from Emeraldia. My friend's name is Cornelia. She's from Emeraldia too, but she's not a fairy. But it might be better, for reasons I can't quite explain now, if you didn't tell people about meeting us.'

'Tell people about carrying a fairy passenger in a silver party dress who told me that icebergs were going to melt because there were too many airplanes? —don't worry, I won't.'

Tansy did her best to try to keep talking, but the effort was too much for her. She could not see at all any more, and then she found she could not speak either, and finally, she lost consciousness entirely; and when that happened, she became invisible again.

'Please talk some more, Tansy,' Cornelia said worriedly, becoming very frightened when Tansy seemed not even to hear her.

To make matters worse, Cornelia could see that the pilot, too, was having trouble staying awake. She could see that he nodded off a few times, but luckily the sudden jerking of the plane when this happened woke him. At each of these sudden rolls, however, Cornelia was aware that she and Tansy came very close to falling out of the plane.

'Please, Tansy, talk to Mr Lindbergh some more,' she said worriedly. 'He's very sleepy, and you could help him a lot. Please, Tansy, please.' But Tansy did not respond, and after trying to rouse her a few more times, an awful thought suddenly struck Cornelia, and when it did, she felt almost sick with fear. 'Tansy, don't die,' she pleaded miserably. 'Tansy, you can't die.'

She kept on frantically trying to wake the fairy until she found that she herself no longer could see or hear; and for the first time since her spirit had been separated from her body, she felt cold: horribly and overwhelmingly cold.

This was all the more surprising because she had not believed she was capable of much physical feeling while she was in this other world with Tansy, and yet this awful coldness now was the most uncomfortable feeling she had ever known. What made it even worse was her sense of total isolation. She couldn't see; she couldn't hear; she couldn't smell; she couldn't feel; and she became acutely aware of how important those senses were to her as soon as she lost them.

She decided she had died, and that Tansy must have

died too. She had never thought that this could happen. She did not even know that fairies could die. She wondered briefly what would happen to her body now, lying on her bed back in their house. She thought about how miserable her parents would be, and poor Barry, who might think he was to blame for all of this.

Maybe that was why she had not been considered good enough to be let into Heaven. She was pretty certain this was not Heaven. It didn't seem like Hell either, because she was sure she would be too hot rather than too cold if this were Hell. It might be Purgatory, she supposed, although what it seemed most like was that place, Limbo, her grandparents talked about: that nowhere place where the souls of babies who had never been baptized ended up.

Her teacher said that Limbo was not real, and that old people had been misled when they had been taught it existed, but now she was thinking maybe her grandparents were right and her teacher wrong because this seemed to fit the general description of Limbo pretty exactly, although she had never imagined it would be so cold.

But then she remembered that she *had* been baptized, so maybe this was Purgatory after all, and that was why it was so uncomfortable, and she would have to stay here, cold and alone, until she made up for all the bad things she had done in her life. She reviewed the bad things she could think of.

She had fooled her parents, of course, about going

inside Josephine, and she had sneaked chocolate and cake from the pantry now and then; and maybe she had overstated somewhat the sins of Oscar, the gander, and caused him to be sent to the butcher's earlier than he might otherwise have been. But then Oscar had been a very wicked old bird, obsessed with jumping on her shoulder, and he had scared her and—oh no, oh not that, she thought. This couldn't all be about Oscar, could it?

In a panic, she tried to look around her in the cold void. Could her dealings with Oscar really be the reason why she was not being allowed into Heaven? And did that mean that Oscar could be with her here right now in this horrible place that might be either Limbo or Purgatory? She had no doubt that Oscar would qualify for either, because he definitely had not been baptized, which would make him eligible for Limbo, and there was no doubt at all that he was mean enough for Purgatory.

So maybe she was going to have to spend the rest of eternity wondering if scary Oscar might appear any moment out of the void and land on her shoulder and peck at her head as he had done on that unforgettable day when she hadn't been able to get him off her for the entire length of the drive; only in this awful place, he would be able to do it forever.

She wanted to cry at the prospect of such an unfair and awful fate, but she couldn't even do that without her body. She hated being dead in circumstances in which she seemed to have been judged to have been a serious sinner, when she had not even known she was sinning, and it was Oscar who had been the great big sinner.

She remained in that terrible state of nothingness, feeling aggrieved, terrified, and almost frozen, for what seemed to her like days and days (in fact it was for eight or nine hours) thinking a lot about her parents and Barry and Freddy and Tickles and poor Tansy, and wondering if she would really have to go on forever feeling this cold and with no one for company except for mean old Oscar, who hadn't appeared yet, but was certain to appear any minute.

It was all very unfair, she thought miserably. Very unfair.

Chapter 47

City Lights

IN FACT, CORNELIA had been the victim of an unprecedented set of circumstances. Tansy had lost consciousness—something that never happened to a fairy before—and Cornelia had been wedged beneath Tansy when that happened. Her own human spirit then had been completely engulfed by the fairy's unconscious spirit, and that powerful, deep unconsciousness acted like a thick layer of opaque ice, cutting Cornelia's much weaker consciousness off from the world.

Fittingly, it was when they were flying over Emeraldia (although Cornelia had no idea where they were, or even what world or dimension they were in) that she felt the first glimmer of hope.

What happened then was that, just for an instant, Cornelia thought she could see Tansy; but this sighting was no more than a flash, and she wasn't even sure it had really happened at all, because immediately she was back in the cold emptiness. But then she got a second fleeting glimpse of the fairy, and at that point, Cornelia thought that maybe there was still some small hope for her and she might be let out of Limbo after all and Oscar would have to stay there forever all by himself.

What caused this much improved state of affairs was that the airplane finally had reached Europe, and revitalising energy at last was drifting up from the land; although by then Tansy was so weak that it took a while before she was visible to Cornelia for more than the briefest flashes.

Then just by chance, at the same magnificent moment as Tansy became steadily visible to her again, Cornelia also saw the pilot lifting a small bag from the floor in front of her, from which he took out a sandwich that he started to eat.

'Wake up, Tansy,' Cornelia said again with a bit more hope in her voice. 'Please wake up. I think we may have died, but we're alive now and Mr Lindbergh is eating a sandwich.'

Being over land made Tansy revive quickly. She stirred slightly; and before long, she was coherent again, even if she remained very weak. 'We're still on this terrible airplane, aren't we?' she said in a shaky voice.

'Yes, but we're almost in Paris,' Cornelia said excitedly. 'I heard Mr Lindbergh say he can see its lights. Maybe you could make yourself visible and speak to him again, Tansy, so he doesn't think we're rude and stopped talking to him for no reason?'

'I don't think I should,' the fairy said tiredly. 'As things stand, he'll probably think I was some sort of hallucination, and I think we should leave it that way. I shouldn't really have told him about the future, although when we were out there over the ocean, that didn't seem to matter very much.'

As they came down lower over Paris and circled the gaily lit Eiffel Tower, Tansy brightened a little at the prospect that she would soon be in contact with the earth again; but unfortunately, her ordeal was not yet over. When they reached the place where the aviator thought Le Bourget airfield should be, the lighting around it looked so peculiar that he wondered if he had made a mistake about the location of his destination, and he kept on flying.

Looking down also, Tansy could see why he was confused, and in her desperation for this horrible experience to be finished, she was tempted for a moment to make herself visible again, and explain that the bewildering lighting was—in a manner of speaking— the pilot's own fault. It was caused by the headlights of countless cars caught in an unprecedented miles-long traffic jam as Parisians in their thousands headed towards the airfield on news that his plane had been spotted overhead.

She restrained herself, however, and before long, the pilot turned around and came back. This time, he brought the plane down low enough to establish the cause of the strange lighting and that he was in the correct location, and then he circled a few times, checking the wind sock and the condition of the grass landing strip. The comfort of being so close to wonderful, restoring land again raised the hopes of the desperate Tansy who said, 'Thank Nature, we've made it.'

At that point, however, the pilot drove the infuriated fairy nearly past the point of endurance by going right back up again to a thousand feet before beginning at long last his final descent.

'If he doesn't land this thing the next time he brings it near the ground, I'm going to land it myself,' she informed Cornelia fiercely. 'It can't be that hard to fly a plane.'

The plane did land the next time, but Tansy had whirlwinded out of it long before it slid to a halt. Her whirlwind was still weak, but luckily it was just strong enough to carry them over the heads of the huge mass of people that came surging towards the aviator, hardly allowing him to get out of his tiny plane.

Tansy allowed herself one look back at that hated machine and at its calm pilot, who she thought was the most self-contained human being she had ever encountered, and then she turned her mind to finding the more civilised transportation they would need to get themselves quickly through the great traffic jam which ran all the way back to the centre of Paris.

'I think we need a policeman and a motorcar,' she said briskly, sounding more like her old self again. 'We have less than an hour to get to the *Place de l'Opéra* and find Finn, or we'll be too late.'

—*Chapter 48*—

Trouble at the Place de l'Opéra

I N FACT, TANSY NEEDED TWO POLICEMEN. She went inside the officer who seemed to be in charge at the airfield, and then he ordered another very surprised policeman to drive him immediately to the *Place de l'Opéra*.

'Go faster,' the policeman in charge kept barking.

'The car won't go any faster,' the driver pointed out.

'Blow your horn. Drive around those other cars. Drive through the gardens. Drive on the pavement.' When these orders were not enough to keep them progressing towards Paris at top speed, the officer in charge cleared the road personally. The sides of the road were filled with cyclists, and the driver was surprised at how often his superior left the car to take hold of these riders and their bikes and fling them off the road and into the bushes as casually as if they were fallen branches.

'Sir, are you sure—?' he began, but broke off quickly when they came to a traffic jam at a major junction, and found that half-a-dozen cars travelling in different directions had become stuck in it and now were blocking their way. 'I don't know how we're going to get around this, Sir,' he said, but he found himself speaking to the empty air as the policeman in charge was already in the middle of that junction and had started tossing these cars on to the grass verge.

'Something important happening at the *Place de l'Opéra*, Sir?' the driver asked nervously when his wild-eyed superior returned to the car.

'We have to stop a murder,' his boss said. 'We have to stop a man being killed there by a gang of apaches.'

'Those apaches again,' the driver said angrily. 'They're savages, they are. But I can spot those gangs a mile away. If there's a single apache within a mile of the *Place de l'Opéra*, I'll spot them.'

When they reached the *Place de l'Opéra*, however, a startling sight greeted them. As had been expected, the area was packed with people celebrating Lindbergh's flight across the Atlantic, most of them laughing, dancing and making a lot of noise. To the astonishment of both policemen, however, half the crowd seemed to be made up of apaches: gangs with scarred faces and wearing caps or berets and gaudy scarves; and these people were dancing and cheering more wildly than anyone.

The senior policeman jumped out of the car and grabbed one of these by the throat. 'Where's Finn?' he demanded. 'What have you done with Finn?'

'Who's Finn?' the man asked. 'Say, you don't think I'm a real apache, do you? Most of us were at a masquerade party when we heard about Lindbergh. Half the guests at that party came dressed as apaches.'

So that was the explanation. But it was not a good lookout for their mission or for Finn, Tansy and

Cornelia decided worriedly. Looking around at the crowd, which was costumed so uniformly as flamboyant gang members, both of them wondered how anyone could spot real apaches among all these boisterous people.

Their only crumb of comfort was the large number of policemen they could see distributed throughout the crowd, all of them stopping and talking to the revellers in apache costume. Seeing this, both Tansy and Cornelia suspected that the telegrams they had sent to the head of the Paris police from the *Aquitania* might have been taken seriously after all.

Nevertheless, Tansy was very worried. In the midst of so many people dressed like criminals and in the darkness of night, she thought it would be very easy for a gang of real criminals to stab someone to death and then to vanish into this cheering, dancing crowd of masqueraders.

'Look, Tansy,' said Cornelia suddenly, pointing to a fat man dressed in evening clothes. 'Isn't that Mr Malo-Alto going into the Opera House?'

The policeman being controlled by Tansy quickly darted after this man, but by the time he got inside the building, Mr Malo-Alto was nowhere to be seen; and at that point, in frustration, Tansy abandoned the bewildered policeman, thinking she had no hope of searching this huge, lavish building with its thousands of doors, and miles of curtain and velvet, if she were slowed by the limitations of a human body.

Inside the auditorium, they saw that what was being performed on stage was the ballet *Swan Lake*. 'This is the ballet that Savannah's friend, Claudette, was to dance,' Cornelia remembered. 'But I don't see her on the stage.'

'I don't either,' said Tansy, and immediately she had a bad feeling that this might be significant. She shot inside a woman sitting in the audience who then stood up and went out to ask an usher why Claudette Lilas was not dancing tonight.

'She didn't show up,' the usher said bluntly. 'They sent people out to bring her in, but no one can find her. They held the curtain nearly two hours while they looked for her, but finally her understudy had to go on.'

'They're talking about nothing else backstage,' put in an usherette who was standing nearby. 'They were even talking about calling in the police after one of the cleaners found her handbag on the floor back there.'

Tansy waited to hear no more. She left that woman and whirlwinded with more power and speed than she had ever done in her existence, searching through the uncountable number of rooms and separate small spaces that made up that glorious building. 'Do you think Mr Malo-Alto did something to Claudette as well?' Cornelia asked her.

Tansy nodded grimly. 'Claudette was one of the people Savannah telegrammed from the *Aquitania*, and I don't see how it could be a coincidence that she would disappear on the same night that we saw Mr Malo-Alto come in here. We've just got to find him,' she said, flitting furiously through half a dozen mysterious rooms filled with props and costumes, and coming to a stop only when she saw a door that had a sign on it saying *'Danger – No Entrance'*.

'It does say *"Danger"*,' Cornelia pointed out uneasily.

'Yes, and I have a feeling about that,' said Tansy fiercely, looking for a way to get past that sign, and spotting that a small window above the door was open very slightly. 'Hang on,' she advised Cornelia, as once again she squeezed through an opening that was only a small fraction of her visible size.

Beyond this door was a corridor with other doors leading off it, including one facing them at the far end which had a sign on it saying *'Extreme Danger – Absolutely No Entrance'*.

'Now it says *"Extreme Danger"*,' Cornelia said faintly.

Tansy did not hear, too preoccupied with wondering how she would get through that door and resigning herself finally to having to go under it. 'This is it,' said the fairy fiercely, as she gritted her teeth and started to push herself through this narrowest of slits. 'I'm sure this is it.'

Tansy's instincts proved to be correct. At the other side of the door, was a huge room so crowded with disorienting props and backdrops that it was hard to know what was actual and what was illusion; but then both Cornelia and Tansy heard a small muffled groan coming from behind what appeared to be a marble staircase, but which in fact was a curtain on which was painted a very real-looking marble staircase. Tansy furiously darted behind the curtain, and the first thing she saw was poor Claudette—who at that very moment should have been dancing triumphantly on the stage—lying on a brocade-covered sofa, bound and gagged. Beside her, Mr Malo-Alto was sitting on a bench, holding a gun.

'The good news,' Mr Malo-Alto was saying, 'is the boss says you're not to be shot. He figures you must be a smart girl to have found the safest place in Paris for Finn to hide those jewels of his—right here in the opera house, mixed up with all the old opera props and the phony jewels they don't use any more. The boss says he always has a job for a girl who's good at using her head. He's even going to make sure you get a world cruise,' he added, as a pale Claudette looked at him in horror. 'To the U.S.A. via Shanghai, no less.

'Your friend, Finn, is finished though,' Mr Malo-Alto added in an indifferent voice. 'The boss needs Finn for only one last job, which is to get himself killed tonight, and I'll be going outside in a few minutes to make sure he's done just that. Not that there's much doubt. If everything's going to plan, Finn should be walking out of this building right now and straight into the arms of some apache friends of mine.'

An ear-splitting screech filled the room then, which made Mr Malo-Alto jump and the colour drain from his face until it was as pale as Claudette's. 'What the— ?' he began, as he stared in terror at a spot just a few feet away, wondering if he could really have seen a momentary vision of a beautiful, but very dangerous-looking, girl in a silver dress. 'You know, maybe they're right about this place,' he added, wiping the nervous sweat off his forehead with the back of his hand. 'Maybe it is haunted.'

In fact, what he had heard and seen was a fairy experiencing the greatest panic of her existence. On hearing that Finn, at that very moment, might be in the process of being murdered in the street outside while she, the fairy sent to rescue him, was hanging around uselessly inside the opera building only a few feet away, Tansy lost control of herself entirely; and for that instant of total panic she could be both seen and heard; and what she had to say was an ear-splitting fairy scream of frustration.

Recovering herself, she whirlwinded out of the building so quickly that Cornelia couldn't even see where they were going until they were back in the crowded square, and then their attention was drawn immediately to a point at the edge of the crowd, opposite the *Café de la Paix*, not far from the opera building. A dramatically glamorous woman with shiny short black hair, wearing a luxurious fur and carrying a fluffy white dog, was shouting loudly: 'Police, Police: a man is being attacked by apaches.'

Looking to where she was pointing, Cornelia and Tansy then saw Finn. He had just knocked a knife out of the hand of a rough, brutish-looking man who was clearly a real apache; and again, for a startling instant, the world became a blur to Cornelia because of the great speed at which Tansy was dashing towards Finn.

By the time the fairy had slowed enough that Cornelia could see what was happening, Tansy had taken possession of a second member of the apache gang who also was carrying a knife which he was just about to sink into Finn's back.

Under Tansy's control, this apache stopped with his arm in mid-air, and immediately turned away from Finn and threatened instead with the knife the three other gang members, one of whom now produced a gun. Moving at a speed that made the startled crowd gasp, the Tansy-controlled apache then kicked the gun out of this other apache's hand, before picking him up by his feet and swinging him around, using this astonished apache as a cudgel with which to knock down the two other gang members.

Police all over the *Place de l'Opéra* were blowing their whistles, and a few of them summoned their wits enough to be able to pick up from the ground and take into custody the two apaches lying dazed and bewildered on it; but others—along with the rest of the large crowd— were just staring mesmerised as one apache swung another through the air in this unprecedented manner. Tansy ignored the police for as long as she could, but finally and regretfully she slowed her spin, tossed the apache she was holding by the heels high in the air, then caught him on his way down and handed him to one of the policemen.

The police, to great cheers, then led away the gang, and Finn was left thanking profusely the person whose shouts and vigilance had alerted Tansy. 'Why, you're Josephine Baker, aren't you?' he said to the glamorous woman. 'I never thought I'd get to meet you. I certainly never thought you'd save my life.'

'Some friend of yours seemed to think I'd be useful,' she told him. 'I got a telegram saying you were going to have a problem here.'

'They really have very good information at the Silver Poodle Club, don't they?' Tansy said smugly. 'Everyone there says she's the most important person in Paris now, and look—she is.'

'Now, Finn, Darling, you're to go right back to Emeraldia,' Josephine Baker was telling him. 'That was in the telegram too. And another thing, it said—'

Worried about Claudette, Tansy waited to hear no more, but hurried back inside the opera house, where she saw that Mr Malo-Alto, still looking very pale, had come out to the foyer and was talking with a man that Cornelia thought at first was Mr Durham, only she could see when she looked closer that it wasn't Mr Durham at all. It was a younger man, who happened to have a similar gremlin-Walter-type face, although he moved away before she could get a really good look at him.

Tansy did not notice the other man at all, as she was having a great struggle with her instincts. What she

felt like doing very much was to lift Mr Malo-Alto by
his ears, whirlwind him up to the highest point of the
building where the statue of Apollo stood, hang him
by his braces from Apollo's lyre, and then perhaps to
whirlwind up a great tornado just around him. Instead of
consigning him to this appropriate and richly deserved
fate, however, she dug deep into her reserves and found
more self-restraint than she had ever displayed in her
existence before.

She would make sure Mr Malo-Alto was sent to jail.
That was all she would do.

She went inside Mr Malo-Alto, and Mr Malo-Alto
immediately went over to the doorman and said: 'Please
call some of those policemen over here and make them
arrest me. I kidnapped your prima ballerina, Claudette
Lilas, and I've left her bound and gagged in a locked
room backstage. I think I ought to be put in jail for a
very long time. And I tried to have him killed,' he added,
pointing to Finn, who had come running up from the
crowd. 'So hurry up,' he added, holding out his hands
as if waiting for handcuffs. 'Get those police.'

The policemen were called, but no one really believed
Mr Malo-Alto until he led a deputation that included
two policemen, Finn, Josephine Baker, and the director
of the ballet past the signs that said *'Danger'* and *'Extreme
Danger'* and behind the curtain where the terrified and
bewildered Claudette was lying bound and gagged on
the brocade-covered sofa.

The police immediately arrested Mr Malo-Alto then;

and all the people who worked at the ballet and Finn and Josephine Baker wanted to call an ambulance for Claudette, but Claudette did not react as they expected. Of course, this was not surprising, because Tansy had gone inside her and wanted to make Claudette feel better for having missed her great moment.

'I want to dance,' she said. 'I want to go on stage and dance. This was to be the most wonderful night of my life—my first night as prima ballerina—and I don't want to miss all of it just because of that bad man.'

Everyone smiled when she said this, and although they all felt sorry for her, no one took what she said seriously. 'But you're not able,' the director of the ballet said kindly. 'You've been lying there bound and gagged. Your body just couldn't do it.'

'He's right, Darling,' Josephine Baker agreed. 'You could hurt yourself.'

'No, I wouldn't,' said Claudette. 'Look.' And then she did a sequence of turns and leaps of such speed, grace, perfection and duration as they had never seen a dancer do before. 'I have to dance. You must let me.'

In fact, the director did have to let her dance, because he just could not stop her. He and the dressers and several other dancers and the doorman all tried very hard to restrain her, but on that night, Claudette was strong as a lion and two dozen men would not have had the strength to hold her back.

She danced the last two Acts of *Swan Lake*, and of course, all of the ballet world still talks about that performance. No one before or after ever danced the part of Odette/Odile as it was danced that night.

'I am ready to die today,' one critic gushed in the next morning's newspaper, 'because what can life offer now to match the perfection—the sheer magic—I saw last night when Claudette Lilas came on stage in Act III of *Swan Lake*?

'But what about the gossip that filled the auditorium, you ask?—that this magnificent dancer had been unable to dance Acts I and II because she had been kidnapped? This writer cannot comment, but knows that, after last night, the whole world will want to know everything about Claudette Lilas.

'That most extraordinary ballerina set a standard that

is unlikely ever to be matched by any other. I am not ashamed to say that I too gasped and applauded as I watched the divine Miss Lilas perform the impossible: one hundred *fouettés en tournant*! One hundred!—her foot spinning all the time in one precise position. What ballerina will dare to dance that part ever again?

'And for an encore, what did this astonishing dancer do? One hundred and fifty *fouettés en tournant*!'

In fact, Tansy might have kept on going and danced a thousand of those demanding turns on one foot in the same position if Cornelia had not begged her to stop spinning. 'I'm not dizzy exactly, Tansy, but Claudette must be.'

No one knows how long the standing ovation lasted. Even after the building was closed for the night, a large crowd of people remained outside on the street clapping, some of whom were rewarded by seeing the exhausted but elated Claudette being carried on a stretcher home to bed.

'I just had to do it,' Tansy explained, after she had left the dancer's body.

'I know,' said Cornelia giggling. 'And it was fun. But now I think we'd better make sure that Finn gets home, and leaves that note he's supposed to leave for May and Fuchsia. And do you know something, Tansy? I want to go home too.'

Chapter 49

A Different World

W HEN CORNELIA WOKE UP on Christmas Eve morning, she felt very strange.

A few things seemed normal enough. Tickles was asleep down at her feet under the bedclothes, and Freddy had his head on the pillow beside her. Strudel was in her hand; Daisy was under her arm; and Jules and Josephine were looking down at her from the shelf beside the bed.

For a reason she could not explain, however, Cornelia felt she was somewhere she had never been before. It was not that anything in particular looked different, at least not in any way she could explain; it was just that she felt a sense of disorientation as she looked at certain objects in the room.

That painting, for instance, hanging on the wall over her mantelpiece: it seemed to one part of her brain that she had been looking at this painting—now darkened with age—for as long as she could remember; and in all that time, she had never stopped wondering about the identity of the brilliantly beautiful girl in the 1920s dress who was its subject.

The picture had been a christening gift from her very famous and exotic auntie Savannah and her great-granduncle Finn; and from the time she was old enough to talk, Cornelia had been pestering and begging Savannah to tell her who the beautiful girl was. Savannah, however, would only say, frustratingly, that one day Cornelia would find out for herself, and she would be one of the very few people who ever would find out; but in the meantime Savannah would not tell her.

But in the other part of her brain that just woke up this morning, she knew, of course, that this was the portrait of Tansy that Savannah had painted on the *Aquitania;* and it was hanging in the place where, in this second part of her brain, she had been used to looking at an old mirror with photographs of her favourite pop stars stuck to it. And this second set of memories was just as real to her as the first.

It was confusing, really. Very confusing. Of course, a dream could have an effect like that sometimes, and she had been mixed-up once or twice before in her life immediately after waking up from a strange dream; but the confusion of this morning was much more profound and significant than anything she had ever experienced previously. This was like she had led two different lives.

Keeping her fingers crossed, she got up from the bed (a tousled Tickles emerging from under the bedclothes behind her) and went over nervously to look out the window. She breathed a sigh of relief when she saw smoke rising from the chimney of the Ryans' house and saw the two familiar fairy forts, both of them looking as if no human had disturbed them for centuries.

And yet she was sure she had seen something very

different and terrible out this window before. Those memories of something different were as real as the green, undisturbed landscape she was looking at now; she was certain of that. But all the same, it was very puzzling. While she was still looking in perplexity at this peaceful scene, her door opened, and Barry came running into the room, stopping with an expression of great relief when he saw her standing at the window.

'Oh, you are here,' he said. 'So things are okay?'

She was not quite sure how to answer this. 'Yes, I think so,' she said uncertainly.

'Hey, I'll bet you woke up figuring something weird has happened too, didn't you?' he asked, looking at her.

Cornelia nodded. 'Very weird. I got out of bed just to make sure that the Ryans' house and their fairy fort hadn't disappeared.'

'I had to come in here to check that *you* hadn't disappeared,' her brother said. 'The last thing I remember, Mom and Dad had you all wrapped up and were carrying you out to the car and we were leaving for France and I'd just made sure that you had Josephine in the blanket with you. And then I woke.'

Cornelia, whose second set of memories was dominated by images of the exotic and the impossible—Paris apaches, the *Aquitania*, Lindbergh's plane, dancing on the stage of the Paris *Opéra*—had no idea that things at home had been as bad as that. 'We were leaving for France?' she squealed.

'Yeah, it's pretty cool that we're still here,' Barry said. 'But I'm having trouble figuring out what was real or not,' he added confusedly, looking around her bedroom. 'It's too weird to think that Finn was supposed to be dead and because of that, the Pickenoses–I mean, hey, the Pickenoses!–were bossing everyone around.'

At the thought of this, both of them stopped being uneasy for a while and started laughing. They both had a clear memory of a grim situation in which the Pickenoses were practically in charge of Emeraldia, but that particular bit of their memory was just too stupid to be real, they both thought. The Pickenoses, for heaven's sake! The Pickenoses were mean and weird but they were never likely to be important or anything.

Okay, Puffy's name had been in the newspapers a lot, but not for the sort of reasons anyone would want to have her name in the newspapers. Like when she'd been a prison guard and was so mean to the prisoners, throwing cold water over them and things, that she caused the biggest prison riot in Emeraldia history, and all the prisoners went up on the roof and refused to come down until they were sure she's been fired, and she'd been sort of famous for that for a while. Then about a week ago the prison gave her a job in the parking lot showing people where they could park their cars, and she became even more famous. What happened then was that dogs started biting her.

And not just biting her: clasping on and attaching themselves so determinedly to her bottom that even vets weren't able to get them to loosen their jaws. A few dogs almost had to be put down because they were so tightly attached to her, and those dogs had let go just in time to save themselves. But then another dog usually would take its place.

So then, just a few days ago, they'd given her a different job inside the prison, in a place where only the prison guards were supposed to see her, but Mrs Ryan's brother, Father Joe, who was a chaplain in the prison, had told Cornelia's father that he didn't think she'd last very long in that job because some of the prisoners were saying they'd heard a loud guffaw coming from the office where she was working, and they passed the word around among themselves that Puffy was back.

After that, there was a threat of another riot, so the prison governor had instructed Puffy to stay very quiet, and also to use the knob when she opened doors instead of just forcing them open, but nobody thought she'd be able to keep up that regime for very long.

Pompeous, in fact, was more of a nuisance to Cornelia and her family, because he was their rubbish collector, and he was not a very good one. He usually left a lot more rubbish thrown on the ground than he took away, but mostly people didn't dare say anything to him about this because of the way he'd stare at them and say really mean things and then leave long, insulting letters—full of words that sounded like Latin but were never quite right—stuck to their doors.

Pompeous, in fact, was a very big nuisance, but the idea that he could practically have been one of the most important people in Emeraldia was so ridiculous that every time they tried to say something to one another about it, the two of them instead ended up rolling around on the bed laughing.

'Did you have this elephant toy?' Barry asked finally, when they stopped thinking about Pompeous and were able to think coherently again. 'And did I go into it with fairies and we stopped a massacre, and then your elephant toy disappeared?'

'Zanzibar,' answered Cornelia. 'That was his name.'

'So do you think that's kind of what's happened now? Did you stop something happening to Finn? I mean, would he have died if you hadn't done something?'

'Oh yes. He was just about to be killed by a gang of apaches, but Tansy saved him. Oh, I wish Tansy would come. Then maybe we'd understand everything better.'

'I think it's like we've led two different lives,' Barry said. 'One with Finn alive and protecting Soldiers' Fort, and the other with him dead and the Pickenoses—' But at the very mention of the Pickenoses, the two of them started laughing again helplessly, and it was a while before Barry could finish his sentence. '—and the Pickenoses in charge of Emeraldia,' he said finally.

They were still laughing when their mother came into the room, also looking confused by something.

'Well, I'm glad you're both up and in such a good mood,' she said, 'because visitors are on their way and they seem to have something very urgent on their minds. I just had the most mysterious phone call from Savannah. She said that she and Finn didn't want to wait until this evening to come over, and they were coming here this morning, because they can't wait a minute longer. She even said the two of them had been determined to stay alive until today, because it was so important that they have a long, private talk with both of you.'

Her mother looked at them curiously. 'So what's up between the two of you and Savannah and Finn, and what on earth was Savannah talking about?'

For once, even Cornelia could not find her tongue, and she and Barry both just looked up at their mother in confused silence.

'Now if that very odd conversation with Savannah wasn't enough to make me almost explode with curiosity,' their mother added, 'your reaction to it certainly is.' She eyed them a moment longer. 'You know, both of you look very guilty. You haven't done something wrong, have you, that Savannah doesn't want me to know about?'

As Cornelia turned bright red, her mother became even more uneasy, but decided to let the matter drop for the moment. 'Oh, never mind. It's Christmas Eve. Listen, put on your pretty blue jumper, Cornelia, and come to me to comb your hair. I want you looking nice for Savannah. By the way, don't make any noise around your grandparents' rooms. They want to rest in bed this morning because they're going to be up late tonight.'

When Savannah and Finn arrived, Cornelia's parents settled the remarkably fit-looking couple at the kitchen table with hot drinks and a plate of Savannah's favourite oatmeal and honey cookies, and then they said they had to pick up a few things from the shop and would be back in half an hour. 'Now you take good care of your guests,' their mother told Cornelia and Barry before she left.

'You know, this is easily the noblest thing I've ever done,' Cornelia's mother said as she and her husband sat into their car to drive off. 'I'd give anything to know what was on Savannah's mind, but she was determined not to say anything, and since it was Savannah—well, what could I do? She's always been so good to the children, and she's never asked for anything before.'

'She and Finn just have their own way of doing things,' said her husband. 'Though when I look at the two them, I'm inclined to think we should all be copying whatever it is they do. You'd never guess their real ages, would you? They look a good forty years younger than they are.'

'The children don't know how lucky they are that Savannah and Finn have always been so interested in them,' said his wife. 'I mean, it still amazes me that, even when they were only tiny babies, Savannah seemed to know exactly what their personalities would be like. What do you suppose that big book was that she had with her?'

Back in the kitchen, Cornelia was as confused as she was thrilled by this most disorienting get-together. On the one hand, she had known these two kind people from the moment she was born, and in spite of their very great age (which they really did not show, and often she thought they looked younger than her grandparents) she had always regarded them as the most glamorous and interesting of all her grown-up relations.

Now, however, since waking from that strange, un-classifiable experience, she was looking at them with her memories rather than with her eyes, and the people she saw sitting at the table with her and Barry were the raging and honest young Finn, obsessed with saving Savannah, and the dashing, talented, brave Savannah who had been such a satisfactory travelling companion and who, dressed as Finn, had been the talk of the *Aquitania.* Or had she?

'Was it real?' Cornelia asked abruptly. 'When Barry and I thought about Zanzibar, we could see how it might really have happened, but all the same—'

'Zanzibar?' Finn said, puzzled. 'The fairies didn't take you to Zanzibar, did they?'

Well, there it was. Finn had said the F-word. 'No, Zanzibar was an elephant,' Cornelia explained, 'but—'

'Cornelia, darling,' said Savannah, breaking in on this most cross-purposed conversation, 'you and Tansy and Barry saved Finn. We know the date you saved him, and we know the date it was here in your own lives when you and Tansy came back home. It was in the small hours of this morning, and Finn and I have had that date marked in our diaries for decades and decades and decades, and we knew we had to stay alive long enough to meet the two of you afterwards, and to let you know that what you remember is true and correct and that Finn and I have the same memories, and that every extraordinary thing you remember about our wonderful Tansy really happened.

'Of course, people might not believe you if you said

anything, and your parents would be frightened to death if they knew, and might never leave you out of their sight again, so that's something you might want to think about before telling them; but at the same time, you must never doubt your own mind. You three darlings—you and Barry and Tansy—changed history, and you gave Finn and me our lives.'

Barry and Cornelia both grew pink at these words.

'Show them the letters,' said Finn. 'Show them the letters.'

Savannah opened the book she had put on the table, and being kept flat inside it were two yellowed and worn bits of paper, one of them headed '*On Board the R.M.S. Aquitania*' and the other headed '*Compagnie Internationale des Wagons-Lits et des Grands Express Européens*'.

'There you are, darlings,' said Savannah. 'In case you need something in writing to prove what you remember is true. I can't tell you how often we've read and re-read those perfect letters. And if paper proof is not enough for you,' she added smiling, 'you can go look at the brass plaque in the maritime museum with the name of Aeneas Finbarr O'Hara on it. Apparently, he still holds the world speed record for hopping in a potato sack around the promenade deck of an ocean liner.'

'Listen to me, Cornelia and Barry,' Finn said abruptly. 'Soldiers' Fort is going to belong to the two of you when Savannah and I are gone, and you have to make sure you protect that Fort. You can't do what I did and go off and abandon it. I'm not saying you have to live in it, but you have to be responsible for it, and get help from the fairies if you ever need it. The jewels will belong to you, too, of course, but don't mind about them. We'd have brought them here today to show them to you except we thought they'd frighten your parents too much.'

'What jewels?' asked Barry.

Cornelia put her hand to her mouth guiltily. 'I forgot to tell you.'

When Barry was told the full story of the rubies and emeralds, he reacted with so much noisy excitement that Tickles was inspired to run around the room in figures-of-eight and Freddy, for once, cast aside his dignity and joined her.

'I think this is about the most exciting day in the history of the world,' Cornelia said happily. 'Except I wish Tansy were here. Then everything would be perfect.'

'I wish she were too,' said Savannah. 'But you know I haven't seen Tansy since 1927. I've met King Fuchsia and Queen May, but I've never seen or heard from Tansy since she left New York with you.'

'But we'll see her now, won't we?' she said anxiously.

'I hope so,' said Savannah. 'May and Fuchsia never let anyone else see the letter Finn wrote to them in 1927, and they've never told Tansy what she did then, just as Finn and I never told the two of you. We're hoping that today, for the first time, she remembers what happened, the same as you two did, and when she does, she'll want to see us as much as we want to see her. Both of us would give anything to see Tansy again. But we just don't know.'

—Chapter 50—

The Christmas Tree

'I want to give her a Christmas present,' Cornelia said after a while. 'It might help her to remember us if we gave her a Christmas present.'

'That would be fun, all right,' said Savannah. 'And Tansy would love being given a present. But do fairies even know about Christmas?'

'Oh, they do,' Cornelia said. 'Tansy says they know about it, but they don't understand it, and they wish they did. Tansy says they have fairy scientists who do nothing except test the air on Christmas Eve night to see what kind of magic is in it so that they can celebrate it too the same as humans do, but their scientists haven't been able to figure it out. Which is very sad because it's the very best night of the year and they don't get any fun out of it.'

'Yeah, but how would you give them the present?' Barry asked, trying to work out the details of the idea. 'Would you just leave something on top of the fort or what?'

'Well, why not?' said Finn. 'You couldn't deliver it any farther. It would be the same as if something were left on your doorstep here.'

'It's hard to know what present one could give a fairy,' said Savannah. 'Maybe—'

'A tree,' said Cornelia quickly. 'I want to give the fairies a Christmas tree.'

'You know, that's an awfully good idea,' said Savannah enthusiastically. 'I suspect a Christmas tree would go down a treat with the fairies.'

'You'd need to ask the Ryans, though,' said Finn. 'That is if it's on May and Fuchsia's fort that you want to put the tree.'

'Mommy, will you ask Mrs Ryan if I can put up a Christmas tree on her fairy fort?' Cornelia asked her mother as soon as her parents came back.

'Will I what? Cornelia, what in heaven's name are you thinking? I can't ask Mrs Ryan something like that. Anyway, you shouldn't even think of putting a Christmas tree on a fairy fort. If there were fairies under there, they wouldn't like that at all. It would be against their tradition.'

'No, it wouldn't be. It would just be different. It would be their Christmas present.'

'Absolutely not. That would be all wrong, Sweetie. I wouldn't even let you put a tree on our own fairy fort. It would be disrespectful. Ask Savannah and Finn if you don't believe me. They'll tell you it would be a wrong thing to do.'

Her mother looked across at Savannah and Finn. 'Can you help me here at all? You tell her how it would be inappropriate.'

The old couple, however, reacted in a way that surprised her. 'Well, I don't know, Kate,' said Savannah cautiously. 'Cornelia feels so strongly about it.'

'What is it she's feeling strongly about now?' asked Cornelia's grandfather, who had just come into the room with her grandmother.

'She wants to put a Christmas tree on the Ryans' fairy fort,' said her mother, causing both her grandparents to start to laugh.

'What put that idea in your head, Cornelia?' her grandfather asked.

'Fairies don't get to celebrate Christmas,' Cornelia said, blushing, 'and I think the fairies who live over there would like to.'

'But why the Ryans' fort?' asked her grandmother. 'You might find it easier to coax your mother to let you put it on your own fort.'

'No, it has to be the Ryans' fort,' said Cornelia, blushing even more deeply.

'They say fairies get you that way sometimes,' said Finn, coming to her help. 'If they want something very badly, they can make a human obsessed about doing it.'

'Well, Finn's the expert,' her grandmother said, pulling Cornelia on to her lap, and giving her a hug. 'It seems odd all right, but maybe the child had a dream or something. Is that it, Cornelia?'

'Oh, come on, Katie,' said Cornelia's father, who had been listening to all of this with growing amusement. 'Are you going to take the risk of spoiling the fairies'

Christmas? If Finn with all his inside information is backing the idea, do we dare go against it?'

'Not you as well,' said his wife, looking at him in exasperation. How on earth am I going to ring up Lucy Ryan and say my children want to put up a Christmas tree on her fairy fort?'

It took a while, but after about half an hour, Cornelia's mother finally gave in. 'All right, I'll ring Lucy,' she said. 'But if she sounds the slightest bit hesitant or reluctant, that's an end of it, and no one is to say one more word to me about it, all right?'

Mrs Ryan, however, burst out laughing as soon as she heard what Cornelia's mother had to say. 'Listen, I'm going to take that as meaning Cornelia knows something about that mound that I don't, and that we really do have fairies in it. You know, I always thought so. She wouldn't mind if Patrick and Mary helped, would she?' she added enthusiastically. 'We have a spare tree-stand, by the way, if it's any use. And all of you come up to the house afterwards for mince pies, so Cornelia can tell me what she knows about our fairies.'

So Cornelia's father cut down a small tree, about four feet high ('any taller, and it would blow over in the wind,' he pointed out when Cornelia and Barry urged him to cut a much bigger one) and Savannah insisted that they call by Soldiers' Fort to collect several boxes of decorations.

'I'm too old to decorate a tree now that's more than two feet high,' she explained. 'But we have thousands of decorations. Pick out the best of them,' she advised. 'They won't be much by fairy standards, but we want to make the best show we can.'

—◇—

'What do you think is happening?' May said to Fuchsia, as all the fairies came up from their fort to look curiously at the cheerful, noisy group of humans and dogs bringing the tree and decorations on to their mound. (Well, all the fairies, that is, except Elder, who was never around the fort any more except when he was having his meals or sleeping, because he was busy all the time scouting the security walls of the prison where Puffy Pickenose worked, trying to work out the best means of getting a dog inside it.)

Cornelia did not keep the fairies in the dark for long, but began to talk immediately to the invisible figures that she was sure were watching.

'I don't think anyone can celebrate Christmas unless they have a tree,' she explained, 'so that's why we brought you one. It's not as big as we'd like, but Daddy says it would blow over if it were any bigger. And you can see that we're not disturbing your mound at all, but we're putting the tree on this stand, which is very heavy and should keep it nice and safe.

'I'm very sorry we don't have lights, which a Christmas tree really needs, but there's no electricity out here so we couldn't plug them in. Some people put real candles on their Christmas trees, but Mommy says those are very brave people, and she didn't even want to hear me mention the idea of candles. But we have very pretty decorations. They're Savannah's, and Savannah always has prettier decorations on her tree than anyone else.'

At first most of the fairies were unsure what to think about this disturbance of their private space. Obviously, these humans were well-intentioned, but all the same—

When they saw, however, that the king and queen were gratified and delighted at what was happening, and saw Tansy actually dancing in ecstatic circles around the tree and its decorator, they all began to see the possibilities for fun that the Christmas tree brought with it.

'You know, we really could do something with this tree,' said the fairy, Basil, looking at it appraisingly, after the noisy, laughing group of mortals had headed off at last to the Ryans' house for the promised mince pies. 'We'll leave the human decorations, of course, but with the addition of some gold and jewels, it would look very festive I think.'

'I think it has to be bigger,' said the fairy Hazel. 'The scale isn't right, and of course, there just isn't room to hang much on it.'

'Wait until dark,' said May. 'The humans will be coming back this way, and I wouldn't want them to know we'd made any changes to it. They might think we weren't grateful for what they did.'

The O'Haras did walk by the fort on their way home, and all of them thought the tree looked surprisingly impressive. 'You know, if I didn't know better, I'd think it had grown since we put it there,' said Cornelia's father, surprised.

As darkness fell, Cornelia's skin began to tingle as it did on every Christmas Eve night. Because she was the youngest in the house, she was allowed to light the Christmas candle in the front window; and as happened every year when she did this job, she began to shiver with excitement.

'Good lord, look at the tree,' said Cornelia's mother, startled, as she looked across at the fort at the other side of the glen. 'I didn't think we'd be able to see it from here even in good daylight, but I can see it clearly even now. Your father is right. It does look bigger. And Savannah, your ornaments are wonderful. Even in the dusk, I can see them reflecting light.'

The fairies found that they had never enjoyed a project as much as they enjoyed decorating this tree. 'It needs gold chains,' Fern said definitely. 'It needs lots of gold chains hanging in swags.'

'And jewels,' Laburnum agreed. 'Fat, round jewels hanging on short lengths of gold chain, but the jewels should get smaller and the chains shorter as they're hung higher on the tree.'

'And everything should be symmetrical,' said the twins, Snowdrop and Barley. 'Whatever we hang on one side, we should hang something to balance it on the other.'

'But the tree itself still isn't big enough,' Spruce pointed out. 'It needs to be in some proportion with the trees growing around it. It should be at least twenty feet high.'

'And it definitely needs lights,' said Arbutus. 'But should they be white or coloured, or should we alternate, and have them white for a while and then coloured for a while?'

'Not lights,' said Fuchsia. 'They'd be too visible to humans.'

'Well, maybe we could have just a little burst of light later on when the humans aren't looking,' said May, 'and we might as well alternate between white and coloured and see which we like best.'

'Shouldn't we give the humans a present in return?' said Tansy.

There was an eager murmur of agreement to this, with only May expressing a note of caution. 'Yes, I'd like to give them a present too,' she said, 'but we have to be careful. Sometimes presents from us can cause problems for humans even though we don't mean them to.'

'Fairy fires,' suggested Tansy. 'We could give them fairy fires in every fireplace in their house. Humans love fairy fires, and they don't do them any harm.'

Most of the fairies thought this would be a very inadequate present, but May and Fuchsia approved of it thoroughly. So when the family sat down that evening around the fire in the big room where they had put up their Christmas tree, everyone who had a cardigan or a jacket on took it off because of the wonderful heat that was coming from it; and straightaway, everyone started seeing in the fire whatever it was they were thinking about.

'It's Santa,' said Cornelia, her cheeks dark red with excitement. 'Santa, and his whole sleigh and reindeer and everything. Can you see them?' she asked ecstatically.

'What I see,' said Savannah, looking at the fireplace in amazement, 'is the *Aquitania*. Honestly, I can see a grand stateroom and Coco Chanel, but mostly I can see a friend I haven't seen in a long time.'

'I can see my parents,' said Cornelia's mother, her eyes growing misty. 'I can see them as clearly as if they were sitting here beside me.'

'It does play tricks on your eyes all right,' said Cornelia's father. 'It makes me think I can see a new glasshouse.'

'That's funny,' said her grandfather. 'All I can see is that new small television we got yesterday for our bedroom. I can see it there as clearly as if I was lying in bed looking at it.'

'Well, to my eyes, that fire is acting just like a looking glass,' said her grandmother. 'I can see all of us sitting here together exactly as we are with the big Christmas tree behind us and all of us in good health and without a problem in the world, and it's a wonderful sight. I just hope that every time I look at this fire, I can see what I'm looking at now.'

'I don't know how any of you can see those things,' said Barry. 'What I see is this place in Africa and a little baby elephant with its mother, and no one is shooting at them or anything, and they look really happy.'

'I just wish you could all see what I see,' said Finn. 'I see Josephine Baker.'

When they left the house at about 11.30 to go to Midnight Mass, they got their biggest surprise. 'What the—?' said Cornelia's father.

The tree by then had grown to about 20 feet tall, and was brilliantly lit with white lights, the fairies having discussed the matter and having decided that the humans would not take offence at seeing the tree lit; after all, they had wanted to put lights on it, but just had not been able. By the time the family reached the gate of the drive, the fairies had decided to have a look at an alternative lighting scheme, and the tree was lit with red, green and yellow lights.

Cornelia and Barry were hopping up and down with excitement, but what was surprising Cornelia most was how calmly her parents were accepting and enjoying things that she would have expected them to say were impossible. 'I'm not even going to question it,' said her mother. 'I've always thought that, on Christmas night, anything can happen. And obviously it can.'

Usually, Cornelia felt a sense of disappointment when midnight came on Christmas night, because although officially it was just the start of Christmas, that special sense of electrical magic that made her skin tingle on that night started to lessen them. On this Christmas, however, the greatest excitement was yet to come.

When she went to bed finally, it was after two in the morning because after they had come home, they had a nice party downstairs and she and Barry were allowed to eat all the cakes and sweets they wanted. For once, the dogs did not come up to bed with her because, glutted with sweets, they had fallen asleep in front of the fire down below; but there in her room waiting for her was Tansy.

'I've been dying to see you,' Cornelia said excited. 'I was so afraid I wouldn't see you again.'

'King Fuchsia and Queen May said I could come and thank you very much for the Christmas tree which everyone thought was the best present we've ever got. Do you like my picture?' she asked, looking admiringly at the painting over the mantelpiece. 'I'm not sure if any fairy has ever been painted before. It's quite good, isn't it?'

'It's beautiful!' Cornelia agreed enthusiastically. 'And you know, Savannah and Finn want to see you too.'

'I'm going to see them in the morning, but they're both asleep now, and May and Fuchsia said I wasn't to disturb anyone who was asleep. Anyway, I can visit *them* any time I want, but do you know what,' she continued worriedly, 'May and Fuchsia say I should be careful about visiting *you* too often.'

'But why?' said Cornelia, shocked to hear this.

'They say I might confuse you and that you might start to think humans were boring when you were around a fairy all the time, and that would be bad because you have to make your life among humans. They say Savannah and Finn are too old to become confused, and that's why I can visit them as much as I like, which is good. But I don't really see why I shouldn't visit you all the time as well,' Tansy added, as she conjured herself a ballet tutu and whirled to each of the four corners of the ceiling, and then came back towards the centre where she settled into a long sequence of upside-down *fouettés en tournant*. 'You don't think I confuse you, do you?'

'Confuse me?' repeated Cornelia indignantly, addressing the spinning, upside-down top of Tansy's head. 'Of course you don't confuse me. People confuse me all the time, but you, Tansy, you've never confused me at all.'

The End

GALWAY COUNTY LIBRARIES

SORTIE